Alpha Jasper

Midika Crane

This book is published by Inkitt. Join now to read and discover free upcoming bestsellers!

Prologue

I face my best friend, my back to the edge of the forest.

"It's not funny anymore," she insists, glancing over my shoulder, desperately trying to insinuate that my need to come inside is greater than any sense of humor I could muster.

"I'm enjoying myself." I grin, glancing around, as if I have a magical ability to see in the darkness. Quite frankly, the light from inside the house doesn't do much.

June, my best friend, hops from foot to foot, anxious to rescue me from... whatever danger she thinks is out here, but she can't bear to risk crossing the threshold of the doorway.

"Thea, please... I'm being serious when I tell you to get inside," she says, her voice shaking, and not from the cool breeze.

I dance around on the spot, autumn leaves crunching under my feet.

"Phantom Wolves don't exist," I chant, my voice carrying itself along the breeze.

June shakes her head, rubbing her arms up and down nervously. "I swear to the Goddess that I am not coming after you when one of them snatches you and drags you away into their rape cave," she tells me. She's not joking.

I pause, my dancing ceasing. Slowly, I turn around, the forest looming over me. It's endless, cold, dark, and I'm not even sure anything lives in there. But I can't help myself.

"June, we need to get inside."

"Why?" She asks nervously, watching me back my way up the porch steps cautiously.

I scream, so loud I'm sure the neighboring Pack can hear. June joins my shrills as I fall past her, straight into the house, and into the clutches of the fur rug on the floor. She slams the door behind us, pressing her back against it.

I turn from where I'm lying face down on the ground. June looks petrified, her eyes glinting with memories of all the books on Phantom Wolves she's read. I start to laugh.

"Oh, I gotcha so good!"

Her terrified expression dissolves into one of pure anger, as she realizes I just pulled off nothing but a prank.

"I didn't see a Phantom, but I did see your face as pale as anything." I fail to keep the humor from my voice. I stand, leveling myself with a livid June.

"You idiot! How many times have I told you. Phantom Wolves aren't something you mess with," she growls, slapping her hand over her forehead as she attempts to gather her wits.

I smile. "Come on June, lighten up."

She sighs deeply, trying to collect herself. Since we were children, June has always believed in the myths the older kids at school would tell us to scare us. And most of these included Phantom Wolves.

"Lighten up? Do you want to be like Alpha Jasper?" She dares me.

I roll my eyes. *Here we go.*

Alpha Jasper disappeared one night and never came back. It was said he was stolen by Phantom Wolves and murdered, just like his father. And this happened years ago. No, centuries ago.

Other like-minded people believe he committed suicide, and no one was up to taking over his position as Alpha.

"Jasper wasn't murdered by Phantom Wolves, silly..." I tell her.

June narrows her eyes at me. "You're right, because he's one of them."

Chapter One

I swing the dog's leash back and forth as I walk, watching the fake leather gleam in the dull light. Above my head, vicious clouds swoop in, looming over me with threatening shadows in their wake. It makes me sigh, irritably.

The Devotion Pack is situated centrally within the Pack Quarter. It can get warm here, but the weather remains typically gloomy and dull. It doesn't put you in the best mood when you look up and see a darkening cloud overhead that never results to anything.

I've decided to return June's stupid dog today. She's my best friend who I visited last night. She wouldn't let me walk home along the path that skims the edge of the infamous Phantom Forest. Her insistence that those mythical creatures called Phantom Wolves may kidnap me and drag me back to their dens to kill me, wore me down. She left me no choice but to take her useless Jack Russell with me.

Might as well do it today and walk home in the daylight. After last night, I decide to take the long walk through the town, rather than delve into that forest. I nearly lost Squiggles (or whatever she calls it).

The village is pretty small. There are other townships within the Pack, but they are all miles away and desolate like our own. It's so tightknit, no one leaves, and no one comes in. At least, not since people started believing in Phantoms again.

Too scared to step foot out of the village, most people have accepted a simple life away from any other civilization. Many people, including myself, have also accepted the idea of never finding our mates. It sucks. But in some people's eyes, it is safer to stay away from where Phantom Wolves are said to lurk.

I smile to myself, as I recall the myths in my head.

Jasper. He was the Alpha's son. Centuries ago, he disappeared, and his father died soon after. Everyone thought it was Phantom Wolves, so they left the Pack. They just got up and moved completely, whittling the population down by plenty. Now ridiculous ideas suggest he is still alive, commanding a Pack of the night-prowling beasts as he kills the innocent in the night.

I chuckle.

When the older kids at school told June and me these stories to scare us, I always believed he had either simply left—since his body was never found—or committed suicide elsewhere. My simple answers helped me sleep at night.

I just won't leave because my dad won't. And as a nineteen-year-old living with her father, who works part-time at the local diner, I don't see myself doing anything else anyway...

The little Jack Russell June calls her guard dog skips ahead on its little legs. I'm not sure if dogs are allowed on streets this close to stores, but no one is really around to question it. It's a Monday, so the small number of children in the area are at school, and everyone else is working.

"Maybe it will actually rain one day," I say aloud, but I'm not sure if the dog really listened to my mindless words. It cocked an ear, but that was it. I just listen to its claws click against the concrete, wishing my life was as simple as his.

Maybe it is as simple. I don't go anywhere. My boyfriend will probably have to mark me on the grounds that neither of us are likely to find our own mates. My dad works most days. My friend is a crazy lunatic sometimes. And I don't have enough money to move out...

Okay, maybe it isn't that simple.

I stare into the store windows as I pass by, wishing I could afford some of the nice clothing and what not. Instead, I am left looking at my own hazel eyes, and frumpy clothes. I need a miracle...

4

Suddenly, my eyes catch on something taped to the store window of a second-hand clothing shop. It has my sneakered feet finding a stop, my eyebrows raising past the line of mussed brown hair that swoops over my forehead.

A piece of paper, newly printed with bold text, with a photo that's surprisingly eye catching. But not as eye catching as the wording.

Missing Person

My heart rises in my throat, as I recognise the name under the familiar photo. *Jessica Holmes.*

I went to school with her. She was the epitome of an introvert—kept to herself, always drawing in her notepad or reading some high fantasy novel. I think she was better friends with the town librarian than anyone in our year.

I stare at the long mass of curly auburn hair that tumbles down her shoulders. She is quite pretty, if you look past her thick-rimmed glasses, and her eyes as cold as chunks of ice. The traits she has, she shares with most of us in this Pack. Dark hair, hazel eyes. Average.

But she had gone missing. Missing? No one *ever* leaves this town.

I am a very curious person. I can't ignore it. I used to read thriller novels before I got a job, and ever since, the slightest sign of a mystery has my heart racing. And since nothing *ever* happens here, I am instantly intrigued.

With a jingle of the bell atop the door, I stroll into the store, poster in hand, having left the dog tied to a pole outside.

The clerk at the desk glances up as I walk in, probably not expecting someone to visit at this time of the day. Since everyone knows everyone here, I don't have any trouble identifying her as Ms Morris. Elderly, cheerful, but the worst gossip in town.

And her partner in crime shifts clothes around on a nearby rack. That is Ms Slater. Both mateless. Both probably the biggest entertainment in this town.

"Thea dear! What a lovely surprise!" Ms Morris chirps, clapping her hands together at the sight of me. I force a toothy smile onto my face, wishing I was as optimistic about life as these two. I can't imagine how they've lived so long all on their own... No mate, nothing.

"I saw this in the window," I tell her, getting straight to the point so I don't have to be stuck with them, talking about how boring my life is.

I slide the piece of paper across the counter top, giving Ms Morris a perfect view of the missing person poster. The moment her gaze touches the paper, her face pales, and her mouth forms a tight line. I have never seen her without a smile.

"Ah yes. Poor Jessica," she says solemnly. I feel Ms Slater stroll up behind me, thick heels clicking against the linoleum floor. She leans over the counter as well, drinking in the sight of the young girl.

"The poor family," Ms Slater muses, smacking her pink-tinted lips together. "I can't believe she would do that to herself."

My heart stops. "Do what?"

The two ladies exchange glances. They look so similar, I realize, as they contemplate whether or not to tell me about Jessica. Both have the same fluffy white hair and sun-damaged eyes. They dress the same, and even put on the same make-up every day. I don't judge though, because it's familiar. I grew up thinking they were sisters.

"She killed herself. She walked straight into the Phantom Forest and those wolves killed her," Ms Morris exclaimed. My jaw clenched.

Just like the rest of this town, these women are one drumstick short of a picnic basket. No one has ever seen a Phantom Wolf, and here they are convincing themselves that they do actually exist.

"Did they find the body?" I ask, wondering why there would be a poster up otherwise. The women shrug at the same time.

"No... but she was a little bit strange. So we don't doubt it was a suicide..."

I want to roll my eyes.

"And we think the wolves are getting closer to town. Maybe she got scared and gave up. It would make sense, since her mother said

Jessica was a little worried about Phantoms," Ms Slater assumes. This isn't the first time I have heard their ridiculous assumptions.

"Do the police know about this?" I ask, my index finger tapping impatiently against the counter top.

Glances are passed again. I mean, our police force consists of two men. A father and a son. The son, my boyfriend. Their job is hardly necessary in this town... Well, until now I suppose.

"No... But we can't think of any other way," Ms Morris says. It takes my entire being not to sigh at the batty old women.

I could have gone anywhere in town and found reliable evidence, but instead I made the mistake of coming in here.

"She might have just left home. She was old enough," I suggest.

"Can't be. The librarian saw her leave, and her parents never saw her come back. She was either taken, or she killed herself," Ms Slater stated, trying to confirm the lack of information.

I take a few steps backward, leaving the poster. *This is stupid...*

People don't leave. Ever. And if people don't leave, then people don't mysteriously go missing. My assumption is that she left home, simple as that.

Leaving the shop, I grab the dog and start on my way again. My detective work for the day is over. I decide as I walk, I'll keep it to myself.

Because I know exactly what June will think...

Chapter Two

"We are going to die..."

I nestle my head between the cushions of June's beaten up old couch, wishing it would completely drown out the sound of her insistent voice.

I showed up here fully believing she wouldn't find out about Jessica going missing. She never leaves the damn house—I even have to buy her groceries for her—and I assumed her parents wouldn't tell her either.

"*Missing?* No one ever goes missing here," she says, sounding so distressed I almost feel sorry for her. Too bad she thinks it's a fictional character that's the cause of the disappearance...

"She hated everyone here," I try to convince her. "It wouldn't surprise me if she just upped and left."

June doesn't look convinced. Her fingers fiddle with the bottom of her shirt, as they do when she's nervous. Her eyes are like mine, hazel, although a little darker. Sometimes we get called sisters, which I take as a compliment more than she does. June is very beautiful. Slim facial features, round doe eyes and the sweetest smile. Her hair is thicker, more voluptuous than mine, and always styled neatly.

Her face is shadowed, as her back faces the window. It is quite a scene, with the thunderstorm currently raging outside.

It doesn't rain very often. And storms occur so rarely it's considered an event. So with rain beating on June's roof and windows, and thunder rumbling in the background, I'm surprised she isn't frightened.

"What if she was kidnapped? What if we are next?" she demands, raking her hands through her mass of curls.

In that moment, she looks a lot like Jessica. "June, calm..."

"I live alone... Oh, Goddess!" She starts pacing in front of me. "I'm next, aren't I?"

I jump up, grabbing June's shoulders. I glare at her, holding her tight as she shakes beneath my hands. She is genuinely scared, and I can't really blame her. Something like this has never happened in our peaceful little town.

All of a sudden the wind howls loudly from outside, and the lights flicker off.

We aren't in complete darkness, but it is enough to make June cry out and dive at the couch, throwing a blanket over herself. The trees outside wave their branches around, the little light from the dark clouds casts strange shadows across the floorboards.

"It's fine... just wind," I croak. Storms scare me. Always have. The thought of Mother Nature's potential casting a terrible disaster across the Pack is terrifying.

The sound of June's whimpering brings my attention back to her. "We just have to wait for it to pass."

Again, the wind picks up, thrashing the trees around so violently a branch snaps off a nearby one, skidding across the deck.

And then, the door blows open.

The force is so strong, it swings back and hits the window, smashing it completely. The crash of the glass and June's scream are similar. Glass scatters across the ground, landing at my feet.

"We are going to die!" I hear June faintly through the sound of the wind in my ears. It is deafening, as I fight my way to the door. The force of the wind is unnaturally strong. *Something is wrong, things like this never happen!*

I grab the edge of the door, glass crunching under my shoes. Using the strength I developed from carrying plates to customers at work all day, I force the door closed, only satisfied when I hear it click.

Relieved, I collapse to the ground, surrounded by glass.

"Thea? Are you alive?" I hear June ask tentatively, peeking out from under the blanket. We lock gazes.

"No thanks to you," I mutter jokingly, patting my hair down.

I don't want to bring up how the wind was the strangest thing I have ever had to deal with. How I found the courage to shut that door, I am not sure. It was as if I was being willed to stop it.

"Where is Squiggles?" June asks, finally emerging from the blanket. Wind still billows through the hole in the window, sometimes sending a leaf in. That isn't going to be easy to fix.

"He was in his..." I break off, as my gaze finds the spot where the dog was moments before. June's face instantly pales. Her dog is her life. Everyone in the entire town knows it. So the second he's out of her sight without knowing *exactly* where he is...

We spend the next five minutes searching June's small cabin for the dog. Under the couch, behind the fridge, around the chairs. Nothing.

"He's out there," June says, her face falling in defeat. She glances at the door, and I know what she is thinking. Instead of being trapped in the small room, full of wind and screaming, the dog had escaped. Into the forest, most likely.

"When the wind passes, I am sure he will come back," I tell her, but the words completely pass her by. She is already at the door, opening it. Instantly, the room is consumed in deafening wind, blowing shards of glass toward me.

I push forward, grabbing her by the forearm to stop her from making her thoughts a reality. Visions of her getting lost in that storm haunt me. No way am I letting her walk out there on her own...

"You stay here. I'll go out and find him," I promise, warily casting a glance outside. The rain is relentless, and doesn't seem to be easing anytime soon. Hopefully the thickness of the forest will be enough shelter.

Despite not wanting to send me out in the storm, June nods, fueled by the thought of her missing dog.

So, mustering as much courage as possible, I run outside, slamming the door closed behind me. Outside, the rain hits me like bullets. This is the first time I've felt rain on my skin in a long time. The feeling is uncomfortable, as the cold liquid winds its way through my hair, and dribbles across my skin.

I head down the same path I had taken last night, the canopy giving decent shelter from the onslaught of rain, but not so much from the wind. I fight against it, my hair whipping around my face as I run.

"Squiggles!" I call loudly.

My eyes scan everywhere as I go, looking behind tree trunks, and under bushes. He's gone. The feeling of defeat sets in only a few minutes of being in the forest. The further I go, the darker everything seems to get. Am I imagining things, or are shadows seeming to crawl out from behind those trees?

I keep walking, shivering at the feeling of my wet clothes against my skin. Now I am starting to regret walking around for her stupid dog. And it's beginning to seem like everything is against me at this point. The wind may have died down, from my position in the forest, but rain stills coats my entire body.

"Squiggles, please..." I croak, stumbling over my feet as I walk. The dirt path has mixed into mud, sticking to my feet—I didn't take time to put on shoes.

Kicking a stick in front of me, I groan in frustration. Not only is June going to kill me for losing her precious dog, I'm probably lost, and the idea of getting hypothermia is becoming more realistic by the second.

Then I hear the sound of a man clearing his throat, from behind me.

I jump, twisting around while praying to the Moon Goddess that it isn't a murderer lurking within the woods.

I see nothing. No one. Nada. Instead of seeing another person, I'm stuck staring at tree trunks and a thick mass of leaves. Like an idiot. Someone, or *something* lives here. And I don't think I'm very welcome.

Calling out 'hello' is probably a stupid thing to do. At least that is what every horror movie I have watched suggests. If whatever is in here doesn't know I have accidentally accompanied it, then maybe I may just get out of here alive. But it sounded like a very *normal* person making a very *normal* noise.

So I stand still, unsure of what to do. But then I see something. A figure. The outline is shadowy—almost fuzzy in a way. I have to strain my eyes to make sure I'm seeing right. Because if I am, there's a man standing farther down the path, his back facing me.

I may have just found someone to take me back the way I came. Because I believe I strayed from the path.

"Hey! Ah... Hello?" I decide to try my luck. Better than dying out here alone. My words carry through the wind, and for a moment, I assume he didn't hear me.

But then his head turns.

I can't see much of him. It's almost as if he's completely consumed by his own shadow. Only the outline can be seen, which shows me he is very tall, and of a much larger frame than I am. Definitely a man. A man who could either help me, or kill me on the spot.

And then, he walks away! Down the path he goes, strolling away without even acknowledging me.

"Wait! I'm lost," I call after him. He disappears around a corner. Well, either I stay out here and possibly die from the cold, or I follow him... The latter presents the only option.

Forcing my freezing limbs into action, I jog after him, pushing violent branches out of my way as I fight through the bush.

When I sight the man again, tendrils of darkness seem to chase after him. I decide I might be going crazy. But I still follow. I still follow the path he strolls on.

Despite the pace at which I chase after him, he only seems to get farther away. The distance between us is agonizing, but every slight turn of the man's head keeps me going. Perhaps he wants me to follow him after all. But right now, I don't have time to ask him.

And then, suddenly, he vanishes around yet another corner. And when I make it around, I'm back at June's house.

I let out a deep breath in surprise. The quaint, old cabin with the broken window stands in front of me, and I can't help but think I'm hallucinating. The man is gone. Like he had been carried away with the wind. And instead, I'm looking at a police car parked in front of June's porch, the rain leaving a slick sheen over the bumper.

Luca. My heart races.

I run up the porch steps, wet feet slapping against the wood. I call through the window, waiting for June to get me out of this vortex of wind and rain. The moment the door opens I stumble inside, yelling at her to close the door behind me.

Twisting around, a frazzled June presses herself against the door, the wind from the broken window blowing her hair around wildly. But I don't really notice her, despite failing the mission to find her dog. I do notice the man standing in the corner.

I stride over to him, throwing myself into his arms. "I'm sorry."

I was apologizing because I know he is going to be mad. Being uptight about safety is his job, and the fact he is my boyfriend, and soon to be forced mate, makes it so much worse. He just happens to be in his police uniform as well.

"I can't believe you would do something stupid like that... Putting yourself in danger," Luca mutters into my hair. I want to roll my eyes. This isn't the first time I've heard those exact words from him.

I pull away from him, glancing over at June. "I'm sorry. I couldn't find Squiggles."

She shrugs. She's visibly calmer now, having had time to cease worrying while I was nearly lost out in the storm.

"I called Luca, because I thought you weren't going to come back..."

"How long was I gone?" I ask. June and Luca exchange glances.

It gives me a decent amount of time to assess the two. They look similar. Not just because they are born into the same Pack, but because they are first cousins. They share the same hazel-colored eyes we all do, but his hair's slightly lighter from working in the sun a lot. But their facial structure is very similar, which at first I found weird. But now I'm kind of used to it.

"Like, four hours," June said. My eyes widen. Four hours? I swear I was only gone for about half an hour. I clutch my head in confusion. And then I remember the strange man.

13

"Someone else was out there," I tell them. "A man."

Luca looks out the window, probably assessing the weather. No way is it possible for him to go out there and look for him now. And who knows if that man was even real? It could have been my imagination, from the cold.

Speaking of the cold, I suddenly become aware of the icy feeling crawling under my clothes and across my skin. June notices, and rushes across to the chest where she keeps all her blankets.

"Dad and I will head out tomorrow to check the area for June's dog, and the man," Luca tells me. He's in business mode. I can spot it a mile away. His shoulders are pushed back, arms tense. His expression is even grim. I hate when he gets like this.

June comes up behind me, wrapping the blanket over my shoulders. I just want this day to end.

And to find out who that man was.

Chapter Three

I lie under my covers, listening intently to the sound of heavy rain pattering against the roof. It's an addictive, lulling sound, making me want to stuff my head into my pillow and sleep for a few more hours.

But I had promised to meet Luca at the diner for lunch before my shift. I glance over at my bedside table, to see I have to be there in an hour...

I'm out of bed in a second, and into the shower. Luca hates it when I am late, and personally I do too. Unfortunately, I'm not the most organized person in the world. So when I am finally dressed, and towel drying my hair, I guess the knock at the door is Luca hurrying me along.

And I keep thinking that, until I open the door.

My towel slips from my fingers, pooling at my feet. Eyes wide, I am stuck staring at the most attractive man I have ever seen. No one gets close to contesting that thought. Not Luca... No one.

"Good morning," he says. And the voice from his mouth is surprising. Those two words he uttered should have been cheerful and light. But he pronounced them delicately, his voice deep and soft. And the accent... so familiar, but exotic in a way I can't even begin to explain.

I just stand, staring at him like an absolute idiot, taking in this 'God' at my doorstep. I can't take my eyes off his own. A deep-set swirling violet, tinted with the darkest ebony-black irises of his eyes; they almost trap me, like hands made from illusory magic that seems to pull me in.

He must have been at least a few years older than I am. Maturity is etched into his expression, as he stares at me as intently as I stare at him. But he doesn't have thick, matted wet hair upon his head like mine. No, just shadowy wisps of mussed black hair, dancing across his sun-kissed forehead. And if my eyes don't deceive me, a tint of violet similar to his eyes is entwined within those strands.

I know normal, and this is *not* normal.

"Ah... I... Hi." The words stumble from my mouth with no filter, probably incoherent.

The more I stare at him, the stranger he becomes. I could never imagine someone looking so beautiful. Almost magical. And, despite the rain pouring down outside, not an ounce of water taints his being. Perhaps the canopy dad had slung up to keep the rain off the deck protected him, but he had to have got here somehow, and I don't see a car or an umbrella in sight.

"I came to return this to you," he tells me, voice low and caressing. My knees want to drop me in front of him.

He holds up his hand, and I see he's holding a leash. My eyes travel down the leash, and I meet the bright eyes of Squiggles.

"Where did you find him?" I ask, bending down with my arms extended. I don't like the dog, but the relief I feel on seeing him alive is too overwhelming to ignore. And for the faintest second, it's more normal than the stranger.

Because strangers don't exist in our town.

The dog runs into my arms, putting its dirty paws on my thighs at it licks my face with a sloppy tongue. I resist the urge to cringe in front of the dog-saving God.

"He was wandering around the forest," he tells me smoothly, voice like the sweetest honey. "This was the first house..."

I'm struck still for a moment. My house is on the opposite side of the woods from June's, which means Squiggles would have had to trek for a while to get here. But the fact this man has approached me with such confidence that the dog is mine is a little unnerving.

Is he the man from last night? No, I have to be imagining that.

He hands me the leash as I stand back up, looking me directly in the eye as he does so. Hoping he doesn't notice my hands quivering from the intimate feeling he is giving me, I tug on the leash for Squiggles to come inside.

"What were you doing in the woods?" I ask. A simple, maybe too intrusive question, but I am curious. But what really has my curious side digging at me is the idea of a stranger being here. And a beautiful one at that.

"I just moved into a house over there," he tells me, twisting around to point further across the woods. I glance over, noticing it's the part no one ever goes to. It's not owned, because of the ideas of Phantom Wolves roaming there. Not until now at least...

We stand, staring at each other for a few moments. Then I realize I should probably be polite.

"Would you like to come in?" I ask, forcing the smile I reserve for strangers or elderly people. Without a second of hesitation, he nods, so I step back, holding the door wide for him to walk in.

And just like that, I have let a complete stranger into my home, who may possibly be a rapist or murderer. I blink, as he wanders into the lounge. Perhaps it was the intimidation factor he used so smoothly and easily.

"It's not really my dog," I tell him, closing the door nervously. I face away from him, my face screwed up as I curse myself internally.

"Oh?"

"It's my friend's. She lives a good walk north," I explain, swooping down to let Squiggles off the leash. He tears away, running off on his tiny legs to Goddess knows where in my house.

I can imagine June's reaction if she saw this elusive man. Either she would fall in love, or accuse him of being a Phantom Wolf.

"The names Thea, by the way," I inform him, turning around to finally face him. He is staring at a wall laden with framed pictures—of my mother.

He pauses, as if he's surprised at being expected to tell me his name. "Ah... Casper."

"Interesting," I muse. Glancing down, I notice my thighs covered in dirt from that stupid dog. I attempt to brush it away, only to stain my jeans in the process. I sigh, strolling closer to where Casper silently stares at the wall.

"Uhm..." I pause, noticing the way Casper looks down at me, a solemn look in his eyes. "That's my mother."

"I'm sorry," he says gently. He knew. The look on his face is sympathetic, but I only feel embarrassed. It is as if his gaze can strip me down, tearing away at the layers I've put on to protect myself. It's been like that since her death.

I cough, stepping back. "Don't be. It was years ago."

I twist around, striding quickly to the kitchen. The house isn't big, so I can still see him from here, but I don't want to. He should leave, before he sees the tears stinging in my eyes. Because I don't want to admit that a complete stranger already knows a big secret of mine.

And I don't even know why he is here... or what he wants. Nothing. I have to brace my arms against the kitchen bench for a moment.

"It doesn't matter how long ago it was." I jump, as Casper has come up behind me. How did he get here so quickly? "A loss is a loss."

He speaks his words from experience. But unlike him, I won't press it.

"Look, I think you should go," I exclaim, maneuvering my way around his massive body. He doesn't say a word, as I fluster around the lounge, looking for my coat and keys. Luca won't be happy if I am late.

And then I look at the clock, expecting it to be nearly noon.

"Four thirty?" I yelp, seeing the clock hands on the most unlikely numbers. I was meant to start work at twelve thirty! I am so dead.

"Crap," I growl, the hunt for my keys suddenly more desperate. How did I allow myself to get lost in conversation with Casper for... four and a half hours? I am losing my mind.

Casper stands close to the front door, keys balanced on his index finger. "Late?"

If I wasn't about to be fired from my only job that would pay for me to leave this Pack, I might have questioned him. How did he not know that time was passing so quickly? How did *I* not know? Something just doesn't add up.

"As a matter of fact, I am *very* late," I tell him, plucking the keys from him while grabbing one of Dad's coats from the hook. Opening the front door, I usher a very calm Casper onto the deck, locking the door behind me.

"I enjoyed..."

"Like I said before, you need to go," I insist, cutting Casper off. His face loses all expression, as he nods blandly.

And without a word, he walks into the curtain of rain, and into the forest.

Chapter Four

The diner has been a special place to me since I was a little girl. Having milkshakes after school with June was a ritual, and I always told the ladies at the counter I would work here when I was older. Fast forward ten years... I am living the dream.

Except the dream is hardly what I thought it would be. Sometimes, it's more of a nightmare.

"Four hours late?" My boss, Janet Dupree says, arms folded over her chest. "Four hours I've spent doing your work."

I sit meekly behind her desk, head hung low. I'm no stranger to embarrassment, but the looks the other two waitresses gave me as I walked in was enough to have me hold up a white flag.

Janet's office is a tiny room tucked into the back of the diner. We always refer to it as The Cave, because sometimes our boss hibernates in it. In the unlikely event you did something foolish, or against one of her rules, we would have to sit beneath the posters of half-naked firemen.

Torture, if it's accompanied by Janet's lecture.

"This is an official warning. Don't let it happen again."

I stand, brushing my uniform down. When I was younger, I thought the dusty pale blue dress with a white apron tied around my waist was cute. No, it's painful and the high school boys make it their job to look under the high hem of the skirt whenever possible.

I wander outside the room and into the kitchen, after muttering a half-hearted apology to my boss. The other waitresses mull around, one at a table, another wiping the main counter. We have one cook working during the day, but we don't usually talk, due to his constant pessimistic mood.

"Girl, what happened?" The waitress at the counter—my good friend, Kera, asks, ceasing her wiping. Big busted, almost too friendly and always showing off her whitened teeth, Kera has been working here for as long as I have. Her eyes are something I've always been jealous of; the clearest crystal blue, like nothing I've seen before. She's from the Wisdom Pack, so naturally very smart, and beautiful.

"I was late," I say blandly, grabbing my name pin from my designated shelf, putting my coat in its place. Kera rolls her eyes, throwing her wiping towel over her shoulder as she strolls over.

"I have eyes, sass." She grins, leaning an elbow against the bench Cook was working at. We call him just Cook, because he refuses to tell us his real name. "Want to tell me why?"

I brush past her, and out into the main dining area. I stop behind the counter, looking for tables that may need assistance. Only one table is occupied and Britney, the other waitress, seems to have it covered.

"Someone moved into the estate in Phantom Forest," I tell her, releasing a sigh of irritation. Kera has come up behind me, her eyes widened.

I've never seen the estate, but I've heard about it. Dad told me *never* to wander into the forest, and after I disputed my belief in Phantom Wolves, he told it was private property.

"Who?" Kera twists her body around so she can look me in the eye. She knows how her eyes always evoke the most honest answers out of me. *Almost like Casper's...*

"A man," I say carefully. Her mouth falls open in surprise. Kera hasn't found her mate, or a man willing to hold down her fiery personality. She's all over the place, taking interest in any man who even looks at her in a day, before something fresh becomes the new objective.

I turn, trying to keep a calm expression, but inside, I'm beating myself up. Luca is going to be beyond mad at me for abandoning him. And instead of wallowing in guilt like I should be, I'm talking about another guy.

"Is he hot?" Kera asks, pushing my shoulder gently so I would face her. Why not be honest?

"Very. Tall, hot, sexy, and his eyes are to die for..."

Suddenly, the sound of someone clearing their throat from behind me has me twisting around again. I meet the eyes I was just about to compliment.

All over again, I am struck with the handsome features that belong to this stranger, Casper. He's dressed differently... casual. A simple black shirt, and dark trousers with his hands shoved into the pockets. He stares at me through silky black hair that brushes over his brow, an amused smile dancing across his face.

Did he hear that? A feeling of utter dread washes over me, as I come to terms with the embarrassment that's showing itself through the color of my cheeks.

"Thea," he murmurs, my name rolling off his tongue enticingly, entwining with his accent to have my hands quivering by my sides. I've completely lost my breath, but Kera on the other hand...

"I must say, we aren't used to having strangers around our parts. Especially handsome ones," Kera says, her voice dripping with sultry confidence. She pushes up next to me, leaning over the counter coyly, blatantly showing her cleavage to Casper.

His eyes remain on mine, like chips of ice, the violet making his gaze so much more intense. He hardly even acknowledges Kera. Any other man would have been enticed by the beautiful woman showing herself to him.

"I'm checking out the town. A lady in a second-hand shop directed me down here. She told me a beautiful girl worked here," he says smoothly, no hesitation in his words.

I glance at Kera (who's realized her breasts aren't going to work) and stand up squarely. I know it was probably Ms Slater and Ms Morris who directed him down here. It was either for Britney or Kera, since I'm the only one in a relationship.

"Well look no further," Kera purrs, and I think she winks when Casper finally drags his gaze to hers.

"We also have great food," I add, taking a step back. I bend down, grabbing a plastic menu we keep under the counter to hand to him. He takes it, a simple 'thank you' his only return.

Backing up, Casper walks off to find a table. Britney walks up to us the moment he's moved away, having finally finished chatting up customers at her table, using words of seduction to lure them into tipping her generously.

"Yum...who's that?" she asks, ripping a piece of paper with words on it off her pad.

Britney is a sweet girl. She's trying to buy her way out of this Pack, like me, and sometimes she can get a little competitive over tips. Her hair is a lighter version of what we typically see on girls' hair. When she ties it up, like today, the gold in her hair can be seen.

"Yeah, who is that, Thea?" Kera asks. Both girls looks at me expectantly.

Grabbing Britney's note with her customers' orders from her hand, I slide it over to Cook. "I don't know. Casper, I think his name is."

They almost jump at the hint of his name. By the way their eyes gleam and they almost salivate at the mention of his name, I decide to not tell them he is the reason I was so late to work.

Suddenly, the sound of a bell tinkling from the top of the door signals a new customer. Except it's not a customer. It's Luca.

He strolls in, a look of determination written all over his face. Dressed in his dark law enforcer uniform, he looks dangerously official, and all the more intimidating. This is someone you don't want to stand up, for no reason.

He catches my gaze, dark eyes wild with emotion, like a thunderous storm.

"Where have you been?" he demands viciously, his voice so loud it catches the attention of everyone in the room. I want to cower. I want nothing more than to hide away from everyone's speculative gazes, to cover our relationship from prying eyes.

"I was late to work," I tell him meekly, as he strides closer till he reaches the counter.

He narrows his eyes at me, as if he believes I was doing something illegal.

"I was looking all over for you... I checked June's, your house, the entire town," he tells me.

This is what I'm used to. Not just his anger, but how he forces the blame on me, victimising himself.

I glance around, seeing everyone's eyes on me. But it is Casper's I get caught on. He stares at me, an unknown emotion flickering in his eyes. Then he switches his attention to Luca, and I see anger. Pure, thick anger he doesn't bother to hold back. To which he responds by standing, abruptly.

And I know, the next few moments will be hell.

"I think you should stop," Casper says, his voice lower, more calculated than Luca.

Luca is driven by a different kind of anger. His is right there, in your face. He couldn't hold his back when it was right there in front of him.

Casper seems to understand his own feelings in a way, not showing a single hint of weakness.

"I didn't know this was any of your business," Luca drawls, eyes alight with fiery hot passion.

I can't help but stand there, stunned that Casper is sticking up for me. He strides closer, hands still casually shoved in his pants pockets, as he stands in front of Luca. His loose stance is like an open invitation, an offering to try anything with him. I would hate to know what the consequence would be for Luca.

"Well, officer..." Casper bends down a little, looking at the name tag pinned to Luca's button-up shirt. "Luca. I don't think it's very professional to be raising your voice to a lady, in public."

This doesn't go down well with Luca. His job is his life. "Back off buddy. Don't give me a reason to arrest you."

Casper smiles. A gentle, taunting smile, not made for amusement. It is calm, exact. He knows what he's doing, and how far he's pushing Luca.

"It would be my pleasure to accompany you down to the station. I'm sure your dad would be happy to hear how you can't even bring your girlfriend to climax with your name on her lips," Casper says casually, not taking his eyes of Luca's once, even to look at me.

Again, I am shocked. Everyone in the diner was listening in, and I'm sure the waitresses behind me are taking great pleasure in hearing such information. Redness flushes my cheeks. I am embarrassed. Because it's true.

Luca hasn't given me an orgasm for a year now. I'm pretty decent at faking it, now. I'm not sure why, but our spark has gone. It vanished into thin air, and sometimes I think we just tolerate each other.

He's not my mate. That's what my dad keeps telling me. Everyday my dad tells me to wait, instead of taking a male to bed whose mate might be just around the corner. But it's easy to love him. Easy to call him mine, to have him be there.

Luca's face is as red as mine. "Harassing an officer is an offence."

Casper steps back, and I almost let out a sigh of relief. I think he's giving up, letting Luca continue without an issue. Instead, he begins circling him. Smooth, elegant strides around my boyfriend, like a beast preying on a small animal.

"Try your luck and handcuff me." Casper sounds menacing. Casper isn't a small man. Muscular frame, tall, he's a threat to Luca.

And the smaller man knows it. Handling Casper would be a nightmare. I shake my head at the thought.

Suddenly, a whiny voice of strange reason steps in. "Stop."

Casper freezes. As does Luca.

"I'm going to have to ask both of you to leave my diner right now." It's Janet, my boss.

And both men instantly know they can't contest the woman who owns the shop. As obediently as I've ever seen Luca be, he turns around, and stalks straight out the building, his pride a little damaged.

Casper apologises to Janet, hands his menu back to me, and leaves swiftly.

I am left completely confused. What just happened?

Chapter Five

His hair slips through my fingers, which tangle around the light brown strands.

Luca is mad. Furious actually. So irked by Casper's comments, he has taken it upon himself to prove he can make me climax. I think he is proving it to himself more than anything.

But as I lie there, feeling the assault of his tongue against the most sensitive part of my body, I don't feel anything but uncomfortable. Fuelled by anger, not love, Luca has decided to go down on me, and I am not enjoying it in the slightest.

For a start, I can't get Casper out of my mind. How he knew about me faking orgasms was chilling. People shouldn't just be able to look at others and tell that from one glance.

So instead of enjoying his tongue against me, I moan when needed, and utter his name as I pretend to finish.

As I pull my clothes on, I notice Luca looking proud of himself. It's boosted his ego, and I don't doubt he will tell Casper any time he sees him.

I decide I need to wander into the Phantom Forest, and find where Casper lives. Because I can't deal with a jealous boyfriend any longer, and because I have a feeling Casper is the main cause of Luca's sudden change of attitude, I'm going to find Casper and tell him to stay away.

Luca leaves not long after. He got a call from his father who reported another girl had gone missing. Despite being worried it might be June, I'm going to find Casper first. The sooner he is out of Luca's and my life, the better.

So I grab a black backpack, and stuff it with a spare jacket, an umbrella, and a flashlight. I am prepared.

I start my walk with the afternoon sun on my back. Since yesterday, when Casper came to my house, and made me late for work, I've wanted to find his house. It's only fair, me knowing where he lives, since he knows where I do.

So I walk at a quick pace down the beaten path I usually take to June's house. I hope she's okay. She locks her house up pretty good, and never goes out much. But with that broken window... No, she would have stayed at her parents' house if it was that much of an issue.

Determined not to let the heaviness of my backpack get to me, I stalk on, pushing away the odd branch from my face, or any bush sticking out of the dirt path from my feet, as I walk.

I have a vague idea of where Casper's estate will be. People have said it was old and falling apart, and stuck out through the undergrowth, which means it won't be hard to find. Nowadays, the only people who go around the property are the ones who owned it, although no one knows who does anymore.

Some rumours even hint that Alpha Jasper and his father lived in it centuries ago, before they both died. I think June told me once that their souls haunt the place.

Not that I believe that.

The walk eats up around an hour of my time. I hadn't expected to take so long to finally find the estate Jasper lives in. And despite there being no hint of this being his residence, it just seems... so obvious.

But it's not exactly what I thought it would be. I expected run-down. I expected chipping away at the edges, broken and deranged. Instead, the house stands proud and tall, sun reflecting off the classic wood. This isn't the estate I was told to be frightened of.

This is a mansion. A palace in its own right.

The garden isn't unkempt either. Plants grow around the concrete walls that surround the property, kept trimmed and neat. Someone has put great care into the home that stands many floors above me, wanting it to look delightful and airy.

27

I slip through the wrought iron gate that has been left slightly open. If Casper doesn't live here, someone pleasant must do. Maybe that's foolish of me to think so, but it's the drive behind the courage needed to actually knock on the door.

The front door presents itself like the gateway to hell. If Casper is really behind that door, then what will his reaction be when he sees me? Is he even home?

I knock twice before stepping back. Why is my heart beating so fast? Why am I asking myself so many questions?

I wait for at least a minute before knocking again. No answer.

My back is turned on the door by the time it opens. I had given up on the idea of him actually opening the door, was already planning how I was going to keep him away from Luca. That was, until I heard the click of the door opening.

Slowly, I turn. Not only am I faced with Casper, but a half-naked one.

I never knew a man without a shirt on could take my breath away until now. Leaning casually against the doorframe, I'm fully aware Casper is watching my eyes drag down his torso. And at that moment I couldn't do anything but.

Not only do his abdominal muscles look as if they're carved from the personification of sex itself, but they glisten with a thin sheen of sweat. What I assume is a tattoo runs from his shoulder down to his hip, curving in and out of the muscles built into his body. I can't be sure it is a tattoo, as it looks like he he'd been born with darkened markings that didn't quite make a coherent shape.

Over his other shoulder drapes a small towel I know was used to mitigate sweat when working out. And boy... does he need it.

I blink. What am I thinking? I have a boyfriend, and yet I'm standing here, staring at the chest of a complete stranger. But who am I to not appreciate a masterpiece of a body? *No, Thea. Stop.*

"What a pleasant surprise," Casper notes, drawing my gaze off his body. He assesses me through thick locks of dark hair that cascade across his forehead in a way anyone would be jealous of. I never really questioned his violet eyes, but maybe I should start to—because they hardly look normal.

I can't force words out of my mouth.

"Would you like to come inside?" he asks. Glancing over my shoulder, I guess he's either worried about the time of day, or the weather.

Finally, I find words. "I just came to tell you something..."

"You should really come inside," he insists, still not meeting my eyes, as if the clouds behind me are far more interesting. I shake my head in protest, until suddenly, a crack of thunder booms in my ear.

To reiterate, I hate Mother Nature. Sure, I had braved the wind and rain the other day, but thunder was different. It may just be a sound, but it always has me cowering for fear, and today is no exception.

I push past Casper in my fright, rushing through the door which he closes behind me. Stumbling into the hallway, I brace my hands against either wall, my eyes squeezed shut. My fear of thunderstorms has overruled my rational thinking.

"Here," Casper murmurs. He drapes a mink blanket over my shoulders, and the feeling of softness against my skin instantly calms my nerves. "You can stay here."

His words are a warm promise. And despite the true reason for coming here, I'm grateful his house is refuge from the storm.

I wince at the sound of another clap of thunder above us. "Sorry."

Why I am apologizing, I'm not sure. Without a word, Casper coaxes me deeper into his home, down the dimly lit hallway. My fingers clutch the edge of the blanket around my shoulders, as I savor the feeling of Casper's hand pressed against my clothed back. Almost as if it's my lifeline.

"Nice home," I point out, drinking in the sight of the gathering-cum-lounge room he's led me into. It's decorated lavishly, and I know from the sight of the old books lining the wall, and the furniture, this place is probably worth more than I am.

"I only just finished putting the furnishings in," he tells me. I sit on the edge of his couch, sinking into plush cushions.

I notice Casper is still shirtless, despite the cold that circles the area. He glances at me. "Tea?"

I nod gratefully. He disappears through a door for a moment, and I can't help but admire him as he walks out. His back is like a machine, with every muscle moving intricately as if to ensure he keeps his elegant gait and stance.

Other than the marvelous silk fabric and tapestries strung around the place, it is hardly decorated. No portraits. No evidence of the life Casper left behind to move to this Pack.

He wanders back in a few minutes later, a shirt now on (unfortunately) and a teacup balanced between his finger and thumb. I catch the gentle smile on his face. It really is a sight to see, and for a moment, I wish he would smile more often.

"Here you are," he says, handing me the tea. "It is especially for calming nerves."

I take the cup, only to be surprised at the contents. The liquid is a thick mixture of swirling black and grey. Gently tipping the cup so I can properly see what is in it, I notice the way the contents lag and spill like sludge around the rim.

"What the...?"

"Will you drink it?" Casper asks, having found a spot on the couch opposite mine while I was inspecting the strange liquid.

He stares at me with such fiery curiosity I feel nerves within me spike. The opposite of what the tea is said to do. "Not if it isn't tea."

"And if someone else offered it to you? Your friend, your dad, your boyfriend?"

His voice is demanding, yet also smoother than silk. Obviously there is nothing more that he wanted to know about than this. But what he asked takes me by such surprise, I have to think about it.

"I suppose so, yes," I say warily.

Instantly, Casper's expression is cold, detached. He even looks slightly angry.

"In the cup is a mixture of herbs meant to sedate someone; make them drowsy and vulnerable," he tells me, looking anxious at his own words.

I gasp, the cup falling from my hands. The china shatters on the ground, the contents within soaking into the carpet by my feet. He's tricked me... I've allowed myself to be lured into his psychopath's home.

I'm up in a second, twisting around to dash down the hallway. The moment I get out of this house, I will call Luca and demand Casper gets taken into the police station.

Except, when I make it to the door I realize, with a sinking heart, it is locked. And I can't see a way to unlock it.

Defeat beating away in my heart, I slowly turn around. I have never felt so devastated. So frightened of inevitable death. Because if he doesn't merely rape and discard me, my future could look a lot worse.

"Please, don't kill me," I whisper.

Casper stalks slowly down the hallway, noticing how I am trapped. His eyes strip me bare, his gait slow and calculated, as if he's assessing which is the best way to kill me.

Instead, he surprises me with his words. "Calm down. I'm not going to hurt you."

But I don't believe him. He stands before me, eyes burning into my mind. Wordlessly, he leans forward, bracing his arms on either side of my head against the door.

Holy...

His head is on the left side of my face, hot breath brushing against my ear. I want to arch against the feeling, savor it. But the fear of being potentially drugged by him pushes through the feeling of his proximity and the heat it sends to my core.

"I'll never hurt you," he murmurs, the words radiating straight through my body. "Because if I were going to, I wouldn't have told you what was in that cup."

Truth. I can see it in his eyes. In my fright, I hadn't thought rationally about what had been in the cup. I had just thought about what it could possibly to do me. Maybe it was linked to the fact that I've probably made a big mistake, walking into this stranger's house.

But the thunder... it has suddenly ceased.

"Then, what do you want with me?" I question, my voice breathy. He seems to think thoroughly about my question.

Right now, I could teach out and touch the soft skin on his face, or even kiss him if I wanted to. Him being this close, is terrifying. But at the same time, a part of me wants nothing more than to feel him against me... *Wait, what am I thinking?*

"If anyone... *anyone* offers you a drink that looks like that, you *don't* take it," he says, as if he's able to predict the future, and can see someone planning to force feed me such a drink. I could laugh in the moment. I could take it as a joke, but the look in his eyes suggests I shouldn't play around, when this is serious.

"Okay..." I mutter, still unable to move.

Casper waits for a moment, and I see a flicker of something in his eyes. Longing? Sadness? It's masked in a second, and he lets me go.

"I should go home," I tell him, anxious to get out of this house. His jaw clenches, and he leans over me, and for a second, I think he is going to trap me against the door again. Instead, he twists the doorknob, and swings it open.

"It is getting dark," he says, and I turn around to see he is right. But how? How does time pass so quickly around him? When I swear it hasn't even been an hour... "At least let me drive you home."

I let him. Despite wanting nothing more than to say no, and walk back, an hour pushing through the undergrowth at night doesn't sound pleasant at all, and if I wander off the path...

I make him park further down the driveway, so my dad won't question who I've shown up with. Perhaps he would demand to see Casper, then intimidate him as much as he intimidates everyone else in the town.

"So why did you come over in the first place?" Casper asks, as I am about to step out of his car. I pause. The true reason I had gone was expelled from my mind when the thunder struck, and hasn't reappeared until now.

I can't get out of this car until he knows. "I need you to stay away from me and Luca."

32

He looks surprised.
Why do I feel so bad?

Chapter Six

Dad is sitting at the dinner table when I walk back inside.

Despite the fact he is slightly balding, and the scuff of dark hair on his chin suggests something like a beard, we look alike. Everyone says we have the same nose, and our eyes have the same dark tint around the outside.

He smiles, setting his newspaper down on the table, letting me get a glimpse of the front page. Jessica's face has been printed large scale, with a daunting title and, most likely, a degrading passage on how she was depressed and how it was suicide. If the town believed that, then no propaganda would surface, and everything would be okay.

"Hey honey," he says, peering at me from behind his reading glasses. I smile at him warmly, dumping my backpack on one of the dining room chairs as I go to sit in the seat opposite him.

"I was just at June's," I lie. No point bringing Casper up.

Dad stands, tucking the newspaper under his arm as he wanders to the kitchen. "You look cold. Would you like a drink?"

"Sure," I say, rubbing my hands together. He has no idea I've shown up here in someone else's car, rather than walking all the way from June's. I know he hates the fact I took a route so close to the Phantom Forest.

Dad rustles around in the kitchen for a moment, boiling the jug, getting the tea ready. In the meantime, I kick off my shoes and hang my jacket on the back of the chair.

"Someone else went missing today," Dad tells me from the kitchen, making my blood run cold. "A boy, this time."

This is the third person who's disappeared from town. It can't be a coincidence. "Who?"

"Ryan Connolly," Dad tells me. I close my eyes, a mental picture of the young boy clouding my vision. Another one I went to school with. His family are very wealthy, living in the best neighborhood, providing him with the best clothes and car. He wasn't a jock, but his money bought him popularity, and even girls.

"What do his parents think?" I ask warily. Prominent figures in this town's society, Ryan's parents are known to hold the town on a leash. Sometimes, we think his father believes he is the substitute Alpha, since no one took over the role since Jasper's father.

Dad chuckles. "Your boyfriend and his father, along with half the town, are out looking for him."

My father loves Luca. *Loves* him. The two get along so well they should be the ones dating. My father was the one to introduce me to the boy, letting us date straight away, unlike other boys I'd had any interest in before.

"Apparently a man recently moved into the estate in the Phantom Forest. He might be brought in for questioning," Dad says, setting my tea in front of me. *Casper... He wouldn't be the reason why they have gone missing, right?*

I sip my tea. "I suppose it is the only lead."

I look down into my cup, taken back by the sour taste it leaves in my mouth. Not the refreshing, tannin taste I was used to. And just as I swallow, my heart sinks in my chest as I assess the contents in the cup.

Thick, black... almost like I was drinking straight oil.

I set the teacup down slowly, trying not to scream. Trying not to cry out. Casper had warned me. But this is my father; he wouldn't poison me.

"Like your tea? It's new, meant to calm nerves," my father says. This strikes my heart with full frontal force. He's lying to me, through his coffee-stained teeth. My own father just gave me a sedative, and won't admit it.

I won't react. I *can't*.

"I think I'll go to bed," I say carefully, already feeling my tongue is heavy and pasty in my mouth.

He really did it. He really did drug his own daughter.

"Tired?" he asks innocently, catching my gaze within his own. I nod, standing slowly so I won't fall.

Whatever he has given me, it's working fast. It seems to be starting at my feet, sinking them to the ground like a weight, before crawling up my legs.

He says 'goodnight' but I don't reply. All I can think about is 'why'. Why would he drug me? What does he want to do with me? I need to get out of here, now, before these questions are answered without me even knowing.

I slam my bedroom door behind me, stumbling over heavy feet, feeling as if my body is wading through something as dense as water. I fall onto the bed, my arms struggling to pull myself up enough to grab my phone.

Luca will come here... He'll save me.

I try to text, but my eyes are blurring, and my thumbs refuse to move, as if my brain has cut itself off from my body. I have to crawl on my hands and knees to the bathroom, bending over the toilet to stick my fingers down my throat to throw up the tea.

After I wash out my mouth four times, I drag my numb back legs to my room, before dizziness hits me like a truck, and I trip face first into unconsciousness.

I wake once. I fight through a heavy haze hovering over my mind, catching the sound of two familiar voices. Still on my bed, I stare through the crack in my bedroom door. Luca and my father are standing there, deep in a heated conversation.

"Now?"

"I had no choice."

"Why? Why rush the next stage so fast?"

"*He's* here. That goddamn man will ruin everything if he finds her. He will take her from us, because she belongs to him."

I don't need to hear anymore. I need to get out of here. And the window is my only option.

The one sip I took must have not been enough to keep me unconscious, because I can feel myself coming back to normal, as I force my window open with absolute stealth. Still talking, Luca and Dad don't notice me rather ungracefully force my body to maneuver through the window.

I fall on my stomach, the ground almost winding me. The moment they realize I am no longer in that room, they're going to come for me, and do Goddess knows what.

I find my feet as my head clears, the drug I had thrown up fading into the distance of my veins. I'm free... but... where do I go?

My own boyfriend has betrayed me... and my dad has, too. I don't know which is worse.

June's. I can trust her. I circle the house, finding the path that leads to her house. I can run there, and never look back.

Then in the morning—but the police are behind what just happened. At least, half of their force is.

Tears flow without me being able to stop them. My mind can't put together any proper thought that makes sense to me. Except one. Casper. He knew about the tea, and that someone would give it to me. He even tested me, and I failed.

Suddenly, a jab of nausea hits me. The drug is still in effect, and it is as if it's on wave two of its infection of my system. I fall to my knees in the middle of the path, confusion hitting me every second.

And then I see him.

He's standing between the trees, shadows curling around his limbs, eyes more violet than I have ever seen. He doesn't look real—like the personification of magic itself. It seems to emanate from him in dark tendrils of the night.

Casper.

He almost looks disappointed at seeing me here, in the middle of the woods at night. Striding forward, Casper kneels down in front of me. Gleaming leather gloves wrap his hands, almost merging into the sleeves of his dress shirt. Why is he dressed so neatly in the middle of the night?

Wait..."Why are you here?"

My voice is raspy, sounding bizarre next to the gentle sounds of the night. And the moment Casper's silky smooth voice could be heard, I sounded deranged.

"Why did you drink it? I warned you," Casper mutters, brushing my hair away with his gloved fingers. I shiver. He isn't telling me why he's here, and for some reason, I know not to press it.

"I didn't expect it," I tell him, staring directly into those violet eyes.

Casper stands, glancing over my shoulder, sighing as he does. I join him, making it to my feet, but not without swaying dramatically first. Luckily, Casper steadies me, hands gripping my shoulder to stop me from falling onto my butt again.

"Why him?" I ask, my voice weak. "Why my own father?"

Casper looks grim. If he did happen to wander into the woods at the same time I did, then he might know why my own father decided to drug me. And maybe why Luca happens to be part of it as well.

"Because of me," he tells me. "He was going to take you far away to somewhere so desolate, so alone, you would never escape, nor see the sun again."

His words take me back for a second. So callous, with no holding back. But what frightens me the most is the fact he did not once flinch, instead staying true to his words of pure honesty.

"Why because of you? What did you do to him?" For a moment, it doesn't look as if he is going to tell me, by the way he begins leading me down the path.

"I did nothing to him. It is about what I will do to him," Casper says cryptically. I frown, not quite understanding what he means.

He looks down at me as we walk. "I have been lying to you about a few things."

"Like what?" I ask warily.

I have been lied to by many people, and now, I don't know who I can trust with anything today. My own father lied. My boyfriend. Everyone I love and care about is turning against me, and I don't even know why.

"My name, for a start," he says. *Casper isn't his real name?*

38

Suddenly, the sound of someone shouting echoes through the forest. We exchange glances, instantly becoming aware of who is in the forest with us.

"We need to go," Casper, or whoever he is, insists. He grabs my hand, the leather if his glove feeling foreign.

He begins pulling me away from the sound of the shout. The sudden change of direction and the insistence on movement has my head spinning, the drug I'd taken earlier begins rearing its ugly head once again.

"I can't," I breathe, my feet skidding against the path. "I might pass out again."

And I'm right. Because as Casper turns, a vignette of blurriness shrouds my vision, and I know at that moment I won't be able to stop myself from becoming unconscious.

And the last memory I have before darkness hits is of Casper catching me in his arms.

"I won't let anything bad happen to you. I'll protect you, I promise…"

Chapter Seven

I wake again, and this time, it's morning.

I sit up, my mind awake in an instant. I'm not sure where I thought I would wake up, to be honest, but back in my own bed wasn't an option I had considered. Lifting my bed sheets, I see I'm dressed in my pajamas. I have never got out of bed so quickly.

Pushing open my door, emerging into the lounge room, I find June sitting on my couch, reading from a book as big as the Bible. I stare at her in disbelief, as she glances up at me.

"About time you woke up," she says. Warily, I wander further into the room.

"What are you doing here?" I feel my eyes narrowing.

For a moment, she looks offended. "I came to show you something."

I sit beside her on the couch. I trust June. She's my friend, and would never do anything bad to me. Despite her being flighty at the best of times, I can rely on her to be honest with me at all times.

"Where's my dad?"

"At work I guess," she suggests, placing the massive book she brought with her on my lap. Was I dreaming last night? It seemed so unorthodox, I wouldn't cross my vivid nightmares off the list. I mean, Casper worried me with his proclamations about a drugging tea. Perhaps it had got to me last night?

I mean, why would my own father and boyfriend do that? It makes no sense, and seeing Casper in the forest last night makes it all the more unlikely. I was definitely dreaming, I decide.

I gaze down at the book, seeing a passage of small font, and a slightly faded picture... of Casper. He's seated on a throne, almost lounging on it. He looks younger, more youthful, and carefree. On his head is a golden crown, bejeweled with glittering diamonds, rubies and sapphires. Across his shoulders is draped a cloak of red velvet. He looks... pure royalty.

"That's Jasper, two days before he was meant to be named as Alpha. A day before he disappeared," June tells me.

My eyebrows furrow. "Why show me this?"

"That new guy... the one who happened to show up in this town the day Jessica went missing. That man has an uncanny resemblance to the Alpha of all Phantom Wolves..."

My eyes automatically roll.

"First, it is just a coincidence. Casper hasn't killed anyone. And, Jasper doesn't have the same violet eyes, his are dark brown. And, Phantom Wolves don't exist. Let's just drop the subject of Jasper still being alive, and let him rest peacefully."

June doesn't look convinced. I can tell she's about to let out a retort of some sort of excuse why Casper is actually an Alpha. But the phone rings. The shrill call cuts short my best friend's words, as I stand, answering the phone to my left.

"Patterson residence," I say, answering the phone how my father typically does.

"Thea, is that you?" Luca's father, Jamie. His voice is warm, comforting... familiar. "I just wanted to call you and ask where your father is. A colleague of his sent in a message saying he didn't make it to work."

I know why they're worrying. Dad works on an orchard, and it's harvesting season—the busiest time of year. As the manager, my father *never* misses a day of work, even when he's sick.

"No, he isn't home," I tell him, warily casting a gaze around the house. "Something weird happened last night."

If there is anyone I can trust, it's Luca's father. Every generation of their family have been cops, and I think Jamie is one of the best. And he doesn't have a temper like this son does...

41

"It was like a vivid dream, no, a nightmare. Dad had drugged me, and Luca had been a part of it too. And then... and then I met Casper, you know, the new guy to town. And then he told me his name wasn't actually Casper, but he ran out of time before he could actually tell me his real name. And the strange thing is, before this all happened, I was at Casper's, and he told me not to drink this drink... which just so happened to be the drink my dad gave me..."

I take a deep breath.

"Wow kid, that's one strong imagination you got there. Ever thought about becoming a writer?" Jamie asks, the laugh he sends down the line full of amusement. He really does think I'm crazy.

"I think I might be sick," I say, glancing at June who's heard the whole thing. She looks alarmed. "I mean, these strange dreams, or hallucinations... I even feel like time is passing by slower than it actually is."

I hear Jamie grumble on the other end. "Maybe you should see the doctor."

But what kind of sickness correlates to me basically losing my mind? Perhaps it has had something to do with Casper. Ever since he showed up at my house the other day, things have been off.

"Unless I was dreaming, my dad said the Casper man would be brought in for questioning," I say, wishing June wasn't in the room to hear our conversation.

"Ah yes, I got him in early this morning. He's clean. Just a normal fellow from another town in the Devotion Pack, looking for a fresh start after he..."

I stop listening. That man is far from normal, and now he's haunting my dreams?

"There's a town meeting tonight. I suggest you attend..." Jamie tells me. "We need to talk about the missing kids. Hopefully your dad will be home by then."

Why aren't I worried about my father? Am I holding some sort of vendetta because of my dream last night? Because I'm sure he never would drug me. Wow, maybe Jamie is right. Maybe I should become an author.

"And ah... lock your doors, okay? I'll get Luca to pick you up," Jamie says, sounding frighteningly wary. "Just for precaution, you know."

I hang up. So something terrible really is going on. Is a mass murderer out there right now, ready to snatch either June or me next? I won't worry her, not now.

I convince her to stay all day with me. It's nice, having someone around after my dream last night. I even tell her more about it. She laughs at how ridiculous it sounds, confirming that what 'happened' last night was just in my mind.

I start thinking less about it, and more about where my father is...

Luca picks us up around five in the afternoon. He's in a bad mood, and on the drive to the town hall, tells me he thinks Casper's a bad man who shouldn't have been let off, as Luca strongly believes he did it. He thinks Casper took those people, and done Goddess knows what to them.

The town hall is the heart of the town. Meetings here are scarce, which leads me to believe something big is about to go down. Anxious for what's about to happen, I clutch Luca's hand. People like him being here. He is a policeman.

The place is packed full of people when we walk in. Despite the low population of the town, we know how to fill a room. Luckily enough, we find seats near the back, just as Luca's dad is clearing his throat for everyone's attention.

"Thank you all for coming out this evening," Jamie greets everyone warmly. "We have a lot to discuss."

The murmuring cuts off, but I know everyone's tempted to start again. 'A lot to discuss' could allude to anything, and since nothing ever happens, curiosity has heightened.

"As you all know, five teenagers have gone missing as of late..." Jamie said. I blanch. Five?

I watch the man, so similar to his own son, cast a glance toward the back of the room. Not being able to help myself, I glance over my shoulder, to see two couples looking stricken. I know right then

43

they are the families of some of those people. One of the mothers cries into her husband's shoulder.

"And they have been found..." Jamie follows, and the way his face pales, the way he looks down at the papers he holds, suggests one thing. My heart falls.

"All five were found dead, hang..." he coughs, unsure if he should continue speaking. But this town is open. "… hanging from trees within the Phantom Forest. Police found a note, and are currently investigating it. We have also spoken to some people, but so far have found nothing to further our investigation."

Everyone gasps, including me. Luca, next to me, swallows from already knowing the news, while June drops her head on my shoulder and starts to cry.

"What did the note say?" A man from the back shouts.

"We cannot disclose that information at this time, but we will be releasing it when all families have given permission," Jamie answers.

That is the first clue. Whatever is on that note is personal.

"So what happens now?" someone else calls from the front of the room. A mother, by the look of her.

"We lock our doors, we keep our children safe while we officers look for the killer... or killers."

The mention of this possibly being the doing of more than one person has my blood running cold. I glance over my shoulder again, wanting to assess the reactions of the families, but instead a violet gaze captures me.

Casper is here. He is a part of this town now, but seeing him leaning casually against the back door takes me by surprise.

"The police force is officially disallowing any more access to the path bordering the Phantom Forest, as well as other walking areas in and near that forest. We cannot take any more risks, therefore we suggest you ensure you are aware of your children's whereabouts at all times." Jamie sounds serious.

June and I exchange glances. That's how we get to each other. Sure, there's the town to go through, but I can already tell seeing June will be harder.

44

But that isn't what I'm worrying about. I'm worrying about my father. He isn't here, and I doubt he's at home. My father is missing, and even the police don't seem to care.

Jamie says little after that. The families have to leave after emotions get to be too much, so Jamie closes the session after a few other notes. Luca goes to talk to his father, and June wants to see her parents who've attended the meeting, so I agree to wait outside.

"Thea," a silky-smooth voice murmurs from behind me. I jump, twisting around to see Casper. He looks smart... just like he did in my dream last night.

"I told you to stay away," I mutter, hoping Luca won't come out and see Casper who's now standing directly in front of me.

I try my best to avert my gaze.

"Last night wasn't a dream," he tells me. I flinch. He grabs my shoulders, fingers digging into the cloth of the long sleeves. "We did meet in the forest, and you did drink that drink."

I stumble back a few steps, but I can't take my eyes off his.

"And I need you to come with me right now, because you are in serious danger."

Chapter Eight

For a good second, I am stunned.

I could choose not to believe him. I could tell him he's crazy, and then walk away. But not only do I see truth in his eyes, he relays what had happened to me with not a single falter in his voice, in his expression.

"What... what do you mean?" My voice is breathy.

"These people, who you trust, are planning something, Thea. Something terrible, and I need to get you out of here before they can..."

Suddenly a hand clamps my shoulder, tightly. I jump, but don't bother turning to see who's behind me. I know it's my boyfriend. His touch is one I always know, especially when he is angry.

"Thea, it's time to take you home."

The look on Casper's face, in his eyes, is something almost impossible to put adequate words to. It could almost be compared to utter malice brewing under his skin, and by the way his fists clench by his side, I can tell he is considering letting Luca get a taste.

"Don't go with him, Thea," Casper says carefully. With every word that comes from his mouth, Luca's hand clenches tighter on my shoulder, but I keep my face passive.

"I am her boyfriend," Luca says carefully. "And I am taking her home."

I can tell what this is... a contest of masculinity. Both of them staring each other down, waiting for the other to turn around and walk away. And despite Casper being far bigger than Luca in size, my boyfriend would never step down from something like this if it killed him.

"I want to know... "

Luca cuts off my words, pushing me behind him. The movement is so sudden I stumble back a few steps. I want to question him, I want to understand why he did what he did last night. What Casper had to do with it...

But he ushers me into his car, and there's nothing I can do. If it truly wasn't a dream, then my father drugged me, and Luca had been a part of that.

And at the last moment, I catch Casper's eye, and I feel this isn't ending here. And my thoughts are confirmed by his next words.

"Don't believe them... I'm going to save you from..."

And then he disappears behind the crowd, as my boyfriend drives me away

***

"Keep your doors locked tonight, okay?"

I don't say a word.

Luca turns back, as he closes all the curtains in the lounge room. He isn't staying. I've told him to leave. I've even told him to explain himself, but he said he would take me to the doctor in the morning, and arrest Casper too.

"Babe?" he snaps, making me look up from staring at my fingers, wondering what I should do.

"You don't think your dad would drug you, do you?" Luca chuckles slightly. "Or me?"

I cross my arms over my chest as I lean back in my seat, still not saying a word. He sighs deeply, obviously annoyed. It isn't like he hasn't told me I get on his nerves with my stubbornness before.

"Just go," I mutter.

With one more furious look my way, Luca turns and walks out the door, slamming it behind him.

Luca and I argue a lot. But nothing like this. Nothing has felt like the current confusion, and disbelief.

Casper remembered last night. He relayed the moments to me like they really happened, but everyone else has told me I am ridiculous. Am I?

I stand up, both hands clutching the sides of my head. What do I do?

Luca closed all my curtains, for safety. It's raining again outside, so everything is naturally darker, meaning I should probably start my thinking by turning on the lights. But the moment I flick the switch, I realize the power is out.

I growl under my breath. Grabbing my phone, I dial my father's number. Not the first time I've done that today. But again, he doesn't answer, letting my worry set in even deeper.

I begin to pace.

I call June, but she doesn't answer. Then I call my co-workers, my boss Jamie, and everyone I can think of who would get me out of here... get me anywhere that isn't this house, without my father, and without power.

Then as I lie back on the couch, my phone rings in my hand. I see the caller ID being a private number. A flicker of concern passes across my mind, as I wonder who it could be. I decide to answer it anyway, seeing no harm in finding out who requires my attention.

"Thea, listen…" Casper. The ease, the smoothness of his voice is unmistakable. But something urgent is there.

"Casper, what do you want?" I don't want to admit I wanted to talk to him. Obviously he knew about last night, and I'm on the tipping point—whether to believe him, or my boyfriend, family, and friends.

"I am coming to get you," he says quickly, and I hear a door slamming in the background. I frown, walk to the window, and push back the curtain.

"Why?" I feel wary.

The rain is beating down as viciously as ever, indicating this storm or whatever it is, is the cause of the power outage. And by the looks of it, it doesn't seem to be ending anytime soon.

"I told you, you aren't safe," Casper reminds me. "I will explain everything when I get to your house. Pack a few things. We will be leaving this Pack as soon as I get there."

His words take me back. The way he spoke has made me want to follow his orders instantly, as if it's second nature. But I make myself stop, and think, before I go and get together a bag of things to leave my home.

"Excuse me?" I splutter. "I am not…"

"Thea, you need to understand—you are in serious danger. Like I said, everything will be explained to you when I get there."

And he hangs up. I'm left staring at my phone in complete bewilderment. Not only do his words ring in my ears, but I am considering them. And after what happened last night…

All of a sudden, the sound of a loud banging comes from the front door. "Babe! Let us in."

Luca. He's back. Looking out the window again, I notice two very large men with him. And, if I am not seeing things, one is holding a wound rope in his hand. I nearly scream in horror.

Casper is right! My own boyfriend is coming here to hurt me.

Glad I remembered to lock my door, I run to my room. It takes a few minutes to pack some clothes and other necessities. All that's running through my mind, is 'am I really doing this?'

Am I about to get into the car of a stranger, because I think my boyfriend may be planning to kill me, or something else?

The banging only gets worse as I sling my bag over my shoulder, and wander to the back door. Every call of my name from Luca is like a stab to the heart. Perhaps I am falling for Casper's trap, I think, as I quietly exit through the back door. But the thoughts melt away as I see Casper's car pull up in the driveway.

We don't meet gazes, and I can tell he is looking at Luca, who is on the other side of the house from me. Without a second thought, I'm sprinting harder than I ever have toward his car.

Everything seems to slow down as I run, rain hitting my face, feet sliding across the grass of my backyard. Just as my hands reach for the door handle, I look left of the driveway, just in time to see Luca's livid expression, and the confusion on the other two men's faces.

"Drive," I snap, the second I'm seated in the car. Casper presses the gas pedal down, dramatically forcing the car forward, making me brace my arms on the dashboard. I even nearly smack my head as he turns around to drive back down my driveway.

I toss my bag over into the backseat. "You'd better explain before I call the police."

Glancing behind me, I see Luca throwing his hands up, and I can sense the phone call I'll be receiving soon if my phone isn't turned off.

Casper looks a little nervous, so I decide I need to be the one demanding answers.

"Were those men there to kill me?" I watch Casper bite his lower lip. "Or hurt me?"

"Yes," he admits, as if it is the most painful thing he has to say. He glances at me anxiously, as we pull onto the main road, the car window wipers moving quickly against the onslaught of rain. It reminds me of how soaked I am right now after the run I made for his car.

I swallow. "Why would they?"

"Because of me. They knew I was aware of what they were doing... of what they are. The moment I set foot into town I was planning to take you away from them, to save you from them, and they knew that. They weren't planning on hurting you yet, but my presence forced them to bring their plans ahead," Casper tells me.

That takes me back to last night... when Dad was talking about starting the next stage. Of what, I don't know.

"How did you know about this?" This is the first question to ask, despite all the ones already mulling in my mind. And by the way Casper is heading toward the exit of the Pack, I have no idea how long I'll have to ask.

"It's a long story," he tells me. I lean back in the seat, wishing my hands would stop quivering.

I shrug. "From the beginning."

"Well, my name is actually Jasper, and I am the Alpha of the Devotion Pack," he says casually. He hesitates, glancing at me so I can get a glimpse of those violet eyes. "I'm your Alpha."

Chapter Nine

I stare blankly at him, whoever *he* is.

He glances back at the road, paying attention to where he's driving for a second. But I can't help looking at him, letting my brain process his words.

"Jasper is dead." I say it clearly, more to myself than him. I want to hear the words so I can understand them, *believe* them.

He shakes his head slowly. "I was dead, but not anymore."

Out of everything that has happened today—my boyfriend trying to kill me and my father disappearing—this passes through easily. Perhaps I am just numb to everything right now, with all the stress…

"Many years ago, my father cursed me," he tells me, his words pronounced as he tries to get me to understand. "He turned me into a Phantom Wolf out of jealousy. My own father did not want me to become Alpha, and as a way to not arouse suspicion, he told everyone I had committed suicide, when really I was sent to be a Phantom with many others in the Pack."

I just sit there, patiently listening.

"I am sure you understand what a Phantom Wolf is. A wolf, half dead. A wolf that can walk as normal, but whose heart does not beat," he explains.

He glances at me, as if looking for permission to continue. I just stare at the rain hitting the windshield, trying to make sense of what he's telling me. And for whatever reason, I'm taking it better than I would expect myself to.

"Recently a few people helped me. That is a story for another time. But I want you to know I have been waiting to meet you for a very long time."

I decide to finally voice my opinion. "The asylum workers didn't do a very good job at keeping you locked up, did they?"

Violet Eyes chuckles. That's my new name for him since I can't help but think he isn't the centuries-old Alpha who supposedly died of suicide. Sure he looks strikingly similar to the Alpha, but that could just be a coincidence, right?

"I know it is hard to believe, but I need you to open up your mind to this," he says, casting me a wary look. "Because I would hate to intervene with..."

"With what? What could you do to me that I already haven't considered?" I growl. I know he's possibly a mass murderer who read about Alpha Jasper and then finally decided he is him. And if my likelihood of surviving by jumping out the car was higher, I'd have done it by now.

He smiles, a feline smile, suggesting something I don't dare question.

"I am capable of many things," he tells me. "But if I tell you, I am sure you will not believe me. So I will show you."

My eyes widen at his words. *Is he going to show me his murdering tendencies? Will he sling me from a tree like those innocent people who were my age? Is that his way of showing me?*

"I have nothing to do with the murder of those people, I promise," he murmurs, making my eyes widen.

Did he just...?

"Like I said, it is hard to believe, but the assumption you think is totally wild is actually very true," Violet Eyes says casually. "Reading minds is something I have perfected over the years, and now I would like to think I am pretty good at infiltrating someone's mind."

"I don't believe you," I say quickly, heat reaching my cheeks, as I am hasty to push away what I think is unrealistic.

Because if he can read my mind... No he can't, there is no way.

"If I can't, then how would I know that you don't believe I am who I am, because you don't believe in Phantom Wolves. Because you don't want anything abnormal to happen to you after your mother was found dead in the Phantom Forest, with the cause of death unknown."

My heart stops completely for a good second, and the fact that I don't go into cardiac arrest is a miracle.

The man, who I am slowly becoming more aware of, places his large hand on my thigh, the warmth spreading through my damp jeans. It may not have been skin on skin contact, but it almost made me calmer, like something had spread from his hand, and flooded through my veins.

Everything almost seems to fit in place, as if my mind is opening to every idea he's presented. Every idea Jasper has presented.

"As I said before, there are many things I am capable of, and a calming touch is very small in the arsenal of tricks I have up my sleeve." He takes his hand away, leaving me feeling as if I have drunk three too many drinks.

"Like magic?" I ask, wondering if that would freak me out, break through the numbness that has shrouded my brain. But when he nods, I feel nothing.

It just seems to make sense.

"It took me many years to perfect a calming touch. But I can safely say my touch does a lot more to you than you think."

I frown. "What does that mean?"

He shrugs, and I can tell no amount of harassing is going to get him to spill anything.

"I feel drunk," I slur. "Does that mean your touch is supposed to calm me down? To make me understand you are into some voodoo magic? And you're some half-dead beast that's said to kill innocent people? Or maybe you've made me feel like this so it would be easier to lure me..."

"Stop. I am not trying to manipulate you. I am trying to help you understand how far my powers stretch. I also don't want you to feel violated when I tell you I have been reading your mind for quite some time now. Actually, ever since I met you..."

Despite whatever magic has been forced into my veins, I am still mildly offended.

"So you're telling me that everything I've thought was right there for you to sift through for your own enjoyment?" I ask; his answering smile is enough. I frown at him, resting my head back on the seat with my arms crossed over my chest.

"Are you mad?"

"No," I admit. "Whatever magic you poured into me is doing its job."

Jasper chuckles. It feels strange, even in the mind I know is right now being violated, to hear the name Jasper, a name people haven't spoken for many years.

"Let me make it up to you. Let me answer your questions, in all seriousness and what not," Jasper promises.

I think for a moment. "Tell me exactly why they wanted to kill me, and why you decided to save me."

"Well, they technically wanted to sacrifice you. Your entire town happens to be cursed, with everyone who is a resident there being a Phantom Wolf. Each and every one of them once were alive, but died in a vendetta, as you know. However, you and your mother were the only ones to not become Phantoms."

I stay silent, not wanting to say a word until he's finished explaining himself.

"Your mother visited your town, and met your father who was already a Phantom, over 100 years old. They had you, and soon after, your mother was sacrificed. As they planned to do to you," Jasper informs me.

"Why?" I whisper.

"There are two kinds of Phantom Wolves. Those turned by what they once did, while others were cursed. I was cursed, as was Luca, and your friend June," he continues. "Their parents decided to turn their children to save them from sacrifice. Your father, on the other hand, planned to sacrifice you since you were born."

Again, I want to ask why, but the words won't come out. He can read my mind anyway.

"The Phantoms within your town believe that the Moon will grant them their souls back, and their beating hearts if they sacrifice enough of the innocent," Jasper tells me, looking as if this pains him to say, as much as it pains me to hear.

"Did June want me dead?" I ask, my voice sounding raspy, as the emotions he had quelled still threatend at the edge of the haze.

Biting his lip, he nods solemnly. My heart falls.

"But she spent so much time trying to convince me Phantom Wolves existed, when I believed they truly didn't," I protest, although he probably already knows.

"I'm sorry," Jasper says. "I mean that. But you are safer with me. I will make sure they never get their hands on you again."

I have so many more questions. So many. But everything I want to know cannot be voiced.

"Will all this hit me like a ton of bricks when the magic wears off?" I decide to ask. Simple enough.

Jasper shakes his head. "No. Once you sleep, your mind will have accepted the information."

That's a relief. I close my eyes for a moment, wishing I could think of anything *but* what has just happened, or what I have just found out. But the numbness is uncomfortable, and a constant reminder of everything.

"We were going to mate," I breathe. "Luca and I."

When I open my eyes, Jasper looks uncomfortable at what I just said. He even sighs deeply.

"You can't force the mate bond. Your mate will find you," he tells me.

I have honestly given up on finding whoever my mate might be. But can he find me? Will he possibly grace me with his presence in his near future?

"Yes," Jasper murmurs, making me jump. He knows. He can read my mind.

Silence stretches between us for a few moments. It gives me time to think about who my future mate might be. What he might look like, and even how he will treat me. And as I let these thoughts fill my mind, I don't miss Luca in the slightest.

"Can I demonstrate another power of mine?" Jasper asks. I nod, probably not having a choice.

"It is time manipulation. I am able to bend time to suit me, ceasing whoever I am with for as long as I want, letting time pass before I let their mind go," he says.

It stuns me for a good second. I have to force my mouth to close. "Wait..."

"I can hold your mind still, and let hours pass. While it would feel long for myself, it would feel like less than a second for you."

Before I can say anything, I only blink and know he has used his strange power. The sky has darkened, doused with different shades of blue and purple, signifying the evening. The storm has passed, and no longer are we driving. We're parked outside a massive wall, that scales higher than I've ever seen.

We are at another Pack.

"Holy shit," I breathe.

Not only does it dawn on me further that he had used a power only hours ago I would have ridiculed—I would have said that it was far from the realm of possibility for existence—but I realize that we are very far from the Devotion Pack.

I turn, catching Jasper's gaze. He smiles slyly.

"Welcome to the Love Pack. Our home for the next few days."

Chapter Ten

The Love Pack is one of the colder Packs. In fact, the sky is significantly darker here, suggesting it might snow. I huddle closer into my seat as we begin our drive into the Pack.

"I wish you'd told me to bring something warmer with me," I note, gazing out the window.

The houses here are exquisite. The entire place looks like something out of a fairytale. Lawns and gardens are neatly trimmed behind white picket fences, with the horizontal siding of the exterior painted to contrast the eaves. People even walk the conventional sidewalks, bundled up in soft fur coats and gloves.

Everything here seems so cliché... *domestic.*

"I'm sure we can find you something," Jasper tells me, glancing over at me while he drives. The speed limit here is tame, to match the pace everyone seems to be living at.

"This town is beautiful," I note, watching the people and places we pass. "Their Alpha must be an amazing person."

To my surprise, Jasper chuckles, and when I cast a glance at him, he looks blatantly amused. I don't doubt he knows all the Alphas, unless none of them know he is still alive, like I didn't. If he does, whoever this Alpha of Love is—who I've never heard much of—must really be cause for laughter.

"Malik isn't as much of an angel as you might think," Jasper informs me with a slight chuckle. I meet the gazes of an elderly couple as we drive swiftly past. Such innocent happiness gleams in their eyes as they stroll through the cold weather, arms linked.

"What's the word for him...?" Jasper muses. "Mischievous, perhaps."

I can't imagine it. "Why?"

Jasper seems to think for a moment. In the meantime I enjoy what I am looking at. Precise uniformity, presented in such a delicate, enjoyable manner.

"No one really knows. He is very... passionate. He shelters his people, giving them a life like no other Pack can offer. He is a possessive man, wanting to protect his possessions with his life," Jasper imparts.

I'd hate to imagine the Alpha of Passion, Desire and Love together. All Packs run off emotions and want, which I imagine is a dangerous mix.

"It is," Jasper cuts through my thoughts with his words like a sharpened knife. I forgot he could read my mind. "The three of those Alphas can be an extremely infuriating mix. Take it from myself, who has experienced many irritating people."

"Is he mated?" I ask, still wondering about the Alpha, Malik.

Jasper gives me his full attention for a moment. His lips quirk up, giving me a good look of the expression on his face that I'm coming to like. Such an easy, laid-back expression of playfulness.

"Why?" he asks coyly. "Interested?"

I can see the game in his eyes and I know, despite the situation, he could make light of any moment.

I shrug. "Maybe."

"Well I know him personally. I am sure he would love you to accommodate his presence for the night," Jasper teases.

Does he enjoy this? Messing with me? He seems to have been doing that the entire time I have known him. I mean, all that magic he has used on me... What about what he hasn't yet told me about?

Jasper manages to find a cute boutique on the street that is close to closing for the night. Since I'm not very well-equipped for the chilling weather, I need at least a coat of some sort. But despite the need, Jasper doesn't look very pleased with the idea of coming in with me.

"No one is in there," I note. We stand outside the car, my hands rubbing up and down my arms in an attempt to keep myself somewhat warm.

"It's not that..." he drawls, glancing at the pretty store decorated in a rich shade of pink.

The pink is meant to attract the good-willed people of this Pack, to influence them to buy the soft shades of fabric apt for the winter climate they perpetually live in. Even if the clothing type in there isn't really my style, anything but the thin jacket I wore for rain will do.

"Come on," I sigh, narrowing my eyes at him. "Malik would come in there with me."

His jaw clenches, and I see the conflict stirring within him. "Fine, but the moment someone else walks in there, I'm leaving."

I could make a sarcastic comment to tease him, but he can read my mind. Instead I just roll my eyes and enter the small shop. Jasper reluctantly follows.

The clerk at the front of the shop smiles pleasantly as we walk in. I notice her look twice at Jasper. I can't blame her...

I watch the Alpha smile knowingly from where he stands close to the door. My eyes narrow on his, as I realize his annoying abilities are working in his favor. *Violet eyes,* I think, specifically so he would notice. Admittedly they are strange.

And I won't for a second admit, even using thought, any kind of attraction.

I end up picking out a thick coat I'm sure will protect me against the elements.

"Good choice," the clerk says as she bags my item. "Looks like it's going to snow."

I follow her gaze to the sky, tainted with thick swirling clouds of intimidating darkness. I've never experienced snow before, living in a Pack where the weather is fairly tame. Aside from recently. I wonder for a fleeting moment whether or not Jasper had anything to do with the wild storms.

Suddenly the staff door opens from behind the girl currently serving us, a man emerging from it.

He looks like the epitome of a Love Pack member. The dark shade of hair, the eyes as cold and blue as ice. It's a mix that suggests so little about them, when really most of them only want one thing. Love.

The man catches my eye. His name tag reads Luke, which makes my heart jump a little. Luke, Luca. It can't be a coincidence...

"You don't look very familiar," the staff member named Luke notices. "Just moved here?"

Before I even have a chance to answer his question, I feel a warm hand land on my back, hand fisting my shirt. It's Jasper who's come up behind me, looming over me as he faces this other store person.

"Just visiting," he says, his tone as cool as the color of Luke's eyes.

"Are you two together?" Instantly I frown, ready to shake my head no, and completely shut down his wild assumption, when Jasper cuts in.

"Yes." His hand presses against my back tightly through my shirt, and in that moment I am grateful it isn't skin on skin contact. "We thought visiting the Love Pack would be good for our relationship."

I want to kill him. What kind of bullshit is he feeding Luke, and why? It seems as if the Love Pack member fully believes what comes out of Jasper's mouth.

"That's a shame. Your girl is very beautiful," Luke says, before disappearing back into the store room.

I take the coat with the bag, and stalk straight out of the store. Jasper warily follows me, obviously knowing what I'm mad about. But I don't even know if I am that mad about it. I think confused fits much better with what I'm feeling right now.

"Care to explain?" I snap, turning around as Jasper exits the store with me. He has his hands shoved in his pockets, looking anything but sheepish, like I expect.

He shrugs. "He was coming on to you."

"No he wasn't," I growl, remembering nothing about that man flirting with me. Jasper shakes his head as if I'm the most ridiculous thing he has ever encountered. Sure, he may be magic and an Alpha, but I still don't appreciate it.

"I can read his mind," Jasper tells me. "Love Pack members are very passionate about their beliefs. He was thinking some wicked things about you, which I had to put a stop to."

I want to slap Jasper, but he'd see it coming... No, *hear* it coming.

"Look, put your jacket on, and let's keep going. The person we are staying with lives deeper into the Pack. We need to get there before it starts snowing."

As much as I hate to admit it, he is right. Perhaps I would have been angrier if I wasn't still under his strange spell. So instead of arguing, I slip the coat on, and follow the Alpha of Devotion back to his car.

We drive for a while longer. We were only ten minutes from the little shop, when ice crystals began to fall from the sky. Jasper seemed mildly irritated by it, while I was in awe.

"So who is this person we are staying with?" I ask.

It has crossed my mind that maybe I should go off on my own. Jasper seems to have done a great job of making sure I don't get into any trouble, but I'm sure our partnership, or whatever it is, will have to come to an end eventually.

Right?

"Well, she doesn't actually know me," Jasper tells me warily. My eyes widen. "I needed to make sure we didn't leave a trail for your boyfriend or your father to follow. So I checked advertisements for someone offering a place in their home to stay."

I stare at him for a good few seconds, in complete and utter disbelief.

"First of all, Luca is not my boyfriend anymore," I tell him slowly. He smiles a little. "And second... we are staying with a complete stranger?"

He nods, giving me a playful smile that suggests a youthful part of him I don't see very often. "Ever heard of living on the edge?"

I close my eyes, falling back onto the car seat. Not only have I nearly been murdered by someone I thought I loved, but I 've been dragged away from my Pack to a completely different one, with people who believe in strange things.

"I know it's hard," Jasper murmurs. "I promise everything will make sense soon."

I sigh, nodding as I keep my eyes closed.

I don't know if I fall asleep throughout the drive, or if Jasper uses his creepy time manipulation powers to pass time, but when I next open my eyes, snow covers the ground, evening has set in, and we are parked outside a quaint little building.

"Our home, for now," Jasper says, as he notices me come to again.

Our. I force a slight smile onto my face. The future is uncertain, but hopefully I can trust Jasper to make it somewhat bearable.

Chapter Eleven

The house this girl lives in is nice. Much nicer than mine back at home.

It dwarfs the other houses in the neighborhood, standing tall against the sinking sun. Her wealth is obvious, I can't help but think as Jasper lets me in through her front gate.

I watch as Jasper knocks on the door, and we wait. My backpack full of clothes useless for this wintery weather is slung over my shoulder, making me feel more and more like a homeless person. I suppose that *is* what I am right now.

The door swings open after a few moments of shivering on my part. Apparently the cold doesn't affect Jasper too drastically. Lucky, because this snow is doing things to me.

The girl who answers strikes me straight away. Mainly, it is her stark contrast to a Love Pack member, as if her ancestors never stepped a single foot out of the Pack, to even be in the presence of someone foreign.

Her eyes are like a glacier, although it is almost like calling the water in a swimming pool blue. Perhaps at first glance you may think so, but it's what's behind it that gives it that color. Something untouchable, something pure.

"Hi! You two must be my new stayers!" she exclaims.

Her Love Pack accent is thick, she pronounces her words fluidly in a way that almost sounds like magic.

"We are," Jasper says in a cheerful, approachable voice I haven't heard him use before. The first impression between us and this girl is essential. "Jasper and Thea."

She thrusts her hand out to Jasper first to shake, and then to me. "My name is Aria."

She invites us inside, with a single glance at the one bag I hold, and I can tell she is wondering if I've brought anything else. Jasper doesn't have anything with him, and he just shrugs when I ask him about it.

The inside is slightly different to the neat, tidy outdoor area. It isn't messy or anything, but the clutter has me fidgeting uneasily. It's mainly books. Everywhere. They are stacked against the wall in a way that could be considered dangerous.

But ultimately, it looks so domestic, and so normal, I feel quite content with it. Luca, my murderous boyfriend, won't find me here.

"I was just cooking dinner," Aria says, leading us through the living room, where she tells me to leave my bag for the moment, and then into the kitchen. I smell chicken, and I can't help the instant stab of hunger that assaults my stomach.

"You don't have to cook for us," Jasper tells her, his voice warm and soothing.

I'm surprised this Love Pack member isn't reacting more to Jasper. Even I can see his friendliness might be perceived as something more. Instead she slips an oven mitt over her hand, and checks the oven.

"I don't mind. I love cooking," she tells us. Aria's dark long brown hair is shoved up into a messy bun, which looks like it suits her perfectly.

I glance at Jasper, but he isn't looking at me. He's looking out the window, at the snow as it falls. The sky is darkening out there, and by the look that crosses his face, I think he wants to be anywhere but here.

"So where did you two come from? You both are very attractive. Maybe it's because you're foreign, and new. I like new," Aria says, her words so quick, I almost don't catch them.

This time, Jasper catches my gaze, and I see the dance of amusement there.

"Devotion Pack," Jasper tells her, as she sets a roasting dish on the bench. She grins wildly, showing prominent dimples on either side of her face.

"Oh how exciting! I heard no one goes there because of some myth about some dead wolves or something? Ghost wolves...? I don't know. But whatever it is, you must be brave to live among them."

I have to lower my gaze to stop my cheeks from flushing. They tend to do that when I'm in an uncomfortable situation.

Dinner is just as uncomfortable, although it's easy to fade into the back of Aria and Jasper's minds, as they chat like old friends. Both seem very charismatic, and conversation flows like it's second nature. I feel very out of place.

After offering to help Aria clean up, which she refuses, I wander upstairs to shower. Jasper stays downstairs with her, and I wonder what lies he'll tell her to cover our situation.

I can't help but cry, as I lean my back against the shower wall, letting the stream of water hit me. The magic is starting to wear off, and although I have accepted what has happened, it doesn't make it any easier to deal with.

My own boyfriend. My own father and best friend. They all betrayed me. They even wanted me dead.

I dry myself slowly, dressing in loose pants and a shirt. I don't feel pretty, as I brush my hair back, but I don't think I care anymore. If I was with Luca in this mood, we might have cuddled. But instead I'm stuck in a house with a half-dead Alpha and a Love Pack girl.

I towel dry my hair to the best of my abilities, until I hear someone knock on the door. It's Aria.

"I brought you extra blankets," she says, handing me a pile. Not that I'm not grateful for her hospitality, but she seems to be quite overzealous with her treatment. I mean, anyone would think Jasper and I are royalty.

"Which room is mine?" I ask her.

She smiles. "Down the hall, with your boyfriend."

I have to fight to keep my expression straight. This is his ruse and now I am going to be forced to commit to it? Despite being a Love Pack member, she doesn't seem bothered by the fact that we have apparently declared ourselves as mates, or something.

"Thank you Aria, you are very kind."

Jasper is sitting on the double bed in the room we are renting. A double bed. I am being forced to sleep in the same bed, right next to the Alpha of Devotion, who also happens to be a Phantom Wolf. Great.

I nearly jump for his neck.

"Have I ever told you I had you?" I question, closing the door behind me as I watch Jasper pull his shoes off. Jasper only chuckles.

"It was the only thing I could come up with."

I sigh. For an Alpha, he isn't really very good at planning things. Unless this is all an elaborate plan that could lead to something very bad happening to me.

Jasper shakes his head, standing again.

I hate having to admire him. *It's as if my eyes are naturally drawn to him, at all times. Any unmated girl has to admit that he is handsome, with those sharp eyes and mussed hair. Sometimes...*

My thoughts are cut off by Jasper chuckling. "So, you're admitting you're attracted to me?"

"Stop reading my mind," I snap, as he takes a step closer. I try my best to stand up tall, not letting him even consider me being afraid of him. Jasper just smiles in amusement, taking obvious enjoyment out of my frustration.

"Perhaps I will teach you later how to keep me out of your thoughts," he pronounces, making me sigh in relief.

Not having to worry about Jasper infiltrating personal thoughts will be a relief. Or maybe he could just decide to keep himself out. But by the way he winks coyly at me, I know that isn't an option.

"Well, I'll have the right side I guess," I say, going to sit on the edge of the bed. Rather than make this more awkward than it already is, I decide to just not argue and go along with it.

Jasper joins me, on the other side, and I keep my back turned as he undresses. How he manages to get clothes here without bringing a bag is beyond me, but something tells me his magical abilities have something to do with it. Who knew conjuring fabric was an option...

"Just let me know if you are feeling homesick," Jasper murmurs from behind me. I'm still perched on the edge of the bed, waiting for him to finish changing.

What can he possibly do to make me feel any better? Console me? Although that idea might seem slightly appealing, I push it away, and take his talking as my cue to turn back around, sitting back properly on the bed.

He is dressed in loose black pants, but his shirt is missing. And holy...

I know he can see I'm blatantly staring, but I can't help myself. A chest smooth, with abdominal muscles almost carved for a Greek god. The personification of perfection. I have never seen anything like it in my life, and I don't think I can breathe.

When I drag my eyes back up to Jasper's, his gaze is dark, predatory.

"I... I'm sorry," I stammer, sounding like a complete and utter fool. But he doesn't seem to listen. He is concentrating on something else... *Me.*

"Why did you ever choose him?" Jasper asks, his voice a gentle whisper. "And why as a boyfriend, over a mate?"

I frown. That's what he wants to bring up, right now? My mind is hardly comprehending very much at all. Never in my life have I ever expected to be in the presence of an Alpha, let alone one like this...

"I don't think I will ever find my mate," I mutter, truthfully. It's something I have thought of many times. But recently I've accepted the idea of having to mate with Luca, so I wouldn't spend my life alone.

"Fate works in mysterious ways..." Jasper tells me, his voice almost whimsically soft. It is enchanting, captivating, like the drug-like magic he used on me.

"I think we should go to sleep." I glance at the bed. That seems to break the spell between us. Whatever it was.

I clamber into bed, trying to keep as far to the edge of the bed to avoid any awkward touching during the night. We haven't had any skin on skin contact, and I want to keep it that way. He's saved my life, but he is not mine, and I am not his play thing. Or whatever my sly mind conjured up moments ago.

Jasper does the same, cloaking the room in darkness as he joins me in bed, turning the light off.

The bed sinks slightly as he gets into bed, making this all the more real. My back is turned to him, my eyes shut so tightly I see colors dancing in my vision. I just want this tension between us to disappear.

"We are safe now," I hear him say. My eyes open, but it doesn't make much difference.

"We are," I reply, and it's as if those words give me the comfort to finally fall asleep.

I don't know how much sleep I get before I stir from my slumber. From the bleariness of sleep, I tilt my head back enough to see Jasper standing at the window. Moonlight douses his skin, making it glow magically.

He's dressed from head to toe in a black suit. He looks handsome, from what I can see. I know he can read my mind right now, but it's as if he isn't. He looks distracted, as he pulls black latex gloves over his hands.

I could say something, but I want to watch him. Whatever is on his mind, the way it's distracting him enough to not realize I'm awake sparks my incessant curiosity.

And it only increases as I watch him slide the window open very slowly, and clamber out. Is he going to scale the building?

But then he jumps. And vanishes.

I'm out of bed in a second, throwing the sheets back as I clamber toward the door. Looking out the window, I see Jasper has reappeared on the sidewalk down below, and is strolling off into the night.

And I can think of only one thing. I need to follow him.

Chapter Twelve

The speed of shrugging on the jacket I bought earlier today with Jasper's money is legendary.

Of course I don't jump from the window like he did, as I happen to be missing a certain power that would allow me to basically evaporate my body mass, before completely rearranging it again once I was on the ground.

If I did try, I am sure I would most likely plummet face first into the snow, and break my nose, or something.

Instead I jog downstairs, trying to keep my steps quick, but light so I won't wake Aria, or lose Jasper. As I pull my last shoe over my foot, I swing the door open and emerge into the night.

After only a few hours, the snow is already thick on the ground, coating it in ice crystals still fresh from the grey clouds above. Bare trees hold the burden of the snow lying innocently upon the branches, which stir only when the crisp breeze hits every so often. This Pack is beautiful, but skin-shivering cold.

Jasper walks yards ahead, pacing through streetlamps' luminous cones of light. He looks like he's simply decided to go for a late night stroll, but I know something isn't right.

The crunch of my feet against the snow is the only sound as I stalk behind Jasper.

Feeling stupid doesn't even begin to cover what I feel right now. Perhaps it is pure evil to invade someone's privacy like I am right now, but curiosity is digging at the edge of my soul, ensuring I follow him like a dog on a leash.

Continuing to follow him, he unknowingly leads me down the street, brightly lit but still with enough shadows for me to conceal myself in. But never once does Jasper turn around.

He leads me to the town square, or at least that's what I assume it is. It mustn't be too late, because the lights illuminating the snow-kissed square show everything is still open. Although, what the stores are, exactly, is indistinguishable, due to the way the frost crawls and twists over the signage.

Jasper walks directly to what looks like a restaurant, filled with merry-looking people, with cheeks flushed by wine, and animated smiles you could only find in this Pack: under a spell of love.

To ensure no one sees me, I keep to the left, rounding the decorative fountain currently capped with ice and off to the side of the brightly lit restaurant, where I press my stomach against it in order to keep hidden from Jasper.

The moment he wanders inside the restaurant, I cringe.

I can either turn around and walk back the way I've come, clamber into bed, and possibly ask Jasper about it in the morning. Or, I can follow him into the room and find out why he's decided to take a night-time stroll, even if it is for a late night snack.

Goddamn my insistent curiosity. It's going to get me killed one day.

Giving Jasper a few moments to get into the restaurant, I follow behind, but this time, I don't stalk. My back is straight with confidence as I stride purposefully toward the door. It is all I have going for me, since I am currently wearing my hair in the wildest bun, in my flower-printed nightwear, and snow-frosted sneakers.

Almost everyone glances up as I walk in. Eyes drag over my outfit, drinking it in with stunned expressions they don't bother to cover. Some stare back down at their food awkwardly, while others whisper to their partners.

Honestly, it doesn't bother me though.

Instead of being offended, I indulge in the heat that wraps around me, licking my frost-touched skin with the softest caress. Just as I cast a glance around the eclectically styled room, I see Jasper's back, dusted with quickly melting snow.

He's being escorted by a man wearing waiter's attire to what looks like a private room. I watch him walk in, the door closing behind him. I would be deterred had there not been a window divider connecting both rooms, with only dark-stained shutters between.

The waiter catches my gaze, and I see him blatantly assess my clothing situation. Can he make the decision to serve me? Not that it matters, since I'm not here to eat. Instead I meet the man in the middle, and smile broadly.

"That was my boyfriend," I tell him. He seems to believe me, motioning with his hand as permission to follow Jasper.

Hardly able to believe that's worked, I wander over to where the room is, and when the waiter turns his back, I tuck behind the couch seat under the shutters.

This is ridiculous. Although now ashamed, I know it's too late to change my mind, so I might as well find out what has brought Jasper here.

The wooden shutters are partially open, and a gentle classical-styled music drifts through. Along with two voices, which aren't coherent.

Braver than I have ever been in my life, I rest my fingers against the edge of the shutters, pulling them back just enough to catch a glimpse inside. And it is beautiful, furnished and decorated to suit the intimacy of the room.

Sitting on the plush couch on the other side of the room, is Jasper. And a woman.

She is beautiful. Stunning. She is the woman form of Jasper; the perfect specimen. Her hair is long and dark, curling down in subtle waves across her chest, and to her waist. The unfamiliar woman bites her red lips, staring at Jasper with dark, sultry eyes.

From what I can see, she leans suggestively on the couch, facing the Alpha of Devotion, who looks like he's resting casually. They're deep in conversation and now, in this position, I can hear them perfectly.

"The extraction plan was a success?" she asks, her voice foreign. It sounds wispy; old-fashioned. Even her outfit looks outdated, but by the way she pulls off the slim fit, you would hardly notice.

Jasper shrugs. "It could have gone better, but for what it is worth, it is over now."

"You must be relieved. I understand she is extremely valuable," the woman proclaims, taking a brief moment to check her long nails out. What in the world are they talking about? Who?

"*Extremely,*" Jasper murmurs.

Are these two together? Am I potentially invading on an intimate moment? The blush that creeps onto my cheeks seems to scold me for what I have committed to. I'm about to pull away, but their next words make me stop

"I know she means a lot to you," the strange woman breathes, her words, her accent almost entwining with the lyrics set within the song. "When are you planning on telling her?"

A strange thought invades my mind, and in that moment, I wish I could swat it away. Are they talking about me? And 'extraction plan'? I mean... that sounds awfully close to what Jasper did for me. But he had saved me.

"Soon, when she is ready. The last thing I want to do is to force this upon her after what she has been through. A man she thought was her boyfriend was planning to kill her..."

I stumble back from the shutters. They *are* talking about me!

The words they said are almost imprinted in my mind, as is the way the woman sipped her golden wine thoughtfully as she listened to Jasper. Listened to him talk about... me? How I mean something to him?

The waiter doesn't have time to question me on what I am doing. The snow hits me like a slap in the face as I stalk outside, the cold seeping its way through my coat, its chilling crystals clawing their way across my skin. My mind whirls like the snow around me, disturbed by my footsteps.

I rest my back against the restaurant, trying to rearrange what Jasper's magic wasn't here to combat.

Just as he graced my mind, he suddenly graces my presence in a rush of cold and shadows. He's right in front of me, violet eyes blazing as he stands only inches from me. The sight of him instantly knocks the breath from me.

"What are you doing here?" I question in disbelief.

His wild magic has allowed him to appear in front of me in the blink of an eye, leaving behind remnants of his power in the form of curling violet and blue shadows that capture falling snowflakes.

"I was about to ask you the same," he mutters. For a moment, I assume he'sgoing to be angry with me, but his lips tip into a flutter of a smile, and I see entertainment glinting in his eyes.

"Who is she?" I'm trying to avoid answering his question. He can goddamn look into my mind if he's *that* interested.

Jasper tilts his head, assessing me for a moment, almost as if I am a strange creature. Then, he surprises me, by leaning forward, close enough so our breath apparent from the cold, mingles. His hands are out of his pockets, pressing against the restaurant wall to trap me in.

"Jealous?" he asks, raising an eyebrow. Automatically, I shake my head.

"No. How did you find me out here?" Out of nowhere, Jasper had sensed my presence that I had been hoping to keep away from him. My plan had been about to work out perfectly, with my head start to getting home much higher.

Jasper only chuckles. "I always knew you were curious."

My eyes narrow at his. He is so close our body heat is being shared; we're only inches away from actually touching.

"I know, you are hopeless at answering questions."

"Would you really like to know what I was planning?" he whispers, and I swear he moved a little closer.

Do I?

"I was going to blow her mind. Give her the best sex she has ever had before. Fuck her until she screamed my name for all those people to hear."

My mouth falls open; I'm completely stunned by his crude words.

He grins. "I'm joking.

74

"In actual fact, I am sure she would rather pursue such ventures with you, rather than me," Jasper tells me, much to my surprise. And here I was, thinking those two were attracted to each other.

"Oh," I breathe.

A silence stretches between us, as we stare directly into each other's eyes. The moment is unexplainable. Reading about the rest of the world disappearing when you're caught up in someone else is something I used to ridicule. Now I am experiencing it, my understanding has increased, like the tension between Jasper and me.

"I'm not happy you followed me out here, interrupted me," Jasper tells me, slicing through the silence. "Perhaps if you were mine, Thea, I would show you exactly what happens to the ones who step out of line. Maybe in a way both of us could get behind."

He tilted his head coyly. "If you know what I mean."

I shiver, and not from the cold. His words are full of unspoken promise, that part of me yearns to pursue. Luckily he doesn't give me space to respond, because I'm not sure I'd be able to without saying something embarrassing.

"Come darling, let's head back before you catch a cold. And if you behave, maybe I will explain everything to you tomorrow."

Chapter Thirteen

Perhaps I would have been maddened by Jasper blatantly refusing to tell me anything about what I've just witnessed, were I not so tired.

The moment the bed is in my line of sight, I forget Jasper will be sleeping next to me. The last thing I remember is face planting into the softest of pillows.

When I awake, it's the next morning, and Jasper is dead asleep beside me. His torso is magnificently bare, and admittedly, I take a few moments to admire the smoothness of the perfectly sculpted muscles I'm itching to touch with my bare fingers.

The sun is rising, its rays going to work on the thickly frosted windows, the remnants dribbling down the window as liquid tinted by encroaching daylight.

Gentle oranges and subtle pinks dance across Jasper's face. His eyelashes brush against his cheeks, his lips are partly open. The bed sheet twists around his limbs, a contrast to his sun-kissed skin. An Alpha, in a vulnerable position.

I slip out of bed, wishing there was a better heating system in here. Muttering to myself, I find fresh clothes in my backpack, and wander off to the shower.

That the temperature has dropped is significantly more noticeable when I step out of the shower to dry myself. Chilling icy cold air drifts around me, as I wrap my towel around myself realizing I probably should have grabbed underwear along with the rest of my clothes.

Jasper is awake when I walk back into the bedroom, my hand clutching the top of my towel. He's stretched across the bed, rubbing his hands over his eyes. The whole situation seems very domestic for an Alpha and a random girl running away from her deranged family who hid the fact that they're Phantom Wolves from her...

I stoop down, rummaging through my bag for another set of underwear.

"Good morning," Jasper murmurs, his voice rough from sleep.

I stand, and Jasper finally catches a glance at my current lack of clothing situation. The way he stares at me, makes it seem as if the towel doesn't even exist, and it sends an embarrassed blush to stain my cheeks.

"Ah... Good morning," I say quickly, before turning and dashing into the bathroom again, slamming the door behind me.

Bracing my hands against the edge of the ceramic vanity, I stare at myself in the mirror, through the subtle condensation clouding the edge.

I look... healthy. After everything that has happened, I thought I would at the very least look sick, or worried. But the side effects of all this stress hasn't seemed to do anything harmful to my appearance. In fact, my face is full and doused with color, my eyes bright and my hair shinier and more voluptuous.

Dressing quickly, I leave the room to see Jasper has done the same.

Downstairs, Aria has left a note about having to go out with her friend for the day. This leaves Jasper I to make ourselves breakfast, which really is just cereal. We eat quietly, and it isn't until we finish eating, and I'm cleaning the dishes, that I speak.

"So, who was she?" I ask.

Jasper looks up from the book he's found on Aria's shelf. They have that in common; a love for books.

"A friend," he tells me, closing the red-covered book. I remember him mentioning something about her sexuality, which I assume is proof Jasper wasn't meeting her for reasons I don't want to think of.

I put the last clean plate between the slats of the dish drainer. "Where is she from?"

"The Devotion Pack. Well, the Devotion Pack a couple hundred years ago," he continues nonchalantly. I twist around, *that* being the last thing I had expected to hear from him right now, and also the last thing I wanted to ask.

Jasper smiles, as he stands smoothly, his eyes holding me almost paralyzed.

"Time travel?" I squeak, that being the only conclusion I could come to. Jasper tilts his head, and I can tell from the glint in his eyes, he knows I don't truly believe him. Sure, I've been exposed to a lot of magic recently, but still, this is traveling through time we are talking about.

Jasper strides toward me, around the counter, the tips of his fingers dragging across the soapstone. I however, have my back pressed against the bench, my shirt probably getting wet from the sink water.

"You don't think, that if time travel ever was to exist, then travelers would be walking among us today?"

My heart kind of jumps a little at his words. Jasper just watches me, as I process what he's said.

"Many years ago, a merchant offered my father the ability to travel into the future, from a man who had accidentally transported himself many years back in time. Of course, I was introduced to the idea, and I have been traveling often ever since."

My mouth falls open in surprise, as yet another tsunami of shock consumes me. No, it's hit me in the face, like a bus.

"But don't worry, I am not going to take you through any realm of time," he says, as if to reassure me. There's no way I would ever agree to it anyway...

Jasper stands a few inches in front of me, looking down at me with something that could be curiosity. Sometimes I think he looks at me like I am the strangest thing he's ever seen.

"You confuse me. Even without my magic to assist you, you have handled this all very well. You are strong, and I respect that about you," Jasper murmurs.

It's strange how much warmth spreads through me from just those few words. Maybe it was the honesty he conveyed, or maybe just the idea of someone finally seeing something in me I haven't seen in myself.

Deciding to be brave, I take a step forward, and rest my hands on Jasper's chest. It isn't skin to skin, which today with Werewolves can be seen as very crude, but it's a gesture I want him to understand. "Thank you. Now can I ask for a favor?"

"Depends what it is?" Jasper says warily, holding eye contact, despite his muscles being tense under my palms.

"I want you," I say, dragging my finger down the line of Jasper's chest, wondering where this confidence has sprouted from. I ruin it though, pushing back, although he only moves a few steps. "To show me how to keep you out of my damn mind."

Jasper grins at my playfulness, catching onto the first good mood I've probably had this entire time. Really, I want a way to keep Jasper out of my private thoughts.

"I think I can do that for you. Shall we go for a walk and talk about it?"

Turning around, I see the window allows the soft gleam of sunlight to light up the room around us. The snow has settled outside, no glimpses of falling snow to be seen. It may be cold out, but a walk won't do us any harm.

Jasper retrieves my jacket and some gloves of Aria's from upstairs, while I lace my shoes. When he strolls downstairs, Jasper has a winter hat on, his dark hair sticking out from under it. He tosses my gloves at me, tugging his own ones on.

"How long are we staying here for?" I ask him, once we are finally equipped for winter, and he's draped my coat over my shoulders.

He shrugs. "However long we need to."

At this point, I'm used to Jasper being cryptic, so I let it pass, planning just to deal with things as they come. It seems to be working for me so far.

Jasper guides me with his hand on the small of my back the moment we step outside. Instantly, my breath fogs in front of my face, and I can feel the tip of my nose turning red. The snow is up to my ankles, compacted by the sheer thickness of last night's snowfall.

"Beautiful, isn't it?" Jasper notes, smiling down at me.

The sidewalk has few footprints from early risers' morning walks, so the snow is not yet dirty, or completely sludge. It still glistens magnificently, almost matching the puffy clouds in the blue sky.

"Very," I whisper. "Now, can you teach me how to keep you out of my mind?"

Jasper thinks for a moment, as we walk with feet crunching through the ice, sinking deeper into the snow with every step.

"What if I told you there is no way to keep me out of your mind?" he asks, tilting an eyebrow up while he gazes down at me, violet eyes glinting mischievously. I, on the other hand, cannot find any humor in the idea.

"Tell me you are joking," I growl, narrowing my eyes at him.

He chuckles, shaking his head. Without any warning, he reaches up, plucks the edge of a tree branch we've just walked under, and lets snow fall down with a sigh and a rustle, straight upon my head.

I gasp, cringing as icy cold, melting snow drips down the back of my coat. Jasper laughs animatedly, clapping his hands in pure enjoyment at my uncomfortable position. I smack him angrily on the arm.

"This is serious," I snap, wishing I could strip off my wet clothes.

Jasper grabs my hand, pulling me back. For a moment, his smile fades, but I still see that warmth, that aliveness that suits him so well. "I like seeing you smile. You didn't do it enough when you were with Luca."

I frown. Never would I have expected him to say something like that. Sure, Luca got on my nerves sometimes, but back then, he was all I had. And Jasper... well, he hardly knew me... us.

"Look, let's make a deal, shall we?" he says, cutting off any chance I have of questioning him on what he's just said.

I sigh. "If it doesn't include snow down my back, then I suppose I have nothing to lose."

Before announcing this 'deal', Jasper turns us around, saying I need to get back before I catch a cold. I don't hesitate to remind him it was his fault. Not that we've walked far anyway, just to the outskirts of the town's square.

"How about I promise not to look into your mind anymore?" he offers. I narrow my eyes at him sideways, not sure if I actually believe him. "On my life."

I stop, making him do so too. He looks at me expectantly.

"Not just on your life... On your Pack's life... Ah, even on your mate's life," I demand, throwing out things I think will mean the most to him. Just saying those things makes me realize I don't know very much about Jasper, although... we did only meet a few days ago.

"My mate and I haven't..." he pauses. "... touched yet."

I roll my eyes. "Well, whoever she is, wherever she is, you swear on her life."

Jasper holds his hands up, almost in a mocking way, but I can tell he's finally taking my claims seriously. Until I hold my pinky finger out, which he stares at as if it's a foreign object never before seen.

"What?"

"Pinky swear," I insist, entwining his finger with mine, completing a superstition I've had since I was a little girl. It reminds me of June, which stabs at my heart a little. "This is the only way I will trust you."

It takes me a couple of minutes on our walk back to the house to explain the importance of a pinky swear. It seals a promise; but he just can't get it. By the end he understands, and we have a mutual agreement about how he is *not* to infiltrate my mind unless I state otherwise.

"I like autumn. It is a mild season," Jasper muses, as we near the end of our walk. We were arguing about our favourite season, mine being spring, because everything blossoms.

Jasper's just about to reply, when I glance to my left, and nearly scream aloud.

Aria's neighborhood is coated in snow, but that doesn't mean I didn't see three men surrounding someone across the road, on her doorstep. The woman at the door is bundled in a grey robe, as she looks at the piece of paper presented to her. By Luca.

He is here.

Chapter Fourteen

Just seeing him sends an entire wall of emotion at me.

His back is turned to me, but I know it's him without any doubt. The man I thought would once be my mate, but who actually wants to sacrifice me.

"We need to go," Jasper says quickly, having seen Luca at the same time.

He grabs my hand, dragging me toward Aria's house, which luckily is right there. My feet sludge through the snow, my burning limbs fight against the drag. Jasper has no problem disrupting the snow around us, but it's mildly heartbreaking to see the beautifully resting fluff being tainted by our footprints.

I keep turning back as we jog across Aria's lawn, making sure Luca and his men haven't yet turned around to see us. Because if he sees us... everything will have been for nothing.

Don't let him find me. He can't find me. If he finds me, I am dead.

"How does he know we came to the Love Pack?" I question frantically, once Jasper has closed the door behind us. Not before checking Luca is still occupied with that woman. "How had they figured it out? Is the whole town out looking for me?"

Jasper looks stricken, and I can tell his plan has just flown out the window.

"We need to go. We can't stay here," he insists, making sure the door is locked before he fully faces me. It's almost like I can see him thinking about our next move, about how he's going to get us out of here without Luca finding out we were ever in this Pack.

"Where? How?" I question, watching him frown as he rakes his hands through his hair.

Suddenly, he grabs my arm, pulling me swiftly upstairs. As he closes the curtains, he tells me to pack my belongings again. I feel tears of stress and fright well in my eyes as I zip my backpack up, after shoving in the gloves I was wearing as well.

"We leave this Pack right now, and we don't look back," Jasper mutters, grabbing my backpack for me.

We run downstairs, just as a knock on the front door resounds through the house. It *has* to be Luca, ready to show whoever lives here a picture of me in an attempt to see if anyone has seen me around.

"Out the back door," Jasper says quickly, ushering me toward it. He hasn't taken a moment to stop and look at me. I am grateful, because otherwise he would see the tears I so desperately try to swipe away.

The moment we go through the back door, as silent and as elusive as we can, I regret not keeping my gloves on.

"This way," Jasper mutters, cutting through my thoughts about how frustrating the coldness of this Pack must be for someone like Aria, who has lived here her whole life.

We sidle along the side of the house, where to the left, is Jasper's parked car. The windscreen is layered by thick snow, dusting the hood, the bonnet and the boot. Pulling his keys out, Jasper makes it to the car to unlock it, while I try my best to scrape snow off the window with my sleeve over my hand.

As Jasper turns the car on, I want to beg him to hurry and pull the car out. I feel my desperation in my beating heart, in the lump in my throat, and especially in my tense muscles that could plead their own case to Jasper.

"Hurry," I whisper, my voice hoarse with desperation.

Snow bursts out from around the wheels as Jasper frantically pulls the car into reverse, and onto the road. My eyes search for Luca, and I don't have to look far. He and the two other men turn as Jasper shifts the car into drive.

Our eyes lock for just a second: surprise, confusion, and anger.

Tires sliding dangerously across the tarmac, Jasper slams the accelerator down, lurching us forward, so I have to brace myself on the dashboard.

Luca disappears from my sight in less than a second, as we drive swiftly down the street, leaving him in the dust... or snow, I suppose.

"We should really stop needing these quick getaways," Jasper says with a slight breathy chuckle. I know he's only saying that to lighten the mood, but I'm too busy recovering from that rush of fright I've just experienced.

But as I rest my head back against the seat, I smile despite myself.

"I can't believe we actually got away," I note, shaking my head. Jasper glances at me, before nodding at the backpack on my lap. How did I not notice he threw that there? Without questioning it, I toss it into the back seat.

"Maybe we are getting good at this," Jasper imparts, which makes me roll my eyes, not sure if I want to be good at it...

As we drive out of the Love Pack, leaving the beauty of that winter wonderland behind, a brooding silence falls over us both. I can't help thinking about what would have happened had Luca caught us. Surely Jasper would have got us out of that situation; but if I had been alone?

"So we just drive until we find somewhere to stay?" I ask, as the snow on the side of the road starts to thin out, becoming less like that silky, fluffy snow, and more a filthy, icy mess.

Jasper shrugs again. He seems to be good at doing that. "Maybe. I have a place to take you, but I don't want to risk Luca following us there. We are going to have to stay somewhere for the night to steer him off our trail."

I'm not sure if I want to know exactly where we're going. Jasper looks tense. I can tell just from his expression that he is apprehensive of taking me there, that it is somewhere special to him. Living by my motto of taking it as it comes seems to be what is stopping all the stress I could be feeling right now.

"How are you holding up?" Jasper asks, casting me a wary glance.

It makes me feel a little warm inside to know that he at least kind of cares about my well-being. "I am fine. Are you?"

"Don't you worry about me," Jasper remarks, smiling slightly.

Staring out the window, I watch the snow begin to disappear, as the trees thicken on either side of the road. Living next to a forest, I am used to trees, but these trees seem darker, tighter and growing more compactly together. I shiver uneasily.

"We need to stop somewhere for petrol. Maybe there will be something to eat," Jasper says after a while. Sitting up with a start, I rub my bleary eyes. Did I fall asleep?

When I look out at the road, we're still driving down a straight two-lane road, with trees lining the side. The shadows they cast through the car make me tuck my legs up on the seat to hug them, in a wild attempt to warm myself up.

"Sure," I affirm, ready to fill the void of hunger that has grown throughout our drive.

Luckily enough, we only have to drive for another 20 minutes to find a gas station on the side of the road. It's beside some eerie-looking motel complex Jasper and I collectively agree we won't stay at.

"You get the snacks, I'll get the gas," Jasper suggests, and I agree, liking that.

While the Alpha stands at the car, I wander inside the petrol station. Fairly run-down, the entire place looks like it was meant to exist a few years ago, and that's it. The man at the front reads a newspaper, and doesn't even look up as I wander in.

Turns out my options are very limited.

I grab two waters from the fridge, that aren't even chilled, a few bags of chips, something unfamiliar I don't want to question, and a couple of chocolate bars. The clerk finally looks at me, putting his newspaper down.

And then he stares at me. And stares... And won't stop staring.

"Ah, I've decided what I want. Can I pay for the gas as well?" I ask, motioning out the window to where Jasper has the nozzle of the gas pump shoved in the car.

The strange man, with thinning grey hair, turns his head enough to see Jasper, before he looks back at me. Without a word, he finally starts to scan my items, putting them into a bag slowly, despite my insistence that I don't need one.

As he bags my items, I turn around to see two other people are in the store with me. Both stare at me, as one grabs a bottle of milk, the other's hands hovering over a stack of newspapers that broadcast the murders from my part of the Devotion Pack.

Grabbing my items after paying, I quickly leave the store, jogging over to where Jasper has just finished filling the car.

"I just experienced the weirdest thing in there," I mutter, as Jasper takes the bag from my hands to inspect the contents inside. "Those people in there wouldn't stop staring."

Jasper pulls a chocolate bar from out of the bag, tearing the packet open. "They are probably rogues."

Rogues? I haven't heard much about them, but I know for a fact that not many people like them, and tend to stay as far away from them as possible. Those without a moral to stick with are very frowned upon.

We get back on the road, looking out for a place to stay the night. Jasper tells me the Loyalty Pack isn't too far from here, but he decides against it, since apparently Luca would be able to find us more easily here.

"As long as Luca isn't there, I will sleep wherever," I admit, wanting to knock my head against the dashboard to end this suffering.

Jasper doesn't want to use his power in case they trace it, so I'm left having to endure the long drive.

Jasper chuckles. "How does on the side of the road sound for now?"

I shrug. We're far enough away that I doubt Luca will find us, at least for now. Jasper has even chosen some side roads in an attempt to draw him off our trail. Now, as the sun begins to set, all I want is to sleep.

Without even waiting for my consent, Jasper pulls over, parking the car within the grass on the side of some country road.

He switches the roof light on as we eat a bag of chips each, and talk about anything other than our current situation. Easy to talk to, Jasper's soft voice begins to lull me into a sleep. Until a loud bang on the roof makes me wake back up instantly.

Jasper's violet eyes are wide as he looks at me, as if to make sure I am actually alive. Something is on our roof.

To my surprise, Jasper immediately cracks the car door open.

"Stay here," he orders. "And don't leave the car until I come back."

Chapter Fifteen

Stunned, I sit, frozen to the seat.

Jasper clambers out of the car, slamming the door behind him. Instantly, the darkness of the freshly settled night swallows him whole, leaving me alone, only illuminated by the car light above my head.

The weight on the car roof is obvious, by the slight indents made on both the right and left side. Something big is above me, and I don't even want to consider what it might be.

Trying my best to catch a glimpse of where Jasper has gone, I try smothering the spike of fear that bubbles in my stomach. Instead of being brave, I lean over and lock every car door, promising I will only let Jasper in.

A few moments pass, each spent with my hands on my lap, fiddling with the empty chip bag.

Whatever was on the roof is now gone. I can tell because the car doesn't shake and creak like it had done before. Has Jasper taken care of it?

Suddenly something hits the window right by my face. I wasn't looking at it, because I was too busy seeing if crumbs had been left over in the packet. But when I do jump, glancing to see what has threatened the structural integrity of the window, I see nothing but grass, dirt and—blood?

I unbuckle my seat belt in case I need to make a getaway quickly, leaning away from the window. *Please, don't be Jasper's blood...*

At one point of excruciating waiting, I even consider calling the police, although I do rethink that. The last time I trusted the police, they nearly had me killed. Anyway, I doubt Jasper will want anyone interfering.

Alphas can look after themselves. Right?

All of a sudden, the sound of someone knocking on the window nearly makes my heart stop entirely. It's Jasper, waving at me through the fogging glass. With a hand over my heart, I unlock the door for him to get in.

"Sorry about that," he mutters, closing the door after him.

I stare at him. He looks as normal as ever, as if he hasn't just walked into the night around an hour ago. Maybe his hair is a little more ruffled, and his cheeks are tinted from the cool of the night, but other than that, it is still Alpha Jasper.

Until he cringes.

"What's wrong?" I ask, noticing the way his posture suddenly changes, as he favors his side a little.

Watching as he lifts his shirt, a gasp escapes my lips. One large red, bleeding, raw cut edges his ribs, staining his skin, dripping down the frame of his torso. His flesh has been completely ripped into, exposed to the naked eye.

Blood has never really bothered me. Plenty of worse things than something that aids our survival. But seeing the red stuff trickling from a gaping wound is not pretty.

"What happened?" I splutter, dragging my eyes up to Jasper's. His face is pale, his expression a grimace. He's in serious pain right now, and I can tell he doesn't want to admit that to me. However, I can hear his short breaths and faint groans of pain.

"It was a Phantom. One of those rogues from the gas station," he tells me, biting his lip hard as if to take away from the pain.

Swallowing the terror that has risen within me, I move to reach out to touch him... to do something. But instantly he shakes his head in protest, flinching away from my insistent fingertips as if they will inflict more pain than he's already in.

I draw my fingers back. "We need to get you help."

Almost instantly, Jasper shakes his head in disagreement to my words. He pulls his shirt down again, and starts the car.

"Jasper, seriously. You're going to bleed out, and no amount of Alpha healing capabilities are going to even touch that wound," I snap. "And unless you're about to tell me you have the magical ability to heal all wounds, then we are driving straight to a hospital."

The health of my saviour matters. Whether it's because he has saved my butt so many times, or because he truly has taken good care of me, I've started to care for him a little. Luckily he has promised not to read my mind, because otherwise I would be more than embarrassed right now.

Jasper stares at me for a moment, jaw clenched, violet eyes blazing, before he steps on the gas, and we lurch onto the road again. "Fine, but any sign we are being followed, we are leaving."

It is obvious Jasper was aware of where we had to be by the way he drove pointedly in one direction, taking roads in the dark I wouldn't have even considered.

Something tells me he takes this route often, heightening my curiosity about where he is taking us.

A small hospital lights up a deserted parking lot, which doesn't surprise me since it's obviously late. One very large, red flashing sign seems to alert anyone who dares take this road that this slightly paint-faded building is in fact a hospital.

"I don't think this place is very safe," I say softly, looking at how the O in Hospital is flickering.

Jasper grins at me, raising an eyebrow. For someone in immense pain, his mood is rather pleasant. Or maybe teasing me gives him a type of rush that could mask any pain. "It was your idea to come here."

Rolling my eyes, I step out of the car, rounding it to help Jasper out, but he refuses any kind of aid, making it a point of getting out himself, while attempting to not show any kind of pain on his face.

"Where are we?" I ask, as we walk across the parking lot and toward the hospital entrance.

Jasper clutches his side. "Somewhere between the Love Pack, and the Loyalty Pack. The Desire Pack is more to the west. We are heading that way after a nurse patches me up."

Only a few people are on shift when we walk in. The lady at the main desk looks stunned for a moment when Jasper bursts through the door, and I begin blurting out an excuse as to how Jasper hs been hurt.

"Oh, ah... Yes, if you take a seat, I will get the nurse," she says, quickly grabbing a clipboard and trotting off down the hallway, fixing her bun as she goes.

Again, Jasper won't let me help him to the waiting area, where he instantly takes up two seats as he lounges with his legs out across the plush blue cushions. To make myself useful, I fill a plastic cup of cooler water, and make Jasper take a sip.

"You're really bleeding," I note anxiously, biting my nails as I pace.

Jasper glances at his shirt, stained with darkening blood, with a chuckle. "Something like that."

The lady, dressed officially for this time of night, brings a male nurse with her, who's dressed in blue scrubs. He brings a wheelchair with him, which I see Jasper grimace at. He really doesn't like being assisted at all.

The nurse, a very kind man—who's accepted Jasper had fallen, and somehow managed this deep cut—stitches him up. I sit in the corner of the room, wincing every time Jasper does, almost feeling his pain for him.

"You're going to want to rest for a while," the nurse said, after he is finally finished.

Jasper nods, but I know that is never going to happen. In a heartbeat, I know the Alpha will fight any other Phantom rogue if it comes down to it.

"Finally," Jasper mutters, once we've left the hospital. Someone is irritable about being cared for...

"Will you tell me how many Phantom rogues there may possibly be?" I ask, as we walk toward the car.

Right now, I want nothing more than to sleep. Jasper, who has explained his lack of need for sleep, seems full of energy now he's been stitched, and the healing process can begin. But other than that, I want him to explain to me where possible danger may lurk.

"I'm not sure. Many Phantoms lurk everywhere, some as bad as Luca and his father," Jasper tells me, as we walk across the car park, only the street lamps showing us the way.

"And everyone else," I murmur under my voice, making Jasper look straight at me.

We haven't talked much about what's happened today. Nor of what could have happened... He won't even tell me about their belief about sacrificing the innocent. I've been left in the dark, and I'm slightly glad of that.

"I promise you, I am taking you to a very safe location, where you will be looked after," Jasper says, as he unlocks the car door.

A smile almost graces my lips at his words. That Alpha of Devotion has a way with words, making me feel comfortable in any situation, including ones that include a crazy boyfriend coming after me. His words make it seem as if nothing bad is ever going to happen.

"Will you be staying there as well?" I ask, as I clamber back into the car. It smells like candy and stale chips in here.

Jasper smiles, through the pain of sitting down in the car. "Would you miss me too much if I left?"

Something is weird about our relationship. We rely on each other, and sometimes I think we flirt. Yet not once have we touched skin on skin before. Would that make whatever is going on between us weird?

"No, I was just wondering," I say, wishing I could nudge him jokingly, but I'm too scared I might accidentally hurt him.

Jasper offers to skip time, which I refuse. He believes the risk of Luca tracking us at this time is low, but fatigue has caught up with me, and now all I want to do is sleep for a few hours, which Jasper says is fine.

The next thing I know, Jasper is shaking me awake gently, calling my name into my ear to stir me from me peaceful slumber.

Blinking warily, I sit up, looking out the window. We're still in the car, and I'm stuck staring at where we have made it to. My mouth opens automatically in complete shock.

"Welcome home," Jasper murmurs.

Chapter Sixteen

My eyes follow the road that is almost endless, stretching miles straight, carving an obvious line through the thickness of trees.

This place is an entire village, a settlement. Average-sized and styled homes stand close to each other, placed to conveniently face the road, which seems to lead into... nowhere. It is all so... so domestic, so normal. Something I haven't seen in what seems like a while.

"What is this place?"

My bearings are way off. These trees aren't familiar, the sky is clouded over, and a soft fog seems to be dancing around the edges of the road. Something tells me this isn't on the map, or at least in any Pack.

"Some people call it a safe haven. A home between the Desire Pack, and the Love Pack," Jasper tells me, as I tiredly rub my eyes.

My sleep was decent, and by the looks of it, the day is just starting again. Although, I have to admit I could really do with another nap at least.

"Why here?" I ask. "Who lives here?"

Jasper turns the car on again, pulling out from where he'd parked on the side of the road. He keeps to a decently slow pace, giving me the chance to look out the window at all the houses. They are all very similar-looking, with nothing looking too expensive.

"My Pack members. Those who fled from the Pack centuries ago. Well, the offspring of those. Terrified of Phantom Wolves, they had nowhere to go, so I disappeared from my old Pack to look after these people where they would be safe," he explains.

I frown. "Are they Phantoms too?"

"Some are, some are not. Those few who are Phantoms do not share that with anyone else, due to a law I enforce. Phantoms must not be spoken of, because of the hysteria it causes. Many aren't even aware I am Phantom," he tells me.

All these people living a lie. They are think they live in a perfect town, free from Phantoms under Jasper's protection.

"Do they not get suspicious that you never age?" I ask him, taking a glance at his perfectly sculpted face with its smooth skin, wondering how he could be so old. But when I look at his eyes, shrouded with memories and experience, it makes sense to me.

Jasper shrugs. "I've made them think a Phantom granted me eternal life, to suffer. With their hatred toward the murderous Wolves they'd spent most of their lives around, it didn't take much convincing to get them to believe."

Staring out the window, I see very few people. Those I do see all look very normal, living their lives without having any idea that their Alpha is actually what they fear most. Their neighbours may even have been one.

"So we are staying here?" I'm wondering what a life here would be like.

"If you please. I brought you here to be safe, but ultimately it is your choice if you would like to stay here or not. I cannot make you stay," he tells me, as I fall into his gaze.

Could I stay? With an Alpha?

I shrug. "Let me think about it."

Where we are driving, I don't know. The road seems to never end, as do the houses. Just the same houses upon houses, with different street numbers printed on their fences. Sometimes we drive past a few stores, but only those selling necessities.

"Why here?" I decide to ask. "Why is everything the same?"

"It is hidden within the trees, secluded. If these people were found... Those other Phantoms would surely kill them. Everything here is fairly basic, to not draw attention to anyone who may happen to pass by. I even enforce a curfew to reduce the risks of lights being seen through the trees."

My eyes widen. I had no idea it was *that* extensive, that Jasper would feel the need to completely shelter these people away like this.

I decide to stop asking so many questions as we continue down the road. Where exactly he plans to take me within this little settlement is still unknown to me. It possibly would have worried me a week ago, but now it just seems normal for Jasper to show me rather than explain.

"This is where I live," Jasper tells me, when finally we catch sight of a home.

His home is beautiful. The place is very similar to where he lived back in the Devotion Pack. Slightly outdated, but it has a charm to it that instantly implies home. The house with its wooden exterior, larger than a one-storey estate, is set separately from the other houses down the street, making it all the more magnificent in comparison.

"It's beautiful," I tell him honestly, as he parks the car outside.

The logs used to structure the home are a rich color, contrasting against the wild flowers native to this strange forest that crawl up the walls, even threatening to block the sun from the large windows on every storey.

"Thank you very much," Jasper says, and I catch his gentle smile. "It's very old, but I hope you don't mind a little history."

Is he kidding? This place looks something more than welcoming. It is almost like it's been waiting for me to come home for a while.

The moment I step out of the car, I'm enveloped in the sweet scents from the flowers and the freshly cut lawn. Even the pine forest has a lingering smell that gives me goosebumps. This place is like a dream.

I grab my backpack from the back of the car as I look around, wondering where that sound is coming from... it's birds merrily singing, their song mixing with the sound of the breeze through the pine needles.

"I had someone prepare your room for you in preparation for our arrival. You can sleep again if you would like," Jasper informs me, in a tone that suggests he thinks it would be better if I did sleep. I have been craving a nap... especially after Jasper had been attacked.

Inside, his house is even more spectacular as the outside.

The fact Jasper enjoys books couldn't be more obvious. Shelves strain under the weight of books piled upon books lining almost every wall in the place. Well, at least those I can see.

All the furnishings match the ones I'd seen in his other house. Everything has an antique look to it, which confirms Jasper probably had decorated this place many years ago, and hasn't bothered to change anything.

No wonder he's had so much time to read...

"Would you like me to show me to your room?" Jasper asks, as I look around his living room curiously.

Nodding, I go to follow him, but both of us come to a stop as we see a woman leaning casually on the door frame, staring blatantly at me. Her familiarity hits me like a bus. It's that woman from the night I sneaked out and followed Jasper to that restaurant.

We still haven't talked much about what happened that night, and I make a mental note to ask him about it tomorrow.

"Glad to see you're finally home," she muses.

Staring at her, it is hard to fathom that, in fact, she's dead right now, having passed away centuries ago. Now, I am staring at the young her, who travels through time to experience every realm.

"Tayten. Glad to see you're still around," Jasper greets her, and I can't tell if he is being sarcastic or not.

Tayten smiles, giving me a good view of her perfectly straight teeth. She really is beautiful, and I find myself almost blushing just for thinking such things, considering her interest is women, over men.

I see nothing wrong with it, but the way she is staring at me makes me a little uneasy. Maybe it's because those dark eyes that don't suggest anything about what she may be thinking.

"I wanted to meet Thea." She strides forward in a way that could only be described as graceful. She holds out her hand, and I shake it gently. She tilts her head as she blatantly assesses me, without holding back for a moment.

I shiver uncomfortably. "Ah, nice to meet you."

"Very... Jasper has told me a lot about you. From what I have heard, he is very fond of you," she tells me, her smile not stopping for a second.

I catch Jasper's gaze. "Interesting."

Tayten is soon excused, after Jasper insists I need to sleep, rather than be stuck in a conversation with her, considering I don't know her anyway. However, she doesn't leave until she's made me promise to speak to her again some other time, which admittedly is a hard pill to swallow. She intimidates me, to say the least.

Jasper leads me upstairs to what will be my room for as long as I need it to be.

"You can decorate it more if you decide to stay," Jasper tells me, keeping outside the room as I wander in. "Stay as long as you need. Forever, if you want."

The room is fairly basic, which I don't mind at all. The bed is large and the room has a connecting bathroom. Everything I could possibly need. If I do decide to stay. Even if forever seems quite daunting.

"Why?" I ask, turning around. "Why do this for me?"

Jasper pauses, as if the question surprises him. He hasn't fully explained yet why he decided to be so kind in helping me escape, as well as making sure Luca and the rest of the crazed villagers don't get their hands on me.

"I knew you were in danger, and I had to save you. Unfortunately I was too late to save the others. They were saving you for last, and luckily I was able to get you out before they could do anything to you. As for letting you stay, I feel I owe you that much."

His explanation isn't much, but it makes enough sense for me to be able to sleep. "Well, I thank you very much."

Jasper closes the door after him, leaving me to get ready for a nap. The curtains are thick enough to keep the midday sun out, and after a shower, I find sleep isn't difficult in the slightest. In fact, the moment I lay my face on the pillow, sleep curls its relentless arms around me, and drags me under its spell.

***

When I wake, I feel groggy and delirious.

Forcing myself from the bed, I plug my phone into the charging spot, and check the time. Nearly midnight, and now I'm fully awake...

Wandering to the bathroom, I wash my face and wonder what to do next. Tying my hair up, not bothering about my night clothes, I decide to go downstairs and find something to eat. My stomach is currently complaining to me how it hasn't been fed a decent meal since the Love Pack.

My feet pad down the wooden stairs, my mind silently thanking Jasper for leaving a few lights on so I can actually see.

It takes me a few minutes to find the kitchen. I'm trying to keep as silent as possible, but the blanket of silence magnifies every movement I make. When I bump my shoulder against one of his bookshelves, I cringe at the sound of one of his books hitting the floor.

Finally I find the kitchen, and turn on the light.

Instead of seeing food, I instead see Jasper leaning against one of the kitchen counters, chewing on a banana. He grins at me the moment he sees me, as I stare at him, completely stunned.

"I thought I heard something," he murmurs, tilting his head slightly.

I let out a deep breath, placing my hand over my erratically beating heart. "You nearly gave me a heart attack."

Jasper strolls to the fridge, opening it before peering inside. I watch him curiously. Again, his torso is beautifully bare, lit by the fridge light that illuminates every muscle. Obviously he has been sleeping too, by the way his hair is mussed from sleep.

"I guess we woke from sleep at the same time. Let me find you something to eat," I hear him say from inside the fridge.

I slip onto a bar stool, resting my elbows against the counter as I watch Jasper rummage for something in there. He pulls out a bowl of fruit that apparently belongs to Tayten, before he slides it across the marble to me, where I begin picking through the assortment.

"Are you okay?" Jasper asks suddenly, cutting through the silence like a knife.

I pause, an unchewed piece of pineapple in my mouth. Then I shrug.

"I heard what you and Tayten were talking about. You said I was valuable. Why?" I narrow my eyes at Jasper, who's standing close to the sink. He sighs deeply, and runs a hand through his hair.

"Not right now, Thea," he mutters, the first flutter of desperation I've seen suddenly appearing. "It will make sense soon, but not yet."

My heart skips a little. I've been able to handle not knowing much about our situation. But this? Obviously he's keeping a massive secret from me, and my curiosity to know what it is digs at the back of my mind.

I go to open my mouth to speak, but Jasper shakes his head at me.

"Please trust me," he whispers, walking toward me with soft steps. I stay completely still, not saying a word as I watch him come only inches from me.

"Why?" I ask him, as he leans over me.

For a moment, I wonder if maybe he will kiss me, or at the very least touch me. How will I react? Will I respond if I feel his lips on mine? Will I finally accept the attraction I feel for him, despite how little I may know?

"I promise I will make it worthwhile for you," he muses, smiling slightly. And then he leans away, stealing the moment between us. It leaves me speechless for a good second.

Then he winks. "I think you should go back to bed Thea, before you tempt me."

I scramble up from my spot on the chair, so surprised by his words; the blush on his cheeks could be toxic. Not looking at him again, I nearly run upstairs to think over what he's just insinuated.

Chapter Seventeen

It's raining when I wake again.

The window of my bedroom gives me a decent view of the forest. The branches of those pine trees sway gently in the wind, suggesting a storm is rolling in, much to my dismay. Lately, I have been sick of dreary weather like this.

The rain batters the window as I change. My clothing situation is starting to become an issue. Perhaps I need to harass Jasper into taking me shopping, since I only brought a few articles. Or maybe a washing machine would suffice.

Wandering downstairs, I find Jasper sitting in his living room, reading. He glances up from the novel the moment I step into the room, before I close the slowly.

"Good morning," he says warmly, setting the book down on the arm of the chair.

"What are you reading?" I nod at the book. I wish I still read as much as I used to, and by the looks of the amount of books Jasper owns, maybe he'll let me borrow a few. And looking at the state of this town, I may just have a lot more time to read.

Jasper holds the book up. "A mystery novel. Those are my favourite."

Maybe he likes mystery books so much because he's one himself. Every time I look at him, I'm caught up in his eyes. The violet in his eyes must be a side effect of being a Phantom Wolf. Still, I haven't questioned him much about the Wolves I've spent most of my life believing didn't exist.

We end up talking more about the book, while Jasper tries to find me something to eat. Apparently he needs to shop for more food or something, which almost seems too domestic for an Alpha to be saying.

"He's been in love with her for many years, and a string of murders in their small town brings them closer together..." Jasper explains, as we discuss the book.

I watch him pull out a carton of milk, check the expiry date, before dumping it into the sink.

"That's ridiculous," I comment, resting my chin on my hands. "Things like that never happen."

Jasper smiles softly, as he closes the fridge. Obviously he hasn't found anything for us for breakfast. Not that I mind that much, since I can't say I'm very hungry. My snack from midnight has filled me enough.

"Well, it is fiction," Jasper muses.

Suddenly any chance of our conversation continuing is stolen as Tayten wanders into the room. Almost immediately, Jasper sighs at her presence. She's holding something in her hand—an envelope of some sort.

"Something came in the mail for you, Miss Thea," Tayten says, moving to take a seat beside me on the bar stool.

Tayten looks extra good today. How she manages to pull off clothing obviously in style centuries ago is completely lost on me. Perhaps if she wasn't into women, I could see her and Jasper together, even though he seems perpetually annoyed by her. Both are too attractive for adequate words.

"Who from?" I question, taking the envelope from her. It has a red embossed stamp on it, making it seem as if it is important.

Tayten shrugs. "You tell me. It showed up on the doorstep."

As I peel open the soft envelope, Jasper rounds the kitchen island, most likely just as curious as I am about what I've received. I can't imagine what it could be...

A piece of paper is tucked inside, which I pull out. A handwritten letter. Frowning, I read it through.

"It's from my uncle," I breathe.

The letter reads that my uncle is getting in contact with me, after he saw missing persons' posters pinned up in the Desire Pack, which basically tells me that Luca and his father have stretched their searching radius to more Packs. He's even admitted to being a Phantom Wolf too, listing off times in my life he had thought about saving me from the Devotion Pack.

Pretty much a bunch of words I struggle to believe.

"I mean, how would he have found out I was *here?* I've only been in this place for a day... not even that," I proclaim, which Jasper nods in agreement to.

Tayten however, looks speculative.

"Well, Phantom Wolves do have magic. Perhaps he used some to send the letter directly to you, without actually knowing where you are..."

Jasper coughs, cutting Tayten off. "Are you aware you can go home anytime you want?"

Perhaps thinking Jasper and Tayten would possibly have been a cute couple was foolish. Just looking at them, and the way they argue, the way they shoot snarky remarks at each other, suggests they seem to be nothing but siblings.

"As I was saying, maybe this is legitimate. You may just have an uncle who wants to save your life just as much as Jasper did," Tayten says, ignoring the look Jasper is shooting her.

I shrug. My father did tell me once he had a brother who wasn't in his life anymore. Back when I was young, I was always too afraid to ask about him, because just the mention made my father so mad.

"Okay Tayten, you can go now..."

Tayten slings her arm over my shoulders, which makes me tense uncomfortably. "Obviously you should think this through fully before you decide to run into the arms of a stranger, but I think it would be a good idea."

"Tayten," Jasper warns, making the girl roll her eyes as she stands.

"Okay, I know when I'm not wanted. Just take my advice over his," Tayten says, winking at me before she saunters out. It leaves Jasper and me standing awkwardly in the kitchen.

Glancing up, I catch the Alpha's gaze. He doesn't look very pleased by what we just discussed. After everything he has done for me, he probably just doesn't want me to wander and ruin his entire plan to save me.

"Don't worry," I murmur, folding the letter up. "I don't think I am going to go."

Jasper almost sighs in relief. It's more than evident on his face, as he ran his hands through his hair. He really does care...

*   *   *

Jasper and I don't talk any further about it. He decides to go to the supermarket, which leaves me with literally nothing in my mind to do.

I explore for a while, but eventually that gets boring, and I'm left in his living room thinking of ways to entertain myself. If I sit here too long, then surely I'll sink into the part of my mind I've tried so hard to seal away. The part that reminds me of the life I've left behind, and the people who've betrayed me.

I look at Jasper's bookshelf, wondering if maybe he wouldn't mind if I read something to pass time. I don't see why not...

Browsing his book selection, I feel a little jealous. Some of them are books on magic, obviously as old, if not older than Jasper. Many have incredible spines, which make me just have to pull one book out to inspect the cover.

After finding some potentially decent reads, I stoop down to check the bottom shelf of one of his bookcases that's in the corner of the room.

Apparently the best books are always hidden at the bottom.

One in particular catches my attention. The cover is a soft purple, but that isn't what made me instantly interested in it. It's the fact my name is printed on the spine, in italic font. I curiously pull the book from its slot. There's no author name, nor an illustration on the front cover..

I stare at the book for a few moments, wondering if I should actually open it.

There is no way this can be about me.

When I turn the first page, I'm wrong. Right there is an intricate drawing of me—just my face. Under the picture, there's a question mark, as if whoever had drawn this didn't know it was me.

The next few pages are drawings again, with my face sporting different emotions. From smiling, to frowning, to even crying. There's no denying—this is me.

As realization hits me, I quickly close the book, not worrying about how brittle the pages may be. This *is* about me. It has to be. But why would Jasper have a book of me, with so many drawings that would have had to have come with extensive observation. The drawings even recorded the freckle on my chin.

Suddenly, I hear Jasper opening the front door. Quickly, I shove the book back into its place, before standing swiftly, ready to face the Alpha who's walking through the door.

"Hey, I'm back," he says, lugging in two shopping bags in each hand.

I force a smile onto my face. "So I see."

I end up helping Jasper put the groceries away while I think. Why on earth would he have that book about me? Unless of course there's someone out there who looks strikingly similar to me, and with the same name. I highly doubt that, but after the kindness Jasper has shown, I can hardly believe he would have a stalking manual like that.

"Something on your mind?" he asks, as I put the last bottle of milk into the fridge.

Instantly I shake my head, and then shrug. "I am thinking about taking up my uncle's offer, of going to stay with him."

Initially, I wasn't going to go. It's been the idea of not being able to trust him, and I heard the Desire Pack isn't an easy place to live in. Girls solicit themselves on the streets to quell the emotion almost all of them feel on a daily basis.

But I would have to deal with it.

Because there is no way I can trust Jasper anymore. That book of his is too much to handle, and now I am too nervous to bring it up, in case he turns into a mass murderer.

"What changed your mind?" he asks.

His expression is grim, as he regards me intently. He had seemed opposed to the idea of me leaving the moment it had come up, and seemed almost relieved when I mentioned that maybe I wasn't going to go. Now, an emotion I can't pinpoint dances in his eyes.

"I don't think that is a very good idea," he murmurs, his voice low and calculated.

We stare at each other, both on either side of the kitchen island. The silence between us speaks volumes, as we come to an immediate disagreement.

"You told me I didn't have to stay..." I say carefully, narrowing my eyes at the brooding Alpha.

He tilts his head slightly, as if accepting a nonexistent challenge that has flared between us. "You can't trust him... whoever he may be."

It takes me a moment to hold back from yelling at him. From telling him I trust *him* a whole lot less than I trust my own uncle. Instead, I close my mouth and continue to glare pointedly at Jasper. Eventually he sighs, seeing my stubbornness from a mile away.

"You don't get to make decisions for me. I'm going there, whether you want to take me there, or I have to walk."

Jasper runs a hand down his face in defeat, before he braces his arms against the bench. My fingers tap against the bench as I impatiently wait for him to answer what I've just proposed.

"Fine." Jasper mutters. "But I take you, and we make sure he is actually your uncle."

I don't want to agree with him. All I want to do is run straight out the front door to escape from him and his book. But I stay still, knowing if I am actually going to get out of here, then I need to be smart about it. And that starts with having a ride out of here. And Jasper is my only option.

"But first, you need to know something that will truly help you decide whether you should stay or go," Jasper says softly, rounding the bench.

I watch him warily, unsure of what he is doing.

And before I can do anything, he stands in front of me, and reaches out to touch me.

Chapter Eighteen

His fingers are only inches from touching me.

Had he touched me, I am not sure what would have happened. Was he advancing on the attraction between us? Was he going to pull me close and kiss me until I was out of breath? I have no idea...

And I don't get this opportunity to know, before someone slaps their hands down on my shoulders.

The look on Jasper's face is what I see first, as he retracts his hand. For a moment, it looks like he's woken from a trance, finally snapping back into reality. Then he throws an angry look at the person behind me.

"Did I interrupt something?"

I want to yell *'yes'*. Because the voice belongs to Tayten, and it really does annoy me that I haven't found out what Jasper wanted. Now, he seems to have recovered his senses, and it's as if he isn't going through with his plan.

Jasper shakes his head slowly. "What do you want?"

Tayten moves around me until she's beside me, draping her arm over me. It seems to be her favorite thing to do.

"I just came to make you aware I am going back home."

Thank the Goddess...

"I'm not sure when I will be back... It depends on how things are back in time," she informs us. Jasper almost looks relieved by the idea of Tayten leaving and, honestly, I am too. Now I hope I can escape both her and stalker-like Jasper.

Jasper doesn't say a word to me about what he was about to do in the kitchen as we drive toward the Desire Pack. After he promised he would tell me later, in a better situation, I don't question it.

Quite frankly, I am nervous. The Desire Pack is not for the fainthearted.

"What should I expect there?" I ask Jasper, as we start to slip into the climate of that Pack. Rifts in the Pack Quarter climate are common, but due to the Desire and Love Pack proximity, the cold seeps into both their communities. The difference is that there is no snow where we are going. Just ice. Lots of sleet and ice.

Jasper seems to think for a moment. "To put it bluntly, a lot of horny people."

I blanch at his words. Rumours of the Desire Pack spur obviously from its name. In school, we were told to watch out for old creatures who use magic to disguise themselves beautifully, luring people to use them for sex. Disgusting, but apparently the curse is as old as Phantom Wolves.

"Everyone?" I ask uneasily.

Jasper shakes his head. "Mainly the younger people. Sex is a way of life over there, a sport. If you find the right people, you could probably avoid those under the spell of their true nature."

Find the right people. I think I can do that.

Time passes quickly, with assistance from Jasper's powers. The downside is that instantly I'm hungry, but that's washed away by the sight of the Pack we are approaching.

The distance between where Jasper's small community is, and the Desire Pack, is small, but the drive still drags us into the beginning of night. However, this is to our benefit. Everywhere I look, bright lights illuminate the entirety of almost every space. The sight is dazzling, as some flicker while others sparkle. Never have I see anything like it.

The entrances to most Packs lead into a smaller town, before reaching a larger city toward the middle to end. This Pack did no such thing, expanding into a large concrete wonderland of mile-high skyscrapers and endless sidewalks.

"This place is crazy," I murmur, glancing at Jasper.

110

His face dances with the vivid colors—red, green, blue—from the lights. Despite the striking magnificence of this place, Jasper looks somehow disheartened.

"This entire Pack is a city. Finding rural areas like in the Devotion Pack is very rare, and any there are can really only be found at the far edges of the Pack. From your uncle's letter, he lives in an apartment in a wealthy part of the city," Jasper tells me.

What Jasper plans to do when I'm no longer his burden, I'm not sure. The idea of him not actually letting me go, after seeing that book, has my heart beating a little faster, and my fingers tapping uneasily on my thighs.

I see Jasper watching me. "Why did you *really* take up this stranger's offer?"

The urge to cringe uncomfortably is strong, but instead I uphold my composure. If he knew now what I found, then perhaps he would resort to something drastic, something I can't combat.

"When I was living in the Devotion Pack, I was always asking for a miracle. Nothing in my life was making sense, and now I have an opportunity to do something new with my life. So who would I be to turn it down?" I say. My excuse isn't much of a lie. In fact, I meant every word I've said, and I know Jasper believes me.

Time is getting very late by my standards, but it seems as though the Pack is just coming to life. People are walking past storefronts, dressed in incredible outfits of glittering splendour, with most being unnervingly risqué.

Jasper seems to notice my expression of awe. "They fondly call this the Night Pack, because most people sleep during the day, and come to life at night."

"Don't they have to work?"

People walk in and out of brightly lit stores of all types. All the owners have dressed their storefronts well, and it seems like there's a competition between them to look the most stupendous and almost inconceivable. The people however, look just as breathtaking...

"If they all live by night, then they all work by night," Jasper explains. "And their fashion is a lot 'flirtier', to fit their nature. Especially since they do not follow the Moon Goddess's religion."

The more we drive, the better everything begins to look. Eventually, I stop believing it could get better, but each block proves me wrong.

"I want to explore," I tell him, wishing I was anywhere in this Pack other than the car. All I want to do is get out on those streets and see what there is on offer. Because it looks as if everyone here is finally happy, and I have to admit I'm a little jealous.

"Maybe later," Jasper murmurs.

Apparently my uncle's apartment is at the top of a building made with a sparse amount of steel and a lot of glass. He must be very wealthy, considering the state of the place, and the type of people who are walking in and out.

Stepping out of the car, letter clutched in my hand, I'm surrounded by a bustle of people and extremely bright lights.

"Wait up!" Jasper calls, as I wander into the crowd, awed by everything.

I had expected it to be skin-shivering cold, and although I could do with a sweater, it's milder than I thought. Perhaps it's all the people around, the hot energy they seem to pass between them.

Jasper comes up beside me, looking around nervously. How can he not be excited by this? The atmosphere. All I want to do is run into the nearest night club, which is playing great dance music, and get lost in the night with everyone else.

"You're getting caught up. Remember why you are here," the Alpha murmurs into my ear, his breath hot against my neck.

He's right. As much as I want to ignore his words of reason, I need to meet my uncle, so then Jasper can leave right away. Then, maybe I might have time to check out the town.

Inside the apartment building, it's just as magnificent as the outside. I think it's the massive chandelier, so completely unnecessary for a place like this. It seems the Desire Pack respects the saying, bigger is better.

"We need to get to the 18th floor," Jasper tells me, making me frown.

That's high. Am I afraid of heights? I mean, there has never been a time in my life where I've had to consider such a fear, so maybe not. Luckily, Jasper reassures me there'll be an elevator, not stairs.

We walk across the marble floor, which has been polished so exceptionally well I can almost see myself in it. No one is around, until we're in the elevator with a woman wearing a white fur jacket and thigh high boots with a threatening heel. I stare at the fur nervously, wondering what she killed to get it.

Jasper leans down, whispering in my ear. "It's faux."

Wishing I knew what he meant, I sidle a little closer to Jasper, still unsure about the woman.

We get off on the right floor, and wander down the hallway to where my uncle's room is meant to be. When we knock on the door, nothing happens. No one answers. Jasper and I exchange uneasy looks, as we wait for someone to answer the door.

"Maybe he's out right now," I say, although he looks speculative.

Suddenly my uncle's neighbor opens her door, making both me and Jasper jump. She looks apprehensive of our presence. "What are you two doing?"

"We are looking for a man who lived here. We believe his name is..."

"No one has lived there for a few moments. Sorry," she says, before slamming her door shut. I almost don't catch what she said because of the thickness of her Desire Pack accent. But when I do understand, my heart sinks.

Jasper looks at me sympathetically, as I throw the letter angrily onto the ground. A lie. It was all a lie, and Jasper was right.

Not once does he say 'I told you so', but I can't look at him. All I want to do is cry, and scream, and curse my own stupidity. Without a single word to Jasper I take off at a run down the hallway, back to the elevator.

"Thea, it's okay!"

The elevator door closes before Jasper can get in, and I descend the building. Hands in my hair, I wonder how I could have made such a stupid mistake. If Luca was still my boyfriend, he would have been so mad.

No, don't think about him.

As the elevator door opens, Jasper is standing directly outside, a grim expression written all across his face.

"Don't use your magic around me," I grumble, pushing past him.

He follows me outside, but I push into the crush of people heading down the street. I want some time alone, so when I lose Jasper within the flood, I'm instantly relieved. Despite it being a hot, bustling mess of people, no one here will in any way judge me...

Some gasp as I forcefully push past them, hoping tears aren't falling from my eyes.

I must have lost Jasper completely at this point, as when I glance over my shoulder, he's nowhere to be seen. A relief?.

Walking down the street, with the throng of people, is an experience in itself. Many of them are dressed so intimidatingly, it blows my mind. But my looks are quite different from most of them, causing rogue looks to be cast my way, as people wonder exactly why I am here.

Suddenly, a woman reaches out and snags my arm, pulling me to a stop.

She's wearing the shortest red, leather skirt I have seen, with a cropped top of black lace, showing me the bra I really didn't want to be faced with. Tattoos snake across her stomach, and silver pierces her nose and eyebrows. It's frightening.

"Hey gorgeous. Want some fun? Our boys are waiting inside..." she drawls, in a voice meant to be sexy. Glancing at the shop she's referring to 'inside' as, it's nothing other than a strip club.

I wrestle from her grasp. "No thanks."

Keeping a fast pace, I continue walking down the street. With that experience my heart is racing, and I'm starting to think less about my fake uncle, and more about how I'm going to get out of here.

The feeling of claustrophobia suddenly hits, forcing me to find the edge of the crowd. No one seems to notice me, as I begin to pant. Maybe I shouldn't have run away from Jasper like that. Maybe I should have thought things through first.

Again, I am grabbed. This time, I'm thrust into an alleyway, caught in the grip of darkness, so no one even sees I have disappeared.

"Well aren't you pretty," someone seethes in my ear. And I know then, I *really* shouldn't have left Jasper behind.

Chapter Nineteen

Making a noise isn't an option, as a hand is slapped over my mouth. The other people keep my wrists together behind my back so I can hardly move. Being abducted or kidnapped was never something I had to worry about back in the Devotion Pack, so the unfamiliarity of it all stuns me now into stiffness.

"You're not from around here, are you?" the man murmurs in my ear.

My mind wants me to do so many things. At the very least, it wants me to lash out and defend myself in any way, so I can escape, but my body refuses the command. I'm paralyzed, and this man has complete control over me until I snap out of my disorientation.

Is this what this Pack is like? Are they all so sexually deprived, they have to kidnap women to satisfy themselves?

Suddenly, my body kicks into gear. Not only is it the idea of what could come from this situation, but the idea of not doing anything to stop it. I've been strong since the moment I decided to leave my home and follow Jasper. Not once have I broken down, and I can't let that all be worth nothing now.

So I kick back, the heel of my boot knocking his shin, loosening his grip as he curses crudely in my ear. Twisting around, I rip my wrists from his grasp, pushing at his stomach with a vicious jab that forces him backward.

Stumbling backward, the lights of the street capture me like a halo of safety. Whoever that man is, he doesn't dare follow me out, as I meld back into the crowd again.

With a hand over my beating heart, I follow the ground again, swallowing the lump in my throat. *Did I seriously just escape that?*

No one bothers giving me a second glance as I begin to run. I can't stay on these streets if I want a chance of surviving another moment. I need to escape the streets and find a safe place to catch my breath again.

Most of the places aren't ones that interest me in the slightest. At first, I was mesmerized by this place, but now, as I discover the secrets behind the bright lights, it's daunting. I decide on a small bar that doesn't seem too occupied. At least no one can lure me anywhere...

Pushing through the doors, I'm hit with the aroma of cheap beer and fries. The only people in here are the bartender wiping down the bench around a drunk man slumped over the counter, with someone else in the corner throwing back cider with what looks like his girlfriend on his lap.

I take a seat on the stool two spaces away from the drunk man.

"Need anything?" the bartender asks. Just a faceless person interrupting my time to think. I shake my head and they leave me alone to wallow in the faint jazz music coming from the speakers at the corners of the room.

Suddenly I turn in time to see the man from the corner's girlfriend storm out the door, swinging her purse over her shoulder in a huff. All I can see of her is her back as she moves out onto the street. From behind, she has the same dark curly hair as him, forcing memories on me. Whoever she is, that man's done something to make her angry.

I catch his glance as I turn around. He stares directly at me with dark eyes. The attention we share between us is brief, as I turn away again.

Resting my head against the counter, I close my eyes. That girl reminding me of June couldn't have come at a worse time. My best friend betrayed me, and somehow that's worse than Luca. Because I loved her. She spent her entire life trying to convince me her own species was real, when I chose not to believe. Why?

I don't have time to think about it, as there's the sound of someone tapping the counter by my head.

It's the bartender. "Take this."

She slides a tall glass of what looks and smells like cider. Instantly, my nose curls up in disgust, as my distaste for alcohol hits. Ever since Luca and I got drunk on our graduation and I spent the entire night throwing up while he continued partying, I have never thought about drinking ever again.

"No thank you," I murmur, planning to rest my head in my arms again, but she nudges it closer.

"Someone bought this for you," she mutters, as if she couldn't care less, but it is her job to endure my attitude. She looks as if she wants to be out on the town like everyone else seems to be, but is stuck here.

I look across the bar, to my left. Not only is the drunk man there, but also the man from the corner, only a seat across from me.

He looks like a creature from another planet. Maybe that's an unfair observation, but he hardly looks normal. His skin is deadly pale, with the slightest violet hue to it, although nothing like Jasper's eyes. This man's eyes are coal black, to match everything he's wearing, and even the color of his teeth. I want to recoil from him, and from the toxic smell of alcohol he reeks of.

"You didn't have to," I say uneasily, knowing immediately it was he who's bought me the drink. I'm not flattered in the slightest... especially after what he did to that girl, and how he had stolen his way into that seat.

He shrugs. "It's the thought that counts, I suppose."

Not bothering to acknowledge him, I lean back on the counter, still needing time to think, rather than be harassed by another stranger. The moment I leave this Pack, the relief I will feel will be instant.

"So, you're from the Devotion Pack?" he questions.

I'm worried he knows where I'm from. Our Pack is known for the bleakest features and the darkest hair, which tends to be our best feature. He probably figured it out from a single glance.

But still, I ignore him.

"You seem really lost."

"Look, I don't mean to be rude, but I have had the worst day today. I have a stalker, a fake uncle and a man walking around who's attempted to abduct me. If you could give me some time to think, I would appreciate it!" I snap.

Taking a deep breath, I slump back on my seat. I hadn't meant to blurt out my problems to him, and probably the bartender, but it felt good to vent. My chest feels a little lighter now I've actually said it, since my habit of keeping things close tends to weigh me down.

Tentatively, he slides onto the seat right next to me. Past the horrific scent of vodka, he wears some kind of spicy cologne applied a little too heavily.

"This Pack can be tough on the best of days. I've lived here my entire life, and I still get lost in the feel of it. It entices you in, but the reality of it can be harsh. You have to learn to live off it, make the best of it. That's why this Pack is so brilliant aesthetically, and our Alpha is the wealthiest of them all. Just... don't wander out alone," he tells me.

His lecture is long, and somehow helpful in an unhelpful way. The sincerity tells me a lot about this strange-looking man. No way do I trust him, but something tells me his advice is meant to assist me.

"What did you do to that girl?" I ask, deciding to bring up what truly made me wary of him.

He chuckles. A weird sound. "I rejected her business offer. If you know what I mean."

I shake my head, not even wanting to think about it. But is that really what had gone down? She seemed pretty mad at him, like it was personal. I decide not to question.

"Are you staying here? Like in a hotel or something?" he asks me.

His question takes me off guard. What am I going to do? Jasper is Goddess knows where in this Pack—either looking for me, or out taking advantage of the town. The latter I highly doubt, but at

119

the same time, it almost worries me that he could have left without me.

What am I thinking? He has a book dedicated to creepy drawings of me. As much as I probably need him, that still makes me wary.

As I think back to the question posed, I scrabble to come up with an excuse. "No. My mate and I are staying here. I should probably go find him..."

Aware my excuse doesn't really match what I've admitted to him earlier, I stand from my seat, deciding I really need to leave. But the moment my shoes hit the floor, he grabs my wrist, thrusting me back to him.

My surprise is instant. Why are men here so desperate and rough with woman? And despite my protest, no one in the bar looks twice, as if this couldn't be closer to normal.

"Let me go," I growl, half on his lap already. He holds me close to him, but I still resist, trying to force myself off his lap.

He grins slyly, as if he is enjoying watching me struggle. "Let me help you get used to the life of this Pack."

His hand finds my thigh, which sets alight a fire deep within me. Twisting my arm, I'm out of his grip enough to slap him across his face. He flinches, as I push myself off him. If I could stay and throw my drink over him too, I'd be very pleased.

Instead, I turn and push back through out the door and into the street.

How it happens, I don't know. The size of this Pack is so large, the probabilities of seeing him were slim. At the moment I leave the bar I see Jasper standing across the street, and I forget that book. I forget everything. I just remember how he has never failed to save me before.

The run I make across the street could have been potentially fatal. I hardly look both ways as I weave between cars waiting for the green light to flash, making a beeline for the Alpha of Devotion.

Our gazes meet for a brief second as I near him. Emotions such as relief, and something like happiness dance there, and I'm sure I mirror it.

I hardly have control when I throw myself at him, my arms encircling his torso. It may not be skin on skin contact, but I still feel his body heat, and smell his familiar scent, as I bury my face in his cotton shirt.

Clearly he's surprised, as he hesitates before wrapping his arms around me.

"I was looking everywhere for you," he breathes, as we separate.

But for some reason, I don't want to move away. Because as much as I don't want to admit it, that simple hug felt like the first flicker of home I've felt in a long time.

Chapter Twenty

We make it back to Jasper's car, a silence stretching between us.

With him by my side, not a single person even glances at me, let alone sneak me a sly comment, or grab at me. Jasper is like a walking wall of security, ensuring unknowingly, no one tries anything with me.

"Where did you go?" Jasper asks once we're in his car, shutting out most of the street noise and tacky shop music.

I made the decision moments ago not to tell him about the man in the alleyway, or the man in the bar. Both were creepy and something I want to forget, and never have to deal with again in my life. This Pack is too much for me, and I want out right now.

"Just a bar to think. I overreacted about my uncle, or lack thereof. I just don't understand who would do that," I say, my comment making Jasper sigh. Even though I can't read minds, it's fairly obvious Jasper wonders the same thing.

Clearly, someone had used magic to find where I'm staying with Jasper, and sent a note that would make me set off on a false idea that my uncle actually exists. He doesn't, and now I'm left wondering why someone would do that. And more importantly, who?

I just have to hope Jasper has enough magic to keep them away.

"I have some questions," I say, as Jasper pulls back onto the bustling road, between swerving cars and bustling trucks. Every time I bring up the want to know more about him, he gets a little nervous, as if he is hiding a secret that can never be revealed.

I breathe in. "In the Devotion Pack, there was a storm. When I went out to find my friend's dog, was that you on the path that lead me back to her house?"

It's a simple question that's been one of the many bothering me for the entire time I've known him. Especially since that moment has never been explained, and now I know Jasper was planning for me to escape the entire time he was there, it would be nice to know if he was the reason behind it.

"I couldn't let you get lost in there, could I?" he says casually, a slight smile on his face.

Looking down, I smother my own smile. "What happened to my dad? Not that I really should care, but I would like to know if you were behind his disappearance."

"He was in the way. I kept him somewhere secure, although I am sure Luca will have found him by now."

The fact he's referring to Luca by his name now, instead of as my boyfriend, is a relief. Just the thought of once trusting him, of once sharing a bed with him, makes me shiver uncomfortably. Shaking my head, I try to convince myself I didn't know, that anyone would have fallen for the exact same thing.

"Why Casper?" I question.

His brows furrow, as he cast a glance at me. "Sorry?"

"Why the name Casper?" I reiterate, a slight touch of humor in my voice. "I mean, I wasn't going to figure out who you were, since you really *shouldn't* be alive right now, but could you have made it any more obvious to someone who doesn't think rationally?"

He chuckles, finally catching on to what I was talking about. "You put me on the spot. I hadn't thought about what my fake name would be. Why does it matter, would you rather my name have been Grant, or Dave?"

I shrug, trying to imagine him with such a name, but failing terribly.

And then I whisper, "Why do you have that book?"

Instantly, Jasper tenses his muscles, and looks like I've just surfaced one of his terrible secrets. The risk of him doing something to me now I've found that book has to be low, since he's saved me so many times, and taken care of me better than my father would have.

But I still eye him a little apprehensively.

"Do you trust me?" he asks, his voice soft.

I pause. "I don't know yet."

As I look at him to read his expression, he's looking around anxiously. Is he looking for an escape? This man is the most confusing creature ever. "I've been having dreams about you. For a very long time," he murmurs, biting his lip.

Staring at him, I let the information absorb. "Huh?"

"Centuries actually. They aren't inappropriate dreams," he tells me. "Well, for the most part."

I stare at my lap, wondering what to do with my hands. Did the Alpha of Devotion just admit he has dreamed about me for longer than I have been alive? I should be unnerved, but for some reason, it doesn't bother me too much.

"Why?" I ask.

"I don't quite know," he says, sighing deeply. "All I know is, I had to draw you, to remember who you were."

Are my dreams because he was meant to save me? Have the wires of fate been working since Jasper has been alive? If so, then clearly I am meant to be sitting in this car with him right now.

"So what now?" I ask, the feeling of bleakness and almost loss from the moment I found out I didn't really have an uncle fade back in. My future is now uncertain again, and all of a sudden, it feels like a weight has been placed on my shoulders.

Jasper smiles slightly. "I think I know a place where we can stay."

"You're happy with it." I noted how his eyes light up with just his mention of it. I don't doubt Jasper is aware of many incredible things in every Pack. He is the oldest Alpha out there.

He doesn't say another word until we leave the bustle of the city, the skyscrapers thinning, although we still remain in quite a busy-looking neighborhood.

I follow Jasper's cue as he points to the right of him. "That, is Alpha Asher's estate. The Alpha of Desire."

Instantly, my mouth falls open. Never in my life have I seen anything so brilliant, so lavish. It's lit spectacularly, in a multitude of different colors. It drips wealth and superiority over the rest of the city, placed upon a pedestal that demands attention.

"You've got to be kidding me," I breathe, not being able to take my eyes off it.

Jasper chuckles, clearly enjoying my reaction. "He is very wealthy, and holds some of the best parties ever seen. I think he would be pleased to let us stay for the night."

My heart skips a beat at his words. Am I seriously about to meet the Alpha of Desire? I have seen him on television a view times. Sometimes his face appeared for everyone in the diner back in the Devotion Pack for visitors to see, and Kera to drool over.

We drive up the hill to his house, but not before being stopped by an immense amount of security first. Luckily Jasper seems to have instant entrance to everywhere he goes.

"Impressive," I muse, once we've made it past what seems like the last wave of guards. Each of them wears the darkest cloak with a small golden pin, signifying their allegiance to the Desire Pack.

Jasper shakes his head, smiling a little.

Lights are entwined in the fence line as we drive steadily up the hill. All I can do is stare out the window, taking in the sight of the city lights glittering and winking brightly. Jasper doesn't seemed fazed at all by how extravagant everything is. I remember the picture June showed me of him, with his magnificent crown and coat. He obviously is used to being bathed in wealth.

Fiddling with my fingers on my lap, excitement merges with nerves, as we make it up into Alpha Asher's courtyard.

"Don't be nervous. He can be a little intimidating, but I will keep an eye on him," Jasper reassures me softly, placing his hand on my thigh. Were I not wearing clothes, I would have probably melted in a puddle. Still, just the feeling on his hand *right there*, makes me tense, wondering what he's going to do next.

Instead of bringing any of the ideas I was thinking to life, he removes his hand and winks at me, clambering quickly out of the car.

I close my eyes for a second, take a deep breath, and follow.

Now I'm not smothered by the heat of people, the brisk chill of the Pack hits me. Luckily, Jasper ushers me across Asher's vast courtyard, toward his front door. Believe it or not, it's lit up a bright pink, like some sort of focal point.

Without even knocking, Jasper cracks the door open, and waltzes straight in.

"Ah..." I stammer, watching in complete disbelief. Music drifts out the door—a soft jazz, somewhat romantic.

Jasper motions for me to follow him, before he starts walking again. Still shaking my head, I enter his house, and the door automatically closes behind me.

Inside his house is even more stunning than the outside. Lights seem to be his favorite thing, I note, as I stare directly up at the giant chandelier taking prime place in the middle of the room, hanging almost dangerously down from the roof. It glitters with glass and diamonds, casting an intricate pattern over the marble floor I walk over.

Should I have taken my shoes off? Should I do something to somehow fit into this place? It must be worth more than I am...

"Ash! Hey Asher, you have visitors," Jasper calls out loudly, his voice echoing off the vaulted ceiling.

He turns back to look at me, violet eyes sparkling as he waits for me to catch up. I almost want to cling to him, to stay in his shadow, to feel valuable in such a home. Instead I keep my composure, standing tall so I appear confident. Really, my insides are jelly.

All of a sudden I feel a hand slip into the back pocket of my jeans, pressing unnervingly close to my butt.

I flinch, and glance up. Someone is looming over me, their stomach pressed against my back. That's how I meet the golden eyes of the Alpha of Desire.

Chapter Twenty-One

"What a pleasant surprise," Asher says delicately. "What did I do to deserve the Alpha of Devotion hand-delivering me such a beautiful young lady?"

Surprised, I catch Jasper's gaze for some sort of assistance in this situation. Imagine if I turned and slapped him for his words, and his unwanted touch: an Alpha. Surely some kind of consequence would follow.

Instead, I stay tense, feeling every inch of his fingers against me.

Jasper, however, chuckles. "You really have quite the humor."

Asher winks at me, but I look away. His golden eyes are taunting, and I have to admit, unnerving. Jasper steps forward, grabbing the cloth of my shirt, gently yanking me toward him, making Asher's hand fall away. Something about the movement didn't seem as innocent as Jasper made it out to be.

"I haven't seen you in quite some time, Alpha. As always, it's a pleasure," Asher says, shaking hands with him.

Then, his gaze flickers to mine. "And this one? She belongs to you?"

Instantly, I frown at him, suddenly not caring about his rank. I've heard much about the values of his Pack, and have even witnessed them first hand. Clearly, they are heavily influenced by this guru.

"I don't belong to anyone," I tell him. "Not you, not Jasper."

At my words, Asher's eyes light up. The way he regards me makes me want to be anywhere but here, as his eyes squint slightly, like he can't quite figure me out. Jasper cuts the moment with an awkward chuckle.

"This is Thea. A friend of mine," Jasper explains. I feel him place his hand on the small of my back.

"Of course. I get it..." Asher murmurs, a sly smile creeping onto his face. "Friends."

I shake off his backhanded comment, as he starts walking off across his marble foyer. He wears a billowing cloak, threaded with gold, in patterns like dancing people across the back. This man clearly enjoys the strange fashion this Pack indulges in. It's almost too unsettling.

"Come, you must be thirsty," he calls over his shoulder, motioning for us to follow.

Jasper casts me a quick glance, before following. It amazes me how Asher didn't even question our presence, but rather accepted it. This fully shows me the extent of their friendship. But how does the gentle Jasper I know put up with this man?

"What does he mean by thirsty?" I question, keeping close to Jasper's side as we walk. At this point, I think I am catching on to Asher's whole vibe. His sexual, seductive vibe.

Jasper just grins at me, shrugging casually. "Who knows with him?"

In fact, he didn't actually mean what I've assumed. Instead, he leads us toward an entire bar setup, with a line of alcohol across the wall. It shows off clearly expensive bottles of all shapes, containing potent mixtures of something I don't want to touch.

The first time I got drunk was on whiskey, at our graduation, and I spent the night slouched over the toilet vomiting my stomach up while Luca kept partying.

"Your preferences?" Asher asks, sliding around the bar, while Jasper pulls a seat out for me to sit on. Nervously, I do so, knotting my fingers together as I watch Asher toss a bottle of Bailey's into the air, catching it swiftly.

"No thanks," I say.

Asher smiles, sliding the bottle back under the bench. As he does so, I take a moment to assess him. I'm sure many girls would find him attractive. The sharp features, those eyes and that dark hair he doesn't seem to mind keeping completely unruly. Nope, he's not my type.

Asher looks at Jasper expectantly, but he holds his hands up defensively.

Almost instantly, the Alpha of Desire's eyes flicker back to me. "Not even some Bacardi?"

"Rum isn't my thing," I say distastefully, screwing up my nose.

Leaning across the bench, Asher gives me a look that mirrors the ones Jasper gives me sometimes. So intense, they have me wanting to look anywhere but there. But this time, I match Asher with as much confidence as possible, which seems to give him the utmost pleasure. "And what is *your* thing, darling?"

Jasper clears his throat, and for a second, I think I catch him shoot Asher a dangerous look I've never seen on him before. But in a second, it's gone.

"Do you think we could just crash here for the night?"

"Maybe I will have a drink," I say, cutting Jasper off. Something to take my mind off everything might just help. And how many people get to say they've had a drink with an Alpha? Or two Alphas at that?

Asher claps his hands together. "That's the spirit!"

Jasper raises an eyebrow, regarding me carefully as if he doesn't know how to react. I look away, hoping he isn't too mad about my decision to stay here rather than go to sleep.

Asher mixes up some potent concoction that doesn't taste too good, but after another, I start to feel myself loosen up. Jasper however, stays with a glass of water, while Asher joins me. Although, the more I drink, the more distant I seem to become from both of them. A buzz has hit me, and both of them seem to be as sober as anything.

"He just couldn't get me there," I mutter, swiping the remnants of my last drink off my chin. "Like, he knew nothing about what makes a girl climax."

Asher smiles, and for a moment, I swear I see two of him, swaying back and forth rhythmically. I've definitely passed my limit, and after not having eaten all day... I'm flat out wasted.

"Such a shame. Perhaps he should spend some time in my Pack," Asher says with a smile, sliding me another drink across the table.

Except Jasper intercepts it, catching it in his hand. "I think she has had enough."

"The story is just getting interesting!" Asher dejects. "Tell me Thea, what would you rather he have done to you?"

Perhaps if I was thinking straight, I would have been offended by his words, but instead I'm eager to answer. I'm just about to list everything Luca could have done to give me the perfect orgasm, when Jasper interrupts again.

"I think this conversation has got out of hand. Thank you for your hospitality Asher, but I think I might take Thea to bed," Jasper says firmly, standing.

Gazing at him, I feel myself pouting. Is he really going to take me away when I've spent all this time getting into a real conversation with the Alpha of Desire? And I've been having so much fun...

"Right," Asher says, and I catch his wink. "Don't let me stop you."

Despite my most demanding protests, Jasper assists me up the stairs by holding my arm. Asher has given us free rein to any of his upstairs rooms. Not that I care. Currently, I am annoyed at him for taking away my fun.

"It's too hot," I complain. "I wanna take my coat off."

Jasper shakes his head, stopping me from stumbling across the carpeted flooring, as he tries to find a room to dump me in. My cheeks are flushed and my body begs to be free from all my clothes. I really have drunk too much.

"In your room," he asserts, making me scowl.

We find a room, but I hardly pay attention to it in the slightest. I'm too busy shedding my coat the moment Jasper closes the door behind us. Sighing in relief, I flop onto the bed in a fit of insatiable giggles.

"Never again am I letting you get your hands on that kind of hard liquor. Or any for that matter," he mutters, picking my coat up off the floor to toss it onto the desk. Kicking my shoes off, I wonder briefly how it would feel to just get rid of all my clothes. Then I wouldn't feel so hot.

"You're no fun," I comment.

Chuckling slightly, Jasper moves toward me, looming over the bed.

"I'm just trying to protect you," he tells me, as I fall into another set of giggles. Why can't I stop? All I want to do is go running naked through the streets of the Desire Pack and curse everyone's names to the wind. How great would that feel, Thea?

"You always protect me," I slur, smiling widely. He shakes his head in wonder, before turning to close the window.

Sitting up, I frown. "Too hot, leave open."

The curtains billow, as the sounds of the city float through. Jasper stands perfectly in the moonlight, as it gleams off his perfect skin. Has he always been so beautiful? I suddenly want to run my hands down his body... with his clothes off...

"Fine, but you'll wake up cold," he says, running a hand back through his hair.

I watch him walk back across the room, his gait almost like he's floating. If I'm still drunk, I don't know. Quite frankly, I couldn't care less. Because suddenly, I have a feeling rising in my stomach, and I want Jasper to answer it.

"I'm pretty warm now," I murmur. Pulling my shirt off, I throw it to the side. "Really warm."

Jasper, who has his back to me pulling the curtains across the other windows that remain closed, doesn't notice me at all. The cool air wraps around my bare skin, caressing my breasts that haven't been this bare to someone since Luca, yet I still have my bra on.

Then he turns around. His eyes meet mine, before they wander down my neck and to my chest, as he takes in the current situation.

"Thea," he whispers. "You should put some clothes on."

I shake my head, as I pull my hair out of its tie. Jasper watches my every movement, as I run my fingers back through my hair, confidently. Now, I'm grateful for this buzz, because never would I have the guts to do this on a normal day.

"Why?" I question, fumbling with the button of my jeans.

Jasper steps forward. It's a simple step, but it has a big impact. Just seeing the way he looks at me, with those darkening violet eyes, sends heat straight to my core. And at that moment, I want him to prove to me that an orgasm for me can really exist.

"It's very dangerous," he tells me, a huskiness to his voice.

"Distracting..." He takes yet another step forward. "Tempting."

Never have I wanted someone so badly. Never has someone communicated fully to my body, taking absolute control over it with just a few movements.

"But not yet," he says, tilting his head.

Instantly, I shake mine, and close the gap between us. Grabbing the cloth of his shirt, fisting it in my hands, I beg with my eyes to take back what he says. I want him right here, right now, and I may be drunk, but at this point in time, I couldn't care less.

"Jasper," I say softly. "I need you."

Chapter Twenty-Two

Groaning, I stuff my head into my pillow.

The burden of what I committed to last night weighs heavily on my shoulders, as does my splitting headache. Rolling over, I stuff my head deeper into the pillow, wishing I could say the word and this hangover I granted myself would just disappear.

Memories of last night are a jumbled mess in my mind. Asher's golden eyes, and Jasper's violet ones are in there somewhere. And did I...?

The way I get out of bed so fast, is potentially dangerous. Flinging the sheets off my legs, I acknowledge my lack of clothes before I make it out the door. I shrug a shirt on with pants to follow. I may be known to make some mistakes, but there is no way I'm letting Jasper or Asher see me in just my bra and underwear.

Jasper is walking back down the hallway, when I open the door, hair a mess, with my clothes in disarray.

"Good morn..."

"Did we...?" I ask, both of us pausing in front of each other. "We didn't, right?"

At first, it looks as if he doesn't know what I'm talking about, until he smiles slightly and shakes his head. Sleeping with Jasper might have been on my drunken radar, but not on my sober one. He's an Alpha, meaning... no possible chance.

"If you mean did I help you back to your room, where you admitted you wanted to have sex with me, before falling straight into a drunken slumber before I even had time to answer? Then, yes."

The blush that infects my cheeks I can't hide, as I realize I've completely embarrassed myself in front of the Alpha of Devotion, because I decided to take Asher up on his offer of a drink. To think I had so desperately thrown myself at him too.

"I'm sorry," I mutter shamefully.

We leave Asher in a whirlwind of thank yous and handshakes. Apparently the Alpha has business elsewhere, so he doesn't mind that we're leaving early.

The Desire Pack in the day is slightly less extravagant, and I know the city has fallen asleep, preparing for another rush that is the night. No lights pollute the cloud-capped sky, giving it a few hours to rest. Perched on Asher's hill, the cold and fog snake up the driveway, drifting around Jasper's and my feet as we walk toward his car.

The concrete under my sneakers is slick with ice, and I slide around trying to find traction. Jasper offers to help me, but I don't want to touch him after last night.

Just the idea of it makes me blush furiously.

"You haven't eaten in a while," Jasper points out, as I pull the safety belt over my torso. My stomach has been dealing with pains it's never felt before, ever since I woke up. Eating has been the last thing on my mind lately, so when Jasper mentions it, I agree instantly.

We can't find a breakfast place in the Desire Pack. As we drive down the main street, I stare out the window at all the shops with closed signs strung across the door. It makes me sigh irritably.

"There will be something somewhere," Jasper tries to assure me. He's told me before how he eats primarily for enjoyment, that he doesn't actually need to. Perks of being a Phantom Wolf I suppose.

However, something else is on my mind.

My thigh itches badly, my fingers trying to find a way to quell the ever growing rash building on my right leg. It's easily concealed under the hem of my shorts, but it has my mind straying every time I try to have a conversation with Jasper.

"Everything okay?" Jasper asks, as I quickly pull my fingers out of the leg of my shorts. Where has this sudden rash come from?

"Just thinking," I say sharply, quick to cover it with an excuse.

Jasper examining my thigh after what happened last night, or rather what *nearly* happened last night, can't happen. It isn't just that, but the thought that this may just be something minor I'm blowing out of proportion.

But geez, does it itch...

We find a quaint diner tucked in the middle of a small town between the Desire Pack, and the Safe Haven. The place looks friendly in here, and Jasper agrees we would leave at the sight of any unruly rogues. Another experience trapped in a car while Jasper fights off vicious wolves is out of the question.

The moment we step inside the building, I'm hit with a wave of nostalgia that has me swaying with vertigo for a moment.

"Woah," Jasper says, grabbing the sleeve of my shirt to steady me. "Steady."

The place looks strikingly similar to home, to where I worked for the last couple of years with two people I thought were my friends. The waitresses mulling around, heaped plates of food balanced expertly on their arms, is too familiar to not look twice at. That was me, just last week.

"I... I can't," I mutter, glancing quickly at a concerned Jasper.

Their uniforms may not be pink, but soft pink was just as cute as ours. The main difference is the fact that the cook looks happy to be there, and the one who looks like the manager or boss leaning over the counter has an actual smile on their face.

"You really need to eat," Jasper insists, leading a stumbling me over to a table at the corner of the diner, by the window. "We can leave as soon as you're done."

I let him pull the seat out for me to sit on, at the table dressed in the checked linen tablecloth, matching the color of the waitresses' aprons. It makes me internally cringe, as I pick up a salt shaker with shuddering hands, using it to distract myself.

"Sorry. It's just this place is just like back home. The memories, you know?" I mutter, meekly raising my gaze to Jasper.

He stares at me through the mussed strands of dark hair he hasn't bothered pushing back from his forehead. Admittedly, he looks good today, and I hate myself for noticing. Luckily, he doesn't react as I note how good he looks in the black jacket that matches the rest of his outfit perfectly.

At least he's keeping his promise about not reading my mind.

"Don't be sorry, not for a second," Jasper murmurs lowly, tilting his head slightly. "I told you to come to me if you ever feel homesick."

I remember him saying that the night we had to sleep in the same bed, before I followed him out to that restaurant, completely embarrassing myself. Then, I hated the idea, but now I'm tempted to tell him that the idea of Luca and my father still bothered me. Even June.

That isn't the only thing bothering me. The itch on my thigh is bad, and I still haven't had time to properly check it out.

"Damn girl, I know your man is attractive, but here?"

My head snaps up, my eyes meeting an amused set of blue ones. A waitress has come with menus, but really is clearly ridiculing the first thing she's come across.

Me with my fingers up the leg of my shorts.

Instantly, I retract them, embarrassment staining my cheeks like an infection. Jasper raises his eyebrow at me, probably wondering what on earth I was doing, especially in public, behind the veil of the table.

"I'm not... I wasn't..."

She doesn't listen to the rest of what I'm trying to say, as she places the menus in front of both Jasper and me, before retreating quickly.

"What was that all about?" Jasper asks, as I nervously fold the laminated red menu open.

A variety of potential meals are printed in front of me, and my stomach instantly swallows any need to itch my thigh, wanting me to give it my full attention. Usually I would have been put off, after watching how most of this food would be cooked, but right now, my food-deprived stomach will accept anything.

"People around here are strange," I reply, refusing to be caught by his gaze.

I end up ordering pancakes from the same waitress, who gives me a suspicious sideways glance before walking away with our order.

When she comes back to deliver it, I eat quickly, wanting out of here as soon as possible. Jasper just watches me intently, almost as if he's making sure I will eat something, until he excuses himself to use the bathroom, and I'm left alone to finish my plate.

"This is probably a really weird thing..."

I jump slightly, looking up to see a girl has taken Jasper's seat. She is most definitely a waitress here, with that pasty pink uniform, her bright blonde hair tied in a bun. The blush on her face is one I've become accustomed to, but why she has it right now is beyond me. Well, why she is even sitting here...

"Ah..."

"Was that your mate?" she asks quickly. "The one who was sitting here?"

Instantly, I'm taken aback by the blunt force of her question. I sit for a moment, bewildered, as I wonder how I should reply.

"No," I tell her warily.

She seems to sigh in relief, losing all that pretty posture as she slouches casually down in the seat. Placing my cutlery on my plate, I watch her carefully, still not quite sure what she wants. I even glance at the male bathroom door in hopes Jasper will show himself to resolve this awkward situation.

"I was hoping you would give him my number," she says suddenly, dropping a crumpled piece of paper on the table by my plate. Staring at it for a few moments, I fathom what she is saying.

Obviously, she saw Jasper from across the room, like any level-headed female attracted to the opposite gender. This girl, very pretty, clearly isn't blind to the Alpha's unspoken charm, and wants a piece. I don't blame her in the slightest. But it makes me a little uncomfortable.

Something about the idea of letting this girl get hold of him makes me unexplainably mad. It's almost as if I want to protect him, to keep him close so he won't stray to any other girl. Why, I have no idea, but it's almost second nature.

Grabbing the paper, I unfold it. There it is, her number.

"I guess so," I say, placing it back on the table.

She thanks me graciously before departing, running back to her other working friends to tell them how successful she was.

I stare at the paper. Will Jasper accept that? Will he call her back? I mean, she is extremely beautiful. The jealously that creeps into my mind is something I try my best to shun. Why am I so touchy about this? Is it this stupid rash?

Jasper comes back seconds later, sitting down. "You didn't finish your..."

"Someone left this for you," I say quickly, pushing the note across the table to him.

Frowning, he picks it up, unfolding it with deft fingers. I watch his expression falter for a moment, before his lips tilt up slightly. When he glances up at me, I point to the girl it was referring to, wishing I could crawl into a hole.

"This is a surprise," he tells me. Then, he takes me by surprise as he slides the piece of paper back onto the table, pressing it down with the salt shaker. "But I think I'll just leave that there..."

"Seriously?"

Jasper shrugs, standing. He pays before we leave, waving once at the girl as we go. I'm still stunned, as I get into the car.

"She isn't my type, that's all," he explains. My eyebrows furrow. How can a girl so absolutely beautiful not be his type? Especially to a man equally handsome, if not more.

He laughs at my expression.

"What is your type then?"

He turns the car on, before backing out of the parking lot. He doesn't say a single word, as I wait impatiently for an answer. My curiosity should surely have attacked him by now.

"A beautiful young female named Thea," he says.

I narrow my eyes at him. "Stop playing around."

"I'm not. That's exactly why I didn't take her number. I have other interests to pursue with someone else, so why go after her?"

He gives me a look I can't quite put my finger on. It isn't amusement, which is what I expect with this kind of conversation.

I sigh. "Your mate."

He regards me for a good second, despite driving the car. It makes me squirm uncomfortably, as he shows no emotion.

"Yes," he murmurs. "My mate."

I don't dare question who his mate is. His romantic life is something I've kept out of, despite that he knows a little too much about my previous one. With my lack of orgasms and such.

Then he speaks again. "And pursue it I will, until she realizes *exactly* how much she needs me."

Chapter Twenty-Three

Jasper offers to skip time for us to get home in time, and I take it.

It passes that day, leaving me feeling slightly disoriented and drowsy. Although, I have to admit that it feels nice to be back at Jasper's house, almost as if I've come home for the first time in what feels like forever. Never have I felt like this before.

"You should head to sleep," Jasper murmurs from behind me, the moment we walk through the door.

I flinch, twisting around. We are in his living room, the space filling with warmth from the moment we step inside. Something to do with Jasper's magic, I assume.

"I like when I skip time around you," he says, changing tack. He leans against the doorway, staring at me.

Sometimes the way he looks at me paralyses me. It's as if he can change his emotions with just his eyes, portraying to me only what he wants me to see. Like right now, it captures me, melting my insides with its intensity.

"Why?" I ask, my voice quivering slightly.

I don't know why he makes me so nervous. But as he stands, watching me like a beast stalking its prey, my hands shake by my sides.

"Gives me time to admire you," he tells me softly, tilting his head as if it would give him another angle to look at me. "Time to observe you."

If it was anyone else, maybe I would have been creeped out. But for whatever reason, it only makes my heart race. "I... I..."

"Not only are you stunning, in my eyes you're interesting. No one has perplexed me in such a way, so I enjoy having the time to at least try to fathom *who* you *are*."

His words have me stunned for a few moments. The sincerity in his eyes is breathtaking, stripping all my insecurity in one instant. I have to clutch the arm of the chair I'm standing beside to combat my legs that threaten to collapse.

Jasper strolls forward, his gait loose and approachable, soothing my legs. "Come on, I'll walk you to your room."

I could make a comment about how I don't need assistance since it's just to the bedroom, but I'm too entranced to say a word. Instead I walk up there with him, hoping he can't tell how his words have affected me.

"Thank you, again," I whisper, as I walk into the room. Jasper remains at the threshold.

"For what?"

Moving to the edge of the bed, I sit on it silently. "For everything."

This isn't the first time I've thanked him, but every time I say it, it doesn't seem enough. I want to prove it to him. I just... don't know how...

He stares at me, time between us seeming to slow down, and not because of magic. Again, I'm enchanted by his gaze, and the moment he steps into the room, my entire body yearns for him.

"You don't know how tempted I am to read your mind," he murmurs, taking another step toward me. "To figure out if my want matches yours."

If his want matches mine, he must be on fire right now. Every part of me has surrendered itself to him, wanting to feel his touch, his lips, his skin. Anything to put a stop to the insatiable feeling pulling at my lower stomach, pulsing at my core.

"I can't breathe...," I say hoarsely, "... when I'm around you."

He doesn't say anything, but his eyes spark alight. I watch as he raises both his hands up, darkness crawling up his wrists, consuming his hands. My eyes widen, as it completely encloses around his fingers in the form of a glove, with a fabric I've never seen before in my life.

Males wearing gloves is a sure sign of *something*. Something I don't want to acknowledge. Only because it's so terrifying. It's known around every Pack that if a male wears gloves, he wants one thing. Sex.

But not just any sex. No strings attached, with no risk of finding out the mate bond. He's going to use his fingers, in a way I don't want to begin to question.

It's more significant than anything else. Just seeing Jasper declare the first signs has my body quivering anxiously, like it's answering him without my control.

He walks forward for another step, and I raise my gaze from his hands to his eyes. All I can see is that he's ready, for what I can only assume is me. The moment he leans over me, bracing both hands on either side of me, pressing against the bed, the breath is completely blown out of me again.

"Why me?" I question, my voice breathy.

Why would he want to even look twice at me, being the Alpha of Devotion. Hasn't he had his fill of women over the hundreds of years he's been alive?

I don't care at this point, I'm on top of the world right now.

His face is inches away from mine, and I would kiss him, if I had the guts. "Because every time I look at you I have to hold myself back. I can't anymore."

Almost as if he's fighting an internal battle, whether or not to kiss me, he runs his fingers down my face. The gloves feel oddly soft and silky, like no fabric I've ever felt before, making me shiver.

"Why don't you just touch me?" I question, unable to fathom why he wouldn't. "You don't need the gloves."

Jasper shakes his head at me, tracing my lower lip with his thumb. "That would take the mystery out of it."

I can't help frowning, making Jasper chuckle. He grabs my hand, bringing me up to standing point. Now, I'm pressed flush against him, feeling his warmth through his shirt, the muscle a contrast against my own stomach.

"I also want to show you how I can give you the best climax you've ever had, without even having to take your clothes off," he murmurs into my ear. "Better than Luca ever could."

I shudder, his words like a spell, captivating me. As he pushes me slowly backward, toward the unfurnished wall, our gazes are locked, his spoken promise brewing there.

"How?" I whisper, hoping I won't regret it.

Jasper pushes my shoulders backward gently, so my back is pressed against the wall, keeping me trapped, at his mercy. I want to do something. Touch him, maybe. But his gaze pins me, and I can only breathlessly wait for him to prove his words.

"Like this," he says, bringing his face down to my neck. His breath is hot, caressing my skin while his fingers draw down my sides, sliding under my shirt.

My back arches the moment his fingers touch my skin. Those gloves are ice cold, despite being warm touching my face only moments ago. The foreign feeling makes me shiver, as he traces my stomach with just the tips of his fingers.

"Jasper," I gasp, but he is quick to hush me.

I've committed to his touch at this point, even if it is just his magical gloves suddenly changing temperature. From cold to warm in a few seconds, he circles under my bra, watching my every movement carefully as if he thinks I'm about to resist.

"The moment you opened the door the first time we met, I knew," he says softly, his fingers dancing along the hem of my pants, having given up on my restricted breasts.

"Knew what?" I ask, as the temperature of his gloves fades back to normal, and it's almost like his real fingers are caressing me.

My eyes close for a second, as he dips below my pants line, dangerously close to my private region. The one place that only Luca has had access to, is now in the control of the Alpha of Devotion. My body wants to belong to him, and in that moment it does.

"That Luca never gave you the pleasure you deserved," he said, pausing his fingers, a silent tease. "That you *needed.*"

"Then show me," I breathe.

143

It's the last part of me snapping. The last part of him that's been holding back. His hands are between my underwear and my pants, not touching anything until the tips of his finger press down on...

I gasp, my hands find his shoulders, to clench into his skin through the thin cloth of his shirt. The feeling is instant pleasure running through me, euphoria filling my veins.

"That's it," he murmurs, as I can't hold back the moan that surfaces.

I've never felt something so intense, so consuming. The way Jasper presses his fingers so firmly against me is something I almost can't handle.

My head is stuffed in his shoulder as he moves against me, creating friction between his fingers and the most sensitive part of my body. I just want him to take his gloves off, I just want to feel him inside me.

Jasper gazes at me, as I writhe against him and the wall, silently wishing the intense pleasure would end, while at the same time begging for more.

Then it hits me square in the stomach. Jasper's name is the only thing on my lips as a wave of pleasure washes over me, my hand on the arm that's doing all the work down there. Never had Luca given me an orgasm so consuming before, nearly having my knees buckling.

Sliding his hand out of my pants, Jasper holds me close to him, as I try to get my breath back.

"That's only the start of the pleasure I plan to give you," he says in my ear, guiding me toward the bed. I collapse down on it, completely clothed—as is Jasper.

Jasper stands over me, my mind still reeling from what I just committed to. That is the most pleasure I have ever felt, and if I wasn't so tired, I maybe would beg for more. Without the gloves. I even would return the favor in some way.

"I can assure you, the moment these gloves come off, then this will have been child's play."

And I don't doubt it for a second.

Chapter Twenty-Four

The sun has hardly risen when I next open my eyes. It has to be at the beginning of dawn, which is surprising since I've never woken this early.

"Oh Goddess," I drawl, running a hand down my face as I sit up.

Did I really do that last night, or was it a wild dream? It can't have been been a dream; I remember the feeling so well. His fingers, his eyes, his everything. It was so real, and so is the fact I committed to it, wanting with every ounce of my body.

Clambering out of bed, I throw my hair into a ponytail, and form a semblance of an outfit that might be suitable for a walk outside. Right now, I need to clear my head.

Jasper is bound to be awake, since he doesn't need to sleep, being a Phantom Wolf and all, so going out the front door isn't really an option. After last night, I don't want to see him yet, and something tells me he won't want me to go wandering outside this early in the morning in a place I don't yet completely know.

Instead, I zip up my coat and open my bedroom window.

The air from outside is sweet against my skin, ice-cold but refreshing, enticing me into the outside world where maybe I will feel a little taste of freedom... of safety.

Sliding across the windowpane, I hook my fingers onto the edge of it, maneuvering my body till I'm hanging completely out the window. This is either incredibly brave, or incredibly stupid. Probably the latter, since my plan is to grab hold of the fire escape, and scale my way down the side of this two-storey house. Perhaps if I break my leg, Jasper might have some magic to heal it.

When my feet touch the ground, crisp with early morning frost, I want to kiss it. Instead, I brush the spider webs from my polyester coat, and stalk around the house.

The edge of the sun peeps slightly over the horizon, as I find the main sidewalk down the street. Where I plan to go, I'm not sure, but just breathing in the air of this brisk morning is a relief.

I'm lost in thought for a few moments, before my fingers unconsciously wander down to my thigh.

The rash that surfaced yesterday had sunk to the back of my mind, being less irritating when distracted by Jasper's devious fingers. Now, it seems to have kicked into full gear, and suddenly it itches painfully. Not only that, it seems to have spread, creeping up my thigh and down to near my knee.

Should I tell Jasper? Will he know why this is happening?

Taking a deep breath, I shake my head. I don't have to rely on Jasper for everything. I'll prove to myself that this is nothing; probably just stress after these past few days.

Deep in thought, the tips of my fingers scratching the rash through the fabric of my leggings, I hardly notice the figure running toward me. Glancing up, alerted by the slapping of sneakers against pavement, I see someone coming toward me at a fast pace.

It's a man. He seems to be on an early morning jog, and as he gets closer, I can see the concentration written across his face, headphones in his ears. The man keeps going past me, and as he does, I take a moment to look at him.

Clearly he is from the Devotion Pack, or at least originally. That same blank, mundane features a lot of us share, with the dusty brown hair and dark eyes. Except he has a strange look about him... something I can't put my finger on. Sure, he's blatantly attractive, especially with the shirt he decided not to put on today. Not stunning, like Jasper, but simply good-looking.

The moment he brushes past me, I glance over my shoulder, to see he's doing the same, slowing down his run.

"Hey," he says warmly, as we both stop.

Talking to strangers is something I was always told to avoid. But for whatever reason, this man seems genuine, not like someone who might kidnap me. Perhaps my ability to trust has been so messed up, I just don't care anymore.

"I haven't seen you before. Have you just moved here?" He has that Devotion Pack accent that's familiar, like we've grown up next to each other.

I can't tell him my circumstance, I know that much. Getting into the reasons why I managed to end up staying with this guy's Alpha might take a while, and destroying any tracks for Luca to follow is priority. So instead, my mind scrambles for an excuse to cover myself.

"Yeah... Ah, Alpha Jasper is my cousin," I say quickly. "I'm staying with him for a while."

He looks surprised, and I don't blame him. Maybe I should have said I was visiting, and avoided him for the rest of the time I stay here. Instead I've opened my stupid mouth and dug a hole I won't be able to get out of.

"Impressive. Has your cousin shown you around yet? This place is pretty simple, but there are some places I'm sure you would like," he offers.

Shaking my head, I look around. I hadn't realized I've walked so far down the straight main street of this place, lost amongst the identical houses with their clipped front lawns, and nothing other than a few decorative pieces to tell them apart. This place is a possible maze I don't want to go missing in.

"I only got here yesterday," I tell him. It isn't entirely true, but it feels like it.

Suddenly, the man sticks his hand out to me. "I'm Cole, nice to meet you."

"Thea," I respond, feeling less anxious about him with every second. His whole persona seems so normal, and so safe, it lifts the pressure off my shoulders. And for those few moments, I begin to think less about Jasper last night, and the increasing rash on my thigh, that might possibly be for an underlying reason I'm unaware of.

He grins, a toothy, friendly grin. If with his lack of shirt, he's getting cold from no longer running, he doesn't say anything. The sun is coming up rapidly now, and I'm sure the place will start to heat up again soon.

"Shall I show you an awesome place to get breakfast?" he asks. An innocent question, which has my stomach growling after a lack of dinner last night. I could really do with some food.

So I agree. Probably a stupid thing to do, but hopefully Jasper will think he wore me out last night, and won't expect me to waken for another couple hours.

We have to walk over 10 minutes to get to the place. It lets me find out quite a bit about Cole.

His parents have lived here their entire life, and he is expected to as well. The vendetta he has against Phantom Wolves is because they killed his great grandparents, and he personally wants to exterminate every Phantom who walks this land. He even chants a mantra about how he respects Jasper so much for what he has done, protecting them against the Wolves he spoke so lowly about.

He has no idea...

I just nod and agree every now and again, hoping he won't catch the blush that's creeping onto my face as I am uncomfortable. He seems like such a nice guy, but he really does hate Phantom Wolves, like June once did. Just the thought sends a jolt of sadness to my heart.

The place Cole chooses is a cute café on the edge of a park. It has only just opened when we get there, and apparently the best place to sit is by the window, where you can watch the sun coming up, and kids starting to come out once the frost melts.

"So, why are you staying with Jasper?" Cole asks innocently, after he's ordered breakfast and a coffee for himself.

I sigh. "Looking for a new start."

This is true. All I want is to forget what has happened with Luca and my father. To move on with my life is so tempting, and I know this place might just be my main choice for a new beginning. I just need a job and...

Just thinking about having a boyfriend scares me. Would Jasper be interested? Clearly I am attracted to him, and he must feel a little something if he was willing to press me against the wall and give me the best orgasm I've ever had last night. But dating him? Just the thought makes me shiver with some kind of emotion I like to keep suppressed.

"This place might be looking for workers... if you need a job," Cole tells me. "Or maybe the supermarket or..."

He goes off listing potential jobs I could have, but I hardly listen. Slipping back into a mundane job like I had back at home doesn't sound very tempting. Just looking at the people who work here reminds me of how it was back home. It may not have been as bad as the diner Jasper and I visited yesterday, but it still makes me feel uneasy.

I can just imagine Jasper telling me to move on already. But will he want me working here? Suddenly my leg begins itching again.

"I'll have to think about it," I say distractedly. Cole is super nice, too nice in fact.

He chats easily about everything, as if we are long-time friends. In fact, we seem to have a lot in common, and sometimes, I feel like I'm slipping into conversation with my old best friend. Still, my mind is on the pain, the itch. There's no way this is normal. I'm going to have to tell Jasper.

Cole has excused himself to the bathroom when I'm finally brought my breakfast. I eat silently, as the man who served me leans toward one of the waitresses who's cleaning the table next to mine, and begins muttering to her.

I can only just hear them.

"I heard the Alpha is back in town..."

"So?"

"What do you mean so? You've been hearing what everyone's been talking about."

"That the Alpha is a Phantom? Come on, no one *actually* believes that."

"You have no idea how many people do. This is serious, Cindy. People are starting to think he isn't actually helping us, but planning something terrible."

My curiosity wants to listen for more gossip about Jasper, but the other part of me wants to intervene and tell them how ridiculous they are. Sure, they're right about Jasper being a Phantom Wolf, but they can't *know* that. But there's no way Jasper wants to hurt them, or is planning something against them. He is too good for that...

Instead of going ahead with both options I've considered, I stand and head towards the door to leave. Just as I do, Cole emerges from the bathroom, his expression falling at the sight of me leaving.

"So soon?" he asks, jogging to me before I can leave.

At that moment, I become more aware of Cole being shirtless, and no one actually questioning it. And these people say Jasper is strange? Actually, they aren't wrong about that...

"Sorry, I just got a call from Jasper, he..."

"He what?"

Flinching, I spin around to see an unimpressed-looking Jasper standing at the door of the café. How did he find me here? Did he do it intentionally?

I hardly have to think, as everyone in the room falls silent, stunned by the presence of their Alpha. We just stare at each other. Last time I saw those violet eyes, they were sultry, and prepossessing. Now, they are brooding and dark.

Then, he lifts his gaze to Cole, who's directly behind me, probably paralysed under Jasper's scrutinizing look.

And something tells me, he isn't very happy.

Chapter Twenty-Five

"Never in my life did I think I would be able to say I actually met my own Alpha!"

Cole's excited exclamation doesn't go unnoticed by Jasper, who looks as if he wants to knock the man out. However, he keeps his anger restricted to his gaze, with which he assaults both me and Cole.

This goes completely unnoticed by the man beside me.

"I just met your cousin!" Cole says pointedly, resting his arm across my shoulders in a way I know is friendly, but hardly looks like it. "She's very sweet."

Poor Cole has no idea what Jasper did for me last night. He has no idea that there is no way Jasper's my cousin. He doesn't even recognize the malice brewing in Jasper's expression.

But to be fair, I don't fully understand why.

"You two seem to be quite friendly, don't you?" Jasper murmurs, his gaze lowering to the arm over my shoulder. The way he looks at the arm seems to add weight to it, making me want to shrug it off to stop all this scrutiny.

Cole looks down at me. "We just met today, but I think we have a lot in common."

Now, Jasper looks at me, and I see a warning there. Is he jealous? Clearly, Cole and I only just met, and there's no way we could have got up to anything close to last night. Why is it, that every time I look at him, I'm pressed against the wall again?

"That's great to hear," Jasper says, although I can hear the cynicism in his voice. "Well, Thea and I have something important to do today, so we must say 'bye for now'."

Surprised, I shoot him a look he just seems to brush off. Instead of acknowledging me, he gives Cole a sickly sweet smile that only I can see behind, and grabs the sleeve of my coat. I want to dismiss him, but I decide to be compliant, to not raise a scene.

Well, not one worse than Jasper has caused, waltzing in all casual and such.

Walking out of the café, I notice how much warmer it's turned already. Morning dew replaces the frost, the sun's lighting everything that was once shadowed. Early mornings and I don't always get along, but I have to admire the change it makes to the park. Young children are out, taking advantage of the warmth to play on the grass.

Jasper doesn't share the mood.

"What's up, attitude?" I mutter, seeing Jasper's car parked on the side of the road. At least we don't have to walk back.

The Alpha sighs deeply, still holding onto me, as we walk toward his car. "I was worried about you."

His words make me blanch slightly. He's shown how much he cares about me, protecting me from the moment we met. He's helped me in the forest, the diner, and ever since then. But he's worried about me? That gives me a kind of warmth my coat can't.

"I was fine," I reply.

He doesn't look convinced, casting a glance back at the café; it's obvious he isn't keen on Cole. Is it because he came on so strong? Does Jasper not like that?

"When I noticed you weren't in your room, I got..." He broke off, biting the edge of his lip. "Worried."

Frowning, I slide into the passenger side of his car, trying to think that over.

"At first I thought it was Luca. I saw your empty bed and open window and the worst thoughts came to mind. I don't know what I would have done if he had taken you," Jasper murmurs, flicking me a quick glance before he starts the car.

I don't know what I would have done either. Would he have killed me right away, or would he have waited to do so? I don't even want to imagine...

"How did you find me there?" I ask, referring to the café.

A sudden look of guilt flutters across his face as he pulls onto the main road. Clearly he's done something I won't agree with, but I'm currently riding on the high of Jasper not doing something to cause a scene back there. I don't think I would have been able to handle that, especially since he is their Alpha.

"I used magic," he told me meekly. "In my defense, I didn't even think you were still in this Pack."

Jasper's worry is passing on to me, it seems. Suddenly, the idea of him knowing it's possible for this to happen worries me immensely. How could I have been so stupid? Leaving like that probably put me at risk of Luca finding me.

My leg starts to itch again, this time close to my knee.

"Why did you act so hostile around Cole? It's obvious you don't like him, but he was nice enough to buy me breakfast. He showed me someone I can actually trust," I say pointedly, finally relaxing a little now in Jasper's car.

A cloud seems to loom over his head, as his expression darkens slightly. I'm beginning to understand his emotions a little more, but still, he can be like a blank canvas sometimes. At times, I want to slap some reality into his face.

"Something about him, the way he acted with you," he mutters, still not looking at me.

A slight smile tugs at my lips. "Are you jealous?"

He shrugs, not catching onto my joking mood. I can't imagine Jasper being jealous about anything, especially about me and another guy. But I can come to no other conclusion as to why he was acting like this.

"Should I be?" he asks, narrowing his eyes at me.

I take his challenge. "It's not like we're together."

"You didn't say that last night," he retorted.

"I wasn't thinking!" I snap.

"Clearly, or maybe you would have been able to stand up by yourself," he replied.

My list of comebacks is all ticked off. Actually, it doesn't exist in this situation. Last night I completely belonged to Jasper, and he knows it. I was at his mercy, and I enjoyed it, and now I'm scrambling to come up with a way to deny it.

"I was fine," is all I can shamefully muster. Again, I'm backed against a wall.

Jasper smiles, but it isn't a smug smile. Did he enjoy last night as much as I did? Is there a part of him that wants to do it again, or even a little more? Like me?

Just the idea of it makes me need to press my legs together, a heat jolting to my core. I have to tuck my head down so Jasper won't see my blush. The fact that I flush at the slightest bit of embarrassment is shameful in itself.

Luckily, Jasper doesn't bring it up again, as we finally make it to the house.

I run straight upstairs to change into some shorts, to let my leg breathe a little bit. And to let myself breathe a little too. Jasper is clearly doing things to my head, and the walk I took this morning was supposed to help. It did nothing.

The moment I take my pants off, I almost faint.

From the top of my thigh, all the way down to my knee, is a bright red, disturbing rash. Ugly, big and inflamed is the best way to describe it. My scratching has made it bleed slightly too, giving it a look that has my head spinning, and my stomach flipping over completely.

"Don't freak out," I mutter to myself.

How this happened, I'm not about to dwell over. I had no idea it had got this bad, and it feels as if it's going to completely consume me in a disgusting, peeling mess.

I wet a towel and lay it on the rash, but it doesn't make it difference. It doesn't hurt, but itches profusely. All is I want to do is tear my skin off in a gruesome act of relief. I have to do something...

Tell Jasper.

Clawing at my hair, I pace, trying to make sure my other thigh doesn't touch it. What will he think... No, I can't doubt this. I *need* to tell him.

Jogging down the stairs, I go on a hunt for Jasper.

I find him in the living room, stooped over a book. Typical, but I hardly bother myself by thinking about that. He glances up as I walk in, his gaze finding my eyes, before he notices the way I'm walking. He looks down at my thigh.

He flinches, blinking a few times, as if he doesn't completely believe what he is seeing.

"What have you done?" He asks in disbelief, not being able to take his eyes from the wound. The few steps he takes toward it are tentative, as if he might get infected by whatever this is too. It dawns on me what this means, making my heart sink dramatically.

He doesn't know what this is.

"It's been itching for a few days," I inform him quickly, thinking back to when it started. "I don't know why."

Kneeling down, he looks as if he's going to touch it, but changes his mind. He just studies it carefully, a deep-set frown tainting his expression. Is he scared for me?

"Do you have any idea? Did you touch anyone who could have passed this onto you?" he asks, his voice rising slightly.

My mind whirls, as I watch his eyes darken suddenly.

"Who touched your thigh?"

This takes me back a few steps. Who touched my thigh? *Who?* I would *never* let someone do that to me. Well, not unless they were Jasper. It couldn't have been Luca, since I haven't touched him for a while before it started itching. Unless...

My mind suddenly snaps on the exact answer.

"A man. In the Desire Pack. When we were separated, a man touched me there, but I was quick to make sure it didn't last," I explain.

I feel repulsed, ashamed. Dirty, even. What had that stranger given me? Could it be potentially fatal?

Jasper stands swiftly, walks to the edge of the room and back again. He looks deep in thought, and I dare not interrupt him. The way his eyes blaze, full of intelligence and life. Clearly he is onto something, and I don't know if I should be worried about that or not...

"How?" Jasper questions, exasperated. "You let a stranger touch you like that?"

That is what he was so worried about?

"Jasper, this is serious. And I didn't even mean to, he was a self-entitled son of a..."

Jasper holds his hands up, silencing me.

I watch as he suddenly strides straight out of the room, forcing me to follow him. When I join him in the other room, he's digging in his jacket pocket for what look like his keys. He wants to take me somewhere. Let's hope it's a doctor of some sort.

"There's only one person I know who might be able to help you," he tells me, holding the keys up for a second before walking out the door again. I follow him.

"Who?"

As long as they're professional, and know something about what might be my problem, then I'll be satisfied. Jasper however, doesn't look thrilled at the idea.

"Someone I'm not exactly fond of. But he has books I don't, and in them is the secret to your... issue," Jasper explains.

I'm lost, as he paces around the room aimlessly, as if he was trying to find something, but doesn't know where to look first.

"Who?" I repeat, not liking this game.

He sighs, finally pausing to look at me properly. "We are going back to the Love Pack."

My eyebrows furrow in surprise.

"We need Alpha Malik."

Chapter Twenty-Six

The closer we get to the Love Pack, the more my nerves set in.

The last time I was there, Luca was too, and the idea of him still being there has me fidgeting anxiously, having to sometimes resort to scratching my thigh to keep my hands from quivering. Not even the idea of seeing yet another Alpha is worrying me as much as this...

Jasper hasn't said another word about what might be wrong with me, and honestly, I'm too afraid to ask. By the constantly stricken look on his face, and the way his hands clench till his knuckles are white on the wheel, I have a feeling this is something I'm not going to like.

The good part about this whole thing is that I'm going back to the Love Pack.

Something about it contents me, makes me feel peaceful and docile. For a start, the snow is a beauty to look at, and in the Love Pack there is no lack of it. Despite the situation, we are going back to the Pack of Love, and I can't wait.

The moment we drive through the entrance, emerging into another world completely, my nose is pressed against the cold window, my window puffing out to emulate the wonderland outside.

The clouds must be on their coffee break, letting the Pack have some sunshine, glistening against the mounds of snow pressed up against people's houses. Does everything here stay flawless and pretty? In the Devotion Pack, wind would have disrupted the peace by now.

"I'm impressed," I hear Jasper murmur.

I don't turn around, transfixed by the beauty of the snow-burdened trees and frost-kissed windows. "Same, this place is..."

"Not that," he cuts me off gently. "I'm impressed by you."

This forces my full attention on him. He stares innocently out the window as we drive, careful of the ice slicked roads and thin traffic. At least he looks a lot calmer, his expression impassive.

"Me? I haven't done anything..." I admit. He's the one who's saved me from a variety of situations. He makes me feel like a shadow compared to him.

He flicks me a quick glance, violet eyes shimmering with something along the lines of admiration. I'm not used to it.

"You handle things so well. I don't even have to use my magic. What's your secret?" he asks, his voice close to a soft whisper. I stare at him for a few moments, trying my best to process his words.

I tilt my head. "Sleep."

He chuckles, and I join him. This is the first jab I've made at him about his lack of sleep. He claims he doesn't need to, being a Phantom Wolf and all. If it wasn't for his eyes, and the slight mention of magic here and there, I would forget completely that he's half dead, but alive for eternity.

Or an Alpha. That slips my mind all too often.

"Fair enough. You still amaze me though, and you can't fight that," he informs me, a truth in his words.

I want to tell him to stop saying that, but I don't bother. With what may be coming up in my future, I decide against arguing with him.

We have to drive quite far from the Pack center to make it to Malik's estate. Jasper tells me Malik's expecting us, which is a relief, since Alpha Asher didn't when I first met him. Let's hope he isn't as intense and so... sexual.

His property covers more ground than I probably have in my whole life. Every frost-tipped blade of grass contributes to an entire land of unfilled wonder, which leads to his actual estate. The impressive building is tucked under a canopy of trees shielding the infrastructure, made primarily of glass, from heavy snow.

It's all strictly protected from behind a massive fence, with an intimidating gate flanked by two guards. They don't look too frightening though, all bundled up and red-faced.

Jasper only has to wind down the window, and they let us in.

"Benefits of being important, I suppose," I say jokingly, although it's true. Jasper can do whatever he wants, whenever he wants, because he's an Alpha.

He just chuckles, carefully driving across the tarmac to park the car near the main entrance. The glass panels that make up a lot of the house allow me to see a lot less than I thought. It was a fogged kind of surface, almost disorientating.

"Now... Malik," Jasper mutters, getting my attention before I step out of the car. "Be careful of him."

I frown. "What's that supposed to mean?"

Jasper sighs deeply, trying to find the right words. After meeting Asher, and having him stick his hand in my back pocket, I'm not sure it can get any worse than that. When I think of the Alpha of Love, I typically assume he's a gentle man with a passion for mates and love. I remember Jasper warning me once before about him— being protective—but I'll keep my mind open.

I have more things to be nervous about...

Listening to the crunch of the snow under my feet as we walk to the front door, I try my best to ignore Jasper's guiding hand on the small of my back. Clearly, he is nervous about meeting Malik, and the backhanded comment he made earlier cemented it. This man isn't someone he wants me alone with.

"You love to invite yourself into places, don't you?" I mutter, as Jasper confidently pushes the main door open without a hitch in his stride.

I'm surprised he knocked the first time we met.

The inside of Malik's house is a shocking reminder of how wealthy Alphas can be. We're enveloped with warmth the moment we step inside the place, which is a surprise, considering the height of the ceiling, and the glass walls.

"I just want to get this over with," he tells me, casting a glance around the main foyer, as if Malik might just be lurking here.

159

This is to find out what is wrong with me. The itch has passed my knee, stretching its radius to my lower leg. It's irritating, but I'm too distracted by Malik's home to worry about it. The entire place is decorated, mainly furnished in deep red hues, and dark wood. Portraits of people I don't know are slung everywhere, covering what had been glass on the outside, but is now real walls.

I don't make sense, but neither does Jasper, and I've accepted him.

"Stay here. I think I have an idea of where he might be," Jasper says deeply, motioning toward a chair for me to sit on. First he doesn't want to leave me alone in here, and now he is abandoning me in a stranger's house? An Alpha's house?

I grab his arm, stopping him from moving any further.

"Alone?" I ask quietly, glancing around as if someone might be near, to judge me. Jasper shakes his head at me, probably thinking I'm completely unbelievable. I just stare into his eyes, giving him a pleading look.

"You'll be fine," he reassures me. "I know where Malik is, and I'll be back in a few moments."

Narrowing my eyes at him, I let him go, backing away a few steps. "Fine, but you'd better hurry back."

He grins, suddenly vanishing into thin air. Although I watch, the sight makes me jump slightly. But at least I'm getting used to it; and at least he doesn't do it often, because I don't think my heart can take it.

Even the seats are probably worth more than me. The moment I sit down on the maroon plush cushions, I feel out of place here.

Suddenly, my thoughts are cut off by the sound of bare feet hitting marble flooring.

Looking up, I watch a girl, around my age, walk down the stairway. She's holding a bundle of clothes to her front, her legs are bare, and possibly even more of her. I can't help but watch, as the beautiful brunette pads down the steps, her hair pushed back out of place.

She looks lost, until she sees me.

In the moment she runs at me, I catch an eyeful of something I really don't want to see. Noticing her mistake, she quickly shoves her boob back behind whatever she's holding, while I shield my eyes behind my hand.

"Sorry, you know how it is," she says breathily, laughing slightly.

Really I have no idea, since my breasts aren't nearly the size of hers. Not that I'm about to tell her, as she sits on the seat beside me. The girl reeks of sweat, sex, and old perfume. I sidle to the edge of my seat a little.

"Are you...?" She looks at me pointedly, and I fidget under her scrutinizing gaze. Her eyes are a frightening blue. "Are you having sex with him, too?"

My eyes widen. "Sorry?"

"Malik... You know, the Alpha," she says, her voice close to what you would hear from a twelve-year-old squealing girl.

This naked girl has just admitted to me she is having sex with Malik. And she thought I was too... I suddenly don't know what to do with my hands, or my legs or even my face.

"You must have me mistaken with someone else," I tell her.

The fact that she ended up in Malik's bed doesn't really surprise me. She's pretty, and obviously quite confident. That she even considered me eligible is actually kind of flattering. Not that I'm interested in whatever those who go up get into.

"He's big isn't he?" she exclaims loudly, causing my cheeks to flush. "Usually guys like that don't know how to use it, but he *definitely* does."

I did *not* need to know that.

"Look, I'm not having sex with Malik. I think you should get dressed, or something," I say, motioning to her current lack of clothing situation, without having to look at it. It doesn't matter, as she stands, dropping the clothes to completely expose her front. She picks up her coat, as I gasp, looking straight down at the floor.

All of a sudden, she squeals again. "Oh, babe!"

I glance up, getting an eyeful of not only the girl's bare butt, but Malik, standing at the top of the landing, staring down at us as he leans casually against the railing. He doesn't even look at the girl. He's looking at me.

Both the girl and I watch as Malik strolls casually down the stairs, letting me get a better look at him, as I ignore the nakedness in my peripheral vision.

He's quite stunning. The black shirt he wears is partially unbuttoned at the front, showing the top of a smooth chest I have to avert my eyes from. Even from far away, I can see the mussed hair, obsidian black, though rather sleek for bedroom antics. Malik walks with a predatory gait, like he's stalking us. It makes me sink back into my chair nervously.

"Victoria, you're still here," he remarks casually, in that Love Pack accent that's easily distinguishable. It entangles itself in your mind, trapping you in a constant spell.

The girl nods. "It's Vanessa, and I was just leaving."

I don't blame her for wanting to get out of here too abruptly. His tone is no-nonsense with her, as he demands her to get out of his sight, forcing her to shrug her coat on to cover her body quickly. I want to apologize for him, but I keep my mouth shut.

His gaze returns to mine. Something about him is so fresh and exuberant, his eyes so blue, I wonder if I should lean in with a microscope to ensure my own pupils aren't deluding me. They are so electric, so intense.

The way he looks at me has me believing for a second he's assessing me, as much as I was him. He didn't even look up when Vanessa turned and trotted toward his front door.

I did though. She flung it open and, without a moment's hesitation, stepped into the snow outside wearing nothing but a thin coat.

"Welcome to my home," Malik says warmly, clapping his hands together once, to force my gaze back to him. He stands in front of me, a fine scent of spice and sandalwood attacking my senses, leaving me breathless for a moment.

He kneels down, smiling sensually. "I've been waiting."

Chapter Twenty-Seven

"I... I... me?"

My hardly coherent stammering doesn't go unnoticed, by the way Malik smiles knowingly. My cheeks redden in response. Where has my brain gone? It seems to have melted under the heated gaze Malik assaults me with.

The first flicker of salvation is like a knock on the back of my head with a very insistent fist. I've spent a lot of my life being intimidated by Luca, and I'm not about to show weakness like that in front of anyone again. Malik may be an Alpha, but I'm a woman who knows how to hold a gaze and cover my emotions with an impassive cloth.

"Sorry you had to see that," he says coolly, standing straight again. Clearly he's referring to Vanessa. "I'm sure you've been waiting for quite some time."

My eyes narrow, as I respond a little too abruptly. "Not really."

Malik watches me carefully, openly searching my face curiously. He's probably wondering what's behind this sudden change of tack, but I'm not about to tell him. I know what he was insinuating... He thought I am another one of his ladies-in-waiting, but he can't be further from the truth.

"Thea, right?" he says after a moment's silence, finally catching on.

Nodding, I stand. But I'm caught halfway by a spike of pain down the side of my legs which sends me hurtling into Malik's arms. He catches my forearms, which was a quick maneuver considering he didn't expect me to throw myself at him so violently.

"At first I didn't think you were so eager," he says, looking straight down at me. "Now I see you've been playing hard to get."

Rolling my eyes, I push myself away from him, not about to let him get any more enjoyment from this. The sudden pain in my leg has already faded as quickly as it had come, which allows me to stand up on my two feet again.

"Where's Jasper?" Malik asks, glancing around his own place, as if Jasper's magic would have him appear instantly in front of us.

Jasper had disappeared in search of Malik, and now neither of us know where he is.

Malik catches onto my expression. "My house is rather confusing at times."

It's a cryptic way of describing things, but it doesn't help the shiver of anxiety up my spine. Jasper won't get lost; not here, not anywhere. Wherever he is, he's not with Malik, because *he's* standing right in front of me.

Then Malik nudges me playfully, making me jump.

"You stress too much, I can see that already," he observes, grinning. "Jasper is waiting for you."

My trust in Malik is next to none, but I willingly follow him through his estate in hope of finding Jasper, who has abandoned me. As I follow behind the Alpha of Love, I do take some time to admire how brilliant his house looks; new hallways and possible rooms open up with every step we take.

Malik wasn't lying when he said his house was confusing. You could take two turns and lose yourself among the hallways and probably never see the sun again. The dark walls and dark-stained wood flooring blend into each other, never changing, no matter how far we walk. All there is to see are wall hangings of people I don't know and am too afraid to ask Malik about.

"Where's he waiting?" I ask, splitting the silence.

Malik only shrugs casually. "You'll see."

And I do, as Malik leads me into a room that is like the outside, and inside of his house: a lot of glass, and confusion. Except this is sterile confusion.

Jasper is at one side of the room, holding something in his hands. His face is pale, his expression distraught as he's closely observing something like a book. Just seeing him makes me feel slightly better, but my heart still skips a beat at how distracted he seems to be.

"What's going on?" My quiet call makes Jasper glance up in surprise. I hear Malik slowly close the door behind me.

Jasper closes the book quickly, sliding it across the counter he was previously leaning against. This room could be one you would find in a hospital, although it misses most of the equipment. Perhaps it would best be suited to a room you would lock someone in, if they were crazy...

White walls, one chair in the middle of the square room with black straps attached to the arm rests...

I watch Malik exchange glances with Jasper. "I was alerted you have an undiagnosed... issue."

My issue being the rapidly growing rash on my leg that sends bouts of irritation, and sometimes pain straight at me. By what Jasper explained earlier, Malik has a way of detecting what's wrong with me. It isn't medical knowledge... it's a book.

And I think it's the one Jasper was just holding.

I'm told to sit down on the very chair I was wary of, although they don't strap me in. I will be out that door without a moment's hesitation if they even try to do that. Instead, I sit calmly in the seat, watching a look of complete seriousness settle over Malik's handsome features.

It's not a look I would expect to see on him. Especially after Jasper's earlier warnings, but somehow, it makes me trust him more.

"I'm going to have to look at it first," Malik tells me slowly, motioning to my thighs which I awkwardly have squeezed together. The way both Malik and Jasper stare directly at my legs has me grateful I put proper long pants on to protect myself from the Love Pack's climate.

I flush under the expectant gazes. "I'm not taking my pants off."

Malik rolls his eyes, while Jasper glances down awkwardly. I watch as the Alpha of Love leans over the counter, grabbing the book Jasper had been holding. He flips it open to show me a page.

It's a strange dialect I've never seen in my life, let alone will ever begin to understand.

"You know what this means?" I'm guessing, still not completely believing Malik had his hand in something like this. Clearly there is a history behind it. It's just... the idea of him being savvy with such things isn't something I gathered when I first met him.

Especially with the first reception I received from his female endeavor.

"How else am I supposed to see what's under there?" Malik questions, ignoring my question. "I can't see through fabric, believe it or not."

"Don't you have a blanket for me to... I don't know, cover myself?" I question, tossing the book that means nothing to me back at Malik. He catches it deftly, all the while giving me a harsh death stare. Probably not used to women not being charmed by him.

I watch him shake his head at me. "You're unbelievable. You have nothing I haven't seen, especially if you're still in your..."

"Malik," Jasper cuts him off shortly, shooting him a warning look. If he would look at me, I would give him a thankful look, as I'm glad he's stopped Malik from further insinuating my need to strip in front of two Alpha males.

Not even for this potentially health-incriminating rash on my leg.

"Fine," Malik mutters begrudgingly. "I'll get you a blanket."

Jasper shakes his head as Malik walks out of the room, closing the door after him. The moment he's gone, Jasper looks straight at me, and I almost melt under the heat of his gaze, which is a contrast to the icy feel of the room. It makes me wary, but just Jasper's presence has my tense muscles relaxing.

166

"You have to let him see it," Jasper murmurs, nodding toward my thigh. "It could be serious."

Something in his tone suggests he knows what is happening, but wants something like confirmation. The moment that thought infects my mind, a spike of fear nearly knocks me back. And it doesn't seem as though either Malik or Jasper are going to say anything until they've seen it...

Malik comes back with the blanket, and I wrap it around myself, before I tug my pants down. It might be stupid, considering Jasper has already taken the liberty of sticking his hands down my pants, but I don't want to give Malik any satisfaction.

"Now, can I see it?" Malik questions irritably, hopefully not noticing how my face flushes in embarrassment.

Slowly, I pull the velvety soft blanket up my legs, letting the fabric slide up past my rash, to where I bunch it over my hips, not letting anything that doesn't need to be seen, be seen. Malik and Jasper just stare, and after a few moments, I begin to fidget under their scrutinising gaze.

"I think..." Malik breaks off, those stunning blue eyes unmoving from the red rash on my thigh.

He grabs the book from the counter, and I notice Jasper look away again. Is he fazed by this? Does it bother him to see this? Something tells me an Alpha wouldn't be bothered by wounds, blood or rashes, so something else has to be behind his discomfort.

Malik flips open the book, thumbing through the pages to where he was originally. He glances up at the wound, then back at the book. By the looks of it, he's trying to figure out whether or not what's in the book relates to what's on my leg.

"You might want to look at this," Malik mumbles, tossing the book at Jasper. Is it an Alpha thing to be able to read ancient dialect?

Jasper looks grim as he does the same as Malik: look back and forth between the pages and my thigh. Then he shuts it, sighs deeply, and shakes his head. Defeat is on their faces.

"What's going on?" I ask, pressing for an answer. I'm starting to quiver, not knowing what both men are keeping from me.

167

Malik runs his hand back through his hair. "Whoever gave you this... They... It's a side effect of being a Desire Pack member."

"What's that supposed to mean?" I growl, sick of the lack of information they are giving me.

Jasper clenches his jaw tightly, his eyes holding back all the emotion I am trying to get from him. It sends me back to when that man touched me, when I thought he was coming onto me. Did he intend this to happen to me?

"You have heard the legends of the Desire Pack members, how they use magic to lure people in for sex?" Malik questions.

I nod in reply. "Do you think the man was trying to lure me for sex? Oh, of course he was," I mutter. "It doesn't... he touched me once... I refused him."

Had I gone along with his plans, what would have happened? I would probably be dead by now, and I wouldn't be having a conversation with two Alphas. But if I had left as soon as he'd taken that seat beside me...

"Exactly. I believe he poisoned you, because..."

"Poisoned me?" I squeak in disbelief. "Poison? That kills people, Malik."

Neither he, nor Jasper say a word. We just sit there and the information sinks in. This... this *thing* on my thigh is slowly killing me, and who knows how long I have until I'm completely dead.

I don't even know how to react.

"We have yet to find a cure for this kind of infliction," Malik tells me, his voice soft. "There's nothing we can do."

Jasper is as unmoving as I am. Numbness is all I feel. It crawls its way up my skin, infecting every part of me that allows me to feel. It leaves me speechless, distant, for a few moments. I think everyone in the room feels exactly the same.

"But there is something I can do," Jasper says, cutting through the feeling of pain that's slowly stripping the numbness away.

I look up.

"I have to kill you," he tells me seriously. "I have to turn you into a Phantom Wolf."

Chapter Twenty-Eight

Jasper paces in front of me.

I sit on the edge of the bed, my leg stretched out in front of me. The blanket is still wrapped around my waist, but honestly, I don't care anymore. Too many things swim in my mind, I'm trying to fit somewhere, but fail, leaving me feeling empty, and numb.

"I don't want to die," I say softly, watching Jasper as he thinks.

Malik has given us some space to talk things through, to discuss how Jasper is going to end my life. However, the moment we are alone, Jasper realises he's going to have to stop my heart from beating, and I realise this is *really* happening.

"I'm sorry to have dragged you into this mess," Jasper murmurs, finally coming to a stop. I've never seen him look so lost, so distraught in a situation. He isn't holding himself together as well as I've seen him do, and it doesn't help my jittering nerves.

I inhale deeply, trying to get some breath into my lungs. "It's not your fault. It didn't... I would be dead by now."

Jasper pauses, before doing something surprising. He falls to his knees right in front of me.

Can he look under my blanket. Yes. Do I care? Not in the slightest. There's so much emotion in his eyes, it's overwhelming. The man kneeling in front of me shows something I've never seen in a man in my life: honesty, integrity, and something signifying a tie to me. He truly does care about me, even if only in this moment.

"I'm going to make this painless as possible for you," he promises, and I don't hesitate in believing him. "We can put you to sleep first..."

Instantly I shake my head, the head of a needle gracing my mind. Just the thought makes me queasy, my mind whirling for a few seconds at the simple idea of it. Storms and needles are my biggest fear. Whoever invented such a painful mechanism of administering medication, is my worst nightmare.

"I can't... anything but that," I mutter, still shaking my head at him, to help him understand my point.

Jasper's jaw clenches, and I can almost see him sifting through ideas of ways to kill me. A morbid subject, but I would rather be strangled to death than have a needle pierce my skin. It may be strange in some people's eyes, but this a fear I've had since a child.

"That's okay," Jasper reassures me. "I could drown you..."

I cringe just at the sound of it, but it hardly measures to needles, in my eyes. Water isn't something I'm all that familiar with. Sure, it is a necessary commodity, but I haven't spent much time swimming in it.

"The more you talk, the more normal dying seems to be," I say breathily, trying to bring some comedy into the situation. Jasper smiles, despite himself.

"So how does it work? And how are you going to bring me back?"

There hasn't really been a time where I've questioned Jasper much on his powers, and what he is capable of, except for the time when we first met. Honestly, just thinking about what he could do to me in a single instant makes me nervous, uncertainty toward his every move being something I want to keep an eye on.

Especially after that moment we had in the bedroom. With his hands down my pants...

"I have to bite you," he tells me warily. My eyes widen. "It's the way of the curse. It has nothing to do with the bite of a mate. If that's what you're worried about."

Am I worried about him accidently marking me? That's hardly on my mind right now. Being mated to Jasper wouldn't be the worst thing in the world anyway, since I've given up hopes of finding my mate, and I don't know about Jasper's.

"I'm not worried about that. How did you die?"

Jasper's face suddenly shadows, and I can tell I've just brought up a sore subject. He was killed by his father... or at least, that's what legends told me. Admittedly, I don't know much about his legend, considering I never bothered to learn about it. Especially not in as much depth as June did.

"I was stabbed."

We both stay silently for a moment. Jasper is still on his knees in front of me, and doesn't look as if he's about to move any time soon.

"I'm sorry," I tell him. Jasper looks down, and I see he's hiding emotion from me. I can hardly blame him... being stabbed is so... intimate. And by your own father? It pains even me just thinking about it. Especially since I'm familiar with having a terrible father.

"They say drowning is like falling asleep, although no one can be completely sure if that is true," Jasper tells me, pushing away any further talk about his father. I don't mind..."

Like falling asleep? That's something I am good at.

"If it's going to be less painful than death by whatever poison that Desire Pack member gave me, then I don't mind at all," I tell him honestly. The pain in my leg comes and goes, and when it does come, it's disorientating, leaving my mind spinning, and my body quivering.

"Tomorrow... That's when it has to be done," he tells me, and reluctantly, I nod. I want to ask him so many different questions about what it's like to be dead. What it's like to be a Phantom Wolf, but he cuts me off.

Jasper moves forward suddenly, back onto his feet. He places his hands on either side of me, on the bed, leaning directly over me. All the breath in my lungs disappears.

"I can't stop thinking about that night," Jasper whispers.

The mood in the room has done a 180. The serious Alpha, who had been discussing the way I was going to die, is gone, now being replaced by a flirtatious, sensual man who I can't take my eyes from.

His proximity allows me to feel the heat of his body, his face inches from mine. His hot breath blows gently against my cheek, and if I move, even slightly, his lips will be on mine. Just the idea has my heart fluttering, and a multitude of inappropriate thoughts that taint my mind have me grateful Jasper promised to no longer read it.

"I can't either," I reply breathlessly, my face flushing at my words. How can one man make me feel so hot?

Without even touching, I'm completely enchanted.

Thea! Get a hold of yourself.

"Your last day of living will be the best one you have ever had," Jasper promises, his voice gentle and soft. It has me trusting him with every word he pronounces. "I'll make sure of it."

His eyes flutter down to my lips, and for a moment, I'm sure he will kiss me. That he will answer the obvious attraction between us that has been brewing for the short amount of time we've known each other. It's a hot kind of chemistry even I can't deny, despite my past history with sexual partners. Jasper is different...

He has proven that to me already.

So what is stopping me? As I stare at the man, biting his lip softly, I wonder why I'm not leaping at him.

Luca! His eyes suddenly haunt my mind in a flash of dark colours and powerful memories.

I jerk back.

His hand. The nights he would come over, furious. When I would disagree with him, and what he does. Even when I hinted I didn't want to force the mate bond. I remember the disapproval he would inflict on me in a number of ways.

And I snap.

"Woah! Woah, woah!" Jasper exclaims in surprise, as I crawl backward across the bed, until my back is pressed against the headboard.

The sting of Luca's hand against my raw skin comes back to me, as I squeeze my eyes shut, trying to push him out. His shadow looms over me, his eyes darkened in pure anger. The cruel grin on his face indisputable. Familiar.

I can feel someone beside me, but I'm frozen, my limbs paralysed. Tears burn hot against my cheeks; it sends me further in, deeper into that night.

That night when Luca...

"Thea, it's okay," I hear Jasper's voice in my ear. Taking a deep breath, I'm out. I'm here, in reality.

Shoving my face into Jasper's chest, I don't care about the tear stains on his shirt. I don't care about his confusion. He is right here. He is real, and I crave that. Forcing him onto the bed, I wrap my arms around his slender waist and sob.

I release the emotion I have hidden all my life. From my friends, from my family.

"I'm not going anywhere," Jasper murmurs softly, as I cling to him. My lifeline, the ground beneath my feet. He wasn't going to go anywhere, and as my breathing begins to settle, the blood stops rushing in my ears, I hear him.

I let him fiddle with a section of my hair. "Talk to me."

My voice is trapped inside my throat. *Like it's always been...*

Slowly, I pull away. Hair sticks to my damp cheeks, my eyes are swollen, and my throat. Looking at Jasper, I can see his concern, I could see his worry. But he won't understand, *no one* can understand.

"I'm fine," I croak, the lie obviously brushing straight over Jasper's head.

Doubt is evident all over his face. "What happened, Thea? You *were* fine, now you're clearly distressed. Talk to me, please, I can't bear seeing you like this."

I swipe my hands across my cheeks, taking a deep breath to fix myself. This isn't my first recovery, and it won't be my last. I'm stronger than this. I'm strong on my own. Jasper may have pulled me out of the trance, but I'm not about to admit to him what Luca did to me.

The past is the past.

"Promise me you won't read my mind," I say quickly, but firmly.

Getting to my feet, I quickly walk across the room, holding the blanket tightly to me. Bending down, I ruffle through the few things that I brought with me, looking for some longer pants to wear. Anything to cover this ugly, painful infliction, dealt me by an equally ugly and painful man.

"Of course," Jasper says, still sitting on the bed, stunned.

When I glance back at him, he's looking at me, strangely. His shirt has an incriminating wet patch on it from my tears, and his hair is mussed. Confusion wells in his eyes, and it would make sense to clear it. But I can't bring myself to admit it.

"Did I hurt you?" He asks, standing from the bed. I shake my head, and he seems slightly relieved by that. "Then what is it?"

I shake my head at him. "Please, not now..."

"Then later," he insists, walking closer. This time, he leaves a decent amount of space between us. He's giving me time to think, and I'm grateful for that. But still, he presses me gently for a reason for my breakdown.

"This is meant to be a good day," I tell him, trying to change the subject. Anything but to address... *that*.

He sighs deeply, running his hands back through his hair. I watch his expression calm, as he realises he's not going to crack anything out of me. I'm showing him I can be strong, even if he has no idea why I'm so desperate to.

"You have to tell me eventually," he breathes. "Today will be a good day for you, I promise. And tonight, there's something you have to know, before we... commence this."

Chapter Twenty-Nine

Jasper gives me space, which I spend in the bathroom trying to make myself look nice. He's promised me we will be going out, to make my last day alive good for me.

I comb my hair through with my fingers, patting down strands that stick out in places. If I had a tie, I would braid my hair. Instead, I push it over my shoulders, and hope it looks somewhat decent. My clothes are rumpled, but I don't have Jasper's magic to conjure up others, and I'm not about to ask him for a pretty dress or something.

This will do. I can still wear clothes when I'm a Phantom.

I refuse to think about what's going to happen tomorrow. Today is all I can think about, as well as Jasper's enticing promise of something special tonight. I have no idea what it is, but he's told me it has to do with a secret he's been keeping.

My insistent curiosity is going to keep me on edge about it all day, I know it.

Rinsing my face, I wash the dried tears from my cheeks.

Luca has to stay at the back of my mind. I hadn't meant to scare Jasper with my reaction to the haunting memories from my past. He's the last thing I should be thinking about, but it was as if he had crept in without my permission.

When I go downstairs to find Jasper, I find the Alpha of Love instead. It's the main foyer I find myself in—too afraid to explore further. With all the hallways and similar furnishings, I'm sure I'll get lost in less than five minutes. The foyer is nothing to complain about anyway, and it's where the stairs lead to.

Malik is on the phone, his back to me. I pause, hands clinging to the banister, stuck still on the last step.

"I know. Father," I hear him murmur. He is looking out the window. "You've clearly made the decision for me."

Oh no. I'm invading his privacy. I take a few wary steps backward, staring at Malik's back. What would the Alpha think if he knew I'm eavesdropping, even if it isn't on purpose? He doesn't seem to notice though, continuing with his conversation without a second thought.

"Just because I don't believe I will ever meet my mate, that does not mean I want to choose who our next Luna may be through some kind of competition. That's utterly ridiculous..."

My brows furrow. What on earth is he talking about? A competition? Slowly, I take more steps backward up the stairs, making sure to keep my eyes on the Alpha, in case he turns and I need to make a desperate run for it. However, he looks deep in conversation, resting his arm against the sill of the window he gazes out of.

Private information, that someone like me should *not* be hearing.

I hear Malik's sigh, despite the broad space between us. "Fine... If you can convince Mother this is a good idea, hypnotising Packs into competing for something like this, then you have yourself a deal."

This is the first time I have heard Malik strike a deal with someone, or be soundly mature. It's unsettling, making the hair on my arms stand up. Whatever this is, I'm not sure I want to know about it, so I turn on my heel and pad as silently as possible up the stairs.

The moment I put my foot onto the landing, Jasper is in front of me.

His use of magic shocks me a bit, but slowly I'm getting used to it. The sight of his magic, drifting around him like smoke and shadows is the only evidence he has used it, and quickly, it evaporates like it never existed.

"I was looking for you," he says, smiling slightly. He probably enjoyed seeing the way he completely drained the color from my face.

I shake my head slowly at him. "I happened to be doing the same thing. Thank you for gracing my presence."

He ignores my backhanded jab at him, giving me a glowing smile. That easy-going air about him always has me envious. I wish I could see things like he does, or ignore the bad around myself instead of letting it get to me. Maybe that will come to me once I'm dead. Or half dead, as Jasper sometimes likes to correct me.

"Come. Today, I have something to show you."

I nod, ready for whatever he has planned. If this is going to be the best last day of my life, I believe Jasper can be the one to give it to me.

***

"I've come to believe you really like the snow," Jasper notes, stealing the silence from the car as we drive. I glance at him, smiling softly. He's right. Having lived in a Pack where the climate is as bland as the people, something as fresh and new as snow excites me. It's so beautiful, and enchanting, and despite being cold, I want to spend all my time in it.

Jasper notices my eager nod of agreement.

"Close your eyes," he murmurs. "We will be there in a second."

Time manipulation. It may possibly be my favourite part of Jasper's powers. What he does while I am frozen between the ripples of time, I don't know. Boredom is a toxic feeling, I don't see how he can deal with it. But never once does he seem to falter in offering it to me.

Trying to smother an excited smile of anticipation of where Jasper is going to take me, I shut my eyes, and place my hands over my lap.

It feels like nothing has happened, when Jasper says I can open my eyes.

I'm struck at first by how bright everything is. For a moment, I have to shield my eyes, before I tentatively raise my hand to reveal something that blows my breath away. Snow, of course—there is nowhere in this Pack where you can escape it. It's thick, soft and voluptuous, coating the lawn, and down what looks like a precipice.

We are on top of a mountain. It makes sense that I didn't see any snowy peaks beforehand, due to the low-hanging cloud that taints this place, so this completely surprises me.

"What is this place?" I glance at Jasper.

The entire place is like a wonderland, almost too beautiful to exist. If there were more breath left in my lungs, I may have something more to say. Instead, I examine the icy-tipped trees, crystal-capped mounds of snow, wanting nothing more than to step outside for a better look.

"Malik suggested it to me. He said it was a romantic place he always dreamed of taking his mate," Jasper tells me, the contrast of his warm voice to the cool air, even in the car, is eminent.

Romantic. Jasper wanted to take me somewhere romantic?

Looking back out the window, I see he's chosen the right place. The mountain towers above the main suburbs of the Love Pack, showing off its indescribable beauty with glittering lights and snow-topped roofs. I want to be out there, getting a better look at it. How the people who live here could ever get sick of this, I don't know.

"Go on," Jasper insists. "Take a look, but don't topple down the side of the mountain."

I don't hesitate, shooting a glare before I pop open the door and step out. My coat does little to combat the cold that curls around my limbs, but I don't mind. My shoes sink into the ice, creating footprints anyone could follow. Quickly, I walk across the untouched blanket of snow until I'm on the edge of the cliff.

Perhaps I could slip and fall straight down, like Jasper warned, but I don't.

The bottom is further coated in snow, leading directly down to what looks like a few houses. That is potentially dangerous.

Especially if there happens to be a slip or something horrific like that.

All of a sudden, I feel something hit the back of my head.

It's a terribly familiar feeling inflicted by none other than the Alpha of Devotion. Snow coats my hair, dribbling down my back in a way that makes me arch back, my face a deep cringe. This definitely isn't the first time I have felt this...

"You idiot!" I snap, although when I turn and see the playful look on his face, I can feel a slight smile tinting my own. "That could have made me fall off the cliff. For *real*."

Jasper shakes his head at me, standing a good few metres away, feet buried deep within the snow. His hands are dusted with snow, giving me all the evidence I need to build a case proving he's the one to hurl that compacted snow at the back of my head.

"I would have caught you if you'd fallen," he exclaims, at which I roll my eyes.

I stoop down, bundling snow up into my hands, which I toss at Jasper. He simply ducks, seeing it coming. It hits his car behind him, with a soft thud. The Alpha doesn't seem to mind, as he beckons me closer.

I follow the motioning movement of his hand, wanting to get away from the edge of this cliff anyway. As I do so, he opens his arms, as if I'm going to run into them and be carried away into the small cabin behind us. My steps closer stop at arms' reach from him.

"Shall we go inside?" he asks warmly, raising an eyebrow.

I shake my head at him. "There is so much left to explore. I haven't even looked at the trees yet."

Without a falter in my step, I slush my way toward one of the large trees creating a canopy over the ground, protecting it from the worst of the latest snowfall. I hear Jasper follow behind me, and I wait till he's right behind me to commence my plan. Call it... a little piece of vengeance for Thea.

I reach up and knock the branch above me. Snow topples directly on top of his head.

He pauses, letting the snow drop off his head, coating his shoulder and back in the cold stuff. He looks mildly amused, and slightly irritated, like he's about to pounce on me. I, on the other hand, laugh out loud, enjoying his obvious discomfort, knowing he'd done exactly the same thing last week.

"Aren't you funny," Jasper murmurs, tilting his head so the melting slush slides all the way off, and back to the ground.

Seeing his fingers quivering slightly, I practically see what he plans to do, before he does it. Giggling slightly, I run toward the cabin, with plans of locking him in there teasing my mind. I make it close to the door, right outside the wooden exterior, when he appears in front of me again. I growl in protest.

"That's cheating," I declare.

He chuckles, and grabs the sleeves of my coat to pull me against him. I can feel his warmth through our clothes, and I savor it.

"Come inside," he says softly. "I have something *extremely* important to tell you."

Chapter Thirty

Inside, the cabin is just as inviting as from the outside. It's small, the furnishings are subtle, and the entire place almost seems to bundle you up in Jasper's magically lit fire's warm embrace.

The moment Jasper ushers me inside, I'm awed by the whole thing. With wooden interior beams on the ceiling, matching what might suffice as wallpaper, the small space seems warm, friendly, and inviting. Despite my wariness of what Jasper calls faux, the rug on the floor looks softer than silk.

Jasper takes my jacket as I shrug it off. "And Malik, of all people, created this?"

The Alpha chuckles. He knows what Malik is like, and if I tell him about the girl—Vanessa, or whatever her name is—then I'm sure he wouldn't be surprised.

"I just find it ironic that the Alpha of Love decided to spend his time with beautiful women warming his bed, rather than actually looking for his mate. I expected him, of all people, to hunt the entire land for her."

"He did. There is a romantic heart in him somewhere," Jasper says, still with slight humor in his tone. He hangs our snow-dusted coats on a hook I hadn't noticed. Admittedly, I like him without his coat on; I can see the smooth muscles on his arms.

He glances at me, probably noticing how I'm checking out his arms. I glance at my feet, to hide my flushing face.

"So what now?" I ask, expecting Jasper to tell this little secret he has been keeping from me.

Instead, he shrugs, a slight grin on his face. The part of my mind where my curiosity sprouts, is desperate for some sustenance to keep it from going insane. But by the expression on Jasper's face, he isn't going to tell me. He's clearly saving it for a better moment, or more likely, the *last* moment.

"I thought you may have some questions... you know, about Phantom Wolves," Jasper says, walking closer to the fireplace. Of course; who better to ask than the Alpha of the species itself?

The closer I get to the fireplace, the closer I get to the heat. It wraps around my bare arms, encircling me like a blanket offering itself to sleep on. It reminds me of a sleeping pill, the feeling of every wave of heat like an insistent tug on the end of my body, wanting me to fall into a deep slumber.

Instead, I settle next to Jasper on the couch. But not so close to get distracted.

"I suppose I do," I tell him, trying to delve into the thoughts I've been too afraid to express earlier. "If you're okay to answer."

He smiles softly. "Of course."

Jasper leans casually against the couch, reminding me of when I spied on him and Tayten—not that it was much of a spy mission, considering he knew I was there the entire time. At least it told me he's comfortable around me, which gives me a warm feeling inside, that the fireplace didn't cater to.

"Will I have any special powers, like you?" Admittedly, I wouldn't mind if I could do something like he can; read minds or something like that.

Jasper bites his lip. "Magic takes a good deal of time to control. I spent many hundreds of years trying to perfect it. Although that was the heavy stuff I hope you never have to see. Perhaps I could teach you, when we get time."

My mind is slightly blown, despite it being such a simple question, and Jasper's reply being so nonchalant. Magic? Just the idea of being able to do something like the Alpha makes me a little giddy, which I try not to show.

"You have eternal life, do you not?" I ask. "Will I share that?"

Jasper glances down at his fiddling fingers. I follow every brush of his fingers over the blanket he's holding, knowing *exactly* what they are capable of doing. Licks of firelight dance across his features, shadowing parts of his expression that make him seem so much darker, and even more mysterious.

"Many die, to rest peacefully after some time. A Phantom's life is much longer than an average Wolf. However, if you do not carry Alpha blood, then you will not live forever, like I will," Jasper tells me. My heart almost sinks a little, but I ignore it.

"Unless..." he suddenly says, raising his gaze back to me.

He looks wary about telling me more, still fiddling with the mink blanket between his fingers. I want to grab his hands, to tell him to stop being so nervous. At least that's what I assume he is, since I'm not fully aware of what he looks like when he does feel that way. He always seems to be so sure of himself.

"Unless what?" I raise an eyebrow.

"Well, unless I marked you," he breathes, biting his lip again. I can't help but stare at it. "Like a mate would."

I don't move for a good second. Mark me? Just the thought sends shivers up my spine, and I'm not sure why. A centuries-old Alpha is sitting in front of me, having just admitted that if he marks me—yet I don't know why he would—then I can live forever. Okay... That does sound pretty sweet.

"That wouldn't be fair on your mate," I remark, letting out the thoughts mulling my head.

He doesn't say anything for a good second as he sits there, thinking. It's at that moment I wish I could read his mind, and see why he looks as if he is fighting an internal battle. Is there something he isn't telling me about this entire Phantom thing? Is it going to potentially kill me, or be more painful than I first thought?

Each thought has the hairs on my arms standing up.

"It's fine," he murmurs.

His short cut answer doesn't swing by me as easily as he hoped. The fact that he's looking down, rather than in my eyes (which he makes a point of doing whenever he can), is unnerving. It makes me want to take his chin and force his gaze to me. Instead, I decide to use words, since there have been times when he's used them on me and left my breath completely blown away.

"Tell me about your mate? Did you leave her behind when you became a Phantom?"

I feel a little bad about bringing it up, but again, that curiosity I wish I could beat down with a stick is raising its ugly head. Jasper shakes his head, finally looking at me. Just the sight of his violet eyes meeting mine, hits me square in the chest.

He really is so beautiful...

All the emotion he holds in those eyes is mesmerising, leaving me speechless, growing the silence between us.

"Fate works in mysterious ways," Jasper tells me, his voice a slight whisper. "He bends time to make it fit to you, or not; it depends on his mood. He chooses who your mate may be, and picks when they will enter your life. It can either make you, or break you."

His words bind me still, as I stare unblinkingly at him. I suppose I never thought about it that way.

My belief in the Moon Goddess is slim; it always has been. Fate is something June once convinced me to believe in, saying he was a cunning man, much smarter and much more real than I would think. Perhaps it is one of the few things she said that actually rubbed off onto me.

"So what's that supposed to mean?" I ask, still not understanding the meaning behind Jasper's expression, and the way he plays with the seam of that blanket like it's the most impressive thing he could look at in this room.

Jasper's eyes blaze. "It means Fate decided to bring my mate into my life, when he saw fit."

Tilting my head, I don't refuse his gaze, which seems to have become more intense with every second that passes by, and with every word we say. Something is going on his head, and I would do anything to find out what it may be. It seems unfair how he can secretly peek into my mind at any time he pleases, without me even knowing.

Despite our promise.

"Do you know where she is?" I ask. If he does, he will be somewhere over me. My mate may be anywhere in this land, in any Pack, with Fate waiting to bring him into my life. He could be Jasper for all I know...

He nods slowly. "Exactly where."

"She must know then..." I say softly.

Has he left his mate to save me, to attempt to save those other people? Has he been such a great Alpha, he's saved me and is now looking after me, despite having a mate at home? What if Tayten is his mate, and he has been keeping it from me? My mind spins with loose ends, not able to come up with just one solid answer.

"She has no idea," he tells me honestly, his gaze hot and unrelenting. "Yet."

I nearly say something about my lack of a mate, but I can't bring myself to mention it. Luca has been my only chance of having something at least close, and just the thought of him sends me back into terrible memories of what he used to do to me...

Instead, I will continue to find out more about Jasper, and his mate. For some unexplainable reason, it's as if my curiosity is demanding I know everything.

And who am I to ignore my curiosity?

"Why don't you tell her?" I ask.

Maybe he's getting suspicious about how I'm demanding to know so much. I don't care though. The night Jasper gave me the best orgasm I have ever had, I accepted my attraction to him, which is definitely potentially dangerous.

"I'm thinking about it," he says softly. "I really am."

It's almost as if everything around us doesn't exist. It's a feeling I could never put adequate words to. At this moment, nothing else around me seems to matter, and more than anything, I can see a storm raging in Jasper's eyes. He's fighting with himself, and I am going to keep questioning him until I find out why.

"You should just do it," I say honestly. "Don't hold back."

Jasper stops, that fidgeting of the blanket in his hands completely stopping. It's then I realize we are close, the heat

185

between us is not from the blazing fireplace. The moment reminds me of that day... pressed against the wall...

All that matters is him.

"Okay," he murmurs. "I won't hold back anymore."

And all of a sudden, he leans forward, grabs my face, and kisses me.

Chapter Thirty-One

I'd always told myself I wouldn't find my mate.

There's an entire part of me that's accepted I would never feel those sparks, or be able to spend the rest of my life with someone I was made for. And there is no way I've thought my mate would be an Alpha.

Let alone the Alpha of Devotion.

However, there is no denying what's going on. Jasper's hands are cradling my face, his lips are on mine... There are sparks, and an undeniable voice in my head screaming.

He's your mate!

Stunned, I stay still, trying to fathom the feeling. Sparks are a feeling I can't put words to. They spread from his hands, through his lips, right across my body, weakening my limbs. I am completely open to the feeling. The tiny electric-like jolts are almost relaxing, but at the exact same time, they awaken a feeling within me.

It is second nature, as I begin to kiss him back. It takes that part of me that controls my consciousness by surprise, but I shun it the moment it tries pushing back. The feeling of Jasper's lips, moving insistently against mine, forces a reaction from me.

His hands slip to the back of my head, fist my hair, pull me closer to him, until I'm pressed against his chest, my arms trying to hold me up despite being so weakened by the feeling of my mate.

My mate. This can't be real.

It's as if he has stolen his breath from me, as he pushes his tongue into my mouth in a gentle, caressing way, enchanting me in a way only he can. My mind swirls with thoughts, trying to make sense of everything, but I can't. All I want is to tear Jasper's shirt off, and touch every inch of his skin I haven't been able to before.

Jasper seems to get the idea. Or rather, most probably reads my mind to see the lust burning there. It's intoxicating as I lift my arms, Jasper tugging my shirt up and over my head, as we separate our kiss only to do so.

His hands are everywhere, and so are mine. While I run mine straight through his silky black hair, he lets his drift across my bare back, caressing my skin with his soft fingertips. This heady mix of his touch and taste almost hurt, paining my heart to feel so much emotion all at once.

I shiver under the feeling of his touch, but something is seeping through the back of my mind, wrapping around every thought of optimism and lust...

Darkness.

It's like the shadows that appear whenever Jasper uses his magic. Except these don't stay; these crawl deeper into my mind, shocking me with a brutal sense of reality that this time, isn't masked by Jasper's touch or kisses.

With a hefty shove, I push at Jasper's chest, making him pull back in surprise.

My breaths are sharp as I shake my head. This man is my mate... *My mate.* The way he kissed me suggested one thing; he knows we are mates. There was no surprise there, which may mean this has been a secret of his for quite some time.

I'm not about to let him out of this, without him knowing how furious I am.

"How could you," I snap angrily, wishing I could slap that look of confusion straight off his face. "You... You..."

"I what?" he questions. "What am I?"

I bite my jaw, anger flaring up dramatically within me. The way he lounges back so carelessly, watching me with an expression of amusement is so infuriating. How could he just kiss me out of the blue like that? Show me we are mates so far into this... 'mildly platonic but not really a relationship'?

"You liar!"

He tilts his head, his eyebrows creasing, despite the half smile on his face. "Now, when did I lie to you, Thea?"

"You didn't tell me we are mates... You've rattled on about having one, and all that, yet you didn't tell me?" I growl, my voice still raised, as adrenaline streaks through my veins. Maybe if he wasn't an Alpha, I would strangle him... or... something.

He shrugs. *Shrugs.*

"I didn't lie. Did I once name a girl who is not my mate? Did you ever ask me if we were mates, and I said no? Than I suppose I didn't actually lie, did I?" Jasper says it so knowingly it makes me scowl even harder at him.

His logic and reason is *not* appreciated.

No," I breathe. "You still kept this from me..."

"I didn't lie though..."

"Well, I get that now. I just hate you for keeping it from me," I tell him. As I say those words, I notice Jasper's eyes aren't actually on mine, but have drifted down my neck, to my chest. When I look down, I notice my lack of shirt, seeing it pooled on the couch, on the other side of Jasper. Great...

Quickly, I cover my chest with my arms. "What were you planning to do back there anyway?"

Jasper doesn't say anything for a few moments, instead he speaks to me with his eyes. I can see how little seriousness he is applying to the situation, despite just telling me, or rather, *showing* me we are mates. Just the sight of that makes me extremely mad. Even madder.

"Well," he says carefully. "I was planning on making love to you."

My eyes narrow at him, and I cast my gaze over to the other side of the couch, where my shirt lies. If I want to grab it, I'll have to lean over him. He follows my gaze, noticing how I'm not acknowledging his comment that, admittedly, sent a wave to my core.

"Want this?" he questioned, holding the shirt up. I look at it, then down at my chest, which aside from my bra, shows too much skin.

"Yes," I say, through clenched teeth.

"Then come get it," he says, the challenge in his voice loud and clear.

For an Alpha over 400 years old, he is being mighty immature right now. Why isn't he taking this moment seriously? Why doesn't he want to discuss this like adults, instead of fuck like a couple who've been in love for years?

"Fine," I mutter begrudgingly. "You son of a..."

My muttering under my breath is hardly coherent as I lean against one arm, reaching with the other across Jasper's body, trying to grab the shirt he holds in his hand. My cheeks flush in response to my partially naked torso against his clothed one. Why don't I take his shirt off instead, to save myself the embarrassment?

"God, you're beautiful," Jasper murmurs, when I unconsciously turn my head toward him, meeting his eyes. Now he can get a full view of my red-stained cheeks...

I take the shirt from his hand, after he loosens his grip. If I stay close to him like that for a second longer, I may fall into the trap of enchantment he loves to set around me, and kiss him again. Then maybe his comment from a minute ago will have come true, and my curiosity will have been quenched.

The moment I sit back on the couch, I know he was using magic on me.

My body seems to relax deep into the cushions, and every ounce of anger, my only combat against him, diminishes, and I'm left with that drunken feeling of happiness. Jasper places his hand on my thigh, and it seems as if calm floods from his fingertips, and I jerk away to stop it.

"You can't use magic on me like that," I snap, trying to find some anger to throw at him. But it's completely vanished, into thin air. I have to remind myself to bring it back up later, when he can't touch me to calm me down.

He smiles softy. "But, you're my mate."

Running my hand down my face, I take a deep, slow breath.

"Look, I'm going to die tomorrow... because of this," I say, pointing to my thigh, after I pull my shirt back on. It hasn't been annoying me, with all the distraction Jasper has supplied. At least I have something to thank him for.

He looks at my thigh, which is covered. "I had to tell you before that."

"I just need some time," I say, standing. Jasper's face drops, and I want to tell him he should have expected it. He's thrown this at me, and now I need some time to regain my composure. I get to my feet.

My mate is an Alpha...

Still, despite Jasper's magic, I find it hard to believe.

"I understand," he says breathily, standing also. "I'll give you time."

"Until tomorrow. Once you turn me into a Phantom, we will talk about this again."

***

The water quivers gently, as the last drop falls from the tap before Malik turns it off.

Who knew a bath full of water could be so terrifying?

This is it... this is the moment where my life is ended forever, and Jasper brings me back to be a walking person without a beating heart. Had I not found out he was my mate, then maybe I would be apprehensive about this. At least I know for sure now he is going to bring me back.

"It's going to be okay," Jasper murmurs in my ear, and admittedly, it makes me feel a little better.

Having my body held under water until I drown to death suddenly doesn't seem as daunting, with my mate behind me. Urgh... What am I thinking? Clearly I'm not... I need to worry about it when I wake again.

If I wake up again.

Jasper holds my arm, as I clamber into the bath. At least the water is warm as it soaks my clothes, and my skin. I sink into the silky water. Malik stands at the bathroom door, looking nervous. Obviously he isn't fully accustomed to the idea of witnessing death. But as an Alpha, he is required to be there, to watch.

"What if this goes wrong?" I ask, holding Jasper's eyes, as he bends down beside the edge of the tub.

A spike of fear slices through me, as doubts plague my thoughts. No matter how hard I try to pretend they don't exist, that everything will be okay, those dark thoughts flood back to me, and my rash starts itching again.

Oh boy, is it bad. It's nearly consumed my entire leg, and I know if we don't do this, I will be facing a more painful death that Jasper can't save me from.

"Trust me," Jasper insists gently. "I will be here this entire time, okay?"

I nod, letting him go. His jaw is clenched, and despite being able to reassure me at anytime, I can tell he's worried. Well, he is the one ending my life, which clearly is taking a large toll on him.

At the end of it all, it is my decision. Moving back slightly, I dip my shoulders under the water, my head close to slipping under.

Jasper rests his hands on my shoulders, looking grim. When I train my eyes fully on him, he tries to look more optimistic, but I see what's behind his eyes. He is nervous about this.

Shoving every thought out of my mind, I wonder briefly if I should take a breath...

How stupid am I?

"I love you," Jasper whispers, and I don't have time to respond before he pushes my shoulders under the water, and I am completely submerged.

Chapter Thirty-Two

My eyes close as the water closes over my face.

The warmth of the water, and the feeling of Jasper's hands on my shoulders. does nothing to quell the fright that instantly consumes me. My body wants to retaliate, as my last gulp of air bubbles out of my mouth. The feeling is nothing like I've felt before, as water slips between my lips. The water, like a hand on my neck, slowly strangles the life out of me.

Forcing my eyes open, I see the shadow of Jasper looming over me, as he holds my shoulders back against the bottom of the tub. I trust him... I *have* no choice.

Involuntarily, as a sudden surge of fright for the lack of breath hits, my legs jerk up, my body convulsing in protest. The water stings my eyes, as I try to see Jasper, to beg him to stop. Doubts run through my mind, easily hurdling all logic. This isn't comfortable... This isn't like falling asleep.

Blinking through the water, I notice what is probably Malik, coming to the side of the bath to hold my shaking legs down. This is serious. They are killing me.

My heart is constricting in my chest, and my lungs burning, as they fight to find air, but it's failing. At this point I am choking and swallowing water at the same time, as my vision begins to be shrouded by a dark vignette. This is it... this is the end, and there is nothing I can do about it.

There's nothing more I can do, no more struggling to delay is the inevitable. And as my eyes drift shut, unconsciousness sweeps me away.

***

Jasper

Malik places his fingers on the side of her neck before we lift her from the bath. Never have I seen this Alpha look so grim, as he nods at me, confirming she is dead. My mate is gone, and it leaves me with with an empty feeling inside. If I dwell on it, I'm sure it will drive me to insanity.

He lifts her from the bath.

"Don't worry about it," Malik insists, once he has set Thea on a chair. I towel dry her body, as if it will make her feel better. Except, she can't feel. Not until I bring her back, as a Phantom Wolf.

Taking a step back, I let the towel fall from my hand.

There is no doubting Thea is dead. Her body lies, lifeless, on the chair, her head lulled slightly to the side, her mouth partly open. Never have I seen her skin so pale, with all life drained out of it by asphyxiation. It was difficult to have to restrain her to the point of death, but I had no other choice. Just looking at that rash on her leg tells me that much.

How could I have let another man touch her like that? I let her get lost in a Pack, under a spell of magic made to lure the innocent and naive into the clutches of the desirous. I didn't warn her enough...

Shaking my head, I turn away from my mate. There is no way I can keep looking at her.

"We get her stomach drained of all the water first," Malik says softly, noticing how I am looking at the ground, struggling to look againat my dead mate, until completely necessary. "We don't want her to wake choking on water still, do we?"

I can't say a word. There isn't any doubt in my mind that this will work. The amount of people I have turned is extensive, but this is different...

This is my mate.

And I've killed her.

"Jasper," Malik whispers. I turn, facing him again.

Malik has given up all hope in finding his mate. Not only do I see it in his eyes, but I hear it in his mind. And unbeknownst to him, he is shoving this information down my throat, and I can relate. I've spent 400 years waiting for Fate to deliver me my mate, when I needed it most.

Whoever his mate is, I'm sure he will find her soon. Unfortunately, his youth suggests his lack of belief in Fate, or even the Goddess. Luckily for him, he hasn't had the joy of meeting the man behind the idea of mates...

"It's fine," I say, although my voice is wary. "Please, just take her away."

It isn't that I don't appreciate Malik as another Alpha. But I cannot imagine any advice he can give me with my head spinning like this. All I want is to force this burden out of me. My magic. It weighs heavily in my mind, but I know I must savour it to fully turn Thea successfully.

Nothing can go wrong.

Clenching my fists, I turn in time to see Malik carrying a limp Thea from the room. Casting a glance back at the bath, water from her struggles has spilled onto the ground. Giving her a death close to mine may have thrown me over the edge of my self-control. She does not deserve the kind of pain I endured that night...

It took Malik's team of professionals over an hour to cater to Thea. Malik had to lie to them, about what was happening. Their confusion must have been distressing but I wasn't about allowing them know about my need to turn her.

What I've told Thea about becoming a Phantom was little. If she knew the true extent of what was to happen, then perhaps she would have chosen death.

My first years were alone. Self-teaching myself what was needed to control my magic, to control my wolf, was difficult. Sometimes, I would beg Fate to take my life, to put me out of pain, and misery. Now, I use my magic with understanding, but there are times where I wish it didn't exist.

Especially when I sense Thea's distrust.

Not once since I promised not to look into her mind, have I. Protecting that promise was my way of showing her she can trust me, that I am not going to betray her like her father had, and that villainous man she once called her boyfriend.

There have been times when I have been tempted. When she pulled away from me... Why?

Shaking my head, I stand. Malik came a couple of minutes ago to tell me I can begin turning her. If I stay in my own head any longer, I might miss the opportunity to bring Thea back.

When I walk into the small, confining room they are keeping her in, I nearly lose it. Clenching my jaw tightly is the only way I can stop myself from punching Malik's face, who stands right beside me. Getting into a fight with him will not change the outcome of this. Thea has to become a Phantom.

I will do everything in my power to keep her out of pain. Even if it means jeopardizing my own health.

She means too much to me.

"This should be interesting," Malik murmurs under his breath, but of course, I hear it. This will be his first time witnessing the turning of a Phantom. It is not that interesting to watch, considering most of the change happens from the inside. However, there is one physical change about her I haven't mentioned.

Brushing my fingers across her temple, I try to ignore the lack of sparks. None will appear again, until she is alive in my arms.

"I have to bite her," I tell Malik, although I'm sure he is aware.

This isn't a mark of mating. To complete such a mark of mating, I would have to be inside her, and when that day comes, I will make it more than perfect.

Her hair is still wet. It feels incriminating against my fingers, as I push it off her neck, exposing a spot perfect for turning her. The feeling is almost natural, as my mind remembers what it was like to turn all those other people. Some are my worst adversaries, while others still live under my name and my power.

Bringing my mouth down to her neck, I take one last glance at my mate's face. Even without breath, she is the most beautiful thing I have ever laid eyes on. The day that girl from the diner gave me her number, I could see Thea's surprise when I refused to even look twice at her.

No one can compare in beauty, inside and out, to my mate.

Placing a soft kiss on her neck, I prepare myself for what has to come. Closing my eyes, I lean forward, bite softly down, on her neck.

To turn her forever.

***

Thea

Death isn't what I thought it would be.

When I am awakened by a surge of pain, it is like being woken from slumber. Thoughts force themselves into my mind, as I force my body up. There is no time to even consider what has happened. Am I alive, or am I dead? Is this what it feels like to be dead? Because it's extremely painful.

With eyes hardly working, or limbs for that matter, I am on my feet.

Someone is on the side of the bed, trying to grab at me, trying to talk to me, but I can't hear or feel anything. This needs to stop.

"What... Who..."

Words stumble out of my mouth incoherently, as my senses start to come back to me. First, my sight. Jasper and Malik stand in the room with me, Jasper trying to come to me, a concerned look on his face.

"Mirror..." I stutter. The only thought in my mind is a need to see myself... to see if I'm real, or if I'm dead.

Jasper grabs my shoulders, while Malik holds a mirror for me. Did they have that on standby? At least I am reassured by their familiar features. I try gather for myself what is going on.

Holding the mirror up, I finally take a good look at myself, while the two Alphas stay silent.

And I realize, I'm no longer the normal girl I once was.

Chapter Thirty-Three

There is no doubting, everything has changed. I am no longer how I was yesterday.

Jasper stands behind me, staring into the mirror as I do. Something is so common between us, there is no mistaking it. Our eyes.

Just looking makes me want to claw my eyes out. That deep-set violet shade has taken over my once hazel eyes, infecting me with the colour I had admired in Jasper. Now it belongs to me too, although it hardly amounts to what I see in Jasper's eyes. His are alight and dazzling, vivid with colour. Mine are still bland and rather lifeless.

Still, there is an uncanny resemblance, which suggests although I'm not actually alive still, I'm not dead either. I'm just a walking body without a beating heart.

"I'm a Phantom," I breathe, running my fingertips down my cheek, an awful transparent colour. Perhaps if I had ever seen a dead person, I could relate myself to them, but Jasper is the closest I have been, and he is like a walking masterpiece.

Jasper moves a step closer, almost wary of me. "You haven't fully developed yet. That will come later."

Closing my eyes for a second, I try to regain my composure. This is real. Maybe if I keep saying that over and over again, I might be able to convince myself, because right now, all I can think about is the need to fall asleep, so I can wake and find this is all over.

I feel Jasper grab my hand. I know it's him, because the moment my skin touches his, sparks crawl all the way through my wrist, and up my arm. Why does just his touch feel so good? He turns me around, so I face him, and I can see concern written all over his face. Is he reading my mind right now, trying to figure out what I am thinking?

"What's going to happen now?" I hear Malik say from the other side of the room, as if I'm not here. His involvement with me is little, and I am still astounded at his willingness to help me, despite the poison I was carrying in my system.

When I glance down at my leg, I notice the rash is gone, completely wiped out of my system. It really has worked...

Jasper stills looks at me, but answers Malik's question. "We wait."

I decide I don't want to question anything. I know Jasper is using his magic. It flows through his fingertips, consuming my entire body in that euphoric, high feeling of contentment. It makes it impossible to scold him for using it on me, as really, I should be dealing with this myself.

"We wait until her magic is developed, then I take her home," Jasper explains, but I hardly hear. My legs sway uneasily, ready to collapse if I attempt to take a step forward.

Jasper grabs my arms, pulling me against him, so I stumble into his chest. With my face against his shirt, I breathe in the fresh, familiar scent I didn't want to ever have to part from... What am I thinking? Is this Jasper's magic that has me so dazzled, or is it the beginning of the mate bond between us strengthening?

Admittedly, the latter kind of terrifies me.

"She needs rest for now," Jasper murmurs, still not bothering to turn his attention to the Alpha of Love, as he trains his eyes on me.

Taking me by surprise, Jasper shamelessly stoops down, putting his arms under my legs, to swoop me up to his chest. The sudden change in my equilibrium, dizzies me for a second, as I cling to my mate's shoulders. He surely knows how to sweep a girl off her feet... literally.

I allow Jasper to walk me up the stairs, as I try hiding my face from Malik as we walk past. I'm embarrassed enough as it is.

"How did it feel?" Jasper asks me, as he sits me down gently on the side of the bed. We are in the room I slept in last night, where I had tossed and turned about finding out Jasper is my mate. Every time I did however, the thought of death drew my thought away. There hasn't been a time yet where I have safely been able to consider the bond between us, aside from when it first happened.

Taking a deep breath, I try to focus fully on him.

He looks lost, like a part of him has been torn away. Shadows are under his eyes, his hair is scruffy and mussed from running his hands through it. Yet still, I have to admire him. I am always confused by the fact he constantly had me entranced, mesmerized. Now I know why...

"I don't want to ever die again," I mutter, remembering the wrapping of water around my neck.

Jasper chuckles. He sits down beside me, the bed sinking with his movement.

Just thinking about the way he died made me feel nauseoss. Being stabbed is like a bad nightmare. I think I would much rather be shot, since it seems a lot less intimate compared to a knife.

"You'll never have to feel that again," he murmurs, brushing the hair from my neck. "Not after I bite you, and give you eternal life."

My entire body tenses, as he leans forward, his mouth close to my neck. Except... he stays still, his warm breath caressing my skin, oddly tender. It feels he has already given me the bite of a mate, by the way my body protests the proximity of his lips to my neck. As he leans away again, I assume he understood.

"I had to bite you... to turn you," he tells me, and I shudder.

However he did it, I don't want to know. However, every thought is instantly dismissed as Jasper cups my face, moving me closer until our lips meet. That is when my body stops protesting, and I forget I was going to berate Jasper for using his magic on me. His lips cure anything.

I can't help myself. I begin to kiss him back, answering his insistent tongue and lips. He tastes so addictive I can't help

200

thinking, as I slide closer to him so our bodies are pressed together, *will I ever get enough of this.*

Jasper's hand snakes around my waist, holding me so close, I almost can't breathe.

This has to stop. But I can't...

With my hands in his hair, there is nothing I can do to stop Jasper, as he uses his strength to lift me straight onto his lap, as I straddle his hips. In this position, I can feel every inch of him against me, with my breasts pressed against his chest, and his hips against my thighs. It's so intimate...

"Jasper," I breathe, pulling away to get my breath back. "This is too much right now."

My hands are on his chest, as he continues to let his lips assault me with pleasure, kissing along my jaw. Despite my protests, my head unintentionally tilts, my body yearning for more of him, and his touch.

"Mmm," he mumbles against my skin, his lips drifting down to my neck.

The feelings he is giving me are almost too much to handle. Every ounce of me is on fire, his kisses and touch send sparks to set me alight. After everything happening today, I need to think. But if Jasper keeps it up, I might just collapse from pleasure before then.

"Seriously," I mutter, my body betraying me, as my hips unconsciously move against his own, trying to get just a little bit of friction to satisfy what is growing deep within my stomach, despite how little Jasper has touched me yet.

I've dreamed about this. The moment when he can touch me without those gloves.

"Tell me you don't crave it," Jasper murmurs. I almost don't catch his words, as he descends further down my neck, his hands drifting at the bottom of my shirt. "Tell me you don't want it as much as I do."

Honestly, I do... more than anything. My head is such a muddled mess, and Jasper isn't doing anything to help it. Instead he is distracting me with his hot mouth, and what seems to be something growing in his pants.

Slowly, Jasper falls backward, still holding my hips like his lifeline. My hands beside him balance me, my body still atop Jasper's.

He changes that quickly though, as he suddenly pushes me gently, so I sprawl across the bed, my back buried within the covers. Crawling on top of me with a slight smile, my mate grabs my thigh, hooking my leg over his hip. Our position is awfully suggestive, but it seems as if Jasper has forgotten to care right now.

"I died today Jasper," I remind him, as he slowly presses his hips down against me. The feel of them has my entire body quivering in just a second, as I truly feel what is going on down there in his pants. "And I know you're excited, but we should talk... or..."

My last words are cut off, as a moan suddenly escapes my mouth.

The feeling of him against my sex sends me into a state of pure ecstasy. My eyes close, and despite the fabric separating us, the jolt of pleasure sends me back to that night Jasper gave me an incredible orgasm. It reminds me of *exactly* what he is capable of.

"I don't have to read your mind to know what you want," he purrs, rolling his hips rhythmically against mine. The feeling is insane as my body shakes in pleasure. All I want to do is to tear his pants off, or at the very least have him do that to me.

But as those feelings overwhelm me, I feel my mind protesting.

"Jasper... No, we can't... not now."

Realizing my tone is serious, Jasper pulls away, reeling back to look at me properly. Again, he is concerned, and I realise he wears that same expression around me a lot lately. As much as I want to keep kissing him, I can't ignore what is swirling in the back of my mind.

Luca. As much as I hate to think about him, he is a recurring thought.

What if Jasper finds out? What will he do if he knows what is really going on inside my head? The memories of who I thought would be my mate cannot be something he finds out about. If he does... he might do something drastic.

"You're doing it again," Jasper notes, rolling back to give me some space. "That look on your face."

Frowning, I shake my head at him, sitting up to try clear my head. If he keeps his promise, he won't look into my mind, and he won't find out. He may be my mate, but he doesn't deserve to have the burden of knowing this shameless secret of mine.

"Time," I tell him. "I just need time."

"Why? You can tell me anything, Thea. You can trust me," Jasper insists, looking pained at the idea of me keeping things from him. I can't blame him, because I would feel the same way, but it is for the better for him that he doesn't find out. So I shimmy off the bed, standing on my feet while Jasper watches from the side.

I shake my head, wishing he didn't question it. "Let me think things through, and when I get back, we can talk about it some more."

Jasper sighs deeply, looking torn, as if he is tempted to make sure I don't leave the room. Instead he simply nods, but not without looking forlorn. There are no words to make him feel better.

So instead, I turn around, and walk out the door.

Chapter Thirty-Four

Luckily for me, it isn't snowing when I venture outside.

Already, from the moment I step out of Malik's home, I feel better. Just breathing in the crisp air, letting it filter all my thoughts thoroughly, is a relief, and for the first time in a while, my muscles begin to relax, despite the difficulty of pushing through the snow on Malik's lawn. If I can just spend a few minutes walking around, then I can go back and hear Jasper out.

Quite frankly, my mind had found it hard to fathom that Jasper is my mate. An Alpha? My rational mind passes many things off as coincidence, but I know for a fact, this is Fate.

And now I know the true reason why he wanted me to escape so badly.

By the time I reach the streets of the Love Pack, snow has seeped into my shoes, and the realisation has hit me that maybe the coat I grabbed isn't enough. At least the struggles through the snow have warmed me up enough to actually make my legs work. Everybody else I walk past seems unfazed by the brittle cold, brushing past me with a merry expression painted on their faces.

It could be worse. I could be in the Desire Pack, with a bunch of people soliciting their bodies.

"Good day," someone says as they wander past. She is a lovely looking lady , dressed in a pastel pink coat that matches the colour of her cheeks. Nodding back in response, I keep on my way.

Has she noticed my eyes? Does she care they are violet?

The stores I walk past are fairly mediocre. Most of them are closed for some reason, and I wonder briefly what time it is. The sky is shrouded by dark clouds, burdened with snow, so it's hard to predict what time of the day it was when I decided to wander out.

"Oh!"

The exclamation of surprise comes from someone I accidently run into. Too busy keeping my eyes glued to the ground, so people wouldn't notice the colour of them, I've run straight into someone who was looking squarely at their phone. We both stumble backwards, my feet nearly slipping on the frosted concrete beneath me.

It is a girl. She is holding a cup in her other hand, from which a little coffee has spilled. She doesn't seem angry though... probably because it was her own fault.

"I'm so sorry," we say at the same time.

Her eyes aren't that iconic blue that seems to be common here. Instead, I'm staring at steely gray ones. She smiles slightly, until she gets a good look at me, then her entire expression falls, and so does my heart.

"You know what's funny?" she says, tilting her head. "You look a lot like the girl on that wanted poster I saw in the shop window back there."

Luca. I know instantly.

"Except it can't be you. Your eyes are... purple? Anyway, I'm sorry about running into you," she exclaims, before she brushes past me, and goes on her way. Taking a deep breath, I close my eyes. This is supposed to be a walk to clear my head, and think things through, rather than being worried about being caught as a wanted person.

Why does Luca have to be a part of the police? It gives him full reign of every Pack, and clearly, he's taking advantage of that, through wanted posters. That means he's still here.

The quicker I get back to Jasper, the better, but first, I need to take that poster down.

It is taped to the window of a small café. No one bothers looking at me as I walk up to it. That is definitely me, however I can see the difference in the eyes as I catch a glimpse of myself in the shop

205

window. It's probably the only reason that girl didn't run me straight to the police... Only Alpha Malik can order them all to be taken down.

All the paper has written on it is how I had committed numerous crimes that resulted in my immediate need to be captured and brought into custody. The text makes me out to be some sort of unruly, unkempt fool who might endanger people within the Love Pack. There is even a section insinuating there would be a negotiable reward if someone spots and reports me.

This is bad... This could be devastating. Jasper and I have to get to a safe haven as soon as possible.

Grabbing the poster off the window, I scrunch it up in my hand and shove it into my coat pocket when no one in the café is looking. The paper feels cold and brittle against my fingers. Incriminating.

"Hey!" I hear someone call out from behind me. Turning, I see it's a decent-sized man. "You're the girl from the poster!"

Seriously? Now?

Quickly, I turn, pretending I haven't heard him. Maybe if I walk fast enough, I can turn a corner and lose him, because there is no way I will get caught by him. If he alerts Luca I'm still in this Pack, I'll probably be caught, and who knows whether I will ever see Jasper again, or even the light of day.

When I glance over my shoulder, I see him shouldering his way through people, pointing at me as he runs frantically. Alarm surfaces in my heart, forcing it to beat unnaturally fast, as I push myself into a run.

My strategy of turning some corner and losing him becomes my main goal.

"Someone stop her!" he screams, following a few metres behind me. People begin to turn, noticing the frantic chase that is going on in the middle of the street. That is when I feel people snagging my clothes, trying to stop me, despite not knowing what is going on. Clearly my eyes aren't doing anything to sway the man's belief that the criminal is me.

Trying to keep my feet from sliding out from under me, I turn a corner and slip into a short alleyway. My sprint to the end nearly knocks all the breath out of me. Running may not be my strong suit, but when it comes to my life, I'm not stopping anytime soon.

However, that heroic thought is brought to an abrupt end, as someone grabs my arm.

It is another man, who looks down at me, anger painted across his face. Just being under his scrutinizing gaze is enough to have me know I've been caught—this man is going to take me to the police whether I struggle or not.

That doesn't stop me though. Growling and pulling I try my best to pry myself out of his grip. In vain. People are already beginning to catch up, and some people even take it upon themselves to grab me too, ignoring my protests. Some even have their phones out, to prove they have been part of my capture.

It makes me sick to the stomach.

Those crudely filming think they are doing the right thing. *They all do.* Finding a criminal is probably the best thing any of them have accomplished in their lives so far.

And I'm not about to be able to convince them out of it.

***

Jasper

I swirl the drink around in the small glass, watching it splash along the edges. Malik sure does have expensive tastes in some of the most mediocre things.

"She'll turn...?"

"Tomorrow maybe," I tell him. "It needs time to get into her system."

Malik doesn't seem to like the idea of the whole curse thing. He even seems to be a little uneasy about Phantom Wolves, which isn't surprising. His age and Pack life didn't influence him enough in that area, considering his lack of knowledge and wary fascination.

"How will that happen?" he asks. The Alpha of Love lounges back in his seat, the light from the television casting patterns across his youthful face. After I had been worried about Thea leaving for a walk, Malik had sat me down and is now distracting me with conversation, trying to insist she needs her space.

If there is anything Malik knows like the back of his hand, it's women.

"She will most likely shift into her wolf. As a Phantom, she has no control over it, so I assume a lot of my magic will be necessary to keep her under control. That is, until I teach her," I tell him, taking another sip of my drink.

Really, I would rather be out looking for Thea, rather than talking to him. She's late, and it's starting to...

My eyes catch the screen.

"As seen here, the criminal who local police from the Devotion Pack have tracked here, to the Love Pack, has finally been found," a reporter from the news channel announces. "A man spotted her on the street, having seen her from wanted posters. With the help of other outstanding citizens, the girl is now in the hands of that brilliant policeman, Luca Frances."

My heart sinks, as I realize *exactly* what my mate has got herself into.

On screen, a man holds Thea by her waist, as she struggles and squirms in protest. Someone had the audacity to film her? That isn't what makes me mad though... It's the fact that my mate is in the arms of her ex-boyfriend. And I have no idea where they are...

I'm on my feet in a second, with Malik joining me.

"Jasper, man... You have to calm down," I hear him behind me, but I dismiss it. No one is going to stop me from finding my mate.

I don't bother putting a coat on as I push through Malik's front door. By the looks of the darkened sky it's about to snow, but that is the last thing on my mind. I'm going to kill him... I'm going to burn him to the ground, the moment I lay eyes on him.

Magic burns in the tips of my fingers, yearning to be released. Oh it will be, when I see Luca. I won't hold it back for a second.

"Listen!" Malik says, following me out into the snow.

Coming to a stop, I twist around to give him my full attention for just a moment. Anger brews inside me, and I may have centuries of dealt-with anger under my belt, but this is different. This is *my mate*, and anyone who lays their hands on her must die. And with their history... Suddenly I want to cast some of this excess magic into Malik, so he can deal with it.

"You can't just wander out like that. If this Luca guy is like you've described, he's smart, and he knows the ins and outs of the law," Malik says calmly. "You need to be careful, otherwise you'll never get her back."

I hate how rational he sounds. Despite my age, I'm not familiar with these kinds of things. This means I need to get in contact with someone who is.

Someone who understands what bad is.

"Fine. Get the Alpha of Vengeance on the phone. I have an idea."

Chapter Thirty-Five

"How the hell did you manage to get yourself into this situation?"

Sighing deeply, I brace my hands against the table, trying to hold myself back from doing something irrational. Thea has been missing for over eight hours now, and we have no leads on where Luca may have taken her. At this point, he could have taken her to any Pack, and we are still here in the Love Pack.

My jaw clenches. The internal battle I've committed to is weakening, but I won't stop for a second, until I'm with Thea again. I won't eat. I won't sleep.

"I was trying to be a good mate," I mutter, raising my gaze to his own. "How was I supposed to know this would happen?"

The Alpha of Vengeance stands in front of me. Aside from me, he is one of the oldest Alphas who lives today. Kaden and I never used to hold the best relationship, but our disagreements have recently been resolved, and I now find him a valuable friend. With what has just happened, I believe he may be the only one who can assist me.

"So what's your plan?" he asks. At first, he had been reluctant to leave his Pack. With a heavily pregnant mate, Kaden feels apprehensive about leaving her alone, however it is his mate who has insisted he help me get my own mate back.

I know what I'm about to announce may not go down well. "I need you to kill someone."

As expected, his eyebrows furrow, and he narrows his eyes at me. Kaden has killed many souls in his lifetime, yet I can see how disturbed he is by the idea of doing it one more time. I have to physically hold myself back from crawling into his mind, to understand what he is thinking. Unfortunately, some time ago, he made me promise not read his thoughts.

Slowly, he shakes his head. "I can't do that. Not anymore."

This is what I expected. The man I knew, who is a merciless killer no longer, stands in front of me. Instead, he is a soon-to-be father, who isn't keen on taking anyone's life in the future.

"Kaden, I need this," I insist, trying to convince him this may be the only favour I will ask him. Never before have I asked for assistance in anything; especially since he never used to be so accommodating. A few years ago, Kaden wouldn't have been able to recognise who he has turned into now.

He would have had no idea who would be his mate.

"Why can't you?" he questions, folding his arms across his chest. "Why not save your own mate?"

I sigh deeply. This is the complicated part. If I get close to Luca, if I could even find him in the first place, then he will surely do something drastic, especially to Thea. His plan to kill her will begin, if I enter his vicinity. Kaden, however...

"I don't know evil like you do, Kaden. You know the ins and the outs of what makes a terrible person do bad things. I don't. The only chance I have of finding Thea, is through you. You can't look me in the eye, and tell me you don't have the knowledge to find the man who has taken her," I say sternly.

Kaden's jaw tics, and I see his mind is whirling. When he looks down at my hands clenched on the edge of the table, I know he isn't about to lie to me.

I'm right, and he knows it.

"Perhaps I can find him, but I cannot kill him. I swore to my mate I would no longer become that person, ever again," he tells me, and I see sincerity in his eyes. Were I in his position, and Thea proposed the same thing, I would have agreed. Anything for your mate. Obviously, Kaden feels the same way.

"Fine. If you find him, then you can bring him back here, and I will end his life myself," I murmur, falling back into my seat. "And I will take great pleasure in that."

This time, I see less reluctance in Kaden's expression. Instead, I see that spark in his eye I know him best for. The excitement of a mission that answers my own vengeance. And since he's the Alpha of it, the temptation I am offering is enough to push him over the edge.

He smiles. "All right, I'm in."

***

Thea

I stare into his eyes, mustering the most indignant glare I possibly can.

Luca only smiles, sitting forward on the edge of his seat. Staring at him now, I can't believe I was ever attracted to him. He has a cruel, sunken look to his face, which I can't remember whether he always had, or if it has come since I left. Still, he holds himself together well. Immaculately shaped hair, that matches what he wears.

That's the Luca I know. Never look unruly, in any situation.

"Bitch," I snap.

Completely unnecessary, but it feels good to say. His smile doesn't falter, and I'm surprised he holds his anger so well. That's definitely not something I'm used to. Something is seriously wrong with him; like he's snapped. While I have been spending time without my mate, he has been tirelessly searching for me.

I don't feel bad in the slightest.

"Such hostility, considering I saved you life," he says, tilting his head. I watch a stray piece of dark blond hair brush over his forehead, which he doesn't bother to swipe away.

"Saved my life?" I growl mockingly. "Is that the new word for *sacrifice?*"

Luca frowns, his smile finally failing. If I wasn't tired to this chair, I would punch that victorious smirk off myself, but I'm bound very firmly. Flexibility isn't my thing either, otherwise I would kick my foot up and give him something to be mad about.

Instead, I'm stuck staring into the same eyes that have haunted me since my early teenage years.

"You seriously took what *he* said seriously? That man is delusional. Everything he said to you was probably a lie," he tells me, trying to sound confident.

I am not about to tell him I know we are mates. Somehow, Luca knows, and as far as I know, he doesn't think I do, and I would be happy for him to keep thinking that. Jasper wouldn't lie to me without good reason to, and after my supposed boyfriend showed up at my house with two men holding rope, it's easy to see who I can trust.

"Is that why I'm tied up then," I say dryly.

Luca sighs. "It's for your own safety."

"For some reason, I don't believe you. Where are we anyway? You're obviously going to kill me soon, so you might as well get it over with."

Maybe it is stupid to taunt him. He seems unmoved. Where we are, on the other hand, I don't know. We are definitely underground, since there is no window in sight in this small room. I can safely assume no one is going to see us. Luca is too good at his job to let that happen.

"No Thea, my darling girl, I'm not going to kill you," he says delicately, and I narrow my eyes at him.

"The sweet release of death sounds much better than being near you..."

Luca shakes his head at me, before standing up. The sound of the chair against the wooden floor has me cringing. I can tell he's trying to intimidate me, but I'm not having it. Why I'm not scared out of my mind right now, I'm not sure. I'm done being afraid of him.

"Listen, you clearly are in no position to be throwing insults at me. You're never going to see that Alpha again. I have prepared for this moment, and I can assure you that when he comes looking for you, he won't even make it within two miles."

The sinister tone of his voice makes me shiver, but I keep my eyebrow raised, as I refuse to look bothered by that.

Jasper will find me. If I don't escape first.

Suddenly he stoops down, grabbing my chin between his cold fingers. "And your eyes... I had a feeling he would turn you. How long have you been a Phantom, darling?"

I turn my head, pulling my chin out of his fingers. He doesn't deserve to know. If he finds out I died only yesterday, then he will know I have no powers yet. I want him to fear me. I want him to worry about me escaping every time he lays eyes on me.

"None of your business," I mutter. "Bitch."

My profanities go unnoticed, making me slightly nervous. Usually Luca gets riled up when I swear, but instead he dismisses it. Not like him at all. He takes his hand away, and before I have time to react, he slaps me straight across the face.

Biting my teeth together, I try to ignore the slash of pain that sears across my cheek. Ouch.

"You've always been a smart mouth. Go on, cry, be pathetic like I know you are," he taunts shamelessly, backing away a few steps. Right now, I want nothing more than to hurt him. The slap was a decent one, and I have a feeling it's going to leave an equally decent bruise.

Don't focus on that. Focus on how much you hate him.

"So, this is what's going to happen," he exclaims. "You're going to live."

Somehow, that seems better than being around him for another second.

"I'm going to keep you here, and you're going to help me with something. Now, your father and I have been looking for many years for the little safe haven Jasper created before you were even born. I have a feeling, you know where that is."

No. I will not jeopardise the safety of all those people, and give up what Jasper has worked so hard on.

Instead, I vow to keep silent.

"Of course, I understand how stubborn you are, and that you probably won't tell me without a little persuasion," Luca says delicately, and my heart falls. "So if you refuse to talk, which I know you will, then we can happily agree on other methods, ones that I prefer."

I know what he means. He wants the information, and he's going to get it. How? I assume he is going to torture it out of me.

"Try your best," I spit, yanking as best I can on what binds me to the chair.

Luca moves back to stand directly in front of me again. He doesn't bother crouching to my eye level. He's giving me no respect, which honestly, I'm fully used to. He has never loved me, and I'm starting to realise I never loved him either. Clearly he used me, and I did the same to him.

"Well then, Thea darling, you'll crack eventually, and Jasper won't be here to save you..."

Chapter Thirty-Six

The water that rushes around my ears, ice cold against my face, reminds me of the day I died. With gritted teeth, I wait for the pain of suffocation to pass, but it only does when my hair is tugged, and I am brought back to air again.

I spit water onto the ground in front of me, trying not to throw up what I have swallowed already.

"Not happening," I mutter.

My chest hurts; it feels like someone is pressing down on it vigorously. My throat burns from the desperate breathing I've had to do before Luca plunged my head back underwater. I want him to stop, but I am adamant about keeping Jasper's Safe Haven a secret. There is a lot more at stake than the torture Luca is forcing me to endure.

"This isn't going to end, Thea. You have to be honest with me for that to happen," Luca says, letting me fall to the floor beside the bucket of water. The ground is wet and cold, and I feel every inch of my weakened limbs quiver.

Crawling backwards, until I am pressed against the wall, I glare up at him. I hate him so much. I hate the way he thinks he can push me around like he always used to. The premeditated sacrifice he and my father had planned for me doesn't seem to bother me as much as what Luca is doing now. It reminds me so much of our past.

Every ounce of thought in my mind is quashed the moment I hear a knock on the door.

Where we are within this building, I don't know. Luca had blindfolded me, and brought me into a small, darkened room. The fact someone is knocking on the door wouldn't have bothered me, had Luca not frowned, and almost paled.

Whoever is behind that door knocks again.

Luca turns to me. "Don't you dare move."

I am not going to. Perhaps I could stand, and make a run for it the moment he opens the door, but my legs are almost completely unusable. Dragging myself across the damp floor is my only option, and as implausible as it may be, I don't move, even when the door is opened and reveals who is standing there.

His face is instantly recognisable. Not because I have ever met him before, but he is an infamous Alpha, who almost everyone alive knows about. The Alpha of Vengeance.

A shiver runs across my skin, as he meets my gaze.

Many people spread rumours that he is the cruelest of all Alphas. Even more people believe it. Now, as I stare at him, I see it. The dark, endless shallows of his eyes, as he registers who I am, as if we have a past together, as if we know each other. Just the sight of him is terrifying. Why is he here?

My first thought is *he is here to hurt me, as badly, if not worse, than Luca has*. What else would a man like himself, who everyone knows to be a merciless leader, be doing here for any other reason?

"Alpha Kaden..."

The Alpha of Vengeance raises his hand, showing me it is enclosed in leather the exact colour of his eyes. Luca sounds confused, but also mildly terrified. No, *very* terrified.

Keeping myself pressed tight against the wall, I watch as Kaden walks into the room, dismissing the protests coming from Luca. He doesn't want Kaden here, so why is he? Everyone knows he shows up in Packs to exact revenge on anyone who murders. If you break the rules you're the Discipline Pack's problem, but if you kill, you're his.

Yet the fact I haven't murdered anyone doesn't give me any solace, or make me any less terrified of him.

"Now, what do we have here?" Kaden asks. His voice is that deep, melodic accent that comes only from the Vengeance Pack. He gazes around the small room, before his eyes come to rest on the bucket in the middle of floor.

I see something flicker in his eyes, before he masks it.

"What do you want? How did you get down here?" Luca asks, trying to demand answers; however his voice is weak. He is just as afraid as I am... maybe more. This Alpha has wandered in here without a care in the world, after Luca went all that way to ensure I was somewhere Jasper could never find me.

I'd be afraid too, if I was him.

"I have my ways," Kaden murmurs, taking a few steps further into the room. He isn't looking at me anymore. "This isn't my first time dealing with someone like you."

Kaden turns around, and I can't see Luca's expression from behind his body. There are a few moments of deadly silence, and I can imagine the stare off between the two. It reminds me of the first time Jasper confronted Luca, when he refused to back down to Jasper, the clearly superior male.

"I'm going to have to ask you to leave," Luca insists.

I hear Kaden scoff, like he can't believe the audacity of the young officer, who isn't even wearing his uniform. From the way Luca talks, I can tell we must be underneath some sort of government building, or maybe even a jail. Hopefully, it's not in the Devotion Pack.

"You haven't heard what I want yet. I can assure you I *always* get what I want, and today is no exception," Kaden tells him carefully.

As much as I am afraid of the Alpha of Vengeance, I am impressed with how easily he got in here, and how confident he is in riling Luca. Whatever he may be here for, I can tell already that Luca isn't going to like it.

"I am currently in the middle of a police interrogation, so I am going to have to ask you to leave..." Luca says, and I can hear the quiver in his voice. Kaden's gaze is enough to tear down a man's confident facade.

As his lies begin, I know I will have to get out of here, now. The door is open, although both stand close to it, and I'm sure they will grab me before I even get close.

But I have to try.

Bringing my feet under me, I almost collapse when I try pushing myself into a standing position. My legs are so weakened from the asphyxiation Luca put me through, any chance of escaping lies in my own will. However, the moment I actually make it to my feet, using the wall to my advantage, I'm hit with a spiraling wave of nausea.

"And what crime has this girl committed?" Kaden questions, still not looking at me.

Not only is my mind whirling, but bright colors are sparking in my vision, and I feel myself almost lose control of my body. A familiar feeling suddenly fills my veins. Something I did when I was a child, and had time to play and hanker back to the reality of my species.

I was starting to shift, into a wolf.

As an adult, I don't worry about shifting as much anymore. Really there is no point, other than to run around and have fun. Then the Wisdom Pack insisted after 'recent studies' they found it contributed to many people arriving at the brink of insanity. Honestly, I didn't believe in their clinical ways.

Yet, I can usually choose when I want to shift. Now, my body is forcing me to undergo the change, as my limbs become numb, and I feel the beginnings of evolution strike my bones. This is going to happen, and for some reason, I can't control it.

Then it hits me. *I'm a Phantom Wolf.*

I can hardly concentrate on anything but the voices in the room, as I fall back onto the ground again, my shirt soaking with the water I have been submerged in. This is why people don't shift. They lose control of who they really are.

"She... that is private, confidential information I cannot share without a warrant," Luca tells Kaden. Does he thinks that's going to stop him? The Alpha of Vengeance? As I feel my body begin to undergo a painful change, these two are still arguing, and still, I'm not sure what Kaden's motive is.

By the time I have completely shifted, my mind now belonging to another part of me I try to keep hidden, there is a heated argument going on.

"What you're failing to understand, is that I have come to retrieve the girl. You are lucky I have not killed you yet. I was told Alpha Jasper would do so. However you really are tempting me," I hear Kaden say. Their voices are starting to fade into one, and I feel myself losing control completely.

I feel a growl escape from my throat, filling every cold gap of this place.

Both Kaden and Luca turn in surprise, while I fight to stop this Wolf from doing something we'll both regret. However, I've lost the fight, and it is the frightened face of Luca that I last see, before I throw myself at him.

***

Jasper

I'm pacing again.

How I've managed to keep myself up for so long, I don't know, but ever since Kaden announced his idea for finding Thea, I have been stressing out immensely. He hasn't told me how he found out where Luca was keeping her.

I didn't bother questioning it either. The Alpha of Vengeance is capable of many things. Things I'm not sure I want to know about.

The moment he graces my thoughts, he is suddenly standing in front of me, having burst through the door. Catching the first glance of him, I am terrified. Across his forehead is a seeping wound that looks a few steps away from being fatal. Blood is congealed in his eyelashes, and across his cheeks and nose, as he stares at me.

That isn't what worries me though.

In his arms is my mate, drenched from head to toe in blood. Yet, I cannnot see a single wound on her body. Gently, Kaden kneels down, and lays her on the floor, before looking back up at me.

"She killed him," he whispers hoarsely. "She killed Luca."

Chapter Thirty-Seven

Thea

I can hardly feel my body when I wake up.

Every previously working limb of mine is now completely insensate. Scraping at the edges of my mind, I try my best to sweep away the fog that lingers around the part of my mind that marks the difference between logic and insanity.

"Fate, I hate you," I mutter through dry lips, hardly recognising my voice as my own.

Obviously, I don't know the devious entity personally, but he is the reason I lie here feeling so foreign and outlandish. Something isn't right.

Everything comes back to me as I sit up, an inordinate wash of memory and feeling slapping me across the face. My legs sink into the plush mattress that is relatively familiar, making me realise I am back in the Love Pack. Maybe I never left in the first place, but this time...

I'm not in Luca's malicious clutches anymore.

Drawing my legs out of the crisp washed sheets, I give my body a quick once-over. Delicate bruises speckle my thighs and down past my knees. When I go to run a tentative finger across the discoloured marks, I notice what plagued the skin on my hands. Clearly someone has attempted to scrub the evidence from my fingers, but I can still see blood I had once cradled.

With quivering legs, I force myself to my feet. I'm dressed in silken pants and a loose shirt, which I don't remember ever putting on; it doesn't take a Wisdom Pack scientist to deduce someone has dressed me.

Just as I look up, the door to the room opens slowly.

Jasper closes the door after him. The grave expression pasted across his face can't be excused. Listening to my sinking heart, the moment I awoke, was right. Something bad has happened, and it definitely has something to do with the blood all over my hands.

"What did I do?" I question him, the moment I know it is just us having this conversation.

My memories from before I lost consciousness are shaded. The torture Luca inflicted on me is still vivid, but after that, what I witnessed has been stolen from me. A flicker of dark, soulless eyes register in there somewhere, but who they belong to, still remains unknown to me.

Jasper strolls forward, not bothering to conceal the grimness of his expression, or even replace it with another. An essence of unease settles over me. The moment Jasper grabs my hands between his, and I feel the headiness of those sparks and the gentleness of his magic, it disappears.

We sit together on the bed. Those moments where I wasn't with Jasper were incredibly difficult, so it's a relief just to be able to look into the violet hue of his eyes again.

"I'm sorry," Jasper whispers, and all of a sudden, chills dig their nails deep into my back. "I'm sorry I wasn't there."

Clenching my jaw to the point of pain, I ready myself to what he is about to tell me.

"Alpha Kaden, who I sent to assist in finding you, tried to stop you, but there is only so much he could do, to stop an out of control Phantom. I didn't want him to know what was about to happen to you, because I didn't think the effects would hit you so quickly," Jasper tells me, his tone dripping with regret and self-loathing.

Had my heart stopped beating, which it got alarmingly close to, then it wouldn't have mattered. Hearing the Alpha of all Phantoms tell me himself that I was one of them, with such certainty, secures the fact in my mind.

"I didn't hurt anyone, did I?" I ask, knowing full well what a shifted Phantom Wolf can do to someone else. An Alpha though... Especially the Alpha of Vengeance, who I couldn't figure out why he would want to help us, of all people. Surely he would have been able to do something to stop me, or even kill me if he had to.

I must have been completely out of control.

"I'm afraid you did," Jasper says, casting his gaze down to the floor. "Very badly, in fact."

Closing my eyes, I try to imagine how I could have brought myself to be so deplorable, to hurt someone to a point where Jasper would be visibly troubled. When you shift into your Wolf, your morals evaporate into thin air, as they no longer become necessary.

I could have contributed to a mass murder, and not known about it.

"Just tell me," I demand, sick of having been deprived of information for so long. Jasper is good at doing that to me, after keeping the news of us being mates for so long.

Sighing, Jasper squeezes my hand a little more.

"You killed him. You killed Luca," he tells me, the abominable tone of his voice correlating to the feeling that consumes my body at that exact moment.

The urge to double over and throw up is so overwhelming, I nearly commit. Through a haze of dread, I cling to Jasper as my lifeline. No tears fall. No sound escapes my lips. I'm completely consumed in an unfamiliar feeling, that my body is trying its best to reject.

"I can't have... That's not me," I reply hoarsely, trying to rein in my feelings, but failing miserably.

My head falls onto Jasper's chest, but I hardly feel him as he holds me close. Tears of remorse refuse to fall, as I struggle to grasp the fact that I *killed* someone. *Me.*

"You avenged them, Thea. You got justice which all those innocent people, sacrificed by Luca, needed. We should be rejoicing. No longer can he hurt anyone else." Jasper tries to reassure me. That is why I can't cry; because a part of me knows he deserved what happened.

Even if it is I who have forever to deal with the repercussions.

***

It takes weeks for me to be able to even smile again. Taking a life isn't something I can easily pass off. Even if the soul that belonged to that body was dark, and utterly evil.

Jasper and I return to Safe Haven not long after I have been saved.

Thanking Alpha Kaden was strange, considering I was half-apologising at the same time. I had left him with a large cut upon his face, that he would have to explain to his mate. He was quick to assure me he had suffered worse, and that he would heal in little time.

Luckily, Jasper has given me a lot of time to think things through, but is always there at nights when I wake drenched in regrets and cold sweat, to convince me Luca deserved worse than death.

As weeks pass, I begin to believe him.

However, Jasper is starting to have issues of his own. Rumors about him are spreading like a raging fire through a brittle forest in summertime. Once his loyal followers, people are beginning to open their eyes, to realize maybe Jasper is what they fear most in the world. A Phantom Wolf.

Being an open person, when he feels it is necessary, Jasper tells me every day what is troubling him. I can't join the conversations with as much honesty, though. Being used to hiding so much from Luca, to keep from fuelling arguments and anger, I find myself falling back into old habits with Jasper, that I can't shake despite wanting nothing more than to be open with him.

So, to stop myself from going completely insane, I spend some nights stooped over the toilet, vomiting up my pent-up thoughts and emotion.

"I was thinking," Jasper says one day. " I could take you out somewhere."

We are in the living room, Jasper reading another one of his favourite mystery novels, while I try to force myself to properly document my feelings into a makeshift diary, which is really a collection of cut paper.

I raise my head in surprise. "What do you have in mind?"

Jasper looks his usual self, which I can't help but be envious of. There is nothing more I want than to get out of this house. As much as I love it, some fresh air might clear my mind and let me think about something other than Luca. 'Other' being Jasper, my mate.

"I'll find somewhere. I think we both need to escape our thoughts," Jasper says, making me narrow my eyes. Is he reading my mind, after I told him he wasn't allowed to?

He can't have. By now, he would have figured why I may seem somewhat distracted.

Suddenly, Jasper's book is on the floor, my pages of useless scribbles joining him. With his insistent hands on my hips, he pulls me onto him, till I straddle his hips. The intimacy of this position warms the cold ache in my heart. It gives me perfect access for touching his face and falling into the gentle gaze he is giving me.

"You've been somewhere else these past few weeks," Jasper notes, and I shamefully refuse to meet his gaze again, using the tips of my fingers to trace along his jawline. "I have concluded I am going to have to bring you back down to earth."

Biting my lips, I glance up to see Jasper watching me carefully. Sometimes I wish I could read minds. Jasper has told me, after I questioned my inability to shift (which he explained was from his magic keeping me sane) I will probably never have the same ability as he does. As unsatisfactory as it may have seemed initially, it makes me kind of grateful for the mystery behind Jasper's eyes.

"And how are you going to do that?" I do try to sound serious, despite being distracted by Jasper's straying hands on my hips. In answer, Jasper tips me backward, until my back is pressed against the couch. I can hardly believe myself when I hear myself giggle, feeling a rush of feelings for my mate I haven't felt since my mind became clouded with sickening things.

"I have a few things in mind," he whispers, bringing his head down to my neck. Perhaps his instinct to assault my neck with his pleasurable kisses and nips is because he knows it drives me to the brink of insanity. The good kind, of course. However he figured it out, and knew to keep doing it, I don't care, because for once, I feel myself fully relaxing.

"Do you now," I murmur, my fingers winding around the soft strands of his thick hair.

I don't mind my mind conjuring up wicked scenes of what Jasper may be capable of. If anything can take and keep my mind off things, it's my handsome mate, who knows it.

"Shall I take you on this date first? Then after, I shall think of some way to fully please you, to really take your mind off things" Jasper tells me, his voice filled with seductive ease. I can't wait, and I know that fact is real by the multitude of shivers caressing my spine on their way up. Only Jasper will ever be capable of doing such things.

Cupping his face, I bring Jasper's lips to mine, and savour the sweet, addictive taste of him.

"I believe you," I murmur, pulling away slightly. "I really do."

Chapter Thirty-Eight

My eyes close, as the blissful feeling of Jasper rhythmically stroking my hair nearly lulls me to sleep.

He has decided he wants to take me on a date, where we won't be interrupted. Somewhere calm, quiet and tranquil, so we can talk, and simply enjoy each other's presence. So, we have ended up at the end of a small offroad somewhere just out of Safe Haven, where Jasper is sure no one will find us.

Having Jasper all to myself for a few hours definitely appeals to me.

"I have no idea why Fate made me wait so long for you," Jasper mutters, brushing a piece of stray hair from my face. I often forget how old Jasper is compared to me.

I twist on his lap, so I can look up at him. "Have you met him?"

The world is so twisted, not everyone can agree on who runs our lands. Some Packs believe fully in the Moon Goddess's power, despite rumours that she can no longer dictate anything. Some believe fully in Fate, and his cruel and manipulative powers. His life exists, to control ours. Personally, I believe more in Fate than the Goddess.

"Indeed. Such a strange man he is." Jasper gazes down at me. "I don't think anyone believes he has any emotions. Being as confusing as he is, I doubt anyone will ever find out."

Something about him sparks an interest within me. However, I'm not about to question it. Playing with Fate is a dangerous game.

"I think Fate made me wait for you, because he knew I needed time to figure out my magic. Then he decided he wanted you to become a Phantom, so we can be together forever," Jasper muses aloud, picking at a blade of grass by my head. I sigh deeply, listening to the gentle sounds of the nearby stream as I think.

I'm scared of what is to come. Learning to control my magic is not something that will come easily, so just the thought of it is very worrying. I have to try, though, for Jasper. He can't keep using his magic to stop me from turning into a murderous Wolf at night.

"How long did it take you to fully learn how to control your magic?" I ask.

Jasper pauses, delving back into his mind to remember his past. He has told me very little about what his life was like before I was even born, however I haven't told him much either. Although, my life has been a lot more bland than his.

"A long time. Many years, in fact," he tells me, his voice lowered. "I had no help; I was self-taught. But you will have me along with you this entire way."

My heart warms at his words. The idea of him being here this entire time makes me think this won't be as hard as I imagine. But using magic is something I am not familiar with, and when Jasper uses it around me, it seems a little daunting.

Jasper runs his fingers across my face. "What I have noticed about you, is that you keep things to yourself. I can't keep acting like I didn't notice that day, when you almost flipped out on me, when I tried to kiss you."

My jaw automatically clenches, almost like a defense mechanism.

Am I ready to tell him about my relationship with Luca? Sighing deeply, I sit up. I can see the surprise on his face as I straddle his lap, so my face is level with his. He watches me apprehensively, probably waiting for me to spill news that might ruin the relationship we have just started.

"You don't want to hear about *him*," I mumble, brushing my hands through his hair. At the hint of Luca, Jasper's face darkens, his expression becomes grim. "I don't want to talk about him."

With a hollow feeling in my gut, I bring my lips to Jasper's before he can say another word.

Once we get back, Jasper directs us to the kitchen to get something to eat. Admittedly, I'm not very hungry, but I agree to eating an apple for the sake of it.

"I had fun today," I tell him softly, watching him across the other end of the kitchen.

Just being able to talk to him is so enjoyable. Suddenly I feel he and I are closer, and all the distrust I had for him to begin with is slowly diminishing. Had I given up his Safe Haven, I don't think I would have been able to forgive myself.

"Me too," he murmurs, and for a split second, I believe I see his eyes darken slightly.

All of a sudden, he is crossing the kitchen toward me. Time almost seems to slow down in that moment, as I realise there is nothing more that I want right now, than him. The closer he gets, the faster my heart starts beating. This is my mate, who I've spent many years believing I would never meet.

Jasper leans over, bracing his hands against the counter behind me.

"I've been waiting all day," I admit breathlessly, the heat from Jasper practically drenching me. I want to tell him how enchanting he has been this entire day, and how badly my body has been yearning for him, but I can't form those words without blushing profusely.

Jasper runs a finger across my cheek, his eyes darkening with every inch of sparks he leaves in its wake. He wants this as much as I do; I can see it written all over his face.

"Have you now?" he teases, a slight smile gracing his features. His gaze flicks to my lips. "Can you tell me what you want?"

The soapstone bench presses into the small of my back. It is a reminder of the reality I face, keeping me from begging for Jasper to respond with *exactly* what my body requests. So I suggest, subtly, by leaning up to softly kiss the corner of his mouth. As I pull away, I drink in the sight of Jasper's curious expression.

"I want you," I say simply, expecting a simple reply. However, my breath is stolen from me, as Jasper suddenly flips me over completely, with little effort.

My hands splay out against the counter, feeling the slick coldness under my fingers. I feel my back pushed against by his front, one of his hands resting on my hip, while the other runs down my back. At the same time as I am surprised by his sudden excited approach, it only contributes to the desire I feel deep within me.

"You want me to fuck you, don't you?" he says sensually, his hands lifting the edge of my dress up slightly, till I feel it bunched against my hips. "Just admit it."

At this point, I'm so turned on by Jasper's existence, I can't think of anything other than his words. The exact words that drive shivers straight down my spine, and across my flesh with no end in sight. I think I might go insane if he does not go through with this right now. I don't need the finalizing bite of my mate right now. I just need him inside me.

"Yes," I breathe, hardly recognizing my voice as my own. "Please."

Feeling Jasper push my dress all the way up makes it all the more real. I am going to commit to this, and I don't care. Not anymore. Right now, all that matters is my mate, who I can't see, but can feel is slowly dragging my underwear down my legs.

Resting my clothes' front against the counter, I close my eyes, feeling Jasper's fingertips tease their way back up my thigh. I'm grateful I can't see him, otherwise I would probably completely melt. His teasing right now, as he draws circles with his fingers across my legs and back, never where I want to, is not appreciated.

"Jasper," I chide, pushing back till I can feel his hard length against me. "Put us both out of our misery."

I hear him chuckle, At the same time I hear him fumbling with his pant zipper. As much as I don't want this to be over, I don't think I can handle another second of his endless teasing touch.

My entire body freezes in anticipation, as he leans down, till I can feel his breath warm against my ear. As he whispers in my ear, a wave of heat consumes me. "I control the rhythm, is that clear?"

I believe truly, just the words from his mouth will be enough to make me climax on the spot.

Before I respond in agreement, I suddenly feel him sink slowly into me, with one smooth thrust of his hips. Gasping at the feeling of immense pleasure that hits me from the inside, I think for a brief moment, finally my mate and I are as close as we ever possibly could be.

There is little I can do, except gasp and moan my pleasure, as Jasper thrusts into me slowly, asking me once if I am okay. I am quick to assure him all I want is more, not the gentle strokes that are astounding, but my body craves more from him.

He answers by pumping into me at a steady pace. As my hands clench into fists, I feel his hands stray from my hips, drifting down between my legs to gently massage the most sensitive part of my body.

All the euphoric feelings build into one moment, as I cry out, screaming Jasper's name.

Jasper follows a split second after, slamming deep inside me. We both take a moment, trying to catch our breath. Slowly, Jasper pulls me back upright, turning me around so I am facing him again. He cups my face and kisses me, while I continue to cling to the counter, as my legs might just collapse out from under me.

When we finally pull away from the kiss, I rest my head against his shoulder, and take a deep breath. Jasper pulls back, and I gaze up at his violet eyes, listening to his soft murmur. "You're amazing."

Wrapping my arms around his shoulders, I smile warmly. "I guess you're not so bad yourself."

After that, I let him pick me up, and take me upstairs.

Chapter Thirty-Nine

Staring at my hands, I assess the batter that cakes almost every inch of my skin. How have I managed to get myself into this situation? My ability to cook is lacking so much, the cookies I have attempted to make are completely deformed, with most of the dough sticking to my fingers at this point.

My token of appreciation to Jasper is currently in the form of uncooked cookies from a recipe I found in one of his kitchen drawers.

Right now, my mate is out dealing with Alpha stuff. When I asked him about it, he seemed apprehensive to tell me, saying it was complicated business he didn't want to drag me into. I kept my mouth shut, primarily because the whole Pack stuff doesn't appeal to me that much.

So, I've decided to take it upon myself to cook him something, despite the fact I truly have no idea what I am doing. Jasper might either judge my skills, or lack thereof,or he may actually appreciate this.

Almost as if he had read my mind, despite promising not to, Jasper is right behind me, wrapping his arms around my waist.

I can't help but jump. However, the moment I feel his warm breath against my neck, and his chest against my back, I relax. Over these past few days, my trust in Jasper has grown immensely to a point I hadn't believed could ever exist.

Ever since Luca, I have been wary of other men, especially in a relationship way.

But now, Jasper is my mate.

"How was... work?" I ask, wishing I could wash my hands off, so I can touch my mate. Instead, I have to hold my hands in order to not get batter all over our clothes, while I question Jasper on something that really isn't his work.

My head tilts back as he kisses my neck softly, before whispering in my ear. "I was thinking of you the entire time."

Rolling my eyes, I pull away from him playfully. I take advantage of the space to wash my hands thoroughly. After last night, I can tell why Jasper is so suggestive. After our kitchen incident, he brought me upstairs and we made love two more times. It's almost like we can't get enough of each other, wanting to spend every breath together. Even letting him get out of bed to leave was oddly difficult to swallow.

He hasn't even marked me. Apparently he is planning a perfect time to do it.

"Is that right?" I say coyly, drying my hands off. "Aren't you a great Alpha."

Jasper chuckles, and I see him staring at my attempt at making cookies. Never have I wanted to return back to the Love Pack, to Aria, the girl we stayed with for a single night, so she could teach me how to cook properly. The likelihood of me accidentally poisoning Jasper is unbelievably high right now.

"What spurred this?" he asks, nodding to the monstrosity that lies innocently on the tray I haven't even put in the oven yet.

I shrug. "I made them for you."

Something tells me Jasper is trying his best not to laugh openly, as I pick the tray up to slide it into the oven. The only reason I knew how to preheat it was because the one thing I am good at, is actually reading a recipe.

"Interesting," he mused. "You didn't have to do anything for me, you know."

"I know," I say softly, checking the fridge for milk. When I find none that isn't dangerously expired, I frown. There is no way we can have cookies without milk. Jasper may not understand that, but I definitely know he would prefer it that way. This means a walk down to the small shop I remember walking past with Cole, the random boy I met in the street.

I turn, staring at him pointedly. "Would you stay here and make sure these don't burn, while I run down to the shops to get some milk?"

Almost instantly, Jasper's expression darkens slightly.

"Is it a must?" he asks delicately, and I nod. There is no way I am going to suffer through dry cookies. Especially the ones I've made.

"I'll only be a second," I tell him, resting my hands on his broad shoulders. He always tenses up when he is unsure of something; almost like a defense mechanism. The internal battle he likes to put himself through suggests he often wonders whether or not he should make the decisions he does.

He follows me to the door as I sling my coat over my shoulders. "All right then. But I must admit, I'm not that great when it comes to cooking things either. I may be centuries old, but I haven't spent *that* much time in this field."

Glad he isn't resisting a simple trip down to the store, I kiss his cheek and walk out the door with only a few coins to my name in my pocket.

***

The small shop selling convenience goods is almost empty when I wander inside.

Bland tunes from the stereo play as I stroll down the aisle, trying to pinpoint where the milk will be. At one point, I brush past a woman, who holds a shopping basket in one hand, and her child on her hip. Her eyes are dark and brooding as she looks at me, with something dwelling in her eyes.

Chills dance their way down my neck and back at that one look. For a mother, she doesn't look the kindest person in the world. Her features are hollow, and her eyes are encircled with shadows. Clearly her young child, who pulls sharply on a few strands of her hair, is giving her trouble.

Casting my glance down, I keep walking.

The milk is right at the back of the store, yet as I grab one, I hear two people talking at the front of the shop, which isn't the smallest in the world.

"Did you go last night?"

"I had to put the kid to bed. Wish I had though; I heard everyone went."

The first voice sounds like a man's. If I remember correctly, the store clerk is a dirty-looking man reading from a newspaper, sipping cold coffee as I'd walked in. He hadn't even bothered to look up, despite the buzz that sounded when I entered. The second voice, however, is clearly a woman's. It sounds shallow and tired. At the mention of a child, I automatically assume it is the odd woman I walked past less than a minute ago.

"They're all agreeing too," the man says gruffly. "It makes sense. The boy brought decent evidence."

What on earth are they talking about? Why am I even listening?

My curiosity raises its ugly head as I walk down the aisle, hearing more of their conversation as I get closer. I can't yet see them both, but I don't want to. Who knows what they will do if they see me peeking between the cereal boxes at them.

"What are they planning? If Alpha Jasper is really a Phantom Wolf, then surely we can't hold some kind of rebellion. He would kill us all!"

Instantly, my heart plummets to my feet.

"Ideas are mulling around. There will be another meeting tomorrow night," the man says.

Does Jasper know about this? The entirety of Safe Haven is scared of him, and are holding meetings to confirm whether or not he is a Phantom Wolf. These people are scared of the beasts that both Jasper and I are. Had that lady seen my eyes properly? I have noticed they aren't as violet as Jasper's. Instead, they look blue most of the time, with the purple appearing only when I am in the sun.

"I'll be there," the woman says seriously.

"As will I. If there is going to be a movement, I want to be part of it. I'm closing the shop early tonight," the shop clerk replies. He sounds so sincere, and so passionate about this.

A movement? I have to get back to Jasper right now. He will know what to do, won't he? This is his Pack, and he should know it and the people a lot better than I do. However, that might not matter, because by the sound of it, people are losing trust in him with every meeting they are holding.

Taking a deep breath, I walk up to the counter, painting on an expression of indifference as the two people turn to look at me. I am right with my assumption of who they are. The unnerving woman with the giggling child, and the coffee-drinking, stained-teeth, clerk. Both look more evil than any other Phantom than I have met.

Well, aside from Luca and my father.

The woman steps back so I can pay. No one says a word; the silence is only broken when he tells me my price.

With the milk in a bag I had initially refused, I walk out, glad to have successfully dug my way out of that thick tension. I can't blame them for being wary of me, considering I am new to this town, and neither of them have any idea who I am.

Walking down the street, I don't have as much time to think. Instead, I bump into Cole. This guy being the one who took me to breakfast a while back, and now he's jogging toward me, shirtless, yet again.

All I want is to get home to Jasper, to check he hasn't desecrated my cookies, and to tell him what I have heard. Instead, I politely stop to talk to Cole.

"Hey stranger," he says warmly, his grin wide and friendly.

I smile back. "Didn't know you jogged mid-afternoon as well as the morning."

I shouldn't really be fueling the conversation, but at least Cole isn't a strange lady and an abnormal store clerk. He has a kind smile and isn't afraid to offer a stranger breakfast, despite not knowing her. He even thinks I am related to Jasper, when he couldn't be more wrong.

"Did you..." he breaks off, frowning as he looks closer at me. "Did you do something to your eyes, or were they always blue?"

My jaw clenches, as I pale.

"Contacts. Am I wrong when I say they are in fashion? I visited the Desire Pack recently and the trend is big there. Thought I would give it a try," I tell him, trying to sound as casual and realistic as possible, despite the excuse not having any substance whatsoever. At this point, my mind is whirling like a hurricane, so I don't think I will be able to come up with anything else.

Cole chuckles. "I suppose that's pretty neat."

"Sorry, I have to get this milk back before it gets curdled or something," I say stiffly, my expression matching my voice. "See you around?"

Before he responds, I saw Cole look over my shoulder, before he smiles warmly. Trying not to be rude, I don't bother turning around. He is probably meeting a friend, so I might as well take the opportunity to to run.

"Yeah, see you around," he says distractedly, tapping my back as he walks past.

I stand there for a moment. Well, that was easier than I thought it would be. Who is he meeting?

I made the biggest mistake of my life, turning around at that moment.

Because as I do, I not only see Cole's back as he walks away from me, I see who he is walking toward. My breath completely leaves my body at that exact moment. No part of me is ready for any kind of shock of that magnitude; my legs nearly collapse out from under me.

I see, standing in the path, none other than my former best friend. June.

Chapter Forty

I see her before she sees me. Something about the way she stands there, side on to me, makes me insanely angry. She is looking at a piece of paper in her hand, smiling slightly. Her hair is pulled back. She never does that. She's wearing dark clothes, which she never does.

This isn't my best friend. This is someone completely different.

I stride toward her, the rational part of my brain buried somewhere deep beneath hatred and aggression. Cole yelps in surprise as I savagely thrust him out of the way, clearing the way for me to get to June. She turns and for a split second our eyes meet, before I push her twice as hard.

At that moment, I feel a part of me clawing at the edges of some sort of invisible shield. I know immediately it is Jasper's magic keeping me from shifting and killing June.

It makes me mad at him. But not as mad as I am at June.

She stumbles back a few steps.

"Stop!" she yells from the top of her lungs. She even sounds different from when I truly knew her. How can someone change so much in the course of only a few weeks? Although, she hasn't turned into a Phantom Wolf who committed murder, as well as found their mate.

"How could you?" I growl, pushing her again. Her feet nearly come out from under her. "How in the world could you?"

June looks terrified of me. That hasn't changed. Her dark eyes are wide as she brings her hands up to shield herself from the anger I can't yet control. Her lies, her manipulation are all I can think about. There's a sick part of me that wants to hurt her while another part of me wants to crumple down on the sidewalk to cry.

"Thea... Please, listen," she pleads, but my ears are burning.

Suddenly I am no longer moving toward her, as she takes shuddering steps away from me. Cole has hooked my arms back, stopping me from truly doing any further damage to June. Nonetheless, I protest by struggling against him, trying to separate my limbs from his. I have little reason to be mad at him, but right now, I don't want him interrupting anything.

"You're a liar. You don't deserve anything," I growl through my teeth, the hostility in my voice doing more damage than I ever could.

June clenches her jaw tightly before she talks again. "You need to calm down."

My mind whirls with possibilities. Why is she here? What has Cole got to do with this? What is their plan for me?

My breath remains harsh and forced, as I finally stop my struggling. Slowly, the voice of reason within me comes back, as I feel myself calming down. This can't end with me hurting her, because it won't give me any information. If I am to be satisfied, I need her to explain everything to me, including why she is here in Safe Haven. The place she shouldn't know exists.

Shrugging Cole off, I take a few steps to the side. There has to be space between June and I, otherwise I may not be able to hold back next time.

"Explain yourself." I don't care we are on the side of the road, with people who may walk past us and hear our entire conversation. Is there a police force here? I am possibly going to get arrested if June says one word out of line.

June glances down at the piece of paper in her hand, before she frowns and looks back up at me. "There's a lot, but you're just going to have to trust me."

I nearly snort at her.

"I don't think there is anything you can say that will make me trust you for even one second."

June flinches at my words, seeing the truth beneath them. What she had done, or at least, what she has been part, of is inexcusable. Had she contributed to all those kids' deaths? If so, then I have every right to want her to hurt as much as they did. It doesn't matter... She is a Phantom Wolf, and that will never change.

"Can we sit? There is so much for you to hear, including things you may not fully understand," June insists, nodding to a bench further down the street.

I fold my arms over my chest and remain adamant. "I'm not going anywhere."

Where is Jasper when I need him? He must be starting to wonder where I am, considering I had promised a short trip to get him some milk. At this point, the bottle is lying back down the street; having been abandoned after I practically launched myself at June. If Jasper is immersed in a book, he may not even think about my absence for a while longer.

June sighs irritably, and I notice her glance at Cole. I hate that they know each other. "How much do you know? How much did he fabricate?"

I know she'stalking about Jasper. Clearly she has no idea I know him, nor that he and I are mates, which means she is still trying to make him out to be the bad guy. Luca had tried to convince me of the same thing. However I'm not falling for it for a second. Jasper may have kept some things from me, but not for my entire life, like June has.

However, what she said about Phantom Wolves when we were younger was questionable.

"I know you are a Phantom Wolf. I assume you were involved in those murders, or as you probably would like to call it 'sacrifice'. Jasper saved me. Luca was going to kill me," I explain slowly, as it's her first time hearing it.

Again, she and Cole exchange wary glances.

"I tried to warn you, too," she admits. "I had to do it subtly, otherwise your father would have had me hanging with the rest of them. I quite literally had no other choice, Thea. I'm not an Alpha. I didn't have magic to save you."

"Warn me? *Warn me?* You didn't do a very good job trying to convince me Phantom Wolves existed," I snap, anger brewing inside me dangerously once again.

Even back at school, June spent all her time trying to convince me they were real. Our teachers would be mad at her for her wild proclamations that scared all the young kids, including me. Was she trying to tell me since I was *that* young? Never did I take her seriously, and had it not been that we had got along so well, we wouldn't have been friends.

"I tried, but you're so goddamn stubborn," June replied fiercely. "The books, the... everything..."

"Why are you here? How did you find Safe Haven?" I demand, wanting further answers. Jasper will have no idea that his Pack is being invaded by such traitors like the ones right in front of me, and those in the store.

Cole shifts from foot to foot, before he speaks up, "I brought her here. We have known each other for some time now, and I needed to get her away from your father. She is here to take part in the revolt. We know Jasper has spent plenty of time in your presence, but you can't trust him."

"I have heard that many times, but I know it's a lie."

June looks frustrated. "His father created Phantom Wolves. He is the first Phantom Wolf to ever live. He defied what people thought was real. Can you not see that he is the main ruler of a species meant to kill?"

Clearly she hasn't caught onto the fact that I am a Phantom too. There is no way I am about to share any information with them, especially not that Jasper and I are mates. Surely Luca told her, but she doesn't know that I do. If she did... I'm not sure what she would do.

"You speak as if what you say is going to make a difference," I say, taking a few steps backward.

Cole reaches to grab my hand, but I am quick to snatch it away. I can't trust either of them. Cole met me that day, already knowing who I was. He didn't question the story I made up, despite knowing it was all completely fabricated. These two are cunning liars, and I need to get back to Jasper to tell him about these traitors in his supposed Safe Haven.

"Maybe it would, if you listened," June insists, sounding exasperated. "There are people who have a better explanation than we do."

I don't want to hear it. I've heard enough at the store, and even at the diner the day Cole took me to breakfast. The rumor has spread through the down like wild fire, and something tells me June might just be the embers behind it all. Cole too. By the way these two look at each other, they are in some kind of relationship.

Something else my own former best friend has failed to tell me.

"Tonight, there is another meeting. People there will be able to explain it better than we can. Please come," Cole says, sounding a lot calmer than June.

Shaking my head, I take a few more shuddering steps backward. I'm not going anywhere with them.

Instead, I turn around. I need to get to Jasper and tell him everything.

Chapter Forty-One

Jasper *is* reading a book when I get back. As I expected.

He glances up as I walk in, my hands empty of any milk. I assume he sees the lack of colour in my face, as a flutter of worry graces his features. How long have I been gone? June and I had been in conversation for a while, and I had taken the time to listen in on the conversation at the shop.

However, when Jasper finds a good book, I've come to realize, very little is going to disrupt him.

"What's wrong?" He instantly knows from just my expression I have witnessed something terrible. Finally addressing the feelings brewing up inside me, I walk straight to my mate, and collapse into his lap.

I hate myself for being so weak, crying into his shirt; but admittedly, the moment his arms wrap around me I feel protected from everything outside. Including June. Including Cole.

"Talk to me," he insists after a few gruelling moments of me trying to wipe my eyes.

It hurts that she is still here. It hurts that she would lie to me, through our entire childhood. She didn't even question my eye colour. It shows me that, deep down, she doesn't care about me and she never has. It makes me so incredibly mad just thinking about her, and everything she did to me without me even knowing it. She can try to knock Jasper out of his position as Alpha, but she will never succeed.

Not if I can stop it.

"June," I tell him. "She's here."

Jasper exhales, knowing what that means to me. Despite not knowing me for my entire life, he tends to be able to understand my emotions better than I do. It does make me a little suspicious that maybe he is reading my mind, after he promised me he wouldn't.

"Did you talk to her?" He asks softly, waiting a few moments, while I attempt to calm down.

My heart contracts. How I wish I didn't have to talk to her, or even think about her, but Jasper *has* to know about what she and the rest of Safe Haven are planning. If he doesn't put a stop to it, I have no idea what they might do to him. His magic can't control every single one of them... especially as a few of them are just like him.

Including June.

"Have you heard the rumours?" I ask him, tilting my chin up so I can look into those violet eyes. His eyebrows furrow as he shakes his head.

I sigh deeply. "People know you're a Phantom Wolf... Well, they *think* they know. And let me tell you, they don't like it. They are holding meetings at night about who knows what, but something tells me it's not in your favour."

An impassive expression drops like a sheet across his face. Despite the look he gives me, I see the way his jaw clenches slightly, and his eyes have misted over. As an Alpha, hearing your Pack, that you spent centuries building, is planning a rebellion against you is *not* something you want to hear. However, Jasper is not the kind of person to lash out. Instead, he sits there, thinking.

"Maybe if I go, I can..."

"No," Jasper dismisses quickly, standing and helping me do so.

I watch as he paces across the room, toward another one of his book cases. What is he doing? Pulling out a dark-covered book, he flips to a random page, plucks a pen from the middle of it. Watching in wonder, I notice the way he scribbles furiously across the page. That isn't a normal book.

When it comes to Jasper, nothing is normal anymore.

"Jasper," I say airily, placing my hand on his arm to get his attention. He doesn't even glance at me. In the book he writes in, there is a language unknown to me. He seems to understand fluently. It's quite hypnotising, staring at the words that coil easily from his pen, into lengthy symbols and sentences.

I tap his arm a little more firmly. "What is going on?"

"I'm trying to contact Tayten, but she's not picking up the damn book," he mutters irritably, still not bothering to look at me directly.

Right. This whole time travel thing I was wary of when he first explained it has suddenly been brought up again. Despite it seeming totally absurd for him to just simply write in a book for Tayten to see hundreds of years ago, I don't question it. There is no point in trying to figure out the logistics behind it, when it will probably all boil down to magic, and Jasper's uncanny ability to use it.

"Why Tayten?" I question, a fluttering memory of the beautiful woman who had an interest in other women. "You're not going to summon her back here are you?"

Jasper nods absently, still scribbling.

Biting my inner cheek, I squeeze his arm rather roughly, finally getting his attention on me. He looks frazzled, as if he has to meet a deadline, otherwise a major consequence will ensue.

"I can do it. Let me go and find things out," I insist.

He shakes his head. However he slams the book shut with finality. Either he has given up, or she has answered and is on her way right now. A part of me hopes it's not the latter. She intimidates me, and having her back here is only going to make Jasper more insane. I've seen the way those two argue.

"I'm not sending you in there with them," he says, narrowing his eyes at me. "If they find out you're my mate, you're dead."

That much is probably true, but I'm okay with taking the risk.

"They know, but they don't think *I* do. Why not, I have no idea, but I can play it off as if you kidnapped me. June isn't the smartest when it comes to thinking on her feet, so it won't take long to win her trust, especially when she is looking for mine."

Jasper doesn't looked convinced at all.

"I'll just listen, I won't say anything. The moment I get what I need, I'll be back here, and we can sort out a plan afterwards," I say, gathering together an idea as every word comes out of my mouth.

"I can't take that risk," he says, the conflict within him rising to show itself in his eyes. He rakes his hands through his hair distractedly. "I'd hate myself if something happened to you. I might end up killing every single one of them, and we all know that won't sort *anything* out."

My jaw clenches. "You have to let me go. I need to do something—myself."

Jasper turns toward the staircase, shrugging my hand off his arm. My eyes roll at him, as he starts up the stairs.

"I don't need to be caught by you every time I'm in need..."

Jasper doesn't stop as I follow him up the stairs.

"Don't you think I can do things for myself?"

He pushes through into his bedroom. We have been sharing it, so I basically call it mine now. It's styled more to his tastes; dark with a hint of vintage.

"Stop ignoring me. I'm not going to let you keep me locked up in here," I growl, more fiercely than I've done before. He is breathing as heavily as I am. I see it in the way his shoulders tense and move slightly. This is our first disagreement, and I want to punch the stubbornness out of him.

Walking to the window, he rests his hands on the sill.

"I'm sick of people thinking they can oppress me. That they can hold me back," I breathe, tears of hot anger burning in my eyes.

Again, he remains silent. How can he be so calm, and so infuriating at the same time? Why isn't he yelling back at me? Anger is slick in my veins, coating every inch of me in the disgusting feeling. I'm craving an argument based on nothing but emotion, yet he isn't feeding me anything.

"Don't be like Luca," I plead gently, the breeze through the window catching the edge of my words.

Jasper's head turns slightly. I've got his attention, yet I don't know how much I want it suddenly.

247

"I don't want to be hurt again."

The urge to cover my mouth to stop myself from speaking is overwhelming. I can't admit this... I can't burden him with problems from my past that were buried with Luca. This is something I should just forget, yet here I am exposing old wounds to my mate, who at the moment probably couldn't care less.

Yet he surprises me, as he turns slowly, showing me a hard expression. "What did you just say?"

He looks so angry, it hurts.

"I said I don't want to be hurt anymore. I don't think I could handle it," I admit through clenched teeth with salty tears spilling from my eyes.

The words Luca used to throw around so casually echo in my head. If he was here now, he would have called me pathetic and told me to sit in this room until I calm down.

Jasper exhales slowly, almost as if he is trying to hold back the anger I see so prevalent on his features. His eyes flare with it, capturing me so I feel the infliction. He doesn't even bother to use his magic, as if he's let it go through the window he was just standing by.

"What did he do to you?" He asks slowly.

His words, demanding honesty, punch me straight in the heart, with a fist of crisp ice. Had my emotions been intact, I would have shaken my head and changed the subject. Right now, my emotions are bursting, and I can't help what comes flooding from my mouth.

"He hurt me," I say, closing my eyes as I turn around. Grabbing the edge of my shirt, I pull it over my head. I knew where it was, etched in my skin. "On my shoulder."

There is a cruel moment of silence, as I stand there, bare, the breeze touching my skin with its cold breath. I can feel his gaze burning to the incriminating spot right by my spine. He would have seen it before, when he bent me across the bench and made love to me the other day. It took an eye of knowing, though, to see the faint scar.

I startle, as I feel Jasper's finger trace the mark.

"How?" He asks, his voice low and calculated. "Why?"

With eyes still closed, the memory paints itself in my mind. I speak my thoughts aloud as I recall them.

"It was the first time he got angry at me. He burnt me, although called it an accident. At first I believed it, but now I know it was just the start of what was to come over the next four years," I tell him, the words toxic like poison on my tongue. "The beginning of hell."

I cannot tell what Jasper is thinking, or how he is reacting. All I can feel are his fingers, leaving sparks across the scar I hate with my entire being. It isn't about that day, which I've been reminded of too often. It is the idea of how I could have escaped him earlier. For the rest of my life, I will have to deal with it...

"I had no idea," he says softly, turning me around. "I should have read your mind. I should have delved deeper..."

I cut him off, by grabbing his guilt-stained face so I can kiss him. Everything makes sense when his lips press against mine. Luca doesn't matter, and neither does my past. Realizing this doesn't get rid of the memories, but Jasper is like my own personal army, fighting off all the hostilities I once had to deal with.

He kisses me back, but is quick to finish it. Too many question dwell in his mind to pass this off.

"He hit you?"

I nod solemnly.

"He didn't force you to..." his voice trailed off, like it was too painful to even begin to ask. I raise an eyebrow expectantly.

"He didn't force you in his bed, did he?" His eyes darken as he asks. The moment my forehead creases, in a way to expel the memories, I can tell he knows. Either that, or he has looked into my mind to find out for himself.

His jaw clenches, and for a moment, I swear I see something like tears in his eyes.

"I shouldn't have left you with him for so long," he said, cupping my face in his hands. "I should have taken you from him the moment I knew you two were together."

It hurt him to say that. I know it.

"Jasper, it's fine..."

249

"It's not," he corrects me. "It should have been me who killed him. Five years ago, I should have killed him."

"No Jasper," I insist, wishing I could grab his shoulders to shake him. "I had to do it. I'm glad it was me."

Still he doesn't seem to like the idea of that. After I take a seat on the edge of the bed I watch him pace . Clearly, he is having a hard time processing all of this, and I don't blame him for any of it. I shouldn't have burdened him like this. The expression of pain on his face is the *exact* reason I have kept this from him for so long.

"There were so many opportunities I had..." Jasper continues, clutching his hair in his fists. It's getting long now. Do the dead get haircuts?

"I saw you once. You walked past me, but you didn't notice me."

I look up, instantly intrigued. "Sorry?"

When Jasper focuses his eyes on me, they are blazing violet, like nothing I have ever seen before. They burst with colour and vibrancy like tiny bombs are going off in his irises, every time he thinks of something.

"It... It's a long story. All that matters is that you walked past me, and I had all the opportunity in the world to steal you from him, and give you a better life. I didn't take it," he says.

I stand, dismissing all his claims. This is a conversation for another time. Right now, I want him to stop thinking and talking about all his regrets, and instead, start thinking about what is right in front of him. Because if he continues, both of us will go completely insane. More than we already are.

If Jasper is sick of me cutting off him off with kisses, he doesn't protest.

His face is smooth under my fingertips, his chest hard against my own. The contrast in itself gives me a brief feeling of ecstasy that reaches all the way to my toes. His hesitation is there, though, like he wants to pull away again. However, with a slight groan rising from his throat he commits to it.

Kissing him forever doesn't seem bad at all. With him around, eternal life seems like it will be a breeze. His lips are something I can never get sick of.

Slowly, Jasper—his hands around my waist—gently pushes me backwards, until the backs of my knees rest against the edge of the bed. Before I fall onto my back, I twist around Jasper's body, until we have swapped positions. He hardly has space for a single word, once he falls back to take the place on the bed originally meant for me.

I smile down at him, tilting my head slightly.

He looks so stunningly handsome, as he looks up at me, cheeks slightly flushed. I could just pounce on him right now...

I do basically that, as I crawl on top of him, straddling his hips while he lies back against the bed, his head sinking slightly into the feather down duvet. This position appeals to me greatly; it gives me a prime place to gaze upon my mate while being able to control a lot of what he does.

"And what are you doing?" Jasper questions lightly. He quivers slightly, and I can tell he is trying his best to make a move of his own. Instead, he patiently watches me, curious to see what I'm planning to do next.

Honestly, I'm not very sure about it myself.

Trying to make it seem as if I know what I'm doing, I pull the edge of Jasper's shirt up, revealing his toned stomach to my greedy eyes. Why I can't just sit here and stare all day, I don't know. Any second now, Jasper may steal my opportunity to seduce him.

"Something," I reply coyly, testing Jasper's reaction by running a tentative finger across his stomach. His muscles tense in response.

He makes a soft noise in his throat. "I like knowing things."

My finger traces its way across the band of his pants like it has a mind of its own. I'm letting myself follow my instinct; otherwise, I'll lose all the confidence I'm trying to exude.

"That's a shame," I tell him, using both hands to unbutton his pants.

Jasper clenches his jaw, obviously not liking the way I'm playing with him, but honestly, I'm enjoying it. Pulling his pants down a little on his hips, I expose his underwear, which doesn't even begin to hide how clearly turned on he is. Okay, maybe I *am* doing something right.

"I'm going to flip you over soon," he grumbles, glancing down at my insistent fingers. "To fuck you until you can't walk tomorrow."

I ignore his words, grinning up at him while I suddenly grab him through his underwear. He gasps, his eyebrows furrowing as he slightly lifts his hips. He wants this. As much as he hates being teased, he wants me to continue, and I am only too happy to do so. I pull him out of his underwear so I can hold him in my hand.

His eyes flutter closed for a few seconds, as I gently stroke him, feeling him harden further beneath my fingertips. Watching his expression contort from pleasure to pain from my endless teasing is extremely enjoyable.

"Want to flip me over still?" I question, biting my lips slightly, as Jasper shoots me an irritated glance.

Clearly, my simple movements are enough to leave my mate completely at my mercy. Deciding to take it further, I lean down, keeping my eyes strictly on Jasper, who watches me carefully, his breathing short.

The moment my lips touch the tip of his cock, I feel him completely fall at my mercy. The groan that slips from his throat is addictive, letting me know I have no other choice but to keep going. Taking him deeper into my mouth, I run my tongue across his silken flesh, my gratification coming from his obvious enjoyment, as he lifts his hips and moans my name through breathy gasps.

Jasper, however, gives me little time before he interrupts, grabbing my shoulders to pull me back up.

Suddenly I'm pressed against the bed, my clothes pulled off at an impressive rate. My hands do the same, trying to get Jasper's shirt over his head at the same time he is trying to get mine off. At this point, I'm so turned on, all I want is to feel his skin on mine.

Just as he pulls my underwear down my legs, my lips are on his again. With my hands down his back, and his in my hair, I can hardly fathom what is happening. All I know is that I can't get enough of him, and I don't know if I ever will be able to. He must feel the same way, as suddenly, he rolls over. Once again I'm on top of him.

I look down at him. We are both completely naked.

"I think I could be like this with you forever," I murmur, admiring the way the sun drags its gentle finger across his face, bringing out his most attractive features.

Jasper smiles slightly, his hands tracing my hip bone.

"Well, it can be."

I nod in agreement, hardly able to contain the feeling of excitement that digs its way into my stomach. With that, I position myself above him, so I can sink down on him before he can say another word.

At the feeling of Jasper inside me I nearly lose all ability to keep myself from collapsing. If it weren't for his hands on my hips, all stability I need to move on him would be lost, and I would be lying on his chest with my breath completely expelled from my body.

Jasper thrusts up under me, taking control so I won't have to. My body is alight with heat.

I rest my hands against his chest, feeling every inch of him inside, and his pace increases. If he speeds up any further, I may faint, yet when he does, still holding my hips, I manage to survive, moaning his name uncontrollably.

"Don't stop," I find myself saying, with a slur of other incoherent words.

My limbs have completely lost control of themselves, as I reach my climax, almost screaming Jasper's name to the point where the whole of Safe Haven would have heard. My fingernails dig dangerously into Jasper's chest, to the point of nearly drawing blood.

Jasper follows, his head tilting back, with his eyes closed as my name dances on his lips.

Gasping, I fall beside him, my vision still spinning colours. How can I explain to him how amazing that felt. I can't say a word, as he brushes a stray piece of hair from my face.

"Sleep, baby," Jasper says gently, and I nod, sinking into the warm sheets. He follows me afterwards, resting his head on the pillow.

Jasper falls asleep quickly, while I stay awake, mulling over ideas. I can't sleep when I'm thinking too much, despite what we've just done taking all my energy. My nerves have me fidget, sitting up in bed while I watch my mate sleep like an angel.

Am I really going to do this? Go to this meeting to learn what they are planning to do to Jasper?

Jasper looks peaceful beside me, despite telling me he doesn't need sleep. Neither do I, but I know I would rather be sleeping beside him than awake and twiddling my thumbs.

Except for this night, I have something to do.

Slowly, I pull the covers back. It takes me a few seconds to dress appropriately, making sure I keep my steps light to not wake Jasper. I *have* to do this. I'll beat myself up for the rest of my eternal life if I don't at least try.

This life even is my only possibly chance...

Glancing back at my mate, I clench my jaw, before turning toward the door.

"I love you, Jasper. I'll be back. I'll save your Pack."

Chapter Forty-Two

It doesn't take me long to find out where they are holding their meeting. Just down the street, a single building is brightly lit, illuminating the street outside. I make a beeline for it, glad the streets are empty of people.

The air is chilly. It matches this entire situation I'm stuck in.

I know I don't have to do this; however, to me I have no other choice. This is for Jasper. This is for all the things he has done for me, that I haven't yet found a way to repay. Him saving me from Luca is enough to sacrifice myself, but what about the rest? Sure, he knew I was his mate, but he gave up so much for me, and took surprisingly good care of me.

A loud chatter arises from the Town Hall as I walk closer.

How am I going to go about this? Am I going to just walk in, or should I loiter under a window or something, to hear what they are talking about?

The place lacks any kind of window, disappointingly enough. The main doors are open. Are they trying to make it any more obvious to Jasper what's going on? Had he not been so distracted with me, I'm sure he would have figured out their schemes and put an end to them.

I decide I have no other choice but to walk through the main doors.

The entire situation reminds me of the meetings we had back in the Devotion Pack. A few people sit on the stage, talking to a large crowd of people sitting before them. They all listen intently to what the man at the front says.

I recognise him as Cole.

My heart stops for a moment. Had he been a part of this when I first met him? Of course he had... both he and June. I hate them for it.

I sidle behind the seats, trying to be as quiet as possible. Hopefully shadows will keep me hidden from Cole, who talks proudly over everyone. My eyes scan the crowd for June, but I can't see her anywhere. She is part of this as much as Cole is, so she *has* to be here.

"This is what we have been waiting for," Cole proclaims, his voice sounding strained. "Why am I still convincing people, when we have all the evidence right here?"

No wonder. Is his plan not going as well as he thought?

A murmur rises again, as people discuss what he has just said. I see his evidence on show. Pictures of Jasper doing rather mediocre things are taped to the wall behind Cole. Some of him in his own property, which surely is illegal. To add to that are sheets with words and pictures on them relating to Phantom Wolves.

I know how we are depicted. Cruel, evil... yet June is one of them. Does Cole know? Or is she keeping that from him as I'm keeping it from her?

"You can't sit here, and tell me you want to be ruled by a Phantom himself. The *exact* creatures behind the death of thousands and our move here. He is playing us, people. Why can't you see that?" Cole questions.

Under this light, he looks extremely passionate about this.

"What if there is something bigger behind all this? Those savages are out there, and they are going to invade this place, and kill us all, if we don't stop Alpha Jasper right *now*," he continues.

This time, he gets a positive response. People start shouting *'yeah'* in support. He is getting them riled up, so they will all agree with him. Mob mentality at its finest. What would Jasper do if he saw this? Right now, I'm finding it hard to keep still and not say anything.

"We *need* to revolt!" He says.

A few people stand, the cheers getting louder.

"We *need* to show him we don't need him!"

More people stand, and the sound in here almost becomes borderline deafening.

"We will lead ourselves! We will kill every Phantom to exist! And we will survive, *without* him!"

At that moment, Cole meets my gaze. His heated, passionate stare sears holes in my terrified eyes. Instantly, he looks furious I am here, since he believes I am Jasper's cousin. He knows I will go back to him to report everything I have just witnessed.

The moment he makes a move toward me, I turn to run straight out the door.

The cool air outside is a slap in the face. No way am I going to stop running though. My sneakered feet lead me onto the footpath, however they stop when I hear Cole yelling behind me.

"Thea! Thea wait..."

"Don't talk to me," I growl, taking steps back to equal his approach. "Don't even come near me."

He pauses on the grass. I wish I could properly see his eyes right now, but the night shrouds him. Moonlight outlines him, allowing me to see enough to keep away from him. Jasper's home is close enough to reach in a straight run. He will wake up the moment I scream for him, and Cole knows that.

"You can't tell me honestly that he isn't a Phantom Wolf... We all know it!"

I shake my head at him in disbelief, although he probably doesn't see it. "So what? Has he not helped you? Has he not been the Alpha you have needed? He won't hurt you... Not all the Phantoms are evil."

His expression is invisible in the darkness, yet I know he is doubtful.

"My family were killed by Phantoms. I'm not about to be trapped by yet another," he tells me, his voice softening. My jaw clenches slightly. I can't tell if I feel sympathy, or irritation toward his stubbornness. I hardly know him, but I would never kill him.

And I'm a Phantom Wolf now.

"You can't keep thinking like this. You need to learn, and teach the rest that not all Phantoms are bad; that the good guys want nothing more than the bad guys to lose," I tell him directly, trying to get him to understand where I'm coming from.

But it's like talking to a brick wall. "I can't trust him and his lies."

I take more steps back, wishing Jasper was here right now. There is no way I regret coming out here, but if Jasper was here, this would be a lot easier.

"I'm sorry Cole, but I have to tell Jasper. As an Alpha, he needs to stop this," I tell him.

He doesn't follow me, as I turn and run down the street.

***

I have to shake Jasper to wake him.

Blearily, he opens his eyes, staring at me with a blank look while he wakes up, still not completely grasping the situation. After a few blinks, concern flutters across every ounce of his features, and he sits up.

For a moment I want to chuckle at the look of him. His hair sticks up in odd places, he's completely naked, with the blanket only covering part of his lower legs, and his eyes are wider than a deer caught in headlights.

"What's going on? Why aren't you in bed with me?" He questions, still looking a little lost.

His eyes cast down to what I'm wearing, and when he discovers it's clothes, which I lacked last time he saw me, he becomes fully alert. He doesn't even bother to cover himself, as he stands, still fully naked.

"Thea..." he growls, when I don't answer. "What have you done?"

I cast my eyes down to the floor. "Could you at least but some clothes on for this conversation?"

I find myself glancing at his crotch for a split second, before I look back into Jasper's eyes. Safer territory. He doesn't look bothered by the fact that *I'm* bothered by his bareness. To him, my clothes are probably the bigger deal.

"Not until you answer my question."

I swallow. "I went to the town meeting. I found out who is in control of it all."

Jasper's jaw clenches, his eyes narrowing. He looks like he wants to turn and punch the wall beside him. But he stays calm, takes a deep breath. His anger is something he likes to bury, but I know how he feels about this. I know he didn't want me to walk out there and potentially put myself in danger.

"You did what?" He pronounces it carefully, every syllable, as if he might explode at any second if he didn't.

"Cole is behind it all. Along with others. They know you're a Phantom..."

Jasper remains silent throughout my explanation of all events. His brooding gaze presses me into giving every detail, including every word I said, that I can remember. When I finish, I watch his eye twitch under the fringe of dark hair mussed across his forehead.

"I can't believe you did this. I was going to leave you alone for a few days, but now I don't think I can," he says, making me narrow my eyes.

I am not about to be treated like a child.

"Where are you going?"

Jasper sighs. Why didn't he tell me before that he was going away? Something in his expression says he is leaving very soon. Without me.

Well... that's debatable.

"The Alpha meeting. Each Alpha attends every month. It's essential I go," Jasper says, yet I can see his distaste toward it.

I know he doesn't like every Alpha, so I can imagine what it is like to spend a few days with them. Would he actually take me along to something like that? The Alphas I have met have been a lot to handle—I might lose my mind being around any more of them. I have to knot my fingers together to stop them from quivering.

"I don't think I could handle going with you. I'll be fine here."

"With Cole? I can't do anything until I come back. If I leave you here, who knows what would happen," Jasper says softly, biting the edge of his lip as he thinks.

I sigh, deeply.

"I trust you Thea. I know you can look after yourself, and I know you can make your own decisions," Jasper murmurs honestly. "But for my own peace of mind, would you come with me?"

I stare at him for a moment. As much as Alphas intimidate me, being with my mate is not a bad thing; especially since he hasn't marked me yet. Suddenly having an option makes it more enticing too.

Walking up to Jasper, I fall into his waiting arms.

"Okay, I'll come with you," I tell him, despite my mind telling me meeting more Alphas is something I could go without. Still, I'm curious to see how this meeting thing works, if I'm even allowed close. Jasper is the oldest Alpha, I'm sure he can decide what happens.

Jasper strokes my hair gently, and I bask in the feeling. My hips stick back slightly, trying to avoid his distractingly bare crotch area.

When I glance up, Jasper is looking down at me.

"No talking to any of the other males while we are there, though," Jasper warns playfully. "I don't trust a few of them with you."

I hold back an eye roll. "Yes sir."

He kisses my forehead, grateful for my compliance.

"When do we leave?"

"Today," Jasper said. "But shall we sleep first?"

260

Chapter Forty-Three

The Alpha meeting is to be held near the border of the equator, which separates the warmer Packs from the colder.

We aren't too far from the border, though it still takes us over 13 hours to drive. Jasper asks if I want him to use his power of time manipulation, but I refuse. It isn't fair for him to sit for so long driving alone, so instead, we talk during the drive, keeping each other company.

"I don't think you can come to the actual meeting," Jasper says, just after announcing we only have another half hour's drive. "Which is probably for the best."

Jasper explains how this is going to go. We're staying in a facility created just for the Alphas. I will stay in our room most of the time, so I won't get in any of the Alpha's way. It was my decision.

Alphas intimidate me.

"As long as I'm safe, right?" I say, not meaning it to sound as snappy as it has. Jasper nods grimly.

"Yes, as long as you're safe."

I've never been close to the equator before. The weather here is dull, with little breeze and an almost desert-like expanse stretching as far as I can see. Driving down the straight road is unnerving, especially seeing the building where we will be staying on the horizon.

Suddenly, I feel Jasper's warm hand on my thigh. "Don't stress. I know you'll be fine."

I really hope so. If anything goes wrong, I don't know what I will do. I will know Alpha Malik, Asher and Kaden, but I'm still wary of them. Especially Kaden. What I know about him is very little, and I haven't seen him since he saved me from Luca. Will he care about that, if we do meet again during this three-day trip?

"I know," I say softly. "I just hope I can see as little of them as possible," I tell him honestly, tapping my fingers against my thighs anxiously.

The facility really is magnificent. It was built many years ago, probably when Jasper was young. The design of the entire place has not been touched, still vintage in taste and style. Mainly it has been constructed of colored red bricks of various shades, sweeping up into massive glass panels that reveal nothing beyond. The place is lit brilliantly, and I can't keep my mouth closed as we drive closer.

"Every month, huh," I say, still mesmerised by what I am looking at.

Obviously, the Alphas are supplied with absolute luxury. The way they light this place makes it look like a melting pot of gold. Its size is so large the whole first quarter would take me at least two weeks to fully explore.

And this place is supposed to be for just business meetings.

Jasper takes a sudden turn right, veering away from the entrance of the building. Instead of going through the main gate, he heads around the back on a smooth cut road. Jasper only smiles coyly, not answering my questioning gaze. Everything was suddenly drenched in darkness as we turned and drove straight under the building, Jasper is driving confidently despite not being able to see a thing.

"Jasper..." I say warily, then suddenly light hits, and we are in an underground parking lot.

My mate grins as he noses into a parking space. No other cars are parked in here, which leaves me wondering if anyone else is actually here, or whether they came in a front way.

"Come on," Jasper says, opening his car door to step out. I follow suit, my shoes on the concrete making a loud noise. "I'm not used to having anyone with me. Maybe this won't be so dull."

I don't think I am ready for this.

We take a flight of stairs up to the main level of the building, which forces us through a few combining rooms till we make it to the point Jasper seemed to be heading to. Really, it has made for quite a trip through short hallways dressed in beautiful rich wallpaper the color of royal blue, until we emerge into an expansive room that steals my breath away.

It's clearly a foyer of some sort, with a roof higher than one I have ever seen. It lacks a magnificent chandelier like Asher's, however, the ceiling is carved with intricate patterns that must have some meaning. Light cast from massive windows that eat up an entire wall illuminate the marble floor that is, surely, worth more I could ever earn at the diner in 40 years.

Yet, that isn't what I notice the most. It is the people.

"You told me..." I growl under breath, as Jasper leads me toward a small cluster of them. "... I wouldn't have to meet any of the Alphas."

Jasper doesn't say a word until we are standing at the outer edge of the circle. The three who stand there, all males, step back. Alphas. Most girls aren't supposed to even be in the near vicinity of an Alpha, let alone four of them. I just hope my cheeks aren't bright red.

The first one who strikes me is the Alpha directly in front of me. It isn't that I know he is an Alpha, it is that he simply carries himself as one. His shoulders are broad, his physique something many would swoon over. It is his eyes.

He stares down at me with a pair of eyes I have never encountered before. Sure, I've heard of people with dual-colored eyes, but seeing them in person is a completely different experience. His left eye is bright blue, like a turquoise crystal trapped in his iris. His other is a stunning evergreen color.

"Ren," Jasper says gently, extending his hand to the Alpha. "Good to see you again."

The man nods, raising an eyebrow at Jasper. What Pack could this Alpha be in command of? Never once have I seen him before, so my curiosity is heightened.

"Thank you. I feel the same. I see you brought your mate along with you."

"Indeed. Thea, meet Ren, the Alpha of Loyalty," Jasper introduces. My heart skips a beat as I hear his position, which I should have known. He extends his hand to me, and I shake it, hoping my smile isn't too awkward. Why am I noticing how warm his hand is?

"I'm Malik, nice to meet you," the Alpha of Love pipes in from beside me.

Despite knowing exactly who Malik is, I shake his hand as if this is our first meeting. Perhaps I should thank him for contributing to my death in that bathtub. His easy smile doesn't even begin to hint at it though, as he lets go of my hand to shake Jasper's.

"And this is Noah, the Alpha of Harmony," Jasper adds, taking my attention from Malik. The Alpha I look at looks familiar, from television. All the girls in the Devotion Pack used to swoon over his easy smile and enchanting eyes. Green doesn't even begin to cover the color of them. Nothing natural in life looks *that* green. Alpha genes can be extravagant, which explains all the strange-colored eyes in the room.

However, Jasper's take the award for the nicest to look at.

I'm left standing there while the three males talk among themselves. None of them pay too much attention to me, as they discuss topics that go straight over my head. The month they weren't here obviously has been busy for them all, since they don't stop talking for over 15 minutes.

I glance over my shoulder, looking at some of the other Alphas in the room with us. A few are arriving late, while others mill around.

Kaden is here, whispering to an Alpha I don't recognize. Is that the Alpha of Discipline?

Asher is here too. However when I meet his gaze he looks away to those he was talking with—the Alphas of Passion and Wisdom. Such a strange group to be talking. They all make me feel so out of my element, as I am the only female here. I'm also the only one who isn't an Alpha, aside from the guards posted at each door.

Something tells me they would be able to look after themselves if something happened.

"Come," Jasper suddenly whispers in my ear, grabbing my arm. Admittedly I jump slightly, after closely observing everyone else in the foyer. "I'm going to take you back to our room."

Our bags remain in the car after Jasper promises someone will get them for us. It worries me that someone would be handling my personal items, but it's not like I have anything valuable in there anyway. So, still holding Jasper's hand, I walk with him to the first staircase.

It leads up onto a dark blue-carpeted landing, where we spend less than five seconds before Jasper leads me down a corridor to our room. Apparently, it is rather close to the other Alphas' rooms, which gives me something else to think about while I try to sleep tonight.

"This is nice," I comment, walking into our room.

It is rather simple. Jasper clearly hasn't bothered to furnish it while he has been here all those times. The wallpaper is a dark, rich color of red that stretches around the room, and has even influenced the color of our bedsheets. Immediately I walk to the glass door that opens onto a small balcony. Not much to see from it, though.

"No books?" I question.

Jasper shrugs. "They have a library here."

I take a few steps toward my mate, slinging my arms over his shoulders. Just seeing Jasper smile down at me makes me unbelievably happy, as if all the drama going on back at Safe Haven doesn't exist.

The moment his lips touch mine, I feel an immense feeling of bliss. Even all the Alphas downstairs don't exist. They don't matter to us.

"What are you going to do now?" I ask, feeling him kiss my neck softly. My hands tangle in his hair, feeling the silken strands slip between my fingers. All I want to is hold him hostage here in this room for the next three days, so neither of us have to be near any of those Alphas. In my opinion, he is the only Alpha who is normal.

He shrugs. "We have a dinner tonight. I want you to come."

"What happened to me staying secured in this room the entire time? I don't remember it being mentioned that I would be flaunted in front of most of them," I comment sourly, making Jasper chuckle slightly.

Of course, he gets a kick out of it.

"I'm sure they are all interested that I brought my mate. I can tell by the expressions on their faces. I like making them jealous. I have a very beautiful mate."

Grabbing his face, I kiss him, stopping him from saying any more words that might make me pin him to the bed.

Chapter Forty-Four

It gets boring sitting in our room without Jasper. *Extremely* boring.

Jasper has told me something about a garden he will take me to see tonight, once he gets back from his meeting in a few hours. Honestly, I don't think I'll be able to sit here any longer without doing something dreadful.

A part of me wants to leave the room and mess around with some of my magic. I know it's stupid, but I'm curious to see what I am capable of compared to Jasper. All I know for certain is, he has been keeping a damper on it, But if I can find some open space, or some plant-like test subjects, I might be able to try out a little .

The idea is stupid, but it's rooted in my consciousness; I can't get it out of my head.

I try braiding my hair to keep my fingers busy, but that gets old after a while. Next I make the bed, then unmake it. I walk through the balcony door and back in again. I even try staring at the wall. But my wicked mind keeps coming back to one conclusion...

I can't stay in this room a second longer.

Jasper didn't bother to lock the door when he left, which is a relief. I wouldn't have let him anyway.

Luckily I remember enough of the way I came to make it downstairs to the foyer again The vast space is completely empty, with all Alphas at their meeting, which Jasper has told me is at the other end of the building. I'm glad I got that much information out of him.

Opening the front doors that are taller than two of me put together, I walk outside. It's quite beautiful out here, despite the unfamiliar weather that makes my skin tingle.

The driveway Jasper decided not to follow would have lead us to a parking area out front on the gravel. To the right of it is a bright green, well-trimmed hedge with a wrought iron gate in the middle of it, that I assume will lead me to the garden.

Biting the edge of my lip, I walk toward the gate, doubting every step I take.

On the other side of the hedge is an entire expanse of lawn, with a smooth path cutting through it toward yet another hedge. Is the garden on the other side of that? Or am I being lead off to somewhere that will get me completely lost?

Oh, I'm sure Jasper is going to love rescuing me from my own curiosity, that has got me into trouble many times in the past.

The garden turns out to be one of the most beautiful things I have ever seen. It stretches out into the depths of a cluster of trees I hadn't seen over the hedge. Tall grass and vines brush my legs as I close the gate behind me. Looking at all the impeccably bright and flourishing flowers blooming under the shadows of the trees makes me feel inexpicably happy.

I just want to explore.

My fingers brush over the foliage as I walk a little deeper into the garden, feeling the sense of life in everything I pass by.

I follow the wall, which probably is a mistake. Because as I walk further, I find myself having one of the biggest surprises of my life. A man sits, casually, atop the wall, as if the fall from it wouldn't break his legs.

He looks down at me, a gleeful smile etched across his rather intriguing features. That doesn't include his eyes, which don't have any white anywhere. Instead, I'm staring into a palette of darkness, that is completely soulless. He would be frightening, if it weren't for his cobalt blue hair, long and scruffy atop his head.

"What in the world...?" I hear myself.

The man tilts his head. "I've actually been compared to death. People say I only visit with bad news."

His accent has no specific familiarity to it, while at the same time, it seems like a combinination of each Pack entwined. He doesn't look like something from this planet, and I consider for a second whether or not I've inhaled something on the way into this garden that's making me delirious.

"Who are you?" I ask warily, taking a tentative step backwards.

I watch as the strange being taps the backs of his heels against the wall, while he continues to smile at me. Could he be more unnerving? I feel as if he might jump at me if I turn my back on him.

"Do you believe in the Moon Goddess?" He asks, bringing his hand up to inspect his nails.

"I don't believe in anything," I tell him honestly.

He eyes me carefully, as if I've said something incriminating to my stalker. It's true though. All my life I have tossed between believing in Fate and the Goddess. Really, I'm indifferent.

Suddenly, the man jumps off the wall, landing on the ground right beside me. A normal person would have broken their ankles, whereas he seems unharmed. All that really happened was that he slightly crinkled the bright blue shirt he had loosely hung over his dark trousers.

"That's no fun," he says gruffly. "You're taking it all out of this."

I'm as curious about this man as I am scared. Okay, maybe a little terrified. I sidle closer to the edge of the woods area, wondering whether or not I should turn and run from him.

"I'm Fate, by the way," he says casually, holding his hand out to me.

I stare at it blankly.

As strange as it sounds, I somehow believe him. How could I not? Out of all the strange things that have happened to me in the past month, this might just be another normal bomb being dropped. Just looking at him, and the slight mystical aura that surrounds him, confirms it. This is destiny. He is the one entity on this earth that controls what steps I may take next.

As much as I've heard he respects free will, he seems a little overbearing. I suppose it's like trusting Jasper with not reading my mind.

I just have to hope Fate isn't controlling me.

"Right," I say.

He narrows his eyes at me, titling his head in the special way he does. "Right?"

I nod. "Yeah."

He pauses for a second, then furrows his dark eyebrows. It's rather disappointing they aren't the same color as his hair. Was he born with that specific shade of hair? Now I think about it, I don't know much about Fate.

"No retaliation?"

"Why, do you want there to be?" I ask.

He shakes his head. "Interesting."

"Listen, I don't have very much time. I actually have a few things to do..."

"I know," Fate mutters irritably, tapping a slender finger against his lips as he thinks. Of course he knows. He's Fate. Doesn't he know everything?

I glance over my shoulder. "So, why me?"

"Huh?"

"Why me? Why did you come here for me?" I question.

He says himself that he comes bearing bad news, which is what I'm most apprehensive about. Have I done something bad that will require him to take me back to whatever hole he dwells in? I can't imagine anything *that* bad...

"Well," he says, clapping his hands together so loudly the sound ripples through the garden. "I'm inclined to believe your mate struck a deal with me. I'm here to let you remind him of his obligations."

My blood runs cold.

"His obligations?" I say nervously. "Please explain."

Fate walks around me for a moment, watching me, while I keep my slightly blurring eyes trained on the tree in front of me. If Fate means every word he says—but I don't think he would bother lying—then Jasper may have dug us both a hole that's impossible to climb out of.

"Around 20 years ago, Jasper came to me, ready to strike a deal," Fate tells me carefully, every word like a heavy bag of anxiety being placed on my shoulders.

Fate comes to a standstill in front of me. "He told me he was sick of waiting for his mate. He wanted me to find a place for you in time, so he could be with you."

My jaw may have fallen open, but I can hardly feel any movement; a numbness is spreading through my veins.

"He agreed he would pay me back somehow, although it was never really specified how. I found a place for you within a circumstance. From there, things blossomed as they needed to, and now that you two are rather happy, I want my pay," Fate tells me.

Jasper can't have been stupid enough...

Fate? He is the last possible person in this land who I would ever make a deal with. As much as I am flattered Jasper wanted to meet me earlier than he was supposed to, I want to smack him for making an impulsive decision.

"This can't be," I say breathlessly, wondering why my lungs are doing such a terrible job. "What could you possible want from Jasper?"

Fate smiles, straight, glinting white teeth showing themselves behind his lips. The look has me shivering.

"Well. I'm sure his Pack would suffice," Fate says softly, raising an eyebrow at my mortified expression. "Or perhaps, something even more valuable than that to him."

I close my eyes.

"Perhaps you, Thea. Perhaps I may have a place for you in my palace. If your mate accepts, then our deal will be over, and I will never interfere with your life again," Fate says keenly.

I grit my teeth together to the point of pain. Is he even a *real thing* to touch, or will my hand fall right through him? I still understand so little about him, and I have no interest in learning. Jasper would never let me go anyway. I can't be more grateful for that.

"That's too much to sacrifice," I tell Fate, trying to figure out if getting on my knees would be enough.

He shakes his head at me. "I don't know if he has a choice."

Chapter Forty-Five

Fate is behind me as I run.

I'm not sticking around any longer to argue with him. I need to find Jasper to tell him about the ridiculous things Fate has told me, especially about the deal Jasper has struck.

I can't tell if I'm hurt or honored he decided to make such a decision that could potentially jeopardise his Pack.

I don't make it very far before I am stopped again, this time, by a woman. She is gazing at a flower near the gate, touching it with the tips of her fingers. Instantly I pause in the middle of the path, watching her, curiously.

What strikes me first about her appearance is her sleek white hair. It reaches her waist, shining softly under the setting sun. She wears a lilac-colored dress that reaches her knees, and her feet are bare. For whatever reason, I hadn't noticed the way she sung to the plant, but now I do, her voice is like the sweetest honey.

To my surprise, the flower goes from a pale white to a soft blue color, that doesn't belong on those petals. The color is mesmerising, but I am more enchanted by her singing.

She plucks the flower off by its stem, and turns to me.

Her eyes wound me for a moment. Almost the exact color of the garden around us, the lush, vibrant green of her irises aren't like anything I've seen. They remind me of Alpha Noah's of the Harmony Pack; however hers are darker, as if to match the native life around her.

Wordlessly, she walks forward, pulling my hair back to tuck the flower behind my ear. Her smile is warm, as she stands back to look over me.

"Beautiful," she whispers.

I'm too stunned to speak for a moment. There is a part of me unsure of her, while another part doesn't want to ever be away from her. She seems to exude kindness, yet I can't help but be wary.

"Faye," she says, stealing the silence as she puts out her hand. "Alpha of Independence."

Of course, I should have seen it. I've heard little of the Independence Pack. I know they live a simple life in the mountains away from other Packs. The fact she is here shouldn't surprise me but it does. It's not often she leaves her Pack.

"Thea," I reply, shaking her small hand. "Ah, Luna of Devotion? Is that a thing?"

"Of course. Lovely to meet Jasper's mate, finally," she says, her eyes alight. Just hearing her say that about me being Jasper's mate makes me feel important, even though I'm not, really.

My finger reaches up to touch the flower in my hair. "How did you do this? Change its colour?"

Faye tilts her head, looking at the flower. Does she have a permanent sweet smile on her face? If so, I'm very jealous, as it suits her so well. Honestly, she is one of the most beautiful females I've ever seen. Then again, she's an Alpha, so it comes naturally.

"People often forget plants are living too. A single note sung can make them do whatever you please," she says slightly, tipping her hand down to touch a vine. Slowly, it curls up around her wrist. "Or sometimes, all it takes is a touch of understanding."

Something tells me I wouldn't be able to pull that off.

"Have you seen Jasper recently?" I decide to ask, anxious to tell him about my meeting with Fate.

Faye's forehead creases. "I'm not sure, probably in the meeting, or his room. I left a little early. I'm not used to being around so many males for so long, and let me tell you, they are insufferable."

I've decided I really like Faye. Something about her is so easy, and so *real*.

"I should probably go find him, if he's made it back to our room," I tell her, hoping Fate hasn't followed me. "He might be worried about me, or something."

Faye exhales softly, and nods. She looks reluctant to let me go, as if she's enjoying my company as much as I've enjoyed hers. For an Alpha, she seems good at listening, instead of jumping to conclusions and letting her head lead the way. She's very sensible, and I like that about her. Too bad she lives all the way across the land in the mountains, which are nearly inaccessible.

"You're very lucky to have your mate. I hope one day, I'll find love as you have," she says gently.

I see the forlorn look in her eyes, and find myself feeling sorry for her. Despite her beauty and incredible ability with plants, she doesn't have her mate. It is something I never thought I would ever get, but now I have it, I don't want it any other way.

Walking back to our room, I have time to think about Faye. Her Pack isn't very mate-orientated, so I can see why she looks saddened at the thought of it. Maybe she thinks she will never find him, as I once thought.

Jasper is sitting on the bed when I open the door.

"Where were you? I thought I told you to stay in this room," he says, his voice quivering slightly. Clearly, he has been worried.

I paint a smile across my features. "I've just been talking to the Alpha of Independence. She's lovely."

Jasper visibly relaxes, knowing Faye as I do. Kind, gentle and sweet. I can't get up to much trouble with Faye. But I can with Fate.

"However," I say. Jasper narrows his eyes. "I also was paid a visit by Fate."

Almost instantly, Jasper shakes his head, his jaw tightening. He knows more about Fate than I do, that's for sure. What I learned about him from June is that he is a very manipulative creature who does a lot for entertainment. I can imagine how living for as long as he has can get rather boring.

"He told you about our deal, didn't he?" Jasper guesses, slumping back on the bed. I sit beside him, taking a deep breath.

"Yeah. He told me he expects his payment soon. Apparently he wants your Pack, which is completely..."

Jasper holds his hand up, and I pause. I know that expression. He has an idea, and I'm wondering if I should be worried or not. If Jasper is stupid enough to make a deal with Fate in the first place, I can imagine how his payment is going to go.

I just have to hope he's not going to give me away, as if he's done with me. We haven't been together for that long.

Suddenly, Jasper's phone rings.

I watch him from the bed, as he stands and walks around the room, his phone to his ear. A look of concentration covers his face, as I hear a female voice wafting from his phone, the words incoherent. She speaks for quite some time, while Jasper stares out the window, eyes blazing bright violet.

I pluck Faye's flower of from my hair, and twirl it between my fingers.

"I'll come back. I have to," Jasper murmurs to the person on the phone. Then, he hangs up, giving me his full attention.

Coming forward, he kneels in front of me.

"I'm going home to Safe Haven," he says, his expression etched in worry. I swallow nervously, knowing immediately something isn't right. Especially not with Safe Haven being so on edge about Jasper right now.

I brush a hair back from his forehead. "Why?"

"Tayten called. They have burnt down my house. I have to go back and settle things down, before something terrible happens," Jasper says, and my heart drops.

Was this Cole and June's doing? Why would they do that to all his belongings, his books, his everything? He must be devastated right now, but he's not showing it. If my mate is anything, he will be brave for me. I just can't help hating June so much more now. She deserves a life in a Discipline Pack prison.

"That's fine. I didn't bring much with me..."

"No," Jasper says, cutting me off. "You must stay here, where it is safe. You can practice your magic with Faye, and I will come collect you in two days."

Instantly I shake my head, my blood running cold. No, I can't be away from Jasper. He hasn't marked me yet, and he expects me to stay here with a bunch of Alphas who don't know who I am? I'm nervous around Jasper sometimes, so I can't even begin to deal with this situation.

"I know, I don't want to leave you here either, but these Alphas can look after you. I can safely say nothing will happen to you when they are around," Jasper says, and I believe him. No one would try anything with an Alpha.

"You know what..." I nod. "You're right. You're an Alpha and that's your priority. And I'll see you in two days."

Jasper smiles slightly, leaning forward to leave a chaste kiss on my lips. I want to grab him and drag him into bed, to pin him and keep him here forever, but instead I let him back up and walk out the door.

For a moment, I'm reeling from what June and Cole have done.

The sun is setting and darkness is creeping in with dark shadow-like fingers through the glass doors that lead to the balcony. I should probably get dinner, but I don't think I could stomach anything right now.

Walking out the doors, I stand motionless on the balcony. The warm air wraps around me, as I rest my hands against the railing.

Someone clears their throat from the balcony beside mine.

The Alpha of Purity, Rylan, sits casually on the railing, one inch from falling straight to his death. He doesn't look fazed at all as he watches me carefully, the stem of his glass of sparkling water balanced on his fingers. The setting sun casts subtle orange hues across his dark hair, the shadows darkening his already beautiful features.

Rylan and I have not talked before, but I know he is knowledgeable. Jasper told me about the issues he has with his unruly mate, and how he has spent the past year trying to find her after she ran away.

And I think I have problems. This poor guy.

"Jasper has a lot to deal with," he murmurs, his voice nearly being carried away with the breeze. "Don't be sad."

I swallow, brushing my hair from my face. How can I not be? He's my mate, and he's gone to deal with his unruly Pack. I want to be with him through this, but I know I would simply get in his way.

"His Pack did him wrong, after he did so much for them," I say, wondering if I'm talking to myself or to Rylan.

He sighs. "Sometimes leaving the problem alone is the best remedy. Sometimes we think there is a complicated answer to a simple question, but really it's the other way around. And maybe, doing something to help your enemies is the best thing."

I have no idea what he is talking about, until I really think about it.

"So you're saying, Jasper should leave the problem? And... the answer is simple?" I repeat, trying to make more sense of it.

Rylan shrugs, taking a sip of his water. "All I'm saying is, Jasper needs to make a decision. One he may not like, although I'm sure Fate will."

I watch as he turns, walking back into his room.

I can't believe I just talked to the Alpha of Purity.

Staring out at the desert land in front of me, I try to think about what Rylan had been saying. Jasper clearly has to make some decision on how Fate is going to be repaid. But one he may not like?

Then it hits me. Safe Haven. He has to give it up. If Fate takes over Jasper's creation, he will be able to control them, and Jasper can go back to ruling the Devotion Pack. Suddenly, my idea is growing in my mind.

My hands tighten on the railing. Rylan is an absolute genius. Goodbye Safe Haven.

I just have to convince Jasper.

Chapter Forty-Six

The next two days are strange.

I spend a lot of time too scared to venture out anywhere, but at the same time, I have enjoyed the time I've had to wander the garden. Most of the time Faye has been with me, however, tonight I'm going on my own.

Dinner was a little too much for me. The Alphas talk like old friends, which they are, yet I feel I don't belong. I want to play around with my magic anyway, before Jasper comes to collect me tomorrow morning.

The Moon casts down splinters of lustrous gold that collect at my feet as I walk. Without them, I would be blind.

The garden gate whines as I pull it open, shuddering closed after me. The Alphas are inside partying before they go home tomorrow. Faye has told me many things have been resolved in the meetings this month, and apparently, they have been some of the most successful. Of course, I'm not allowed to know what is going on with any other Pack than the one I am the Luna of.

Some don't even count it, as Jasper hasn't yet marked me.

The garden is a perfect canvas for me to practice on. The deep greens gleaming under the moonlight are like the subtle sweeps of a paintbrush against the shadows of the rest of the woodlands. If I wasn't afraid of what may lurk there, I would have explored.

Mainly, I'm afraid of Fate being there.

I glance down at my palms. Faye has taught me what she knows about magic, which is little, but the basics is all I have to know. There is no way I will ever be able to replicate her beautiful voice to make plants grow or anything, but apparently my touch works just fine.

Her words echo in the back of my head. *Clear your mind. Think about what you are touching, and the stem of life within it. Don't command it, teach it.*

It took me four hours to get a little response from a daisy by my feet yesterday.

Faye says frustration is a mask, but when I feel it, I want to give up. Now, as I kneel to the ground in front of a small yellow flower, glowing brightly under the light, I'm sure I'll be able to do it. If I can't, then how am I supposed to ever be able to perfect magic? Jasper himself has told me it's difficult, which doesn't make me any more confident.

Especially since it's supposed to take years, and I don't think I have that much patience.

With gentle precision, I place a tentative finger against the edge of the petal, trying to clear my head of everything poisoning it. The silky membrane becomes my entire world in that moment, as I imagine it growing to the size of me.

Of course, nothing happens.

My eyes scrunch together, as I try to delve deeper inside myself, wrecking the well-armored centre that holds me back from truly accessing the deepest part of me. I imagine a pair of metal tongs sliding into the crack my desperate fingers attempt to hold open, prying it open till the rock splits.

An unexplainable surge of power comes from the base of my skull into my veins, letting magic pour into them before it reaches my fingertips. The flower grows at the same time I open my eyes. The bright flower fills my palm, caressing my skin in a thank you.

I fall back, and my head is in the grass.

My fingertips are bright red, as if I have just stuck them into a bowl of berries. Aside from a mild vignette of blurriness around my vision, I feel fine. Actually, I feel *alive.*

"I'm impressed," I hear someone say from behind my head.

I sit up, mildly aware of the grass sticking to my hair as I look up. It is Alpha Rylan, barely visible with his back to the Moon.

Even through the darkness and shadows that shroud his face, I can see his insanely blue eyes looking down at me with curiosity and, if I'm not hallucinating, amazement.

Scrambling to my feet, I dust myself off. "I'm sorry..."

"Why?" He asks, tilting his head coyly.

I look down at my feet, unable to handle the smooth lines of his face and eyes that would make the purest of girls want to sin. For a man of Purity, he is rather intimidating, with the way he enjoys constantly staring, and observing. Who knows what's going around in his mind.

"I was just playing around," I say, motioning to the flower that now has petals well overcompensating for its small stem.

Rylan follows my motion, a dark eyebrow raising curiously. A lot of Alphas aren't fazed at all by magic, despite not being able to control it themselves. Rylan, on the other hand, looks enchanted by what I have just done.

"Quite the talent you have," he comments absently. "I've never seen that before."

I can't help my smile. Wordlessly, Rylan stalks over to a fallen log on which he sits. He's breathlessly tall and slender, although well-built to the point where he could pick me up and throw me. Jasper has told me little about this man, which ultimately intrigues me. I've heard a few rumors about his mate, yet not many discuss it.

Apparently, it's a subject he is rather serious about.

"Faye taught me... I mean, Alpha Faye."

Rylan nods, drawing his gaze away from where he had been intently scrutinising the flower that slowly tilts its top-heavy body sideways. He stretches his long legs in front of me, his finger tracing across his thigh.

"She is a rather talented woman," he comments.

I nod. "Very much so."

We stay in silence for a while, me standing, and Rylan sitting. He stares up at the Moon, seeming deep and thoughtful. I can't really tell him to leave me to my magic, since he's an Alpha. I'm left wondering why he is out here, so I decide to bring it up.

"You aren't partying with the rest of them?"

He bites the side of his lip, and I can tell he is extremely distracted with something. I believe I know exactly what it is about. He only confirms my assumptions.

"Too much on my mind," he murmurs, resorting to tapping his chin and tapping his foot. "My mate killed one of my men."

My blood turns to ice in my veins. Seriously? His mate is a killer? I've heard he has had issues with her, after she ran away the moment they found out they were mates. He's been sending his men after her for years now, which I can imagine would be tough for a girl who is probably my age. How does she cope? She should accept her mate...

"I understand why she's running. She doesn't want a life trapped in a Pack," he says, his teeth clenching after his sentence.

I take a step back, leaning against the tree. Slowly, I slide down it.

I'm interested.

"Is she a Purity Pack member?" I ask.

He shakes his head. "Desire."

My eyebrows rise in surprise. Fate is surely cruel enough to pair a Desire Pack member with a Purity. Those two are starkly different in morals, which leads me to imagine they would surely have an interesting relationship. The average person struggles to hide from the temptation of a Desire Pack member, but what about an Alpha?

Of Purity? By the looks of Rylan, and how beaten up over this he looks, it wouldn't take him much.

Especially after over a year without her...

Now I know how Jasper must have felt, having to wait such a long time for me. I would have gone insane if I had known my mate wasn't going to come for centuries. I can hardly handle a few days without him now that I know.

"What's she like?" I question lightly.

"Beautiful. Stunning. She's the only female in the world who I can look at, and have my breath completely stolen. She makes me feel things a man of Purity shouldn't feel. It's been a year without, which is why I'm going to do everything in my power to get her back."

I can see the heartfelt plea in his tone. I don't doubt him for a moment.

"I don't know what she has been doing without me. If she is with a male... I think I would kill him," he tells me honestly, as he frowns deeply.

My mind whirls. "I'm sure her eyes are for you only."

"I can't help but be possessive," he says, his voice deepening. "I want her. I *need* her. The next time I see her, I'm not letting her go anywhere."

At the same time as understanding, I want to tell him to leave her alone. His mate must make the decision for herself, she must want to walk into his arms. It's his job to make her want to, to convince her a life with him is a better than a life on the run.

I tell him so, and with every word, his expression softens.

"I know, I'll do everything. I'm going to save her from her life in fear of me. I'm going to make her understand," he tells me, and I smile.

I bend down and grab the flower, plucking the stem from the ground. Its source of life is suddenly stolen, so I place my finger on the bottom of the broken stem, to breathe some life into it. For some reason, it suddenly comes naturally, flowing out of me like a gushing tap. The flower seems to stretch out, brightening lushly in my hands.

Before anything more happens, I pass it to a wary-looking Rylan.

"Just be careful with her," I tell him firmly. "Look after her."

Rylan looks from the flower, then to me, and nods.

"I have to find her first."

Chapter Forty-Seven

When Jasper comes to collect me the next day, I couldn't be happier to see him.

As he steps out of his car, his face is grave and ashen. It alerts me instantly that something isn't right back in Safe Haven. At least he isn't hurt, I remind myself, as I throw myself into his waiting arms.

"I've missed you," I breathe into his chest, relishing his familiar scent. The feeling of his arms around me gives me the first sense of home I've had in awhile. "Like, I *really* missed you."

I'm tempted to hang onto Jasper forever like this, so he can't wander off unexpectedly.

"I know. Tell me, did you at least have fun?"

Fun... that's a word that can't apply to this experience. Yeah sure, I have enjoyed my time with Faye, who strangely doesn't seem like an Alpha of Independence. Rylan seems kind enough, but something about him worries me. He's very persistent and protective, and seems on edge most of the time. Lack of a mate does that to you. I would know.

"Something like that," I mutter, pulling back enough to give him a chaste kiss on the lips.

Our drive back to Safe Haven is silent, even after I tell Jasper I don't want him to use time manipulation. Just sitting near to him keeps me sane; it lets me think about things without worry seeping in. Yet every time Safe Haven comes to mind, it comes back to me. How could it not? That place isn't so much of a Safe Haven anymore, but really, it's all either of us have.

Well... unless...

"We should go back to the Devotion Pack," I tell him, suddenly snatching the silence from the room. I watch his jaw clench almost immediately, his expression turn grave.

The Devotion Pack is my home. Plenty of terrible things happened there, but it is where I'm from, and where I belong. My father may still live there, but Luca is gone, which will allow me to feel a little more comfortable being there. And it's not like Jasper can't handle my father... Right?

"Thea," he says carefully. "I don't think so."

My face screws up in response. "Why not? Don't you think it would be safer there, compared to a place crawling with people who want both of us dead?"

"Have you seen what those Phantoms from your town did to those innocent kids? They murdered them, and I'm sure they will do that to you too, the second you step back into that Pack."

Okay, he has a point.

I sit back in my seat, looking through the window, trees rolling past at fast rates, blurring together in one sad image. As long as I'm with Jasper, I don't care where I end up. I'm still going to do as much as I can to get him to take me back to the Devotion Pack. It's where we both belong, as Alpha and Luna.

Jasper rests his hand on my thigh, his warmth spreading comfortingly across my skin. "Don't stress, okay? Leave that to me."

I shake my head at him. "We are in this together."

Jasper may have centuries of experience on me, even though he never mentions it, I see it in his eyes. But I can hold my own. I will be as brave as he is, because he's done doing things on his own. That's what his life was like years ago. Not anymore. I'm with him now, and I'm not leaving his side.

He smiles down at me, and I'm relieved to see it reaches his eyes, lighting them up so they look more violet than blue. "Of course, Thea. Of course."

It starts to rain another hour into our journey.

Jasper narrows his eyes as the sudden onslaught of rain only thickens, pelting the windscreen angrily. I haven't seen a storm like this since the day Jasper saved me from Luca. It has come on so suddenly too, the clouds barely having time to fully cloud over before they let go of all that water.

Storms. They scare me, as Jasper remembers from the second time we really met.

"It's okay, it will pass," he tells me, rubbing my leg in the way he knows calms me best. I try my best to smile, but it's shaky. Jasper doesn't look so sure of himself either.

This is probably a foolish time to bring up Fate, but something about this storm reminds me of his unpredictability.

"So, Fate." I say softly.

His fingers clench on the steering wheel, turning them white. There is no flash of anger across his face at my words, but I van tell they have bothered him. I know my mate.

"Did he hurt you?" He asks calmly, his voice hard like his stony expression. I shake my head.

"No. He threatened you. He wants his end of the deal done Jasper. He wants..."

The car brakes are slammed on, the car lurches forward, skidding across the wet tarmac. My head is flung forward and smacks unceremoniously against the dashboard. Pain cuts a path down my neck and back, as my vision blurs for a moment. At that point, I am certain I will pass out.

Jasper swears, and I can tell this wasn't his doing.

I drag my aching head back until it rests against the seat, feeling Jasper touching and talking to me. Blinking through the haze shading my vision, I see four pairs of violet eyes swimming in front of me.

"I'm sorry..."

"I don't know what..."

"Are you hurt?"

I can only hear chopped parts of his sentences, but it hardly registers. It takes a few moments of clutching the car handle and

Jasper's arm before I start seeing things properly again. My mate looks concerned, although not at all worried about the fact our car just stopped in the middle of the road.

"I'm fine," I croak, wondering for a moment if that is really me talking. "I think."

Jasper leans over me, unclipping my belt so it slides off. I climb over to sit on his lap while he holds me. The rhythmic sound of the rain helps soothe my head. So does Jasper as he kisses my forehead once, twice... over and over. Maybe he's using his magic on me, but I don't care.

A knock on the window grabs our attention.

Cobalt blue hair, matted from rain; dark eyes; soaked clothes are all I can see through the window. Oh, and a sickening smile.

Fate.

He waves in a taunting way, staring in at us with tilted head. My blood runs cold, as I realize this is all because of him. He created this storm. He caused this car to stop and me to hit my head. This man can do whatever he pleases, being the dictator of everything.

Jasper tenses underneath me, as Fate pulls open the car door.

"Well, isn't this sweet," he says, cynically, a fake smile across his features. I would punch him, however I don't doubt he would rearrange fate to go his way. Right now, Jasper and I have no other choice. We are at his mercy.

"Stalker," Jasper spits.

I don't want us to be in this position when talking with Fate. I don't have a choice though, as Jasper holds me firmly against him. I have no other option but to stay close to him, while we face Fate, the man who could have killed me a few minutes ago.

"Stalker, huh?" Fate mocks, testing the words on his tongue. He seems unfazed by the rain battering him, as he rests his arm on the top of the car. "That's new."

"What do you want?" Jasper growls.

Would Jasper try to fight him? Of course not, he's not that stupid. Hopefully Jasper will use his way with words to sway Fate out of this. He's stopped us in the middle of nowhere, having created a vicious storm; I'm sure he knows I hate them. Who knows what else he feels like doing today.

"I think you know," Fate says coyly, leaning into the car slightly to run a wet finger down Jasper's cheek. I see the way my mate tries to hold himself back. "Alpha."

A low growl rumbles from Jasper's throat.

"You're not getting my Pack. I'd rather you kill me," Jasper says firmly, and my heart almost stops.

A part of me is tempted to cover his mouth with my hand, to stop him from digging any deeper a hole for himself. Fate wants what he wants. He could easily play with Jasper's fate and have him agree, or let him make the decision and get himself killed. The latter is a lot more fun for Fate, so I suppose it's the only option.

"Kill you?"

Jasper nods, clenching his jaw tight.

"How about kill your mate?"

All of a sudden, I'm no longer in the car. How he got me out of there off Jasper's lap is beyond me. But in an instant I'm standing the rain, with Fate's ice-cold hand around my neck. Staring into his eyes, I'm sure I'm not going to get out of this.

"She's so beautiful, Jasper. It would be a shame..." Fate drawls, his hand tightening so breathing becomes even more difficult.

Fright shoots through me, as I remember being drowned a few weeks ago. This is much worse, having this unpredictable man quite literally holding my life in his hands. Jasper gets out of the car, hardly fazed. Fate, as he holds me securely, stares at me with smiling eyes.

Jasper doesn't make any move to touch him, as he is fully aware it might end up getting me killed.

"Please, let her go," Jasper pleads gently, meeting my gaze. I choke for a moment, as his fingers close further around my throat.

Fate chuckles. "You know what I want."

"Give me a few days," Jasper almost begs. It's the first time I've seen him like this.

Fate looks thoughtful, as I claw at his hands. Right now, I want to tell Jasper to just give up, to let me live and not go through this once again. But the words are stuck in my throat, unable to get past Fate's hand. Instead, I plead to my mate with my eyes.

Then Fate lets me go.

"You have two days. Remember Jasper, I'll be back for your Pack. Don't let me down..." Fate glances over at me. "... or your mate."

Chapter Forty-Eight

Jasper cannot hold me closer, as he gently runs a towel over my damp hair.

The moment we get back into the car, Jasper doesn't negotiate time manipulation with me. In a blink, we are back in Safe Haven, I am a little drier, and I have a blanket around me.

I am also in Jasper's arms, which I don't mind in the slightest.

He has brought me to another house he's been thinking of selling, but still owns. He hasn't said much to me about his home that's been burned down, but I can tell it has devastated him. Right now, it looks as if we will be staying here until he can rebuild. I don't mind where we are, as long as it isn't near Fate.

"Are you okay?" he asks gently, and I notice him looking down at my neck.

Back there, I had been convinced Fate was going to kill me. He had Jasper in the palm of his hand, and with all his power, he could have easily ended the lives of two Phantom Wolves, no question about it. Dying at Fate's hand seems significantly worse than my bath infliction.

I nod. "I'm fine."

Jasper bundles my hair in the towel, squeezing it tenderly. I hate to see the pain in his eyes as he handles me like a delicate piece of china, about to shatter at the slightest touch.

"Seriously," I say, grabbing his wrist to stop his movements. "I'm perfectly okay. Well, I will be, if you agree to this."

Conflict dashes across his face.

I don't blame Jasper for not wanting to give Safe Haven up to someone like Fate. He has built this place from the ground, saving innocent people from destructive Phantom Wolves who easily could have ended their lives. As an Alpha, he has been working on this for centuries, which is longer than I or most of them could fathom.

"I can't," he tells me, his voice strangled.

There is nothing worse than seeing your mate beat himself up inside. I grab his face gently between my hands, as he drops the towel to the ground.

It's not that I think kissing him will change his mind. It is that I think kissing him helps both of us cope with everything. The moment our lips meet, nothing matters anymore but the two of us. The delicious feeling of his lips against mine makes me giddy, yet relaxed at the same time. Never have I got this feeling ever before with anybody else.

Jasper isn't about to turn me down. Not now when we are both under so much stress. And what better way to relieve that?

Fisting his hair in my hands, I increase the pressure of my kiss, wanting more from him than the subtle, teasing kisses he's giving me. I didn't mean to force myself onto him, but I can't help myself as I clamber onto his lap, relishing the feeling of his hands finding their place on my hips.

The taste of him is something I could have every day. As he runs his hands under my shirt, across my stomach and waist, I wish the back of this chair wasn't there, so I could push him backward to really get hold of him.

Jasper gets the same idea, as he picks me up, wrapping my legs around his hips as he stands.

There is no question about where this will end up. Spending time with him like this will take our minds off the problem at hand. As long as Fate doesn't decide he wants to show up during the midst of it... otherwise *I'll* be the one strangling *him*.

Jasper confirms my thoughts, as he rests me back against the bed.

Right now, I am in no position to question his control, his desire to vent his feelings in a way both of us are going to enjoy. He pulls his shirt over his head, giving me a good look at his darkening eyes, as he gazes down at me, while I shimmy my pants down over my hips.

No time is wasted as Jasper rids us of our clothes like they are on fire, discarding each item over his shoulder carelessly. As he bends down, he brings his mouth to my neck, where I expect his lips. However, I get his teeth.

Without breaking skin, he lightly bites me, his warning.

Before I have a chance to say a word, although I know what he is insinuating, he's inside me. I clutch his shoulders, unable to hold back the moan that surfaces in my throat. His teeth remain on my neck, preparing me for the marking of a mate, that I am so desperately ready for.

Both he and I have been waiting for the right moment, and with Fate threatening me, this is needed.

"I love you," I murmur in his ear, and he still inside me.

He pulls away, looking at me in a way that is more than special. It's personal, and I know he heard every word I said, and taken it in. Just his gaze in itself reciprocates the feeling.

"I love you too," he breathes. "More than you will ever know, Thea."

It is then his head swoops down, and his teeth sink into my neck. Instantly I cringe, pain sweeps from my neck to my head, assaulting my body with an onslaught of pain.

The moment his gentle thrusting returns, the pain becomes insignificant.

I can do only little but wrap my legs around Jasper's back to bring him even closer to me, even deeper. In this position, I am at his mercy, being only able to lift my hips up to meet his every powerful thrust. My hands have a mind of their own, as they scratch at his back, and delve into his hair.

I can't get enough of him.

I don't last long, and neither does Jasper. In the heat of it all, and our angst and stress, I crumple under Jasper and his incessant strokes before he finishes inside me. I could die with pleasure at this moment of the feeling of my mate. All I want to do is to replay this moment, with this man, over and over.

Jasper kisses me deeply, in a heated manner, despite my need for air. As he pulls away, I see his quivering muscles.

He rolls off me. I look at him, propping myself on my elbow.

"Finally," he murmurs, casting a glance at me with a soft smile on his face. "Now it is confirmed—you are mine."

I grin, running my finger across his chest. "It was always confirmed. Fate did that a long time ago."

Jasper's face falls at the mention of Fate, but he knows we have to talk about it. Now he has marked me, this is the next thing we need to focus on. At this point, Jasper and I don't agree on what is going to happen. I just need him to see it from my perspective.

"Think of the favour you will be doing for them," I tell him, slightly brushing across his muscle with the edge of my nail. Jasper watches my every move.

"How so?"

I pause, before I continue. "Fate could protect them better than anyone, and you know that. Not only that, he will control them, and after what happened to your home, you can't tell me you still have a handle on this."

A flicker of some dangerous emotion shows a glimpse of itself for a moment. It's frightening to see him think like this about something he is passionate about.

"I put so much work in..."

"I know," I say softly, although a little urgently. "If you don't do this, they are going to do nothing but retaliate forever, Jasper. And what else would you give Fate. We could go back to the Devotion Pack to start again..."

I am cut off by the sound of a rather heated, incoherent chant.

Grabbing a blanket to wrap around my bare body, I stand and walk to the window, to see what is going on outside. Jasper follows me, after sliding his legs into a pair of pants. Resting my hands against the windowsill, I look out, only to be shocked at what I see.

293

A long line of people, who could be the entirety of Safe Haven's population, walk directly down the street toward us. My heart falls to my feet at the sight.

Jasper immediately pulls me away from the window, but not before I get a good glimpse of who leads this line of protestors. They are bringing them to a place that isn't even our house, to do who knows what... June and Cole.

It takes Jasper a few moments of staring out there to fully understand. This is his pride and joy walking toward us, malice and vengeance written all over their faces.

Slowly, he turns back to me, and I swear I see tears in his eyes.

"Okay. The Devotion Pack it is."

Chapter Forty-Nine

"How sure are you about this?" I question, clutching his hand tightly in my own.

Doubt is written all over his face, leaving no room for anything else. Of course, I understand why he feels so reluctant to be coming here. He's giving away Safe Haven to Fate, which I can imagine being one the most difficult things possible.

"Not very," he says, casting a glance at me by his side. "I have no other choice, though."

He's right, he doesn't. We had to escape through the back door of his own home after the protest that began on his front lawn. His reasoning through the top storey window had been dismissed, people wanting him dead for being a Phantom. At that moment, he had decided to call upon Fate, which despite having travelled outside Safe Haven walls, he hadn't yet done so.

As he drives, I decide to bring it up. "When are you going to summon Fate, or whatever you do?"

"He will be watching," he says softly, looking ahead onto the road we are on. "He's always watching."

I shiver, feeling a little uncomfortable at that revelation.

Fate's ability to see all makes him almost omnipotent. He must be invincible, being able to see our futures before we have a chance to live them. Jasper told me about the limitations of Fate's power, and how there are ways to trick him, and perhaps kill him even, but I didn't believe him.

Admittedly, Fate terrifies me.

"Don't be scared," Jasper says calmly, pulling over onto the side of the road in a smooth sweep.

I glare at him. "Are you reading my mind?"

He shakes his head at me, violet eyes alight. They tend to do that when he has the ability to prove me wrong in some way, or even tease me a little. "No, silly. I can sense it. Plus, your face is screwed up."

Okay, he's got me on that one.

"Come," Jasper demands a second later, popping the car door open. When I look outside, I see nothing familiar. We are near the Devotion Pack, so the trees are thick and the air is balmy. I have an idea as to why we are here: to meet Fate. It makes sense not to see him in Safe Haven, where both Jasper and I are vulnerable. He doesn't want to hurt any of them.

Once out of the car, we walk toward a thick line of trees, as Jasper explains the need to meet him somewhere he can't play with us. Trick us. Also, no one must see us and this meeting of strange circumstance.

"What happened the last time we saw him will *not* happen again," Jasper reminds me, squeezing the hand he had been holding.

I believe him. Fate's getting what he wants today, right?

The trees close around us the further we walk in, shading the path with shadows of various shapes. Not once do I dare take my hand from Jasper's, as I'm nervous of what might make an appearance at any second.

And he does.

With one turn of my head I see the cobalt blue-haired man leaning against one of the trees. He has a familiar smirk on his face. I don't know what made me jump more: his presence or that look he likes to give us whenever he is near.

"Took you long enough," Fate muses, stepping back from his tree to stroll closer. He holds his gaze with me, until he notices the mark on my neck.

A feline-like smile spreads like a blush across his face.

"We had things to discuss first," Jasper says from beside me. His voice makes me flinch a little. Both these males are making me on edge. At any moment, I don't doubt, he will try his luck, attempting to hurt Fate. He may be centuries-old with experience, but his emotions sometimes get the better of him, and I can't say I want to witness that right now.

"Discuss it?" Fate says condescendingly. "Over what? Sex?"

My face flushes, and Jasper clears his throat uncomfortably. Of course he knows, but it doesn't make me any less sick to the stomach.

"I won't expect to understand what the mating bond is like," Jasper mutters cruelly. I feel myself nod in agreement, before I can stop myself. Fate is already concentrating on me, more than on Jasper.

Fate chuckles at the Alpha's remark. "Perhaps no mating bond... However, something similar. Give me some credit. I do still have your mortal male parts."

The gleam in his eye makes me screw my face up in disgust. I did *not* need to know that.

It is at that moment that a rather disturbing thought enters my mind. Does Fate have a mate? Has she come into his life yet, or has he outlived her by a few millennia? I can't imagine anyone being able to tolerate him for more than a couple of minutes. Especially not with all the power he possesses.

"Listen, we are here to discuss this bargain. I'm willing to give you Safe Haven," Jasper admits, and I hear reluctance trying to rein in his words. "If, and only if, you agree to look after them."

Fate's face lights up almost immediately. It makes me nervous to see how delighted he is to see this kind of deal work in his favour. He had to have known, yet he's clearly drawing out his win over Jasper. The tension in the air could easily be cut with a knife.

"Of course, of course. I'm glad you came to your senses," Fate says brightly, stepping forward.

Nervously, I don't move an inch, afraid of those hands that raise toward my neck once again. He traces his hand over the mark on my neck, which is still tender. I try my best not to flinch or cringe, wishing I was anywhere but here. I can feel Jasper wondering whether or not he should make a move to stop Fate.

I shoot him a look out of the corner of my eye, warning the distraught Alpha not to do anything stupid.

"Took you a while, Jasper," Fate murmurs, the tips of his fingers cold against my skin. "It's a shame about her condition."

This time, I flinch away from him.

"Excuse me?" I sputter, glancing at Jasper, who looks just as confused as I must. "What did you just say?"

Fate's eyebrows furrow, then, he smiles slightly. "Oh? Did Alpha Malik not tell you?"

My mind whirls back to the day I was turned into a Phantom. Quite possibly the worst day I have ever had to go through. The pain of suffocation reminded me of what Fate had inflicted, but that's not what this is about. It's about *why* I got turned into a Phantom... It's about the man from the Desire Pack.

"What?" I ask warily.

"The infection left you with some pretty bad permanent effects," Fate tells me. Then I see a flicker of real life emotion, and it sends worry straight to my heart.

I swallow, as he looks at Jasper.

"I'm afraid it left you infertile."

My heart stops.

I haven't thought about kids since I was young. It never really was something I wanted after I met Luca. What he did to me isn't something a child should have to deal with. But now that I am with Jasper... everything has changed. Jasper and I could have had beautiful, happy children.

"You're serious?" I ask, my fingertips turning numb, before spreading to the rest of me. Jasper doesn't say a word.

Fate looks grim. "Children are not something you will be granted within your future."

My future... that's forever.

"Unless of course..." Fate cuts in on my thoughts, raising an eyebrow. I feel Jasper grab my hand, the spark reassuring, like a lifeline. "... we make another deal."

Jasper shakes his head. "We don't have anything you want."

Fate shrugs. "Not yet, but you will."

Jasper and I exchange looks. A little hope has blossomed in my stomach, but is soon swallowed by fear. We are standing here primarily because of Fate, and his wicked bargains. Would we be willing to trade again?

"You will give me your firstborn child. I will ensure she is female. When she is 23 years and five months old, *exactly,* she will be mine," he says delicately.

"No," I say instantly.

Jasper looks torn.

"Aren't you going to ask me why?" Fate questions. "Oh come, I'll take special care of her."

"No one deserves to live near someone like you," I spit, anger surfacing in the color of my cheeks. Even if he promised to look after her, could I trust him? This man is one of tricks with little reason to his name.

Fate sighs, seemingly bored. "I need someone for a certain job in 25 years, exactly. I'm sure a child of the great Alphas would suffice."

"Tell us what it is," Jasper demands, his voice surfacing for the first time.

"It's a secret," Fate chuckles. "Like I said, I would take great care of her."

As I look at Jasper, I see him torn to pieces over this. He wants a child; he's mentioned it before. It makes sense that all this unprotected sex has lead to nothing, for a reason. I can't have a child, and that has devastated both of us. Yet, could I agree to Fate's wishes? Could I sacrifice my first daughter for an heir to Jasper's legacy?

"On one condition," I breathe.

Fate perks up, whereas Jasper only pales.

"I'll give you my magic, if you swear on your life to keep her safe, and happy at all times," I say carefully, forming my words in a way he cannot twist into something else.

"What need do I have for your magic?" Fate asks.

I could feel Jasper looking at me, but he hasn't said a word. This is my magic, and I have no interest in it anyway. It would be a blessing to Jasper if it was taken, so he wouldn't spend a life having to protect me from it. This could work...

"Please," I whisper.

Fate seems to think, watching me with his unnerving eyes.

"You know what," he says suddenly. "I like that idea. Then I can pass it on to your daughter. Give her a little fire in her step."

Instantly, I hold my hand out. I don't need to think about it. My daughter would be working for Fate, but she would always be happy, and I can live with that. Perhaps Jasper could teach her how to protect herself, and eventually take down the evil mastermind in front of us.

What joy that would bring *everyone*.

Fate looks at Jasper for confirmation. His jaw is clenched, his eyes are dark as he looks at me first. He sees my idea in my eyes, and I feel as if he's searching my mind, understanding all of it. He nods.

Fate bends down, placing his lips to my hand.

And suddenly, the deal fills the air. Thick and heavy it feels, as a ripple of magic blows through us. Fate and I will be tied to this deal for 25 years.

And my daughter will be forever.

Epilogue

A month later

Jasper's arm around me nearly lulls me into sleep, as we sit together on the couch, the volume of the television turned low.

He nudges me. "Don't fall asleep, it will be on soon."

It's late in the Devotion Pack, compared to where the live broadcast is to be shot in the Love Pack. Jasper has insisted we support Malik by watching this, but I have had a hard time sleeping at night since we officially moved here from Safe Haven.

Not that it's Safe Haven anymore. The Pack of Fate, it has been named. After the man who controls them.

"The future Luna will be announced with them," Jasper says, as if that is supposed to excite me more. Personally, I believe Malik should be waiting for his mate, and the rest of us just have to hope Fate can pull a few strings to get them to meet. Although, I doubt he would do any Alpha that kind of favor...

I roll my eyes as Jasper turns the volume up.

I've admittedly been in rather bad moods lately. I haven't had much sleep recently after I'd agreed to give Fate my firstborn child, even though I knew it would be for the best. My daughter may just save the world from his sickening way in the future.

It doesn't make me feel any less guilty.

The reporters begin speaking from the TV screen, discussing something I don't really have that much interest in. I do however, enjoy seeing the pictures of the girls that follow, making internal assumptions about who may be chosen.

It doesn't affect Jasper or me in any way. Well, unless she is a terrible Luna, and under some circumstance I have to spend time with her. Then, I suppose, she should be the one worrying.

"Aria Quade," the lady says, announcing one of the members from the Love Pack.

I find myself staring at her, my eyes drawn to the screen at that moment. Jasper has stilled beside me, his arm rigid over my shoulder. Aria... The girl who had kindly let us stay in her house within the Love Pack, when we were running form Luca. She was competing? That doesn't make any sense...

There is no photo to show her to us, but I still remember her warm eyes and bright smile when we first met. Something about her natural, easy beauty could get her far.

But does she want to?

When I met Aria, she had talked about wanting her mate badly. There was no question that she was willing to wait for her mate, so the fact she has applied, and managed to get in, makes little sense to me. Jasper seems to think the same thing, until he turns his head to look down at me.

"Fate," he whispers. And it all makes sense.

Speaking of Fate reminds me of what really has been bothering me for the past hour. Jasper hasn't let me leave the room long enough to check the pregnancy test I have been too afraid to check, yet I can't think of anything else to do.

Jasper lets me leave after I excuse myself to the bathroom. I have to check sometime... and I won't be able to concentrate on Malik's competition until I have.

Wandering to the bathroom, I see it on the bench.

It sits there, looking guilty of some crime. My feet find a stop at the doorway of the room, staring at it from a few metres away. Why am I so worried? It has to be because of Fate's bargain I stupidly accepted. Now, our daughter will have to undergo his torment. What if she fails to take him down, as Jasper and I have planned ever since that day? At least we know nothing bad will happen to her.

Exhaling deeply, I step forward, until the result section can be seen in my view. It takes me a few seconds to look at it from behind the hands I'm cowardly holding over my eyes.

Positive.

I sink to the floor.

Time is non-existent as I sit there on the bathroom floor, my feet curled under me, my right hand on my stomach while my left braces against the wall. My mind fails to believe it. It fails to fathom what my eyes have just seen, and what is coming in my future. This may be the inevitable, but it still surprises me.

My heart doesn't know whether or not it should be breaking right now, or fluttering with happiness.

I hear Jasper muddling around in the kitchen, which must mean the broadcast has finished. I can't yell out to him or anything, I'm so stunned.

"Thea?" I hear him call before I hear his footsteps.

He must have been wondering what is taking me so long. As I sit there, I become more and more aware of how terrible I must look. Tears streak down my face, and I'm sitting with my legs moved close to my chest on our bathroom floor.

Jasper's expression falls when he sees me.

"What's happened?" he asks frantically, bending down to me. He ushers me into his arms, wrapping them around me. "What's wrong?"

Pushing my head against my chest, I cry silently for a moment, not bothering about my tears that stain Jasper's shirt. He patiently sits there, waiting for me to talk without saying a word. What will he say? Will he be mad at me?

"I'm pregnant," I whisper, unable to hold it in for another second.

I fist his shirt, waiting for his reaction.

He is silent for a moment, processing the information. Then he gently pushes me away from him, holding me tightly by the shoulder. Staring into his eyes, I see emotion blazing amidst the violet, making them brighter than I have ever seen them. The confusing, impassive Alpha is gone, and in his place, is a man who I never would have believed to be so open.

He smiles, and I can't help but smile too.

"Don't be scared," he murmurs, bringing his hands up to my face, where he gently cups my cheek.

"I don't know what we are going to do," I say. "What if Fate doesn't keep his word?"

Jasper helps me crawls onto his lap, so I can properly get a look into his eyes, and see his expression. He looks happy, which makes little sense to me. Maybe I am just being emotional, as a side effect of this entire thing.

"He won't. He is a man of his word, and he will look after her like we made him promise, trust me," Jasper tells me. The lack of doubt in his voice creates a little flutter of hope in my stomach.

I kiss the side of Jasper's mouth. "This doesn't feel real."

He smiles softly, brushing the tears off my face with his thumbs.

"I've waited over 400 years for this. It had better be real," he says jokingly, and I smile at his infectious humour.

"Thank you for saving me," I tell him, my tone finding seriousness again.

Jasper shakes his head. "No, thank you for saving me."

We embrace silently. This is forever.